PATH OF CONQUEST

PATH OF CONQUEST

RUTHLESS BOOK 1

D. J. Rintoul

Podium

Podium

PATH OF CONQUEST

CHAPTER ONE

Derailed

The Florida sun was hot and bright in the sky, and James Robard suddenly felt every bead of sweat dripping down the back of his neck as the light fell on him through the shattered driver's side window.

"Just put the gun down, man," James said. His hands were up from sheer instinct. The man standing next to him, grasping him by his necktie, seemed far from stable.

"Keys, asshole!" the other man pronounced. "Outta the car, and gimme your goddamn keys!"

What the carjacker lacked in eloquence his pistol more than made up for in bleak intimidation. The black barrel stared James in the eye, daring him to make a move.

Off to the side of it in his field of vision, the timer continued counting down as if mocking him: **[01:11:32]**.

"Damn it!" James cursed under his breath. He could think of no way out of this situation that didn't risk imminent death.

To think, just fifteen minutes ago he'd been sitting in a dull meeting!

For the associates at Barry, Pesca & MacDougal, it had seemed to be a morning like any other.

The subject of the morning's meeting: integrating the latest developments in artificial intelligence into firm workflow. Computer geeks were labeling this latest stage as "true artificial intelligence," annoying everyone else who didn't understand the difference between this and the last six stages of artificial intelligence, which had been trumpeted so loudly over the previous twenty years.

However, the firm's founder, Brendan Barry, had insisted that every member of the firm participate in presentations on the new technology. So it seemed that everyone was about to learn those fine distinctions.

James, the only Black associate at the firm, had seated himself as far from the projector screen as possible. He was perhaps the least interested in the presentation of all the participants. Every face in the room was a gray blur. The voice of the presenter was a dull Charlie Brown-style "Wah wah wah wah wah wah."

James wondered for the thousandth time if there was another profession he could have chosen where he wouldn't feel this way every day. An unanswerable question, but one he was prepared to ruminate on rather than pay attention to this meeting. But before his mind could wander away fully, the monotony was interrupted.

There was a sound at the door, a shuffling, scratching noise as someone pushed weakly on the other side.

Already keen to be out of there, James darted out of his seat before anyone else and maneuvered around the table to open it for Alan. The oldest partner in the firm, Alan Roget was rail-thin and pale-skinned. A wreath of ivory hair crowned the sides of his head in a thin layer, growing ever thinner.

"Thanks, James," he said, slowly moseying in with his briefcase in one hand and coffee in the other.

"My pleasure, sir," James said softly.

Alan was his favorite person in the office. Not just because he knew that the old man wanted to be at this meeting as little as James—though he did know that—or even because Alan was the nicest partner on a personal level—though he was that—but, more importantly, because the skinny old guy felt to James like something of an outsider too.

Alan was the only partner who focused on an area other than torts, and it was a mystery to James how the old man had ended up there in the first place. Alan's laid-back style and background in trusts and estates seemed inapposite to the aggressive, competitive, efficient culture the firm fostered in all its associates.

James was grateful for the interruption Alan presented by knocking Sadie Bigelow off her presentation game. Distraction worth more than the old man's weight in gold. It was a pity that Alan couldn't more thoroughly derail the proceedings—maybe start throwing things at the screen and raving like the old newscaster from the film *Network*: "I'm as mad as hell, and I'm not going to take it anymore!"

But, of course, as soon as the old man was seated, the presenter launched back into her presentation. Efficiency triumphing over all once again! James died a little more inside as he heard the words, "Where the real potential of AI lies is in . . ."

What James wouldn't give for a more lasting disruption. A fire drill. A power outage. An emergency alert that a giant asteroid was falling from the heavens, about to smash into their building first. Right now, even that would be prefera—

[**Greetings, heroes!**]

What the fuck?! He heard and saw strange words. The visual display was on a screen in front of his face, like some virtual reality technology from a science fiction movie.

[**Greetings to my dear villains as well! Greetings also to everyone in between! Greetings to all those lucky souls who will soon be initiated!**]

The voice was silent for a moment, and the presenter issued an awkward chuckle.

"Heh. Well, I don't know what that was . . ." She seemed to be preparing to resume.

[**This announcement is to give everyone hearing it time to prepare. Your world is being processed into the System. Think of it as sort of like a software upgrade for reality. Upgrading from boring old Reality 1.0 all the way to Reality 5G—a multi-generation leap!**]

Was that some kind of a joke? Do mass hallucinations have a sense of humor?

[**For those of you wondering, this is a completely serious matter. Deadly serious. As in by the time it's finished, a sizable portion of your planet's population will be dead. A sadly necessary sacrifice for the Orientation.**]

Well, you're able to speak into all of our heads and alter what we see. Even if this is a hallucination, I have to take it seriously.

[**You have one of your hours and twenty-three minutes until Orientation begins.**]

A timer appeared in the corner of James's vision with the corresponding amount of time. *Great,* he thought, *now my hallucination has a sense of urgency!*

[**Please pardon the mess as you prepare for Orientation. Your new world is still under construction.**]

What the hell does that *mean? What mess?! And what sort of construction?!*

[**Take the remaining time to make your careful preparations for Orientation. The task we set before you will not be easy, but whether you believe it now or not, it is necessary. In time, those of you who live may come to agree with us. We hope for the best of you to succeed. *We're rooting for you, James.* You *were meant for bigger things.***]

He swiveled his head around the room wildly at that, looking to see whether other people were getting the same kind of personalized message as he was, but it was no use. They were all looking at their screens in varying degrees of confusion or alarm, but there was no expression on anyone's face that would give away whether they had been personally singled out, as he just had. And he couldn't see anyone's screen but his own.

As the words sat in front of his eyes, a strange excitement came over him.

All his life, James had been singled out by teachers, aptitude tests, and peers as someone special: smart, a possible leader, someone whose future was written in the stars—and then nothing big or important had ever happened to him.

It was the disappointment of his life. He had not dared greatly; he had pursued natural next steps for whatever situation he was in. If anything, he had underperformed people who were similarly competent and intelligent to himself.

James had been his high school's valedictorian! Some of his peers had gone on to military or business success far beyond what he'd achieved, while he had allowed himself to grow dull and complacent, a drone fueled only by caffeine.

It was as if he had been saving himself up for something, reserving his powers and strength for some critical moment all his life, but that moment had never come.

Until now.

Far from needing more caffeine, he was now filled with all the energy and tension of a coiled spring.

What to do with that energy? The announcement appeared to be over now. James wondered when the opaque screen would disappear, and as if in response to his thought, it did. *I have a bad feeling about this.* He experimentally tried thinking that he wanted to read the announcement again, and it reappeared in its entirety, taking up almost his entire field of vision, this time sans the voice of the announcer.

He rushed through it one more time just to take in any details he might have been too stunned to absorb before. It was unchanged. *Am I hallucinating? Is this real? Is it a dream?*

It felt more like a video game than anything else. Then he remembered what video games were like, and a silly idea occurred to him. *Well, this would confirm whether or not it's real, maybe . . .*

Extremely self-conscious, he whispered the word, "Status."

Miraculously, a new screen appeared in front of his face.

[Status

Name: James Robard

Race: Base Human

Class: Blocked

Job: Blocked

Health: Blocked

Mana: Blocked

Stats

Blocked

Skills

Blocked

Talents
Blocked
Titles
Blocked]

A pop-up appeared above his head just after the very unclear status menu had popped up.

Great, there's enhanced spam in Reality 5G, James thought. *Now I can't even escape by leaving my devices behind.* Then he started to read it, and his mouth dropped open.

[Conditions met! New Title obtained: System Pioneer!]

System Pioneer? I wonder what that title does.

An explanation immediately populated.

[System Pioneer: As one of the first fifty humans in your universe to interact with the System beyond receiving announcements, your nature is like that of a pioneer: to rush forward into the unknown and embrace unquantifiable challenges. As such, enjoy a 10% bonus to all stats when entering a setting no other human from your universe has explored before or an engagement with a type of opponent no other human from your universe has defeated before. Don't do anything too reckless, now!]

That sounds quite good, James thought. *Besides that warning at the end. Since it's a percentage increase, it'll scale with my base stats and*—James realized he was thinking about the real world like it was a game and forced himself to stop. *Back to reality!*

Now that he had semi-reluctantly accepted that this was real, James immediately felt a strong impulse to rush home to his wife, Mina. A burst of panic. He'd hesitated too long already. If people might really die during this "Orientation," he needed to be there to protect her.

With a thought, he whisked the screens away. Other people were starting to murmur among themselves by this point. No one had disturbed him as he seemingly stared silently off into space. They could probably tell he must be doing something with the universe's new interface, and besides, he wasn't that close to anyone here; he wouldn't have wanted to join any of the clustered whispering groups anyway. He didn't like any of these people that much except maybe Alan, the only person besides James who was still on his own. *Typical.*

He rose sharply from his seat. If what he was thinking was right, this job didn't matter anymore. These people, whose opinions he had spent hours worrying over and trying to shape in his own favor, were now of no particular account. *Thank goodness. Now I can finally be myself again and do what I want.*

All eyes turned to him, as he was the only person standing.

James ignored them, apart from taking a dark satisfaction in ignoring them, and he marched out of the conference room.

As the door slowly closed behind him, he heard a scraping of chair against floor as someone—two someones?—got up in a hurry. James turned his head to see who was following him.

"Just where the hell do you think you're going?" Cliff Rogers demanded. "A little light show, and you think you can just waltz out without a word—"

"I have to see about my family, Cliff." James found himself unable to just completely walk away. Cliff was moving as if to cut him off.

"What, you think this is real?" Cliff said. "Just hackers, man. Probably fuckin' Russian hackers! They got into the projection system, and they got into the loudspeaker system, and that's all it is!"

"And they somehow projected *individualized messages* in front of all our faces? What's *wrong* with you?" James's voice rose unintentionally to a near shout before he controlled himself. "Just—I have to leave."

He brushed off Cliff's efforts to grab him and pushed through the double doors.

Cliff shouted after him, "You leave here, you're done!"

James didn't even turn his head. As far as he was concerned, he was done at Barry, Pesca & MacDougal.

But another person darted through the doors after him.

"James!" This other voice was more reasonable, and James felt compelled to at least respond to it.

He turned and said, "Dean, I can't stop to talk right now! I have to get to my family!"

"Okay, I get it, man," Dean Crocetti said. "I'm not trying to stop you. Just wanted to encourage you to come back—with the family if you can. If the worst is happening, the office is as good a place as any to make a stand. The walls are good material, there's plenty of space, and there are people you know here."

That last was certainly true. Whether James really wanted to know these people anymore was another question. If the System was real, and not merely mass hallucination, it was a very open-ended question.

But James trusted Dean's survival instincts, at the very least. The forty-something partner was something of a prepper, and he and James had occasionally kicked around ideas about how to survive possible apocalypses. James thought Dean was a survivor type.

"Thanks for the invite, Dean. I'll keep it in mind. Really." Both men turned away from each other, and James rushed toward his Honda Civic, keys in hand.

He unlocked the old car. Got in. Started the engine. Began driving.

His mind moved a mile a minute as he sped away from the office, trying to process all the implications of the world being "processed into the System." *Do people have levels now? Special powers?* It was weirdly energizing to think about.

We're rooting for you, James. You were meant for bigger things.

He felt goosebumps rise on his skin. Then he shivered slightly and smiled to himself.

James turned right at the gas station nearest the office, but then he met traffic and had to slow down to avoid hitting the driver in front of him. He leaned his head out of his window to see how many cars were ahead of him, and it was quite a line. The further he leaned out, the more he could see, stretching off into the distance on what was normally a quiet road. But this was anything but a normal day.

"Damn it!" he swore loudly, punching the dashboard.

He checked the timer that still hovered at the corner of his vision, absurdly video-game-like: **[01:16:21]**.

Stuck in traffic, he thought. *What a mundane thing to keep me away from Mina and Yulia on the last day of the world*. He shook his head.

Whatever. He wouldn't let the traffic get him down. He took his phone out, opened his favorited contacts, and tapped the top slot.

He could at least dial Mina and see if she was okay.

Or maybe he couldn't.

A pop-up appeared on the phone screen this time—rather than simply in his field of vision—indicating that he had no service. James looked at the phone more carefully for the first time since unlocking it and saw that he had no bars.

There went any plans to call Mina, Yulia, his mother, or his sister Alice. He sighed, shoved the phone back into his pocket, and began to turn to look back at the road.

And then there was a smashing sound at the corner of his awareness. Shards of glass entangled themselves in James's hair and clothes, and as he turned toward the noise he was lucky that none of them struck him in the eyes.

"I want the car!" a wild voice declared.

James turned to see a Caucasian figure with darting eyes and long brown hair, but he found it difficult to focus in on any of the details with the black handgun shoved directly into his face.

CHAPTER TWO

Pay It Forward

I want the car!" the man demanded.

"Come on, man. You don't wanna do this—" James began.

The carjacker drew back and pistol-whipped him, slamming James's head forward into the horn. His vision swam for a moment. Suddenly the stranger was much closer to him, reaching into the car and grabbing him by the necktie.

"Jus' put the gun dow', man," James said, slurring some of the words slightly.

"You thought I was kidding. I know! I know it!" the man yelled. "But I'm fucking serious, asshole!"

The sight of the barrel of the gun right in his face brought James back to full reality, even as his head felt like it was going to split down the middle.

"Just put the gun down, man," James said, much more coherent now.

"Keys, asshole!" the other man pronounced. "Outta the car, and gimme your goddamn keys!"

The timer continued grimly counting down in the corner of James's vision, mocking him. [01:11:32]. There was no way he could walk home from here in an hour, even if he had limitless endurance.

"Damn it!" James cursed under his breath. He could think of no way out of this situation that didn't risk imminent death. And he couldn't die here.

"I'm doing what you asked!" James said loudly. He lowered his right hand and put the car in park. Then he turned the keys in the ignition and shut the engine off.

"Great work!" the man said. "Now get out and give 'em here!"

"You got it, boss," James said, forcing a smile. He pulled the handle to open the door, and then he took a step out of the car.

"The voice said they was gonna get me," the man was saying excitedly, "but I know they ain't!"

"The voice spoke to you too, then?" James asked, curious despite himself.

"What's it to you, dickhead?" the man screeched.

"Only that the voice said something to me too," James said carefully. "The voice with the screens, right? What did it say to you?"

The man suddenly looked very afraid. "S-spoke to you too? The voice told me, 'Jerry, don't let them put you back in that cage!' I ain't never going back, you understand?" At the end, his voice had climbed almost to a yell.

James nodded eagerly. "Yeah, I understand!" *So it really is personalized*, he thought. *And oddly specific for this guy. Maybe I'm not so special after all.*

"You understand? Then hand over the keys! I gotta get away from here!"

"I can give you a ride to wherever—"

"No, no ride! I need the car. Gimme the goddamn keys!"

The carjacker's voice had become heated again, and James tried to inject a soothing note into his own voice, to calm the situation.

"Jerry," James said, "why are you trying to take my car? You trying to get away from this?"

"Yeah," Jerry said. He nodded frantically. "If I can get far enough away, clear my head—"

"Jerry, you can't drive away from the voice," James said. "It'll find you. You need to let me help you—"

"No, I—I can get away!" Jerry was gesticulating wildly with his gun now, and James chose to back away.

"All right, Jerry," he said. "Take my keys and drive as far as you can!" James threw the keys overhand at Jerry's head, but off to the side slightly and far too hard for Jerry to catch them in his agitated state. The keys flew past Jerry, landing somewhere in the long grass that grew alongside the road. As Jerry turned to look at where they had gone, James began sprinting away.

He heard a loud sound that might have been a gunshot and might have been a car backfiring, but he didn't look back, and he didn't slow down.

He ignored the noises, as well as the dizziness and slight nausea that he traced to the pistol-whipping. He felt his gorge rising, but he held back vomit and kept moving, running past the other stopped cars and back up the road toward the firm. They started honking, probably at James's stopped Civic ahead of them, but he didn't stop to look around and find out. He stayed low and continued moving at a brisk jog until the terrain changed a bit, and he felt he was far enough away.

Finally, James turned around and made sure no one was behind him. Seeing no sign of Jerry, he slowed down, collected himself, and assessed his situation.

He felt he'd scored a small victory against the carjacker, at least. Jerry wasn't pursuing him and was now out of sight. If this apparently apocalyptic situation they were in was real, he'd made it unlikely that the other man would escape whatever was coming in this area, assuming that the System was geographically bound as Jerry imagined.

Even if the System was some kind of mass hallucination, James had still made it a lot harder for Jerry to steal his car. And once James got cell signal again, he could call the police.

But James couldn't fool himself into thinking his situation was good. How would he get home before the timer ran out? If he failed, what would happen to him and his family? He felt that death was a realistic risk because the voice from out of the sky had said as much. He wasn't willing to let Mina and Yulia face that alone.

The timer said **[01:04:11]**.

James set his jaw and resolved that he would get home, come hell or high water. He started walking back to the gas station he'd passed driving away from the office, a vague idea in mind that he would find some way from there. He was technically getting farther away from home and walking back toward the office, but at least at the gas station there would definitely be cars.

He would find some way to get a ride there, whatever it took.

After several minutes of marching, the gas station loomed into view across a field of long grass.

James broke into a sprint, cutting across the grass toward the station. He was moving fast, landing forceful footfalls with every step, which explained why he didn't notice any resistance when he put his foot down in a certain spot, instead receiving just an alert:

[You killed one Partially Mutated Frog, Lv. 0. Blocked experience gained.]

Partially Mutated Frog, huh? James felt only a modicum of surprise at this, he realized. By tomorrow, he would probably be taking everything in stride. But today was beginning to feel like it would be a very long day.

His mind raced as he ran the rest of the distance. *I guess I get experience by killing animals of any kind. Or maybe only System-altered ones. That might be all animals now, though. Do modern weapons still work? Would I get experience for shooting an animal or is that against a rule of some kind?* There were always rules in game-like worlds, both in video games and in fiction, and breaking those rules was either a way to get incredibly unfair power-ups, or it was a fast-track to oblivion. Usually, it would be the latter in any setting with a half-decent story.

As he reached the station, he couldn't resist bending to look at the bottom of his shoe. Sure enough, there was a smushed bit of amphibian stuck there. It looked weirdly blue for a local frog, but he supposed that must be related to the "Partially Mutated" description.

I don't have time to unravel the mysteries of this frog, he decided after staring for a long moment. He scraped off what was left where the grass met the parking lot pavement, and he moved forward. His mind was still slightly muddled, but as he moved, his eyes took in everything.

There were more than a dozen pumps at the station, but most of them were unoccupied. He could see two of the people who were using them moving frantically between pump and car, rushing to get their tanks filled and get back on the road. Even as James looked on, a big Ram truck pulled out of the station. The driver, a beefy, red-faced man, looked like he was in a big hurry as his truck veered, screeching, out of the gas station lot.

But James didn't concern himself with that man. *Five cars left*, he thought. *Five chances to either convince someone to take me home or . . .*

He began walking toward the pumps.

There was a part of James that was prepared for death beside his family. Apocalypse situations tended to have high death tolls by nature, and he wasn't naïve enough to assume that he was destined to survive. But he was not ready to die, or to let his family die, because he hadn't taken the situation seriously enough.

He peered through the glass storefront of the gas station building. There were only one or two figures inside. Everyone was moving quickly; every motorist was in a hurry to get back into their car and get away from here. They were unlikely, James guessed, to consider bringing on extra passengers who would only slow them down and provide no corresponding benefit beyond possible gas money.

He checked the timer. [**00:59:22**].

Fuck. Less than an hour now!

It was time to consider drastic measures.

James untied his tie and unbuttoned his collar, and he wrapped his tie around his right hand. Then he started looking around for someone who would be easy to carjack.

He saw a little old lady wearing a black hat and limping toward her driver's side door. She had a black cane in hand, and she seemed to lean heavily on it with each step.

Without really thinking about it, James started to move closer to her. He paused, ten feet away from the old woman and her car.

Am I really thinking about doing this? he questioned. *Jesus, she looks a little like my grandmother. Surely I'm better than that, right? I just got carjacked, and now I'm doing it to this innocent old woman?*

He took a deep breath and let it out. He resolved that he would find someone else to carjack, if carjacking was really going to be necessary. *Someone who can put up a fairer fight*, an inner voice commented darkly.

James ignored that voice, turned around, and began looking for someone else he could deal with—though whether through force or persuasion, he hadn't decided yet. The timer read [**00:52:45**].

But he hadn't gotten more than five steps when he heard a cry from behind him.

"Ahh!"

James turned and saw a large man with a tire iron in hand standing in front of the old woman. The big fellow had a grease stain on his cheek, as if he'd just come from trying to work on a car. *He probably has just been working on a car,* James realized. *His own.*

James was not too alarmed by the situation to note that this old woman had terrible luck.

"I need a ride, lady," the big guy was saying. "You can come with your car, or I can leave you here. Up to you."

Not my business, not my business, not my business. This is a distraction I can't afford. James's thoughts were a flood of inconsistent emotions and contradictory impulses. *I need to worry about me!*

Yet he ignored the sensible words, and his feet carried him forward instead. He found himself closing in on the old woman and the man with the tire iron, very much against his better judgment.

When he was within five feet, he stopped. Both of them had already taken notice of James, half turning to face him.

"Is this guy with the tire iron bothering you, ma'am?" James asked loudly, almost shouting.

I need to attract spectators, people who might intervene if this guy gets violent.

"Hey, it's not like that," tire-iron guy said a little uneasily, taking a half step back. He was looking around as if there was some movement behind James, and James just silently prayed that there were other people moving to help.

James took a few more steps closer.

"Do you need help, ma'am?" he asked, voice still elevated, striding up to stand halfway in between her and the man with the tire iron.

Tire-iron guy's weapon hand moved unsteadily back and forth, as if he were conflicted about whether to raise the tire iron and strike or not. James thought this was probably the man's first attempt at crime. If James were in his shoes, he'd be on the fence about whether to resort to violence or to turn and run away.

James liked to think he would be more resolute than the other man seemed— though, of course, he had also just barely decided he would not rob this woman himself.

As tire-iron guy stood indecisively sliding back and forth between violence and peace, James tried to calculate how quickly he could lunge and grab the tire iron from the other man's hand, but realistically, he knew it wouldn't be possible. The other fellow was bigger than him and looked stronger too.

And he seemed to know his way around the tire iron from the way he was gripping it. All he would need to do would be to raise it in the air, and a swift downward motion would break either James's wrist or his skull. Either way, James would be out of the fight for good.

Then tire-iron guy could do what he'd planned to do before James stuck his neck out.

This is so dumb. Is this how I'm going to die? James wondered. *Trying to stop someone from doing something I was considering myself? This is such a stupid fucking way to go. Me and my big, fat mouth!*

CHAPTER THREE

Lucky

As James thought the situation might be hopeless, a voice sounded from behind him.

"It's all right, sonny," the old woman said, her voice loud and reassuring. "I was just telling this nice young man that I would drop him off at his house on my way home."

Tire-iron guy visibly relaxed.

"Thank you," he said, eyes at his feet.

"Are you sure?" James asked, turning to face her. The words were completely pro forma. He was still sweating, and it wasn't just the heat. He couldn't help thinking he'd dodged another metaphorical bullet.

The old woman made eye contact with James, and there was no fear in her expression, just quiet acceptance.

"I'm sure."

She turned and stepped into the driver's seat of her car, and then James heard the doors to her car unlock.

The man with the tire iron walked around and got into the front passenger seat, and they pulled away. James stood there, half-dazed, for almost a full minute before he realized he'd probably just missed his best chance at a ride home.

No, don't worry about it, he thought. *They just headed in the opposite direction from where I live, and who knows if it's possible for all three of us to get to our homes before time runs out.*

He checked the timer again. **[00:49:56]**.

How the hell am I going to get home, though? His head pounded as he had the thought, and he wondered if it was possible the pistol-whipping had given him a concussion. He didn't know what the symptoms were.

He turned and looked back at the other cars that were still there, and he noticed that someone he didn't recognize was watching him.

The stranger, a slim woman with soft features and mousy brown hair, stood staring at him as if he were a zoo animal.

He turned and waved awkwardly.

"Hi, there," he said.

"Hello! I saw what you did just now," the woman said.

"Oh," James said. He didn't dare to hope, but was karma about to pay him an instant dividend?

"Are you a prosecutor?" she asked. "I feel like I recognize you."

"I was," he acknowledged. *Where is this going?*

"I knew it!" she said. "I recognized your voice."

Oh god, who is this woman? James wondered. *Does she have a grudge? How do I know her? Is she a defendant or a victim?* He couldn't place her face.

"Oh, you don't remember me," she said. "I guess you used to see a lot of people in court."

James felt for a moment as if he ought to be worried.

"Yeah," he said. He chuckled awkwardly. "You have me at a bit of a disadvantage."

"Well, thank you for helping me. When I was in court, I might have looked a little different. I was using at the time. I think you saw me on a retail theft charge. Maybe you'd remember my name. Avery Daniels?"

James face-palmed. "Yes, I remember you. And yes, you looked completely different. I don't want to be rude, but it's really night and day. Wow! I guess rehab really worked out for you?"

She's skinny now, but she looked half-starved when I saw her before. I was never entirely sure if I was helping the people who agreed to do rehab, James thought. *The only way I knew if they were doing well was whether they showed up in court again.*

"Yes," she said, smiling. "Yes, it really did. Anyway, I just wanted to say thank you. You and the public defender really helped me out. It's nice to see you're still, uh, fighting the good fight." She gestured in the direction the old woman had driven off in.

"Yeah," James said, sighing. "Well, you can't win 'em all, I guess. I hope that lady will be all right."

"It sounded like she felt she could handle herself," Avery said. "Where's your car?" She looked around as if suddenly realizing James was near the edge of the gas station lot, with no vehicle nearby. "Do you need a ride?"

"Yes, please," James said, nodding eagerly.

A few minutes later, they were moving down the same route James had driven earlier.

"So, he pistol-whipped you?" Avery asked. Her voice drilled into the pain in James's head, bringing the point home that he had indeed been struck with a small but heavy piece of metal.

"Well, it's a crazy day for everyone, I guess," James said. He'd only mentioned the previous incident to put her on her guard. He wasn't looking for sympathy. He just wanted to prevent any further carjacking incidents from derailing his second ride home.

He was fairly certain lightning wasn't going to strike twice and give him another friendly stranger.

As they drove, they passed a wreck on the side of the road. Fortunately, the car was completely in a ditch, so it didn't block traffic, but James got a decent look at it as they passed.

Is that my car? Probably not. Surely he hadn't been the only Honda Civic on the road that afternoon. But the color was the same. *I wish I'd checked the license plate.* He hadn't seen the driver's face either, although there was definitely someone still in the car, hidden behind the driver's side airbag.

It would be ironic if it was Jerry, James thought. *Maybe I avoided an accident by getting delayed.*

Avery's old Beetle arrived in James's apartment complex without further incident.

James thanked Avery for the ride, and she smiled and waved him off.

"Give your family my love," she said.

James said that he would, but he had resolved that he wasn't going to say anything to his family about what had happened. He didn't want to worry Mina, not in this emergency situation when every minute counted.

He tried the door knob on the apartment, and to his surprise, it was unlocked. He went in, taking the stairs three at a time, ignoring the pounding in his head, wary of what he might find.

Mina was not at her usual daytime spot in her home office but was instead sitting on the sofa in the living room, wearing a light jacket over a maternity dress, a single pale hand resting on her very round stomach.

"I hope you don't blame me for not standing," she said gently in her lightly accented English. "I really am very happy to see you."

Wordlessly, he rushed into her space and pulled her into his tight embrace. He let out a long breath, and a shaky smile overtook his face.

"Mm," she sighed. "I love your strong arms holding me."

Immediately he pulled away against her resistance and became serious again. There simply wasn't enough time.

"How are you?" he asked. "How's the baby? Is Yulia here or still at school?" He rested a hand on her pregnant belly as he spoke, his tone urgent.

"I am doing fine, skapi. Please don't worry about me and the baby right now.

We're okay. As for Yulia, she just got home, and she's in her room changing. The school had the decency to put the kids on their buses before they dismissed early for the day."

"Thank goodness," James said. The school wasn't far, but he wasn't eager to try making that distance on foot in the time remaining. He dropped onto the sofa beside her, tension draining from his body.

"Are you all right?" she asked.

"Me?" James said.

She arched an eyebrow, and James realized he probably looked like a mess.

"I'm fine, I just"—he shook his head and smiled again—"just finished moving heaven and Earth to make sure I got here in time. Maybe I'll tell you about it some other day."

"What do you think all this means?" Mina asked. She had said she was fine too, but James could hear worry in her voice.

"I don't know," he said frankly. "I just have theories."

"What kinds of theories?"

"They're really dumb and basic. It's not like I know anything you don't."

"Try me. I want to see if your dumb theories are as silly as the ones I came up with."

"I guess that disclaimer gives me some cover." He smiled. "It has to be a mass hallucination, a delusion for just me that has my imaginings of other people in it, or there's a real world of magic or science out there so advanced that we can't understand it. So advanced that it makes no difference if it's magic or science. I mean, if alchemy had been a real, effective thing back in the Middle Ages, that would be the science now—"

"I think your second theory is a bit insulting, though," Mina interrupted, cutting him off before he could spiral down a rabbit hole.

"Insulting how?"

She touched the tip of one long, dark-red fingernail to his lips.

"Do you really think you could imagine everything I would be doing and saying in this situation? Let alone everyone else? Because that would have to be true for this all to just be a delusion—just *your* delusion."

"I don't know—I guess not."

"Well, don't guess. *I know.* I'm too complex for you!" Her voice had a teasing edge now. Any hint of annoyance, he knew, had just been her playing. That was a bad habit of hers, so he never knew for sure if she was serious the first time she said something.

The first time she'd suggested they try for a baby he had taken it as a joke. After a couple of more hints with no reaction, she had taken more initiative, to mutually satisfying results.

"Then I guess either we're both crazy, or this is totally real," he murmured.

He leaned back on the sofa and rested his head. This was already turning out to be a *long* day.

After a minute or two of quiet, there was a sound of movement in a corner of the apartment, and James opened his eyes. He would have to find his second wind sooner rather than later. The three of them needed a plan *now*, before they were yanked into Orientation.

The door to Yulia's room creaked open, and as he looked over, James saw she was joining them. Sometimes she seemed reluctant to bother them when James and Mina were in the middle of talking, but this time, she had only waited for a lull in the conversation before she stepped out. A sign that she understood the situation was urgent.

"It's good that you're here," he said. "It's time for a family meeting."

Yulia was Mina's fifteen-year-old youngest sister, and James and Mina had adopted her after Mina and Yulia's mother died, so technically she was James's oldest child—and would be the new baby's big sister as well as its aunt, once the child came in two months or so. Yulia was similar to her older sister in appearance, almost a smaller version of the pale, long-haired brunette.

Yulia looked a little nervous at the prospect of a sudden meeting—the last one had been about setting down ground rules for hanging out with boys—but she quietly settled into a chair across from James and Mina.

As he thought about what to say, James felt anxious himself. Yulia was all of five foot two inches and ninety pounds soaking wet, and while Mina would ordinarily be somewhat more imposing at five foot six inches, she was now heavily pregnant. The advent of the System had not found them at a good place in terms of readiness to face physical danger.

"Have either of you done anything to prepare for the Orientation that the System mentioned in its messages?" he began.

"The System is the voice that talks in our minds, sis?" Yulia asked. Her English was imperfect, as both she and Mina were Bulgarian by birth. As the first born, Mina had spent much longer learning English, and she had always been the smartest of the four sisters that made up their family. Mina spoke English like a native already, while Yulia was much less secure in her proficiency.

Mina nodded. "That's right, Yulia." Turning to her husband, she said, "We haven't done much, James. I didn't know if there was much to do. I grabbed our emergency bags"—she pointed to three backpacks sitting in the corner of the room—"and I'm packing heat." She patted her left shoulder, indicating that there, under her jacket, was where her gun was holstered.

"Well, I guess that's just about the best we can do," he said. "We have no idea what to expect, except that it's dangerous. Where's my gun, by the way?"

"Packed it in your bag. Don't worry." Mina smiled. This was a role she knew well and enjoyed: making sure the family was prepared. She had always been more of a planner than James, and it had been her idea for James to buy, and the family to practice with, the two firearms. The pleasure of being well prepared almost managed to wash out the fact that it wasn't a picnic they were getting ready for, but a dive into the great unknown of the universe.

James dove into his bag, retrieved his gun, and handed it to Yulia.

Mina frowned. "Are you sure about that, James? Yulia hasn't practiced with them nearly as much as we have. You'll be defenseless, and she might not be able to use it under pressure."

"It's just for now," he said. "I'm giving it to her in case something happens when the countdown finishes, and we get separated. We should put more food in the bags than we typically have too. And some of our silver coins. We have no way of knowing if whatever is happening will take away what we have on us, and we'll show up somewhere naked, but we might as well be as prepared as possible for as many different possibilities as possible."

"Well, the silver is packed," Mina said. "I figured that should be in the emergency bags months ago, so it's been there."

After she said this, James grabbed a folding knife for himself and put it in his pocket, then gave his other folding knife to Mina. He also distributed three sharp kitchen knives to keep in their bags as backup weapons in case something disarmed them.

"How about food?" Mina asked.

James first grabbed a half-dozen cans of tuna from the pantry, then looked inside the refrigerator and noticed it wasn't cold. He turned to look at the stovetop clock, which was blank. *The power's out.* He wondered how long the electricity had been gone.

When he asked, Yulia confirmed that by the time her bus left school, around fifteen minutes before he got home, the power had been out there too. *The power is probably out at the firm now too.* Not that it mattered at this point. James's coworkers were on their own.

As he had that thought, the ground began to shake.

[Ten of your minutes remain!]

CHAPTER FOUR

Big Sea

Ten of your minutes remain!]

"All right, already!" James shouted nervously, as if the voice of the System was really listening to him. Then again, maybe it was. The quaking stopped eerily quickly after he raised his voice.

We're rooting for you, James, he remembered the announcement saying.

There was no other answer besides the quaking stopping. James didn't waste time waiting for anything else from the disembodied voice, which had just produced a small earthquake in a part of the country that didn't get earthquakes, as if shifting tectonic plates was as easy as setting a phone alarm. Maybe it was for the System.

He pushed into high gear, hustling to complete any preparations he had yet to make. He rushed around, looking in closets and under the bed and behind the sofa. He double-checked the bags and made sure that everyone was physically touching their go-bags.

Finally, after triple-checking that everyone had adequate rations, assorted supplies, and armaments—and seeing that Mina and Yulia were growing nervous from how on-edge he seemed—James sat down next to his wife and her sister and tried to relax. He put an arm around Mina, and she leaned in close and laid her head on his shoulder. He could feel her shivering slightly, so he leaned to the side and grabbed a blanket that was lying next to them on the sofa.

Once Mina was adequately covered, he resumed thinking about what was likely going to happen next. If the world was going to go through some dramatic change into a magical version of itself, there would probably be a choice of what kinds of abilities each person would specialize in.

Unless it was based on some innate traits. *Status.*

The Status screen toggled with the thought.

[Status
Name: James Robard
Race: Base Human
Class: Blocked
Job: Blocked
Health: Blocked
Mana: Blocked
Stats
Blocked
Skills
Blocked
Talents
Blocked
Titles
Blocked]

Still blocked, with less than ten minutes left to go. No clues there. I'll assume we have a choice.

"You should both go to the bathroom," he said. "Then we should have a quick strategy session."

"Leaving it to the last minute, I see," Mina said, looking into the air where her timer must be. Then she went.

Yulia went next.

Then the three huddled around the kitchen table, wearing their backpacks at James's insistence.

"I think the situation we find ourselves in is a bit like a video game or a table top role-playing game," James began.

"You're not going to the bathroom too, my love?" Mina interjected.

"We only have six minutes. I can wait until we see what the Orientation looks like. Anyway, if I'm right, we're all going to be assigned classes and have the opportunity to learn some sort of magic or fighting skills. I've been thinking about this, and I want the three of us to be able to form a fighting party together. Yulia, you've played video games, right?"

"I like video games, yeah."

"You know what a team usually looks like in a fantasy game where players form parties to fight together?"

"Umm." She shook her head. James suspected it was the language barrier at work.

"We need a front-line fighter, a magic user with long-range attacks, and a healer to patch us up when we get hurt." Now he'd put it in the simplest terms he could, and he saw very quick comprehension on Yulia's face.

"I volunteer to be the fighter," James added. "That means you two split the other two roles."

"But I always wanted to be a warrior woman, like valkyries," Mina said, pouting.

On the timer, [00:04:32] remained, and James was not amused by the last-minute joke. His facial expression must have conveyed it.

"I volunteer to be the healer," Yulia jumped in. "That way, Mina gets to cast lightning bolts and fireballs or whatever." She had a reflex to try to diffuse conflict whenever she thought it was brewing; James had noticed it many times before. Sometimes, he found it ill-advised. A conflict avoided would just bubble back up later. This time, it was absolutely essential.

"Thank you, Yulia," he said.

"Well, since the two of you have so generously taken on the boring roles, I suppose I will agree to be the magic user in a hypothetical party, in the event that the System is magical and offers us a choice between different magical paths as James imagines."

The faintly ironic tone of Mina's response put the cap on the absurdity of the situation, and James again seriously considered the possibility of the System and all its messages being a mass hallucination. But he couldn't quite buy it.

The three of them quieted down a little now, with all James's outstanding questions settled, knowing something was about to happen that might change their lives forever.

"I love you," James said quietly, looking at Mina.

"I love you both very much," Mina said back, taking both of their hands and smiling.

They sat like that for the last few minutes, holding hands in a semicircle around the kitchen table. James resolved not to let go; he thought somehow, irrationally, that they would get separated if they let go, but if they kept hold of each other, they would stay together, despite the fact that this was a System that had the capability to speak into their minds and shake the earth beneath their feet.

He was looking into Mina's eyes when the world faded to white.

It wasn't like passing out. He could still feel his body, and he knew he was wide awake, but he couldn't feel Mina's hand or the chair beneath him.

He didn't think he could move. There were no geographic features to the white space he now occupied. It was like being in the middle of a blank page.

Then a material space emerged around him. It was still white, but now there were walls, a ceiling, a floor, a bed. It was like a hospital room from another dimension, so clean it was almost antiseptic. There was complete silence.

James realized he had regained his ability to move, if it had ever been lost, and he took an experimental step forward.

"Hello," a gravelly voice came from his side.

James jumped six inches into the air and twisted in mid-jump to face the voice. It looked like a moving clay sculpture with clumps of gray flesh and few other distinguishing features. The thing didn't have a real face, only a mouth attached to the general shape of a head, which was perched atop a vaguely humanoid figure.

"Who or what are you?" James asked once he'd landed. He kept his voice steady. The thing didn't seem hostile, and he wasn't intuitively scared of it. He finally had someone to answer his questions.

"I am a homunculus created by the System," the clay man said.

"Homunculus? An artificial life-form, right?"

"Yes, that's correct."

"Can you tell me why I'm here? Why the System is doing this?" James asked, cutting to the chase. He figured pleasantries would be wasted on what was effectively a robot.

"As for why you're in this place right now, you are to receive a tutorial from me prior to Orientation, so you will not be lost when it starts. As for why the System does what it does, the answer is complicated, and my explanation might be more misleading than enlightening. Knowledge of the deep functioning of the universe is outside my parameters."

"All right, then. I'll save that question for someone whose answer will hopefully be enlightening rather than misleading. What are your parameters, to save us some time?"

"I can explain your interface with the System and what happens next. I can also offer you your choice of starter Classes."

I knew it! Hopefully, Mina and Yulia stick to what we discussed, and we'll be able to function as a party.

"That's great! Could you explain why my Status screen shows everything as blocked to start with?"

The System Homunculus seemed to frown. "It shouldn't show everything like that anymore. It was only because you tried to access it before you got here, while the System wasn't properly up and running yet."

"Eh, up and running enough," James said. "It influenced one of the people I met into attacking me and stealing my car before this tutorial started."

There was a slight pause. "Influenced how?"

"He claimed that the System voice was telling him he needed to escape the region or that he might be caged again."

"That seems unlikely. It's not supposed to happen. The System does not send individualized messages. My information indicates that your Earth was a dangerous world before the System arrived. Are you sure of what you're saying?"

"Positive! I had a full conversation with him while he aimed a weapon at my face! Then he pistol-whipped me. For reference, that isn't a common occurrence for me. Or it wasn't, before the System. Since this apparently wasn't supposed to happen, I don't suppose you could do anything to heal my injuries?" James didn't really hope for much, but he thought he might as well ask. Nothing ventured, nothing gained. His head *was* still killing him.

"You are to receive a starter kit of supplies when you enter Orientation. I could give you the potion from your kit right now."

"Well, then I'd be at a disadvantage compared with everyone who didn't use up their potion before the big event starts," James complained. "What about you just giving me an extra? I promise I won't tell anyone."

"I am not authorized—"

"I get it," James cut him off. "It's not within your parameters."

The System Homunculus nodded. "Exactly."

"Homunculus," James said, channeling his best Karen energy, "could I please speak with your manager?" *Well, if he was willing to give me a potion early, there might be some leeway if I can talk to the right person.*

"You mean the proctor for the Orientation," the Homunculus said.

"Sure, whoever," James said. *Fingers crossed that whoever the proctor is doesn't turn me into a frog or something for the impertinence.*

"Now dialing the proctor," the Homunculus uttered. A ringing sound began to emanate from his head. *This is like something out of a cartoon*, James thought. *I wonder if there's a handset that detaches from his head!* He snorted to himself.

The ringing stopped abruptly, and James somehow *felt* that another presence was in the room, inside the Homunculus's body. Accompanying it came a great sense of pressure, as if James were an ant, and there was a large child standing above him, holding him in place with a single massive finger pressed down across his whole body. It was almost paralyzing.

Then a very accented voice came out of the System Homunculus's head, and it took a part of the psychological tension in the room with it, although James's body still felt as if he could be forced to his knees at any moment. The voice reminded James a bit of a young Joe Pesci.

"Hey, Sisco, what's the deal? I'm trying to sleep here. The Orientation isn't set to start yet!"

"Oh. Hi, Mr. Proctor, sir," James said in his best earnest schoolboy voice. "I was just explaining to, uh, Sisco here that I was injured, before I was pulled into the Orientation, by someone who was influenced by a unique System message that only he received. We were talking about him healing me, so that the System wouldn't have put me at a disadvantage relative to everyone else before Orientation starts. He said we needed your approval."

"Kid, I think you've got a lot of moxie, lying right in front of Sisco's face like that. I admire that. For future reference, even if a proctor played dumb or wasn't already watching you before you called, I could just go through the Homunculus's recently recorded memories and know that you were full of crap."

"I may have slightly exaggerated. I'm just extrapolating where the conversation was going before you joined in."

"Were you going to mention the part where he offered you access to your starter kit early so you could heal yourself?"

"I'm sure you and I would've gotten there eventually," James comfortably lied through his teeth. It had always been a skill he was proud of.

"A world-class bullshitter!" the proctor exclaimed. "Kid, I think your nose is growing!"

James pretended to check his nose, and the proctor chortled.

"All right, kid, I'll do you a solid this once. Like we said, pardon our mess. Errors in the functioning of the announcement machinery are on us. We've been a little busy, and you know, even the best of processes can be interrupted or *interfered with* by one thing or another. The transformation of Earth took us a little by surprise with how quick it was. Like you were all eager for it or something! A lot of our attention was diverted there. A couple friendly words of advice, though. First, once you arrive at Orientation, it's free game! Whatever happens to you from there, it's on you. Asking to talk to the manager won't do you a lick of good there!

"Second, for future reference, sharp negotiating with a representative for an omnipotent, omniscient System would usually not be a good idea. Maybe even suicidal, which would be a shame, you being a family man and all." James felt a chill run down his spine. "You're floating in a big sea, and you don't have a paddle yet. Hell, you don't even have a boat! But that's why I like you, though. You've got big brass ones! I think you'll go far, kid. Now hold still. First heal is on me!"

A pale green light appeared all around James, and he swallowed and waited to see what effect it would have.

CHAPTER FIVE

Tabula Rasa

James needn't have worried about the effects of the light. It was exactly as benevolent as the proctor had indicated. He felt his body mend itself completely from head to toe. He felt as good as he had when he woke up that morning. Perhaps better.

"Now that's done," the proctor's voice said, "I should really get back to preparing for the Orientation. Good luck! I'm pulling for you, personally. Say hi to the wife and kiddies for me!"

"Wait, wait," James raised a hand as if he could stop this seemingly non-physical being from leaving by grabbing him. "What's your name?"

"Vincent," the voice came after a pause. "Vinny to my friends."

"Well, I won't presume to declare myself your friend when we've just met. But thank you, Vincent. I feel better than I've felt in months."

"Yeah, I may have actually cleared up a nascent case of diabetes as well as a concussion. Later, James!"

I was getting diabetes, huh? James thought.

"Shall we resume the tutorial?" the System Homunculus asked.

"Sure thing," James replied instantly. He wondered if Vinny was still listening, then decided it was all but a certainty that the proctor was. It seemed as if maybe the System did have some kind of a special interest in him, or at least some of its appendages did.

"It is customary that we begin by selecting your Class and then take a look at your Status menu."

"Wait, what? Why wouldn't we look at the Status menu before we make a permanent decision about what kind of fighter I'm going to be? We should at least find out what I'm good at first."

"Erm, it is *customary*. The Class decision is not a permanent one, anyway. It will evolve as you grow."

"Yeah, I don't think I want to abide by this custom, Sisco. Status."

[Status
Name: James Robard
Race: Base Human, Lv. 0
Class: None
Job: Attorney (Pre-System)
Health: 25/25
Mana: 40/40
Stamina: 25/25
Stats
Strength: 7
Agility: 8
Stamina: 5
Fortitude: 5
Dexterity: 4
Perception: 6
Will: 4
Intelligence: 10
Free Points: 0
Skills
Anthropophagy, Lv. 0
Emotional Control, Lv. 0
Empathy Control, Lv. 1
Empathic Projection, Lv. 0
False Impression, Lv. 1
Identify, Lv. 0
Persuasion, Lv. 1
Pillage, Lv. 0
Situational Intelligence, Lv. 1
System Interface
Universal Language Comprehension
Talents
Cannibalism, Lv. 0
Cool-Headed, Lv. 0
Manipulation, Lv. 1
Selective Empathy, Lv. 0
Titles

System Pioneer]

These are interesting, James thought, a little stunned. *I need to moderate my reaction. Vinny's probably still watching, waiting to see how I respond to these wonderful Talents.*

"Where exactly do these Talents come from?" he asked.

"Your initial Talents are based on who you were leading up to the beginning of the System upgrade of your world. Rarely, the System even generates unique talents for particularly unique individuals."

Externally, James nodded and put a finger to his lips as if thoughtfully considering the explanation.

Internally, he thought, *What is wrong with you people? It's been ten years! Ten years I've been trying to do the right thing! Why can't you recognize that? Why do you see only the worst in me?* James felt a seething rage boiling up within him at the System's interpretation of who he was—effectively a judgment of his entire life based on the Homunculus's description—but he knew he had to restrain it. The only external expression of this train of thought was a clenching of the fist that he held down at his side.

Just to be sure, he asked, "What exactly does the System look at when it makes these determinations?"

The System Homunculus spoke, a vaguely perceptible trace of something like confusion in its voice. "The Talents generation process is objective, based on the inclinations you've demonstrated over a lifetime. It does not see only the worst in people. It looks at everything."

This is who you are, it seemed to be saying, and in such a way that it almost seemed to be responding to his underlying thoughts rather than what he actually asked. But James couldn't just accept that at face value. He decided to abandon beating around the bush.

"How the hell is cannibalism one of the *inclinations* I've demonstrated over the course of a lifetime? Give me one example of a person I've taken a bite out of, please. Take your time. I'll wait!" He tried to keep his voice calm. This situation was already a little embarrassing, and he didn't want to lose hold of himself and wind up looking like a complete fool.

He'd had a bad day. Now he learned that what he had thought could be a fresh start was already polluted. The Talents that were supposed to mark him as special would instead single him out as a person who had been defective, a liar, and possibly even a killer before the System—the latter of which he'd never been.

It's marking me as a villain, he had time to think. *Permanently. Like Jean Valjean.*

Then—whether via the Homunculus or the proctor acting through him—the System responded, after a fashion. The status screen in front of James's face suddenly zoomed in, something he hadn't realized until now that it could do at all. A description of the Talent appeared.

[Cannibalism: You've lived your life taking advantage of others by taking more from them than you give in return. Your long-standing life pattern marks this as a fundamental aspect of your character. In the changed world of the System, you can take this to the logical extreme by taking everything from those you feed on, at no cost to you. Generates Skills Pillage and Anthropophagy.]

The System was *judging me*, James thought. It was judging him with breathtaking harshness, in a way no human ever had, at least not to his face. Was it wrong about him? If he was being honest with himself, he couldn't say. And that probably said it all right there.

"You do have an alternative option, if your Talents displease you." The screen zoomed back out to normal as the Homunculus spoke.

"The System can look at other parts of my life and come up with another slate of Talents? Why didn't you say so before? Show me what we're working with."

"Not quite. The option is a Talent called Tabula Rasa, which would replace all existing Talents and Titles. Most of your Skills would go with them. It's a Talent virtually all babies born into a System-inducted world start with. It means you have nothing. No Talents or Titles except those you earn with your conduct going forward. Not even System Pioneer, which our records indicate you acquired this morning."

James thought it over. He looked through his other Talents first, and he realized that by focusing a little harder on one in particular, he could manually produce the zooming in effect that the System had demonstrated with his Cannibalism Title.

[Manipulation: You've spent years honing your skill for directing the thoughts and actions of others. You have shown a deep ability to influence and deceive, especially when others don't realize what you're trying to do. In the changed world of the System, the greatest manipulators have a heightened chance to change the structure of the social hierarchy using the power of their words alone. Generates Skills False Impression and Persuasion.]

I met a good woman and turned over a new leaf, he weakly protested in his own mind. Mina knew what he was behind the mask that he wore for everyone else, but after he had come close to getting jail time nine and a half years ago, he had promised her he would change his ways. And he credited the magic of love with the fact that he hadn't conned or stolen from anyone in these last nine and a half years.

Instead, he did some research, studied for the LSAT, and attended law school. It turned out that law firms valued employees skilled at manipulation and possessed of a cool-headed demeanor and selective empathy.

So, he'd remained on the straight and narrow for years, and now he was almost ready to be a real family man when this happened.

Be honest with yourself, a voice deep inside him said. *You want these Talents. You* want *to be bad. And the System is giving you* permission. *It's a new world. No one to punish you. If they do, you just kill them. Then keep killing until you're on top. And then you make the rules.*

James listened to his dark side for long enough to make his decision. As a purely practical matter, even if he knew what that little voice was saying was wrong, he couldn't ignore how useful the Talents, Titles, and accompanying Skills seemed. *I need these to increase my chances of survival,* he told himself. *I'm my own man, not the System's creature. I'll take the decisions about right and wrong as they come.*

"All right, I'm keeping my Talents. Show me the Class options."

Another new screen appeared before he could even finish the sentence.

[Available Classes

Light Warrior

Medium Warrior

Heavy Warrior

Rogue

Healer

Mage]

Well, those names at least speak for themselves. He started zooming in on each in turn.

[Light Warrior: A basic, unevolved Class. Lightly armed and armored warriors who emphasize Agility over Strength. Quicker and with better reflexes than medium or heavy warriors, at the cost of lesser attack strength and durability. Typically uses subtle weapons such as rapiers, daggers, or small swords. With each level, gain +3 Agility, +1 Strength, +1 Stamina, +3 Free Points.]

[Medium Warrior: A basic, unevolved Class. Moderately armed and armored warriors who place equal emphasis on Agility and Strength. Quicker and weaker than heavy warriors, but slower and stronger than light warriors—a balanced Class. Uses the widest variety of weapons of the basic Classes, albeit with less proficiency in heavy or light weapons than the Classes more specialized in those. With each level, gain +2 Agility, +2 Strength, +1 Stamina, +3 Free Points.]

[Heavy Warrior: A basic, unevolved Class. Heavily armed and armored warriors who emphasize Strength over Agility. Stronger and hardier than medium or light warriors at the cost of lesser Agility and slower reflexes. Typically uses heavy weapons such as greatswords, two-handed axes, or halberds. With each level, gain +1 Agility, +3 Strength, +1 Stamina, +3 Free Points.]

[Rogue: A basic, unevolved Class. Lightly armed and armored fighters who place emphasis on stealth, precision, and evasion. Specialized in ranged weapons, smaller melee weapons, and sneak attacks. With each level, gain +2 Dexterity, +2 Agility, +1 Perception, +3 Free Points.]

James stopped there. He wasn't interested in the Healer Class, and he didn't want to tempt himself with the Mage Class, considering what he'd discussed with Mina and Yulia. Once that was eliminated, the decision was pretty easy.

He didn't want to take the Heavy Warrior option, because he didn't want to be a walking brick. They could find someone else to be a tank for the party if needed, but it wasn't going to be him. Light Warrior, too, was out because based on descriptions alone, it struck him as an inferior version of the Rogue, overly specialized in Agility. Fragile without any enhanced powers of Perception or Skill. Perhaps it would evolve into a Class he'd envy, but James needed to be able to either see danger coming every time or to be able to take at least a few hits, or he'd die before getting a Class Evolution, whenever that was.

That left Rogue and Medium Warrior as the Classes that most suited him. Although something in his nature pulled him toward the Rogue, he decided on the Medium Warrior. It was a moderate approach that should let him adapt and adjust as situations unfolded. The medium armor would protect him from attacks better than whatever protective covering the Rogue Class came with, without turning him into a slow-moving target. All around the best of all possible worlds!

James felt himself growing excited about the prospect of adventure again, a feeling he had quickly quashed the previous times it rose in him. This time he allowed a smile to touch his lips.

[Select Medium Warrior? Y/N]

He selected "Y," and a few pop-ups appeared immediately.

[**Congratulations! You have become a Medium Warrior!**]

[**You acquired the Skill Basic Proficiency–Common Weapons**]

[**You acquired the Skill Quick Strike, Lv. 0**]

[**You acquired the Skill Stubborn Defense, Lv. 0**]

[**You acquired the Skill Loot, Lv. 0**]

[**Superior Skill Pillage detected! Inferior Skill Loot merged into Skill Pillage.**]

[**Sufficient experience accrued. Pillage leveled up!**]

[**You acquired the Medium Warrior's Starter Kit!**]

Alongside the quick barrage of messages, a few pieces of dull gray armor that looked straight out of a medieval castle materialized in front of James and then clattered to the floor. A sack that looked empty dropped right next to it.

"Well chosen," the System Homunculus said after a brief pause. "Now that's done, I'll transport you to the Orientation grounds."

"Wait, I'm not read—"

The world faded to white again, but only for a moment. James reappeared instantly in what appeared to be a large clearing in a forest.

"Jesus, Sisco," James muttered to himself. *I think maybe he took me going to his manager personally. Do homunculi feel emotions?*

The armor and sack of gear again dropped to the ground next to him, and he bent to pick them up. He still didn't even know what was inside the sack, and he couldn't afford to lose any gear so quickly. He also reached to his shoulder and checked that his backpack was still there. It was.

With his items in hand, James slowly rose from his crouching position and looked around. At a cursory glance, he appeared to be surrounded by hundreds of people, most of whom looked to be as confused and disoriented as he felt. Unfortunately, he didn't recognize any of them.

CHAPTER SIX

Into the Woods

The first thing James did was to take his backpack off and put on the armor. It wasn't as complicated to do as what he'd seen in movies, perhaps because he had only been given a moderate amount of armor compared with the Heavy Warrior type. Once he had the chest armor, greaves, and vambrace on, he was virtually fully dressed.

The last piece, the helmet, he left off so as not to obscure his own view, sticking it into the sack with his backpack. It only slightly surprised James at this point that the sack didn't seem to change shape, size, or weight when he added a backpack and helmet to it. *Magic satchel*, he noted, and he tied the satchel to his belt, then directed his attention to the other people around.

Others, he noticed, were also dressed, or dressing, in their varying levels of armor, though there were also a large number of people who seemed to be dazed from the recent transportation and were just standing or sitting around, as if waiting for someone or something to give them direction. Those people, he suspected, would be among the first to die here.

James wanted to call out for Mina so that he could consolidate their party and make a quick exit from among the sheep, but he couldn't see any sign of her, and he didn't want to draw the attention of any hostile creature or entity that might be watching.

Perhaps most pressing, he had a strange feeling as he looked around at the mass of unfamiliar people. He'd thought at first that it was a sort of feeling of vulnerability that hit him because he wasn't wearing the armor he'd been provided in this situation, but putting on the armor hadn't helped.

It was hard to put his finger on the feeling exactly. There was nothing similar in his previous experience except goosebumps, but that was like comparing a sunburn to a burn from being on fire. This was like an intense chill that was just hovering in one particular place on the back of his neck, the way he imagined you might feel if you could somehow tell that you were about to be stabbed in the back of the neck.

This situation felt wrong. Dangerous somehow. James slowly backed away from the group and continued to look around, trying to figure out what was setting off this unfamiliar sense of danger. He suspected it was coming from the Skill Situational Intelligence, though for the moment he was more concerned about what in the environment was giving him this feeling.

James found his eyes drawn to a raised area of ground in the clearing, near its very center. A humanoid figure stood atop the mound, and as James's eyes rose up the body of this figure, he saw that it was clothed all in red except for its face, which was hidden behind a marionette-like mask. James felt a tremendous pressure overtake him when he met where the figure's eyes should be with his gaze, and he knew without a doubt that this was where his feeling of danger originated.

The pressure he felt was almost identical to what he'd felt from the proctor before. It just felt slightly more restrained. He couldn't understand how the people standing closest to the mound seemed to be ignoring the figure in red.

I need to get away before that thing attacks, James thought. He began backing away from the middle of the crowd of murmuring people, eyes peeled for Mina and Yulia.

He'd just made it to the edge of the crowd when the voice entered his head.

[Welcome to your Orientation, my dear Class of what you would number as the year 2042!]

Vinny? Well, he really shouldn't be surprised that the proctor's voice filled his head. But why did it feel like it came from that marionette-like figure in the middle of the field? Was that Vincent's real appearance?

James looked to the crowd, and many people were now staring at the same figure in red. He used Identify on the figure, and an all too brief description appeared above its head.

[Vincent Virgo, Lv. ????]

So it is Vinny. The name was a rainbow of color, which James suspected meant something important, and the level was a series of question marks, which James guessed meant he shouldn't be staring so much as trying to slip away.

[Sufficient experience accrued. Identify leveled up!]

The proctor continued his spiel.

[Lucky citizens of the world chosen for today's induction! Your circumstances were dire and your need great, and we have come in answer. It is your

privilege and my responsibility to begin this initiation of the 73rd Earth into the System that binds the other surviving member worlds.]

While he spoke, James had been using Identify on random people just to test out the functionality of the Skill and see if he could more quickly level it up if he used it on more people. The results had been interesting.

[David Rodriguez, Lv. 0]
[Jaime Rodriguez, Lv. 0]
[Isaac Roland, Lv. 0]
[Victoria Robertson, Lv. 0]
[Aaron Rolf, Lv. 0]
[Heather Rolf, Lv. 0]
[Terrence Rockington, IV, Lv. 0]
[Sufficient experience accrued. Identify leveled up!]

Not only were some families clearly together—besides the two Rodriguezes, there were other people who he hadn't bothered to identify who appeared to be related, and the Rolfs were clearly husband and wife as well—but not many people seemed to have moved from where they started. There was no one besides him, in other words, who appeared to be walking around looking for family members.

James's heart fell. The people here appeared to have been sorted by last name, with everyone he'd seen so far going by a last name that began with "Ro." If that was right, he wasn't going to find Mina or Yulia here. For immigration-related reasons, Mina hadn't been able to legally change her last name to Robard yet, so she wasn't going to be here. Mina and Yulia would both be in some D-sorted group for Danailova.

[As mentioned earlier, the Orientation is a deadly culling process where only the fittest are to survive. Fitness takes many forms, so don't be too arrogant, those of you who think themselves strong. The System has a way of balancing things out among the newly initiated. The Earth itself will be fairly dangerous once the System has completed its construction work there, so consider this your opportunity to adapt to the newly heightened level of danger. The Orientation will last ninety days, or until there's a last man standing.]

So I would need to kill everyone else to get back to Mina early? For a single wild moment, James considered how he might do it—he knew himself enough to recognize he would have few qualms in the moment of decision about slaughtering strangers to get back to protecting his family—before he reminded himself that Mina was in a parallel situation, and surely a seven-months-pregnant woman was not going to slaughter hundreds or thousands of people single-handedly just to get back under the umbrella of his protection. *So throwing my humanity away like that would be pointless.*

[There are no rules for how you survive Orientation. Just live, and there will be rewards commensurate with performance.]

Sounds like my cue to get out of here. This specific place within the Orientation space still felt incredibly dangerous to James, and the speech seemed to be winding down. Undoubtedly the prelude to violence. Even if it continued and began providing helpful information, it was being broadcast into his head, and James doubted there was a range limitation.

Without hesitating or looking back, he walked into the woods. The voice continued, and it didn't grow any quieter as James gained distance.

[I could explain more about how your personal interface with the System works or about the hierarchy of the new multiverse into which you're being initiated, but I find that lessons stick best when you learn them yourselves, through experimentation rather than just being told.]

James was getting some seriously deadly vibes from the speaker's tone now, so he slowed down and turned to see what was happening back at the clearing.

He had booked it into the forest, moving as quickly as he could without being too noisy. James was now so far away from the group that he could barely see them through the thick tangle of forest growth. He could, however, begin to see a rustling in the trees around the people he'd left behind, and he climbed up a tree nearby to get a better look.

Meanwhile, the proctor explained the situation further.

[As mentioned before, only half of your number, at most, is allowed to survive this Orientation. I'm sorry, but the System really must weed out the weak. If you fail to achieve this, we'll randomly eliminate half of the surviving members of the Orientation group, which will result in even fewer surviving than if the attrition had occurred on its own.]

Even from where he was, James could hear the low rumble of objections and arguments at that.

[Yes, we expect this to be difficult for many of you to accept, and for that reason, we're helping you out in three ways. First, you get a counter in your System screen that will help you keep track of the numbers.]

A number appeared in the corner of James's vision until he mentally swiped it away to keep his field of view clear.

[3,468/3,468 Survivors]

[The second thing is that we've scattered around some weapons and lots of opportunities for you to make yourselves deadlier.]

James pulled himself onto a branch to relax, listen to the end of the announcement, and observe. He had been forced to climb rather high to get a good view of events, but now he felt he could see everything.

The first thing he noticed was what a large group there really was in the field. In his closed-off corner, he hadn't realized how large the whole space was, but the area occupied was the size of a football field, and that space was *crowded.*

The second thing was that there was a contingent of people like him who were moving away from the field. He could see them by how the trees were moving around them. These people must still be moving in groups, rather than individually like him, or tracking their movements would be harder. Some of them had started moving almost as early as James, it seemed, but most had started just now. Even those remaining in the field looked a bit restless.

The third thing he noticed was a large number of trees moving together increasingly close to the crowd that still remained in the field, a group which must, James thought, constitute at least half of the population of the Orientation. Something—or rather, some *things*—were coming to get them.

[The third helpful thing is that this setting is full of monsters like those that you'll find once you've returned to your Earth. You can give them experience if they kill you, and they can give you experience and possibly loot if you kill them. This is how you get those weapons I mentioned. It should also help you with thinning the population out a bit. Now, my friends, I sense that the time for my explanation is nearing its end. Let my last words to you for now be "good luck!"]

A final pop-up appeared.

[Quest unlocked: Survive the Orientation!]

James saw a great plume of red smoke appear where Vincent had been, near the center of the field, and he knew intuitively that Vincent had disappeared.

There was little time for the people in the field to reflect on his words. Out of the trees, from multiple sides, came running a pack of what looked like massive wolves, beasts almost the size of men.

Well, I'm awfully glad I'm not down there, James thought. *Now, how do I secure myself to make sure I don't fall out of this tree?*

After he felt comfortably positioned enough at a fork between branches, he looked harder at the Quest itself, and the details populated.

[Survive the Orientation: You have entered the System's culling grounds for the new world, the Orientation. Half of those in your group must die before this Orientation concludes. Survive this process. Reward for Quest Success: Variable dependent on contributions. Penalty for Failure: Death.]

Useful in case I forget that I'm in a death game, James thought ruefully. *Some* additional *details would be nice. I guess there are no safe zones or other useful tips they're going to mention.*

As he began to hear the screams of men and women being torn limb from limb far off in the clearing he had come from, James tried to ignore the brutal noises while finally going through his starter kit of gear as quietly as possible.

Besides his armor, which he was still wearing out of a now quite vindicated concern for his safety, he found that the magic satchel—its real name was Small Bag of Deceptive Dimensions, per Identify, but he liked his name for it better—contained one Health Potion, one Mana Potion, one Stamina Potion, a Basic Dagger, a Basic Shortsword, and a Basic Buckler.

James observed that he could pull a particular item out of the bag by thinking of the one he wanted and reaching in. Putting an item away was equally simple: put it near the mouth of the bag, open the bag, and think of putting it away again. *Neat!*

James prepared for what would come next by strapping the buckler to his left vambrace and pushed the sheathed blades into his belt on opposite sides of his waist. Even if he hadn't wanted to be in the slaughter now unfolding in the open field, he did intend to do some fighting today. It was necessary to get experience, or the next day would only be harder.

And the truth was, he was excited to start killing monsters. Maybe it was childish, and he felt a little guilty, but now that he knew he had no way of reaching Mina and Yulia, there was no one and nothing he had to worry about here but himself and his personal growth. James was looking forward to cutting loose.

As he was grinning to himself, he heard the sounds of growling and movement approaching fast through the shrubbery below. It seemed an enemy was coming to him.

CHAPTER SEVEN

Solitary Man

As the creature James heard moving below approached closer, he pulled his dagger from its sheath and steeled himself. If the creature appeared in his line of sight, he wanted to make an ambush. While most of the other monsters he'd observed thus far were still fighting in the clearing, this one sounded like it was on its own.

James had the benefit of gravity and surprise on his side. There would never be a better opportunity to score a first kill.

Sure enough, the beast stepped into his field of vision near the bottom of the tree, and before James could identify more than a furry exterior, he was pouncing. The creature seemed to become aware of him as he fell. It tilted its head up at James and had just enough time to bare its teeth in a nascent snarl before he fell upon the beast. It was a wolf, probably the same kind as those in the clearing, with thick dark fur, flashing yellow eyes, and prominent canine teeth that looked almost as long as fingers.

James had a moment to doubt whether this was a good idea, and then his knife was plunged by his momentum and strong grip into the wolf's back. The wolf made a pained groan and lunged at its attacker. James was forced onto his back instantly by the wolf's movement, but he was able to pull his head back from the snapping jaws, and the wolf just barely fell short, jaws inches from his neck.

Its claws were scratching against James's armor as well, but it couldn't do any real damage there, and it was limited in its range of motion by the dagger James was still holding stuck halfway to the hilt in the wolf's back. Every movement made it sink deeper or rip sideways to damage the beast's body further.

After a few moments of struggling with the pain, the wolf overcame it and managed to lunge closer to James's throat again.

James forced his armored forearm into the wolf's wide-open mouth to keep it from landing a fatal bite, and with his other hand he pulled the dagger out of the wolf's back and began stabbing mechanically as quickly as he could into the wolf's side.

After a few moments of this, the wolf made a desperate whining sound and tried to pull back from James's blade, releasing his arm. That was a mistake, though.

Now that he could move freely, James threw himself on top of the slowly retreating beast. He used his armored left arm like a club and slammed the wolf's head down into the ground. Then he plunged the dagger down into the hollow of its throat, and an alert sounded almost instantly.

[You killed one Feral Forest Wolf, Lv. 1. You gained 10 exp!]

[Medium Warrior leveled up!]

Amazing, he thought a little numbly. A surge of energy rippled through his body, and he could feel he had grown noticeably stronger from the fight. It was exciting. The fight had been harder than he'd expected, though. *Probably killing humans would have been a lot easier*, he couldn't help thinking.

He assessed his condition.

James was scratched up in many places, he could feel bruises forming up and down his left arm where the wolf had chomped down on it, and even his dagger hand felt sore from maintaining his brutal death grip on the weapon. He forced himself to relax it now. Then he pulled the knife out, wiped it off on the wolf's pelt, and stuffed the blade back into its sheath. Mostly, he was tired.

All that effort for one measly level. He looked at his left arm again. *This had better heal on its own. I'm not wasting my only potion on this. I probably need to find someone and form a party. I'm going to need emergency healing sometime in the future, even if this bruising is gone tomorrow.*

He looked at the wolf corpse and back at the tree. He wanted to climb back up to rest and wait for another opportunity to ambush an enemy, but he was also aware that the wolf was meat, and he hadn't found any food in the magic satchel. So he needed this.

Let's see what this Skill does. He pointed a hand at the wolf. *Pillage!*

The wolf's body instantly took on a gentle glow. Then the alerts came streaming in.

[Feral Forest Wolf's body processed.]

[You obtained Common Wolfskin Pelt, 3x Wolf Meat Bundle, and a Wolfbone Dagger!]

Nice!

[Designate a target for Pillaging: Stats, Skills, Talents, or Titles.]

James had no idea what this was about, but it sounded pretty good. *I probably ought to finish properly going through all my Skills.*

Without thinking too much about it, he mentally selected Skills. There wasn't much to it; he just figured that this was a predatory animal, and even at level one, it must have some pretty decent abilities.

[Skill Obtained: Crushing Bite!]

[Sufficient experience accrued. Pillage leveled up!]

This Skill had better not be more of the System trying to get me to eat people, he thought irritably. His jaws already felt slightly different, though. Stronger. Something he might test later.

He looked down, and he found it curious—and very cool and magical, though he would admit it to no one—that his Pillaged loot was all that was left of the wolf. The rest of the body had apparently returned to nature.

He gathered up the wolf's meat, which was nicely separated into three large packages wrapped with butcher paper and string, and he put them in his magic satchel. Then he picked up the pelt and dagger.

[Common Wolfskin Pelt: The pelt made from James's first victim. Contains the residual durability of the wolf. Boosts Fortitude by 5 when worn. Grants access to Skill Basic Cold Resistance.]

[Wolfbone Dagger: A dagger crafted from James's first victim. Contains the residual ferocity of the wolf. Boosts Strength by 3 when worn or wielded. Grants access to Skill Wolf's Bite.]

Again, good stuff. Nice job, System! I wonder how this loot compares to what I would've gotten with the inferior Loot Skill. Maybe I can run an experiment once I have a party and find out.

He threw the pelt on over his armor immediately and stuck the dagger beside its brother in his belt. Then James climbed up the tree again. He was a little stronger this time, but he was also a lot more tired, so it only felt slightly easier climbing than it had been the first time. Finally, he resumed his perch on the same branch from which he'd sprung down on the unsuspecting wolf.

All right, I'm all alone. I'm as safe as I can be for the moment, and I just barely won the fight. It's time to actually figure out what my Skills do, or the next fight might not be so easy. Status.

[Status

Name: James Robard

Race: System-Boosted Human, Lv. 0

Class: Medium Warrior, Lv. 1

Job: Attorney (Pre-System)

Health: 28/100

Mana: 40/40

Stamina: 12/36

44   D. J. RINTOUL

Stats
Strength: 9(12)
Agility: 10
Stamina: 6
Fortitude: 5(10)
Dexterity: 4
Perception: 6
Will: 4
Intelligence: 10
Free Points: 3
Skills
Anthropophagy, Lv. 0
Basic Cold Resistance
Basic Proficiency–Common Weapons
Crushing Bite, Lv. 0
Emotional Control, Lv. 0
Empathic Projection, Lv. 0
Empathy Control, Lv. 1
False Impression, Lv. 1
Identify, Lv. 2
Persuasion, Lv. 0
Pillage, Lv. 2
Quick Strike, Lv. 0
Situational Intelligence, Lv. 1
Stubborn Defense, Lv. 0
System Interface
Universal Language Comprehension
Wolf's Bite
Talents
Cannibalism, Lv. 0
Cool-Headed, Lv. 0
Manipulation, Lv. 0
Selective Empathy, Lv. 0
Titles
System Pioneer]

James bypassed the Stats section of his menu, interesting though it seemed—
The wolf did all that to my Health?—to focus for now on his Skills specifically. He
needed to know everything, but these were most pressing. Just like in the tutorial
space, focusing on a Skill pulled up its information.

**[Anthropophagy: The bearer of this Skill can consume their own kind to
grow stronger. Consuming meat of your own species will cause your injuries**

to heal more quickly and increase your gain of Stats and Skills. Receive no penalties for eating the meat of your own kind, or raw meat of any non-poisonous creature.]

I thought the word "anthropophagy" looked familiar, he thought. *It just means cannibalism. What the hell, System? I get the hint, already. You want to see me eat people! It's still probably never going to happen!* Onto the next Skill, which he thought ought to be less irritating.

[**Basic Cold Resistance: Grants low-level resistance to cold environments and cold effects.**]

[**Basic Proficiency–Common Weapons: Grants a basic level of proficiency in a wide variety of commonly used weapons, including weapons used by all of the basic Classes.**]

Basic, but good.

[**Crushing Bite: Your powerful jaws can do great damage. Passively strengthens your bite and increases your likelihood of biting through both flesh and bone.**]

Okaaaay. That's useful, though it sounds like exactly what the System would give me if it wanted me to eat people.

[**Emotional Control: You retain control over your emotions under all but the most overwhelming circumstances. Your mind, rather than the fight or flight reflex, dictates your actions in a crisis, and you retain the reaction speed and decisiveness of action possible using the fight or flight reflex at all times.**]

That sounds like it might low-key make me a badass all by itself. He imagined himself getting into a bar fight and calmly dodging all the opponent's strikes before delivering a chop to the enemy's neck and putting him down with one hit.

[**Empathic Projection: Place yourself in another's shoes and find yourself generally aware of what they are likely to do next. The more time spent with someone, and the more they reveal of themselves, the more effective this Skill is.**]

Isn't that something I already do? If it actually lets me predict people's actions, that would be useful, but it doesn't sound like this is that level.

[**Empathy Control: Consciously choose whom you want to empathize with, and how much. You retain the ability to place yourself in another person's shoes for purposes of predicting their actions, without incurring any unchosen feelings of obligation or sympathy.**]

That's a cold Skill. He thoroughly approved, though he again thought that this was something he already did.

[**False Impression: Give the impression you wish to give, regardless of the reality. Boosts efforts to alter one's appearance, smell, or voice, forge items or documents, and make deceptive statements. You can also alter the way your Status screen appears when viewed by others.**]

Mm-hm. James would definitely want to look into the effects of this further in the future, for completely honest and morally righteous reasons of course.

[Identify: Basic identification Skill common to all sentient beings in System worlds. Allows you to identify things.]

No shit.

[Persuasion: Talk is cheap for most people, but you make it expensive. Boosts your ability to convince intelligent life-forms to do your bidding, even at personal cost. Effects scale with Will and Intelligence.]

That will require some further investigation.

[Pillage: Take from your vanquished enemies everything they have. Allows you to steal a dead or dying life-form's property, including body parts, as well as take from one of their inherent attributes of your choice: Stats, Skills, Talents, or Titles. Within the selected category, the individual attribute seized is random. You may only use Pillage once per instance of an individual life-form dying or drawing near death.]

James knew immediately that this was going to become his bread and butter. The idea of stealing other people's or monsters' abilities sounded extremely broken and overpowered to him. The phrasing of the ability was also interesting and suggested potential for abuse, such as by healing a near-dead enemy after using Pillage, then killing them and hitting them with it again. *I made the right choice not to take Tabula Rasa.* Onto the last set of Skills. Almost all basic stuff, by the looks of it.

[Quick Strike: A moderately quicker-than-normal attack movement. Activation cost of 10% of base Stamina. Effect scales with your Agility.]

[Situational Intelligence: A passive ability to intuitively sense whether your surroundings are dangerous or not, accompanied by intuitive guidance about how best to avoid or counteract the threat.]

[Stubborn Defense: Allows you to put up a moderately stronger-than-normal defense against an attack—whether with weapons, tools, environment, Mana, or body parts—than would normally be possible. Activation cost of 10% of base Stamina. Effect scales with your Strength or Will, depending on whether the defense applied is physical or magical.]

[System Interface: Basic ability to use the System, view your Status, and modify it.]

It's interesting which Skills don't have levels. I wonder if that means they can't be upgraded.

[Universal Language Comprehension: Ability common in System worlds to speak, read, and write in Tongues. From now on, anyone integrated into the System will understand and be understood by you.]

[Wolf's Bite: A fierce attack with any pointed, penetrating object(s) or body part(s). If more than one pointed object strikes, attack may deal crush

damage as well as penetration damage. Activation cost of 20% of maximum Stamina. Cooldown of 30 seconds. Effect scales with Strength and Will. If more than one penetrating point strikes the target, damage also scales with number of penetrating points.]

Some very interesting abilities there. A couple that arguably quietly changed the world, like System Interface and speaking in Tongues. But the most interesting thing short term was the damage-dealing potential of Wolf's Bite, which he could imagine himself using with a shield that was covered in sharp spear points to deal massive damage. Completely counter to the probable intent of the ability, but the joy of power was only as great as the amount of abuse you did.

James wondered idly if his arm had fallen victim to that crushing damage. *More importantly, what would have happened if that arm hadn't been armored?*

Before he could give that question more thought, though, he heard the sound of more movement through the trees. More than one thing moving this time, though he couldn't see yet what exactly was approaching him. At least three creatures, all converging on James's tree.

He drew his sword and smiled grimly.

CHAPTER EIGHT

Distress

I just need to wait for them to get a bit closer, James thought. *As soon as I see the yellows of their eyes.*

He assumed it would be more of the wolves, whose eyes were a creepy yellow color.

Sure enough, after a few long moments poised with his sword pointed down, a wolf emerged from the tree line. It stopped running and stood facing the direction of the other movements, completely oblivious to James's presence. It was apparently waiting for its friends. Instead of staying put in his tree until the other wolves made their appearance, James dropped straight down, sword held out point first toward the wolf.

Once James was a foot or so above, it seemed to recognize something was entering its space, and it turned its head to look behind it, but the movement was too little, too late. Momentum carried James through into stabbing the wolf, and this time, the much longer blade of the shortsword penetrated far deeper than the dagger had.

As James's body landed beside the wolf, he braced himself for a sudden lunge that never came.

A pitiable yowl escaped the wolf's throat, and James saw that he had fully impaled the creature right through its center of mass and into the ground. It didn't look like it could move anymore without hastening its own death.

A closer look at this wolf also seemed to show that it was markedly smaller than the previous one. *Maybe a teen wolf?* James thought, smirking.

Nevertheless, wary of those very developed, adult-looking jaws, James carefully placed his foot at the tail end of the beast, reached down to the hilt of the sword, and began to pull.

The wolf feebly tried to reach back with its jaws and bite James's hand, but he managed to grip the sword while keeping his hands safely out of the broken beast's reach. The creature could barely move its head anyway, and it was visibly losing large quantities of blood before his eyes, even more as he pulled the sword out of its body.

He had just managed to retrieve his sword when he saw movement shaking the bushes directly in front of him. He quickly reached his hand out toward the dying wolf. *Pillage!*

The creature began to glow, and James heard it make the most pathetic whine he'd ever heard, as if it were being dissected alive or something. Maybe it was; he *was* Looting it like a dead body.

[Juvenile Feral Forest Wolf's dying body successfully processed.]

[You obtained Juvenile Wolfskin Pelt, 2x Wolf Meat Bundle, and 6x Wolfbone Bolts!]

So it was *a juvenile*, he had time to think before he found himself dealing with a new problem. Three humans had burst through the bushes and were engaging a pair of wolves in desperate combat, ignoring James's presence.

He distractedly selected Stats as the attribute he wanted to steal and put his loot away as he stared at the scene in front of him. He was going to need greater Strength or Agility or something as soon as possible. *Of all the people to see here*, he thought, *it had to be them.*

Very busy dealing with their own troubles and seemingly having hardly noticed him, Cliff Rogers and Alan Roget from work stood grouped up with a woman who looked about Alan's age. The three were barely holding on against a pair of wolves.

Cliff was shouting curses mingled with confused orders, trying ineffectively to coordinate his movements with Alan's. The woman was shushing Cliff, seemingly aware that his noise might draw additional wolves. They stood in a small circle, backs to a nearby tree, as they tried to fend the beasts off.

James faced a decision. He could back away from this fight and leave his coworkers and the woman with them to their fate, or he could step in and pull their bacon out of the fire. The decision would have been easy if it were just Alan and the unfamiliar woman, probably his wife. But Cliff wasn't someone James really wanted to save, nor did James think he would be good to have around in a life-or-death struggle.

He was always a pain in the ass to work with, but do I really want to leave him and Alan to die? James sighed. The answer was clear without much thought.

He turned to the wolf again, put his foot down on the beast's throat, and quickly crushed it with as much force as he could, until he heard the ding and received the announcement.

[You killed one Juvenile Feral Forest Wolf, Lv. 1. You gained 7 exp!]

Now he could safely go after the other wolves. Thanks to his quick action and quiet killing method, the other wolves still hadn't turned away from their prey. James used their preoccupation to his advantage.

He approached slowly and quietly at first. Then, *Quick Strike!*

He lunged at the nearest wolf, which was snapping at the woman, and James's shortsword stabbed almost all the way through it.

[Sufficient experience accrued. Quick Strike leveled up!]

James angrily dismissed the notification with a thought. Fortunately, the split-second distraction didn't take away his advantage.

The wolf let out a cry of pain. It had enough fight left in it to turn its head and try to bite at James, but it only succeeded in impaling itself further, its jaws still inches away from his fingers.

James let go of the sword and drew his two daggers. The wounded wolf charged him as he readied his stance, but it was too slow now to get the jump on him.

As it entered striking range, James closed in with the two daggers positioned like pincers on the wolf's sides. *Wolf's Bite!*

The blades penetrated the wolf on both sides of its chest, and then the beast was on him, jaws predictably going for the throat. James reflexively blocked with his left arm, which turned into a wolf chew toy for the second time that day.

As he held the wolf's jaw back and tried to ignore the pain in his left arm, James's right hand pulled the Wolfbone Dagger forward through the wolf's body, hoping he would cut into something important. The wolf's hot blood poured down onto his chest, and after ten or fifteen seconds of this, the wolf's bite strength began to noticeably weaken. James thought that more of its blood must be outside its body than in it by this point.

Now that its bite lacked the force needed to truly injure James, he was able to pull his armored arm out of the beast's jaws and give it a hard whack with the buckler mounted on the vambrace. The wolf reeled back, and James pulled himself to an upright position. Then he pushed himself onto the wolf and held it by the throat to keep it still while he sunk the Wolfbone Dagger into its eye.

The wolf's body spasmed for a moment and then stilled. A ping.

[You killed one Feral Forest Wolf, Lv. 1. You gained 8 exp, based on your contribution to the fight!]

[Medium Warrior leveled up!]

[System-Boosted Human leveled up!]

James didn't feel he had time to allocate his Free Points or even use Pillage on the wolf corpse while there was another wolf in the vicinity. Instead, he jumped to his feet—only to find that the other three were finishing off their own wolf. It was engulfed in what James would bet were magical flames, and

Cliff was hacking away at the creature with a sword, which appeared to be of the same variety as James's. Alan was also rather weakly striking the creature with a white staff.

Well, they really should be able to do this much, at least, James thought. He was somewhat glad he didn't have to do more; he was starting to feel pretty tired. He returned his attention to the wolf he'd just killed. *Pillage!*

[Feral Forest Wolf's body successfully processed.]

[You obtained Common Wolfskin Pelt, 3x Wolf Meat Bundle, and a Wolfbone Dagger!]

He put the loot away in his bag, selected Stats as the target of Pillage again, and reviewed his notifications from the Pillage of this and the last kill.

[2 Points of Strength gained!]

[2 Points of Agility gained!]

Interesting. Against a stronger target, I would definitely want to Pillage something besides Stats, then. Those points are making a noticeable difference at the moment, since it's basically like I leveled up an extra time, but the Skills are where I'm lacking right now. I need something brutal that deals a lot of damage. I want to kill these things with one strike.

He took a quick peek at the Status screen.

[Status

Name: James Robard

Race: System-Boosted Human, Lv. 1

Class: Medium Warrior, Lv. 2

Job: Attorney (Pre-System)

Health: 22/100

Mana: 40/40

Stamina: 5/49

Stats

Strength: 13(16)

Agility: 14

Stamina: 7

Fortitude: 5(10)

Dexterity: 4

Perception: 6

Will: 4

Intelligence: 10

Free Points: 6

Skills

Anthropophagy, Lv. 0

Basic Cold Resistance

Basic Proficiency–Common Weapons

Crushing Bite, Lv. 0
Emotional Control, Lv. 0
Empathic Projection, Lv. 0
Empathy Control, Lv. 1
False Impression, Lv. 1
Identify, Lv. 2
Persuasion, Lv. 0
Pillage, Lv. 2
Quick Strike, Lv. 1
Situational Intelligence, Lv. 1
Stubborn Defense, Lv. 0
System Interface
Universal Language Comprehension
Wolf's Bite
Talents
Cannibalism, Lv. 0
Cool-Headed, Lv. 0
Manipulation, Lv. 0
Selective Empathy, Lv. 0
Titles
System Pioneer]

Seems as if I get one Race level to every two Class levels, if the pattern so far holds. Looks like I still have plenty of Health. Thanks to these guys, I just haven't given myself time to recover it. What do I need more of to fight more effectively? He recalled the composition of the Rogue build he'd almost selected. Dexterity was the key Stat for them. *It would make my strikes more precise, so my low Strength and Agility wouldn't matter as much. I'm also going to need more Stamina if today is representative of how much fighting we'll be doing here.*

He allocated four Free Points to Dexterity, one to Stamina, and one to Will. The relevant areas of the menu updated accordingly.

[Status
Name: James Robard
Race: System-Boosted Human, Lv. 1
Class: Medium Warrior, Lv. 2
Job: Attorney (Pre-System)
Health: 22/100
Mana: 40/50
Stamina: 5/64
Stats
Strength: 13(16)
Agility: 14

Stamina: 8
Fortitude: 5(10)
Dexterity: 8
Perception: 6
Will: 5
Intelligence: 10
Free Points: 0]

So, now I know that the Stamina bar is the Stamina Stat squared, while Mana appears to scale with both Will and apparently Intelligence. That'll be important if I ever get any abilities that use Mana. That gave him some new thoughts about the starting area. *I have Mana aplenty but no magic Skills, and I have crossbow bolts with no crossbow. I need to go Pillage some bodies, assuming the fighting there is over.*

He dismissed his Status screen and looked over to the others. The other wolf had finally died.

[One Feral Forest Wolf, Lv. 1 killed. You gained 1 exp, based on your contribution to the fight!]

Good to know you can get experience from a fight even if you don't directly strike the enemy, he thought.

"James, good to see you!" Alan was saying from among the group. James could tell from the gentle green glow around the group that Alan was already healing Cliff and the woman with them, though neither looked as battle worn as James himself was. "Get over here and let me give you some healing!"

Well, I can't say no to that. James walked over, and he felt, when he entered the green radius, as if he'd stepped into a warm bath.

"Ahh," he sighed quietly, eyes closing. He felt his cuts and scratches closing up, his bruised and battered left arm slowly regaining its strength and returning to pristine condition. The sensation was much like what James imagined a pre-System spa day would feel like, tendrils of energy reaching deep into his tissue and massaging his body into recovery.

"James, why did you leave the office?" Cliff asked.

James sighed under his breath and opened his eyes back up. Cliff looked the same as he had the last time James met with him in his office: impatient, graying, and doughy, only now with a side of bloodstains on his slacks. He was still wearing the same clothes he'd had on in the office under his System gear.

"Just let me enjoy the healing, Cliff. You know staying at the office wasn't an idea that made any sense for me."

"The hell it wasn't! We were making a plan together!"

"Did the plan involve us being transported to another plane of existence sorted by last name?"

Silence from Cliff.

"Then that was a plan to make at a later time. I needed to see about my family. I told everyone at the time why I was leaving." James failed to keep the irritation out of his voice.

"Fellas, let's try and keep this conversation civil," Alan said. "You both made reasonable decisions for the circumstances we were in."

"I suppose," Cliff said, sounding unconvinced. "Where is your family anyway? We could definitely benefit from a larger group."

"Stupid government gave my wife trouble about changing her last name. She and her sister are in a different orientation!"

"Sorry to hear that," Cliff said.

"Is your family here?" James asked.

"Yeah," Cliff nodded. His voice sounded tense. "Yeah, they are."

Based on his tone, James decided not to ask follow-up questions for now. There was silence for a few seconds.

"Speaking of family, James, this is my wife, Mitzi," Alan said. "Mitzi, this is James from work."

James turned to get a better look at the older woman. Frankly, she looked a bit tougher than Alan, having retained more of the weight and strength of youth. Her right hand held a simple wooden staff. She had strongly ingrained laugh lines around her small mouth and thoughtful gray eyes. She wore her hair in a long gray ponytail, and now that he had a good view of her clothes, he saw she wore a purple dress covered in spiderweb patterns.

"A pleasure to meet you," he said. "Alan is always talking about you and the family. I don't suppose any of the rest of your little clan are here?"

"The pleasure is all mine, young man," she said. "We're the only Rogets here as far as I know. I think there's a pretty small geographic range limitation to who was pulled into each orientation, and our family doesn't live near us."

"That's a shame. As soon as I saw Alan, I was expecting to meet his whole family in here!"

"Sadly not," Alan said. "Are you guys just about fully healed? I'm starting to get tired. I think the, uh, healing is running out."

"Oh, you're running out of Mana?" James asked.

"Uh, sure, I guess that's it," Alan said, a little uncertainly.

"Well, I'm good," James said, looking at his Health bar. "I have a Mana Potion in my bag in case you need to use it later."

"Likewise. I feel great!" Cliff said. He did not seem to James to be checking his Health bar at all, though it was hard to be sure what someone else was looking at.

"I'm ready to do something else, although I love the way your Mana feels, darling," Mitzi added.

The light faded, and James instantly missed its warm glow. With his aches and pains now gone, he thought he wouldn't mind being injured again so much if that was what the healing process would be like every time.

"Thank goodness we survived all that," Mitzi said, voice reflective.

"Thank you for coming in and saving us, James," Alan added. "I'm not sure what would've happened if you hadn't jumped in."

"It was my pleasure," James said, "and I would gladly do it again."

"Well, gang, let's find shelter," Cliff said.

James shook his head. "I think we should go back to the field. I know it's dangerous, but we need more equipment, more weapons and potions. And we can definitely get some there." *Off of the dead bodies*, he left unspoken.

"I don't know how that's as valuable as finding a safe place to ride this thing out!" Cliff argued. "We find a safe place, looking for *living* people as we go, and we get safety in numbers and a defensible position that way."

James could sense that they were about to reach an impasse.

CHAPTER NINE

The Lesson

James decided to give arguing one last chance to work before he would just abandon this group and go it alone.

Although he was at full Health for now—and his Stamina was recovering with each passing minute—he didn't especially want to wander the forest by himself after having enjoyed the benefits of a Healer.

He recalled he had a Skill specifically for this situation. *Persuasion!*

"If our goal is to recruit other people, we're better off near the starting point than wandering deeper into the forest. Some people will definitely stick around there, so there's a much better chance of us finding allies. And I don't think we're going to find anywhere safe to hunker down in this whole place. What we're going to need to do is go around hunting and killing these creatures until we reestablish who's at the top of the food chain."

[Sufficient experience accrued! Persuasion leveled up!]
[Required conditions met! Manipulation leveled up!]

Cliff looked as if he were seriously considering what James said but didn't want to be persuaded. He opened his mouth to say something, but Mitzi spoke first.

"I think we need to go with James's plan. It seems like we're inevitably going to get into fights, and at least some of the people who died back there had potions for Mana. I hate to disrespect the dead, but this Orientation is a game for the living."

James just looked at her and wondered if the Skill had worked, or if she naturally agreed with him.

"I'm a little surprised to hear you say that, Mitzi," Cliff began.

"Cliff, let's talk just a minute in private," Alan said quietly but firmly. He took Cliff's elbow and led him away a short distance, but far enough that James couldn't hear them.

James and Mitzi stood there awkwardly while they waited for Cliff and Alan to get back.

"Oh, has this wolf been Looted yet?" James asked. He'd had his eyes closed while Alan healed him, so he hadn't noticed.

"I don't know, but probably," Mitzi said.

He tried Pillage, nevertheless.

[Feral Forest Wolf has already been Looted. Designate a target for Pillaging: Stats, Skills, Talents, or Titles.]

So, it does still work. He picked Stats again. Now that he'd had a little time to reflect, he suspected that the Skills, Talents, and Titles of the fodder animals the proctor sent to attack them on day one of Orientation weren't going to be very good.

[2 Points of Dexterity gained!]

By contrast, Stat points were always going to taste sweet!

"Get anything good?" Mitzi asked.

"Ah, no, Cliff or Alan must have already Looted it." He didn't want to make clear to anyone that his specific corpse-looting Skill was a little different. If the wrong person found out about it, that information could make James look like too much of a future threat. He couldn't afford to give out that kind of information so early.

Before they could make any more awkward conversation, Cliff and Alan returned.

"We agreed that we'd like to follow James's plan," Cliff said. "I have a couple of questions for James, but we can talk on the way."

James smiled. "I will answer whatever I can, within reason, as long as you're willing to extend me the same courtesy."

Cliff raised an eyebrow but just said, "Sure."

They set out. The group followed James's lead, he was pleased to observe as he crept quietly through the forest.

Reading the mood, Cliff kept his voice down as he spoke.

"So, James, I was wondering, to start with, how many of those creatures you've killed."

Easy enough question. "Just a couple before I ran into you guys, including one juvenile."

Cliff visibly relaxed a bit. It was subtle, but James knew him well enough to spot it.

"That leads right into my next question," Cliff said. "How'd you get away from that slaughter fest at the beginning? I'm certain hundreds of people died there, and when Alan, Mitzi, and I got away, we were chased. The only reason we lasted as long as we did was that other people ran away along the same route we did, and we, ah—outran them."

James tried to contain a frown. Something about that last sentence had made Cliff nervous as he spoke it. James thought he detected a lie, and he wished he had a Skill for that. It also didn't make sense to think of Alan or Mitzi outrunning anyone. The two senior citizens were much too frail to win a race against almost any of the people James had seen at the starting grounds. For that matter, Cliff was also very out of shape. *Did Cliff trip people or something so the three of them could have a chance to escape?*

"I slipped away at the very beginning, before the wolf pack showed up," James said. "I could smell that there was something off about that place. It felt like a killing field."

James wasn't going to ask any questions about how they had escaped, of course. He didn't care what ruthless acts Cliff might have committed to get away. If anything, he was impressed that Cliff had some of what was needed to survive in a setting where half the population was required to die by the end. But he would need to avoid putting Cliff in a position where he could save his own life at James's expense.

He found himself missing having people around him who he could actually trust to watch his back. His thoughts turned to Mina and Yulia. Were they all right? *Hopefully, wherever they are is a little safer than this forest.* But he wasn't optimistic. *Do what you have to do to survive*, he found himself praying—to what gods, he wasn't sure, but he was *emphatically* praying. *Be ruthless.*

Mina, he knew, had a thread of that quality in her just like James did. But she would take longer to default to it. She was more civilized, which would make her vulnerable. And Yulia was even worse off! She was far too sweet and gentle for her own good. If she and Mina were to get separated, he didn't even want to think about what would happen to the teenager.

James was pulled out of these worries by the sound of Cliff's voice.

"I guess that does it for my questions, then," Cliff said. "You had something you wanted to ask me?"

James looked at Cliff's face carefully. *Can't ask why he's lying. Can't ask what happened to his family based on the tone I got earlier.* He resorted to asking a question that would only be important in the far future, if ever.

"Did the office ever come up with any kind of plan for after Orientation?" James asked.

Cliff looked visibly relieved again by the direction James chose for his questioning.

"Yeah, Dean wants to fortify the office building and establish control over a perimeter around it."

Of course Dean does, James thought. *I've had similar ideas when I imagine that I end up surviving this.*

"Neat idea," he said mildly, trying to downplay his interest. "That might work for you guys if the office is still there after Orientation. The way the System is changing the world, I wouldn't be surprised if there's a forest where it used to be instead."

Cliff's face turned a bit sour at that.

"You must really not be intending to come back," he said.

Ah, and of course he still takes any negativity as a perceived criticism of him. I tried so hard not to ask or say anything that would push a button for you, Cliff.

"I didn't say that," James replied. "I know the law firm is over now, but I think the idea you and Dean are talking about sounds like a reasonably good pivot. Whether I joined in or not would depend on the terms and conditions."

"You're being more direct than usual, huh?" Cliff said. "Not worried about your job anymore. I guess you really believe the current shift in circumstances is permanent. I like this new and improved James." He didn't look like he liked it; he looked like he'd just bitten something sour.

"I don't think there's any chance of things going back to normal from here, so thinking about how I keep my job doesn't make much sense."

Cliff looked like he wanted to say something back to that, but suddenly James put a finger to his lips and raised his left fist, signaling for the whole group to slow. He had seen these movements in a military movie—perhaps several movies—that he'd seen pre-System, but they got the message across. Something was coming, and they needed to be still and prepare for a fight.

Alan simply stood back, white staff held in front of him defensively. Mitzi held her staff in one hand and quietly chanted something to herself. James saw an aura—magical energy, he guessed—which appeared to flow, visible and bright orange, from within her body to all around it as she chanted. To his credit, Cliff managed to quietly loosen his shortsword in its sheath. As for James, he drew his two daggers, and he listened.

As he observed and waited for the enemy, a part of him introspected. When he'd been killing monsters thus far, he hadn't felt much of anything that he could recall. Just the excitement and energy of the moment. A desire to preserve his own life and take theirs. A brief concern for his family, but only that. Brief.

And as he was waiting now, anticipating more enemies? He realized he *wanted* them to come. He wanted to bathe his daggers in blood. Wanted to fight again and win. *I'll have to be careful about this bloodlust,* he thought clinically. *It could lead me to act recklessly one of these days.* Underneath that thought, so quiet he was barely conscious of it, he thought, *I hope to God things never go back to normal.*

The wolves burst through the brush with no thought for stealth. There were four of them, and they must have thought they made a dangerous force for an enemy to deal with, given their numbers. They weren't moving cautiously. James leaped in close as soon as the first one cleared the shrubbery. He delivered two cross slashes with the daggers aimed precisely at the beast's throat, and blood burst forth in a torrent. The wolf tried to pull back, but James followed, ignoring the warning snarls of the other wolves.

As they leaped toward him, he used Quick Strike and suddenly closed to within inches of the wounded beast. The daggers delivered another pair of twin slashes that overlapped the cuts he'd already made. James could see through the wounds down to the bone now.

The wolf made a clumsy lunge for his throat and then collapsed, gurgling on its own blood. There was a ding.

[You killed one Feral Forest Wolf, Lv. 2. You gained 20 exp!]
[Medium Warrior leveled up!]

James barely had enough time to register the victory, or the surge of power from the level, before the next beast was on him, leaping onto his back and trying to sink its fangs into his neck.

The attack landed in his blind spot; he just felt a weight land on his back. He noted that it wasn't as heavy as he remembered the wolf being in his last fight, and he had time to think, *Oh, I really am getting stronger*. Then he felt crushing pressure on the back of his neck.

What saved him was the combination of his starting armor, which covered his neck, and—he suspected probably more importantly—the wolf pelt he was wearing over it. The pelt made it impossible for the beast to really see where it was biting. James could hear the armor crunching under the creature's teeth, but it couldn't seem to get much purchase through the fur of its fellow wolf.

All this happened in a split second, and James was on the ground rolling, desperately moving to get the wolf off of his back and land some hits of his own. The wolf jumped off his back as he landed, but as it tried to lunge for another bite, he managed to stick the Wolfbone Dagger into the side of its neck. The beast still bit him, but the bite sank into the vambrace on his arm rather than actual flesh. And then James heard an ominous cracking sound.

The armor shattered beneath the wolf bite, and James felt the crushing force snap the bone of his left arm. He retained his presence of mind and enough will to fight that he managed to pull the Wolfbone Dagger out of the wolf's neck and stab it into the head, right behind the ear. The wolf made a choking sound, but it remained locked on James's arm, pulling back and forth on it like James was a chew toy.

Tears burst from James's eyes, but he retained the focus to pull the knife out of the wolf and stick it in again. And again. And again. One final time, it went in through the ear canal, and the wolf suddenly went limp and collapsed, dragging James down by its locked jaw.

A ding sounded.

[You killed one Feral Forest Wolf, Lv. 2. You gained 20 exp!]

As he gingerly pulled at the wolf's head, trying to get the jaw to release its grip on his broken arm, James had a better idea for removing the body. *Pillage!*

The wolf's body gently glowed.

[Feral Forest Wolf's body processed.]

[You obtained Common Wolfskin Pelt, 3x Wolf Meat Bundle, and a Wolfbone Dagger!]

I can always use another one of those. James selected Stats to steal, and he got two points in Perception, but the Pillaging really hadn't been about the items or Stats this time. He cast Pillage on the other body too, since it was close by, and he obtained identical prizes. He directed the loot into his satchel almost absently.

Then he waited, and a little under a minute later, the first body had faded away. *Weird but convenient how that happens.* Now his broken arm was free with a minimum of painful wiggling.

While he was waiting for the wolf to disappear, James observed the rest of the team. They had done some damage to the two wolves they were fighting, which bore both scorch and sword marks, though he wouldn't say the fight was going well. The three had now split up, which looked to James like a mistake.

Alan and Mitzi were beating away one wolf with their staffs, while Cliff was dueling the other one-on-one with his sword. It struck James that this was almost exactly the situation he had rescued them from when he first encountered the group, and it was a little bit darkly funny that they weren't doing much better this time around.

Except that it wasn't. For now, they were *his* group, which meant he needed them to find a way to fight efficiently together. *There has to be a better way than this.* But no plan of battle would do them any good now that they were already in combat.

For now, he readied himself to join the fight with his one good arm. He winced when his left arm smacked into a tree as he advanced, but he made himself walk forward despite the pain.

CHAPTER TEN

Lessons Learned

As he moved forward, James heard a ding again. A new notification popped up.

[Conditions met! New Skill recognized: Pain Resistance, Lv. 1]

The pain in his left arm instantly became markedly less pronounced.

Now, that's something I can use!

He charged forward with a renewed sense of enthusiasm, aiming for the beast that Alan and Mitzi were struggling with. If he could open up some space for Mitzi, James thought she could probably take out one of the wolves with those flames of hers.

He was proven correct. He had only stabbed the wolf a couple of times, once in the back and once in the front, and drawn its attention for perhaps fifteen seconds, before he felt something hot approaching. The wolf turned to look at the fireball, and James took the chance to wrap his good arm around the beast. He kept it from moving until both wolf and arm were engulfed in flames. At that point, he released the beast and fell away to the side.

When you are engulfed in flames, it's usually for the best to stop, drop, and roll, but considering the condition of his left arm, James elected instead to press his right arm firmly into the dirt over and over until the flames were out. The process was agonizing, and he could see horrifically raw layers of skin that reminded him of Freddy Krueger, but at least he didn't fracture his left arm any further in the act of extinguishing the fire.

The wolf couldn't take such a limited approach with its whole body wrapped in fire, and it didn't seem to be in the right frame of mind to practice proper fire safety anyway. In fairness, the heat was melting its eyes. It was impressive that it retained the fortitude to repeatedly slam itself into trees and bushes, as it in fact did, seemingly trying blindly to get the one that had started the fire rather than to save itself.

Finally, it collapsed in a smoking heap. A fatal ding sounded.

[One Feral Forest Wolf, Lv. 1 killed. You gained 4 exp, based on your contribution to the fight!]

"Alan," James managed to say, "need a heal please." Despite Pain Resistance, he could barely hold himself upright.

"Be right there, James!" Alan rushed into close range with him and began muttering quiet words to himself that were hard for James to distinguish. The old man got so close that James could smell his cologne, which reminded him of his own grandfather, who had passed a few years back.

James felt and saw a more intense green glow from Alan this time, most of which concentrated itself around James's right arm. The flesh and skin knitted itself back together at what modern medicine would have termed a "miraculous pace." The rest of his body healed much more slowly, but he felt the green glow everywhere.

"Thank you. The other arm is broken." James awkwardly flopped the limb over top of his stomach and winced. Alan focused the green light there next.

With his virtually fully recovered right arm, James reached out to the dead wolf. *Pillage!*

[Feral Forest Wolf's body processed.]

[You obtained Charred Wolfskin Pelt, 3x Roasted Wolf Meat Bundle, and a Charred Wolfbone Dagger!]

James selected Stats as his theft target.

[2 Points of Strength gained!]

I was really hoping to get some Fortitude, so I can stop getting hurt so badly, but I guess the odds of that aren't so great. None of the wolves have given it yet. Maybe it's because they're higher in other areas. I'll just throw some Free Points into it.

Outside his field of vision, James could hear the sound of the last wolf yowling as it burned, mingled with the noise of Cliff hacking away at it with his sword.

After a minute, there was another notification.

[One Feral Forest Wolf, Lv. 1 killed. You gained 1 exp, based on your contribution to the fight!]

Jeez, the wolf was level one, and it took them that long? I would have been dead over there dealing with the other two if I were that slow.

The green light suddenly stopped, and Alan collapsed to his knees next to James. His face was covered in beads of sweat, and his usually pallid complexion was flushed bright pink.

"Hey, Alan, are you okay?" James asked nervously. "Don't go dying just so you can fully heal me." He flexed the fingers on his previously broken arm experimentally as he spoke and confirmed they indeed responded to his commands again.

"Just—hah—out of—ahh—Mana, kid," he gasped between heavy breaths.

"We'll have to manage that resource more carefully, then," James said. "I don't like seeing you in this condition."

"Don't feel too bad," Alan said, catching his breath and beginning to grin. "I leveled up from healing you that time!"

James just snorted a little laugh. *Of course you did, Alan.*

"Why did you want to be a Healer, anyway?" James asked. Shadows loomed over him and Alan as he spoke. Just Mitzi and Cliff, thankfully.

"He wanted to keep me safe," Mitzi answered.

"Doing a bang-up job so far," James said, smiling at Alan. "Keeping us all safe."

"Yeah," Cliff agreed breezily. James looked and saw that the man had hardly a scratch on him, which he supposed was good since the Healer was tapped out. It was a little annoying that Cliff hadn't gotten hurt, though, since James had killed half the wolves himself and helped with another, while Cliff hadn't killed a single one until Mitzi came to help him.

"Let's do a postmortem on the fight while we recover our resources," James suggested. "Come up with how we can work together more efficiently."

The postmortem after an important case was a Brendan Barry signature procedure. Completely non-billable, but practically enforced, with the idea of improving the competency of the associates. The upside for associates was that he allowed them to treat each hour spent on postmortems as half a billable hour for purposes of meeting their annual requirements. And James knew how Cliff admired Brendan and his organization of the firm.

"I thought that went pretty well," Cliff said. "But I'm always open to improvement."

"Excellent. Because I had a few questions and a couple of suggestions for how we could fight more efficiently as a group. For starters, there's me. I'm sure you guys saw; I rushed in and drew their attention." He did not mention the rush of excitement that role gave him. "I probably should have told you guys I was going to do that. Because there were a couple of moments there, when they were trying to get at me, where they grouped up, and that would've been a perfect opportunity to hit them as a group with fire. If that hits, the enemy should probably all be on fire. Then Cliff and I poke at them from the sides until they're all the way dead. In this plan, Alan would stay back by Mitzi, protecting her for the duration of the fighting. He only needs to engage if something gets past us. I wasn't able to watch what you guys were actually doing during the last fight, though I have some idea based on the way the wolves moved. Could you explain in your own words, though?"

"We were trying to limit the attention they paid to you," Mitzi said. "I hit one with a fireball, and he followed after me. Cliff also drew one away."

"Yeah, we didn't want you getting dogpiled," Cliff said. James grimaced at the dad joke.

"That was a very fair and thoughtful way to react to the situation as it actually unfolded," James said. "But I think we're only as effective as we can be if we find a good way to let our Mage get into an area of effective attack."

"What about you and me?" Cliff asked.

Alan said something that was halfway under his breath, but clearly intended for Cliff to hear, and James heard it as well, "When you have Terry Bradshaw on the team, you let him call the plays."

"Yeah, yeah, I know," Cliff muttered back. *So that was what they were talking about earlier? They're under the impression that I'm good at this stuff?* Well, they could be forgiven for thinking so. And maybe that wasn't totally inaccurate. He was certainly better at this than legal writing.

"There is a viable alternative strategy where Cliff and I take the lead, and Mitzi takes potshots at the enemies that are on the edges of the fight. I just think that doesn't make the best use of her Mana. Also, if we're outnumbered, and she's only taking shots at the edges while you and I are the primary damage dealers, we'll be too slow to take the enemy down. Once one or two get away from us, they'll go for her and Alan, and she'll be unable to focus on casting, which I think is what happened this time."

Cliff was nodding along now. "Yeah, you're right! That is a problem. Okay, we can try it your way."

They really are treating me as a quarterback, James thought. *This is a little weird.*

"Solid. Let's all recover our resources for a little while before we move on, and we'll try those tactics against the next enemies we face. Unless it's just one or two. Then Cliff and I can take them on our own." He gave Cliff a thumbs-up.

"Sounds good, bro," Cliff said.

James suppressed his instinct to cringe.

"I can be ready to move whenever you want to get going, James," Alan said.

"We should probably let you recover a little more, darling," Mitzi said gently.

"She's right. You're the Healer, Alan," James said. "We shouldn't move until you're in top condition. And don't take a Mana Potion right now, either. We want to save those for emergencies. There's no rush. I hope you're not worried about us leaving you behind. Cliff and I are a lot more expendable than you. There aren't going to be many Healers."

There's no way I *would've chosen to be a Healer*, he thought. Most people here would be thinking about themselves first, not choosing support Classes.

A couple of notifications appeared.

[Sufficient experience accrued! Persuasion leveled up!]

Was I using Persuasion just now? James wondered. He realized he was staring into space at his notifications, and he looked around, a little paranoid that the others might figure out what sort of notifications he was getting. He didn't need to be worried, though, or so it seemed. Everyone else was also looking off into the empty air now, perhaps reviewing their Status screens.

James called his own Status up with a thought. *These things are going to be worse than smartphones.*

[Status
Name: James Robard
Race: System-Boosted Human, Lv. 1
Class: Medium Warrior, Lv. 3
Job: Attorney (Pre-System)
Health: 93/100
Mana: 50/50
Stamina: 32/81
Stats
Strength: 17(20)
Agility: 16
Stamina: 9
Fortitude: 5(10)
Dexterity: 10
Perception: 10
Will: 5
Intelligence: 10
Free Points: 3
Skills
Anthropophagy, Lv. 0
Basic Cold Resistance
Basic Proficiency–Common Weapons
Emotional Control, Lv. 0
Empathic Projection, Lv. 0
Empathy Control, Lv. 1
False Impression, Lv. 1
Identify, Lv. 2
Pain Resistance, Lv. 1
Persuasion, Lv. 2
Pillage, Lv. 2
Quick Strike, Lv. 1
Situational Intelligence, Lv. 1
Stubborn Defense, Lv. 0
System Interface
Universal Language Comprehension
Wolf's Bite

Talents
Cannibalism, Lv. 0
Cool-Headed, Lv. 0
Manipulation, Lv. 1
Selective Empathy, Lv. 0
Titles
System Pioneer]

He decided to throw his Free Points into his weakest Stat, Will, since he had the feeling that his build was going to be based in significant part on manipulating people, whether he wanted that or not, as the System was making that easier and easier for him to pursue.

James walked around for a few minutes after that, trying to seem casual. He was actually looking for the other dead wolf to Pillage it. The body had vanished, however, after Cliff or Mitzi had Looted the corpse.

That's what I get for keeping my abilities a secret, he thought. But it still seemed like a good choice on balance. The odds of some future encounter where someone went after him just for his unusual Talents were too high to ignore.

"So, could we talk about the elephant in the woods?"

James looked up. Cliff had approached him. Mitzi and Alan, he saw immediately, sat tenderly holding hands under a tree. Within sight, but out of earshot unless he and Cliff started screaming at each other. So clearly in love that James was almost distracted by jealousy. He forced himself to remain rooted in the present and respond to Cliff.

"Which elephant?" James asked. *Where the hell's your family?* he wanted to say. That was the elephant he didn't know how to broach, since Cliff had pushed the subject away so awkwardly when they last came near it.

"Looting." Cliff looked at James as if it were obvious. "We should talk about, eh, division of spoils."

This was the last thing James was interested in. He intended to be openhanded with his comrades, and there didn't need to be any formal agreement to that effect for him to behave accordingly. But perhaps Cliff had some other ideas. *Greedy as hell, even here.*

"I think the 'keep what you kill' system we've got right now is sort of working," Cliff went on, "but there could be conflict later, right?"

"You mean when there are more people in our group?" James asked. He really wasn't getting what Cliff was driving at, and it was a pain in the ass just listening to him when he wanted to enjoy the quiet before they moved on.

"Well, yes. Then, but also potentially now. What if, within our group here, we disagree about the division of spoils?"

James decided to try and steer Cliff the way he usually had in their preexisting relationship—by playing to his ego a bit.

"Cliff, realistically, the ones doing most of the killing are going to be you and me. The two warriors in the group. I feel like what you're wondering about is whether you and I are going to fight over gear." He opened his magic satchel. "As far as I'm concerned, you can have anything that you want of what we've Looted so far, but the wolves give pretty much the same things every time. Like these daggers, which only you and I can use anyway because we're the only ones who have any weapon-handling Skills. The only conflict you and I could have is over some unique gear that a one-of-a-kind monster might drop. In that case, the 'keep what you kill' system is the fairest, and it gives us both a chance to jump into action. If there's a controversy about who did the most to kill a beast, and you and I really can't agree, then we can have a secret ballot vote on it or flip a coin or something. After all"—he smiled at this—"you and I are men of the law, of order. But both of us are so reasonable that I don't anticipate much disagreement." He winked.

Cliff nodded, a bit half-heartedly, and the two left each other to muse on their own. James thought that the reasoning he'd given Cliff was good enough, for now.

Would Cliff become a problem later, though, if they ever actually had some really valuable loot? *Hard to say.* No, actually it wasn't. Cliff would absolutely be a problem if his beady little eyes thought they spied a real treasure. James would just have to watch his back in that unlikely event.

Including the time he wasted talking to Cliff, there was a good twenty minutes until Alan had almost completely recovered his Mana, which wasn't an unreasonably long time to wait. This was only day one of the System's reign, and James would have willingly camped out overnight if necessary. So far as he knew, the human bodies that he wanted to rob weren't going anywhere.

The party set out again, and the remainder of their path to the starting point clearing was remarkably smooth and quiet. They didn't even hear creatures moving in the distance, which made James's Situational Intelligence throb a silent alarm inside his head. He suspected they might be walking into an ambush of some sort.

As they reached the clearing where the slaughter had happened, they were within sight of their goal. Bodies lay in full view, some scattered, some stacked like kindling in piles.

It was even quieter than it had been farther out. Too quiet.

CHAPTER ELEVEN

Somebody's Watching

We need to look around to try and figure out if this place is a trap," James said. Since the group was treating him as a leader for the moment, it was time to act like one. He wasn't going to lead them into a massacre if he could help it.

James suggested they make two groups of two and scout in a circle around the clearing, looking for signs of a trap. Anything that might be watching, lying in wait.

Difficult as it was to ask, he suggested that the casters be divided into two groups so that they wouldn't be overwhelmed in close combat.

That meant James with Alan and Cliff with Mitzi. James's reasoning was that Cliff and Mitzi had a balanced firepower together. Cliff probably couldn't do as much damage as James or Mitzi, but he could hold off an enemy or two while Mitzi blasted them with fire. James, on the other hand, had a more aggressive style of fighting—almost bestial—and had tended to get himself injured in the process, which meant the pairing with Alan made sense.

The old man looked worried about his wife, but he quietly assented. *He's trusting in my judgment,* James thought. *Trusting me to keep him and his wife safe. Just because I'm pretty good at fighting.* It was a bit humbling. James would have to do everything he could to live up to Alan's trust.

They moved slowly around the clearing, staying just out of sight of any potential threats, shielded behind the tree line.

As they walked, eyes open for anything suspicious, James tried to open up a whispered dialogue. "So, Alan, have you thought about what you want to do differently in life once we get home, now that the world's changing so much?"

Alan looked back at him quietly for a long moment. "I don't assume I'm going to get home, James." Then he smiled, but it looked to James like the fakest smile he'd ever seen. "I'm trying to take things moment by moment and make the best decisions I can for right now."

He's scared shitless, James realized. *He's* sure *he's going to die here.* It wasn't nearly as much of a surprise as the fact that Alan had elected to put his life in James's hands. He himself had been starting to feel like this was some grand adventure, but he knew others probably weren't as psychologically abnormal as him. *Alan probably chose the Healer Class because he didn't want to fight and kill. He wanted to be out of this whole situation as much as possible.*

"I'll keep you alive, Alan," he found himself saying. "If something dangerous appears, you just stand behind me." *When did I become so reassuring?* But Alan *did* look genuinely reassured.

[Sufficient experience accrued! Empathy Control leveled up!]
[Required conditions met! Selective Empathy leveled up!]
James mentally dismissed the alerts that were ruining the moment.

On the opposite side of the clearing, Cliff and Mitzi were having a quiet conversation of their own while trying not to look too closely at the carnage in the field.

"I'm just saying that his approach tends to be a little bit less cautious than I'd prefer," Cliff was saying.

"I know," Mitzi replied. "You wanted us to go hide and see if we could manage that for the duration. I wonder how that would have worked out once the timer started getting low, and the population count in here remained above fifty percent."

Cliff pulled up the current population number.

[3096/3,468 Survivors]
The total was still pretty high, considering the bloodbath they had seen at the start of the Orientation.

"You're assuming that in just a few months, a group of people who have largely spent their whole lives in a modern first-world country will resort to murder to avoid a hypothetical risk of being randomly killed by the System running this place. Not only will they kill in cold blood, your assumption goes, but they'll also go out of their way to hunt us down in whatever hiding place we've dug ourselves into by the end of the ninety days. They will also need to be better at seeking than we are at hiding. That's the only combination of assumptions that makes sense of our current course of action."

"Any human being is capable of killing somebody else, Cliff. Especially when their life is on the line. That's one of my basic assumptions about life. I grew up on a farm. I know I'm capable of chopping the head off of a chicken. Killing a person is different, and I'm not volunteering to do it, but choosing inaction here is choosing death."

"Unless the System is bluffing," Cliff said. "It hasn't killed anyone yet. Maybe this is some kind of a test. Maybe this is the Rapture."

"Don't kid me in this situation!" Mitzi snapped. She was in a bad enough mood now, worried about Alan. She would never forgive either herself or James if the youngster's plan to split the party resulted in harm to her husband.

"Sorry," he said. They lapsed into silence. Lost in thought, neither Cliff nor Mitzi noticed a gentle shimmer in the air in a certain spot they passed in their trek around the clearing. Possibly neither of them would have made anything of it even if they hadn't been distracted.

They quickly passed it and circled to the opposite end of the oval to meet up with James and Alan.

The silence between them persisted.

"Well, since you asked me," Alan said, "I'm guessing you must have a pretty good idea of what you want to do when you get home."

"Absolutely," James said instantly. "Hold my wife in my arms, along with the baby whose birth I'm going to miss through System voodoo. After that, aim for some level of dominion over the area we live in."

"Whoa! Ambitious, aren't we? Actually, a bit like what Dean was talking about back at the office, I think."

"Yeah, I know. It sounded radical and maybe even a little crazy at first. But I don't think the government is going to be able to keep order anymore. If half the people in this Orientation die, what about the one the president is in? Members of Congress? The military? Once those folks come back, they'll only be looking at how they can help their own families survive this. I don't even know if military-grade weapons will be able to hold their own against a low-level monster in the System's preferred version of Earth." James realized he sounded energized, so he tried to make his voice more somber. "All of which is to say, the Orientation is only the beginning. We probably need to prepare for survival of the fittest outside too."

"When did you start to have these thoughts?" Alan asked. "Just after you heard Cliff mention the idea?"

"Oh, no. I've been trying to predict what would happen after Orientation since we got here."

In just the few minutes of silence since the last exchange between James and Alan, James had gone further, trying to predict the future actions of world leaders in response to the descent of the System with Empathic Projection. The precision was naturally iffy since James didn't know many world leaders—or any, actually—very well, but it should be directionally accurate unless someone important in a position of great power was significantly more competent in the ways of the System than James expected. Empathic Projection had leveled up twice as he made these broad projections, and Selective Empathy once with it.

The predictions had come remarkably quickly, faster than James would normally be able to accurately anticipate another person's behavior, especially given that he was mostly occupied with looking for signs of an ambush. But he couldn't tell Alan about this; he still wasn't ready to share the details of his abilities with anyone.

James was pretty sure this wasn't how Empathic Projection was intended to be used, though. Trying to divine more details about the behavior of people he'd never met, and had only read newspaper headlines about, actually gave him a minor headache. He imagined—hoped—that using the ability on people he'd interacted with would function better.

It was a relief when he and Alan finally came back within sight of Mitzi and Cliff. James could stop focusing on trying to predict the future decisions of people he didn't know and focus instead on the people around him again. He realized that he'd likely been using Empathic Prediction on all of them without recognizing it for the last couple of hours while they'd been together, just as he had apparently used Persuasion without being aware of it. Only his combat abilities seemed to require conscious activation.

"How did the search go?" Cliff asked.

"It was suspiciously quiet," James said. That was the response they had agreed upon beforehand so that Cliff and Mitzi would know it was the real James and Alan.

"All right," Cliff said, letting out a sigh. "So, we going in?"

"There probably is some sort of trap somewhere," James said, "but as long as we're not heavily outnumbered and outgunned, we should be able to run away. And it's an open field, so we should be able to see anyone coming before they get into melee range. The rewards speak for themselves. So, yeah, let's go."

The group emerged from the tree line, and as was becoming his pattern, James rushed forward with a bit more of a spring in his step than the others. He wanted to specifically make sure he reached the Healer and Mage corpses first, since they would have Skills and Talents to steal that he thought he could not naturally obtain on his own.

He needn't have rushed, though. The others moved much more slowly, either because they were still wary of the possibility of a trap—a very real danger—or because the field into which they emerged was so gruesome. In the tree line, the group had been able to avoid looking too long at the grisly scene that now presented itself before their eyes. Now that they stepped into it, it was impossible to ignore.

Bodies lay everywhere, some of them partially consumed with great bestial bites taken out of vital areas or places with lots of fat. Shields, armor, and weapons were scattered around, but the overwhelming impression was of a large number of lightly armed or unarmed people who had stumbled into an ambush by a pack of monsters and been unable to fight back effectively.

This was, of course, not far from the truth, as James knew. The only off detail was that the System had set the ambush.

Some bodies were gathered in small piles, and from the positioning—as well as the size and condition of the people involved—James could tell that among them there were families where parents had died protecting their teenagers or older relatives had fallen protecting the younger generation. There appeared to be no children under the age of thirteen or fourteen, a fact that he filed away in the back of his mind for later thought.

In the center of the clearing there stood a great heap of bodies, as if people had repeatedly climbed over an existing pile of corpses while trying to get away from pursuing creatures.

Or as if someone deliberately made a big pile of corpses, a dark voice in James's mind suggested. *Bait? Someone expected that people would come to Loot the bodies, so they rearranged some of them to get the scavenging humans to step into a certain area?* It was the center of the clearing, so there was no cover anywhere near the corpse mound besides the bodies themselves. James resolved to save the possible Looting of those corpses until the very end.

He approached his first body, a woman dressed in a dark-colored robe and clutching a staff, and he used Pillage.

[Mage Rachel Roper's body processed.]

[You obtained Basic Mage's Robe, 3x Mage Meat Bundle, and Basic Mage's Stave! Designate a target for Pillaging: Stats, Skills, Talents, or Titles.]

James winced a little at the fact that Pillage had treated the body like any monster's body—as a source of meat. Then he selected Skills.

[Skill Obtained: Basic Elemental Magic: Water!]

Very nice, James thought. *I can steal magical powers too, so I was probably right not to worry about missing out on the Mage Class.*

A lengthy sequence ensued of James using Pillage on body after body, trying to get to every corpse he could. He tried to reach corpses the others had already used Loot on before they faded away, since he could still steal a Stat, Skill, Talent, or Title from those bodies. He still felt a little odd about the corpses turning into meat, but he nevertheless directed the meat straight into his magic satchel.

Hopefully, the magic satchel magically keeps meat fresh too, he thought, a bit disgusted with himself. Then, with resolve, he thought, *Well, if I need it, I'll have it.* Maybe the Cannibalism Talent was already twisting his mind.

Over the course of using Pillage on a long series of corpses—he counted one hundred and twenty-eight that he reached personally—James replaced his broken piece of armor, found three crossbows to use his bolts with, acquired backups of his starting equipment—as well as heavier and lighter options—obtained a variety of useful Skills, selectively increased his Titles and Talents by stealing those from the bodies that looked the most unique, and massively bolstered his

Stats. He felt incredibly powerful—far too powerful for his level. His body positively crackled with energy.

He hadn't even gone through his Status screen since this began. It would just be out of date two minutes later.

Perhaps most importantly, after Pillage reached level five, he unlocked the additional Skill Mass Pillage, which allowed him to target groups of bodies within an area of effect rather than requiring him to point at a specific corpse. This made the rest of the work much easier, until the set of cadavers to steal from was almost exhausted.

There was just one more set of bodies to steal from: the towering pile of bodies that had almost screamed "Trap!" in James's mind when the group entered the clearing. The bodies definitely felt like a trap. It had been so obviously a trap from the beginning that James had asked his group to leave that pile for last, in case Looting it triggered an attack.

And the more he looked, the more improbable it was that such a large pile of bodies would have formed naturally in that location given the limited number of people killed. The vast majority of the people in the Orientation had escaped the clearing, after all. James had the feeling the wolves were actually a sort of starter monster, whereas whatever might be triggered by approaching the corpse mound was likely more powerful.

Despite all of that, the mound of bodies was a source of power too substantial to ignore. With Mass Pillage in his repertoire, James didn't have to designate the specific body he wanted to Pillage nor did he have to get very close. Ten feet away worked. If there was a trap, he would willingly trigger it and, he believed, survive the wrath of whatever the System was about to throw at him. If it looked too dangerous, he would just run away.

Maybe the decision was hubris, but with both magic and muscle at his disposal now, he felt invincible.

So James told the others to stay back—they backed off to about twenty feet from the pile of bodies—while he got within range and activated the ability.

As he activated Mass Pillage, the mound of corpses began gently glowing. James felt as much as saw the ensuing flurry of notifications, as his muscles became noticeably firmer and more densely packed with power, and his perception expanded.

Besides selecting Stats as the Mass Pillage target at the very beginning, he blocked all notifications for now. Keeping the pop-ups out of his vision was a trick he'd learned over the last half hour of Pillaging. All it required was a tunnel-vision focus on what he was doing, which seemed to effectively generate a "Do Not Disturb" signal to the System.

This didn't quite come naturally to James, as evidenced by the fact that he hadn't discovered it while in the midst of combat with wolves. Apparently, even a life-or-death fight did not always command his complete attention.

When he mentioned his discovery to the group, he learned that Mitzi had noticed it first. She had only mentioned it to Alan, assuming that the two close-combat warriors would have already noticed.

In the present, he blocked the notifications because he wanted to be ready to move if something attacked.

Very quickly he realized his caution was not misplaced. Because as the corpse pile began to glow, it also began to move.

CHAPTER TWELVE

Blood Hungry

A single massive gray claw emerged first, then a second on the opposite side of the pile, both bursting through the bodies like they were wet tissue paper, sending semi-congealed blood and viscera flying through the clearing.

Each claw consisted of four long, gray digits ending in sword-like black talons. The claws looked to James like heaps of long-dead flesh that had condensed themselves into a pair of ugly, half-rotten limbs. The rest of the body remained hidden beneath the mound of cadavers.

James suppressed his natural disgust to think as analytically as he could. *Is it undead? Does the Orientation—or* the world—*have those now?*

He aimed Identify at one of the claws. Then he began to run.

James had never bothered using Identify on a creature that was right in front of him before since his natural inclination was to just try to kill them before they could kill him. He was glad he made this monster the first time.

The sheer size and physical features of the creature he could see so far were daunting enough, but the description provided by Identify read like the diary of a nightmare.

[Corpse Eater, Lv. 7: An abomination born from the miasma issued by desecrated corpses, typically contaminated in necromantic rituals. Though it likes to live among corpses and eat them as they rot, this ghoulish creature constantly hungers for the meat, blood, and bones of the innocent living, and it especially enjoys the tender flesh of newborn babies. Possesses Strength and Agility beyond its appearance, as well as unlimited Stamina. Weak against holy power and fire.]

In theory, level seven wasn't so far beyond James's level, but he could tell at a glance that this was one of those monsters that would punch a bit above its weight class, if its description hadn't clued him in. Even if he might be able to win a one-on-one match with the Corpse Eater, he had no confidence that his team would all survive.

So, James began to run away, yelling at his comrades to do the same. He heard rather than saw them following his warning.

After a few seconds, he slowed down slightly and turned his head back to look at the creature. That impulse might have saved his life.

One moment he was running forward at a near sprint, and in the next, he was bending backward at an awkward angle to avoid a wall of razor-sharp black talons that ripped through the space where his upper body had been.

James had a moment to breathe before the creature could adjust its momentum, and in that time, he drew his sword.

"Everyone, get away!" he yelled. Then a blur of talons smashed into James's defense. He was strong and fast enough to block the claw with his sword, but he was still thrown backward.

As his body flew backward, James saw Cliff, Mitzi, and Alan facing the monster. Their stances were aggressive; they weren't running away. *Idiots!* he thought. *What are they thinking?*

With some distance opened up between James and the Corpse Eater—and his party members now rushing toward it rather than away, despite his shouted instructions—the creature turned to strike at them. A long, almost whip-like limb came down on Cliff's arm.

For a moment, James thought the older man's armor had protected him, until he saw the severed limb drop onto the ground, blood gushing from Cliff's stump of an elbow.

The Corpse Eater's attention seemed to fixate on the bloody limb, and with a long-taloned limb, it scooped the severed flesh up, tilted its head back, and dropped the arm down its maw.

James got his first good look at the monster's face as it crunched on Cliff's arm bone, momentarily oblivious to the humans all around it. There were multiple eyes scattered haphazardly across the monstrous gray head, a great, wide-opening jaw with rows of jagged yellow teeth—like a cross between a giant snake and a great white shark—two noses on each side of its head, and a ring of ears that had grown around its neck like a collar.

Its mouth was curled in a grotesque mockery of a smile.

Then a big fireball impacted the creature's front and brought it out of its feeding trance. The monster flinched backward and let loose a sound that was half wail and half roar.

"Guahhhhh!!!"

The beast tried to slap at its burning chest with one claw while at the same time aiming its other long forelimb at the heavy-breathing Mitzi, whose spell seemed to have taken a lot out of her.

The claw was a foot away from her head, closing fast, and she was not moving sideways quickly enough to avoid it.

Quick Strike! Several crossbow bolts embedded themselves in the claw that was sweeping toward Mitzi, and although they didn't appear to penetrate very deeply, they knocked the limb off-course enough that Mitzi avoided being maimed.

The Corpse Eater turned its attention to the shooter, James, once again, flailing its claws wildly in his direction. He sidestepped easily. The little bit of pain the group had inflicted was showing in diminished coordination in the creature's movements. *We could whittle it down like this*, James assessed. *That fire did a lot of damage. We're really doing pretty well. Mitzi and I could take turns hitting it, keep it from focusing on any one of us. But looking at what happened to Cliff*—Cliff was crumpled on the ground, clutching his arm—*one hit would definitely take Mitzi out of the fight. I'm not sure if I could win by myself. Maybe it has more tricks than just swinging its claws. And even if I could win on my own, I'm not alone. They're here.*

While he was thinking, there was the sound of shouting off in the distance. James instantly shifted his gaze to look at the tree line where the sound was coming from.

"Run!" a small group of people in that corner were saying. "It's more dangerous than you think! This way!" When James looked closely with his now very enhanced vision, he saw there were five of them, three men and two women.

James thought there was something off about this. Their appearance was too sudden. The moment felt timed. As if they were waiting for something to make themselves known.

Even as James thought that, his comrades started moving toward the little cluster of people. Even Cliff was staggering in that direction, supported between Mitzi and Alan.

But the Corpse Eater was turning to look back at them again. Having failed to strike James with its claws, it aimed for the easier targets once more.

James sprinted into melee range before the monster could deal any further damage to his party members, and with the creature's back turned, he embedded his shortsword to the hilt in a central part of the body. The Corpse Eater turned its head slightly to lay an eye on him, and the long claws closed in so quickly that James had to throw himself backward and leave the sword behind. It had penetrated so deeply that any normal living creature would be dead.

Of course, the Corpse Eater wasn't a normal creature. It was an abomination, likely born of a necromantic miasma, with unlimited Stamina. From its expression, James had only made it angry.

The creature charged after him, wide maw snapping and clicking as it swung its claws back and forth in front of it like swords.

All James could do was dodge and move backward as he tried to think of a better way to kill the monster. He had several forms of basic magic in his Skills now, courtesy of Pillaging over a hundred people's bodies, but he had yet to try any of it out. He definitely did not want to try closing to knife-fight range against a monster with talons long and sharp enough to chop him in half if he made one wrong move. His shortsword was trapped in the monster's flesh, but he had backups if he could get a little breathing room to go into the magic satchel.

Slash-dodge, slash-dodge, slash-dodge, slash-duck. The dance continued with James only suffering minor grazes because he had the Corpse Eater outmatched in Agility. Even so, he had no room to shift his focus and draw another sword. And he could feel his Stamina was starting to get low. Another few minutes of fighting at this pace, and he wouldn't be able to dodge.

On the positive side, he could see his party getting farther away, slowly but surely making their way to the other group waiting for them in the tree line.

Now I need to get away, James thought. The idea of winning had to be set aside for now. He could always come back after he gained a few levels or simply regained his Stamina. Now he needed a distraction so he could get away. He had only one idea that might work.

He focused on the Basic Elemental Magic: Fire ability, and words in an unfamiliar language began to flow into his mind.

Continuing to dodge, but with less and less breathing room, James whispered a chant under his breath. To the outside observer, an orange glow could be faintly seen around his body. For James, there was a feeling of warmth radiating from some place in the center of his body outward.

A slow movement of Mana from within his core into the aura around his body became increasingly visible as the chanting went on.

James dodged to the side again, and the Corpse Eater managed to slash a vein in his arm, seemingly beginning to read James's moves, but even as blood poured down, he never stopped chanting.

As the creature wound up for a heavy slash at his center of mass, James darted forward suddenly at a near-inhuman speed. *Quick Strike!* The purpose wasn't a sword swipe at close range this time; James didn't even have a weapon in his hands. Now, though, the creature was taken off-balance, and James was far from where it had been preparing to attack.

He closed to touch range, and it was ready. *Fire!* He put a hand on the Corpse Eater and directed the flames into the wound still open from his sword strike. A brilliant orange light flared up as the sickening gray flesh erupted in flames. The creature let out an ear-splitting scream right into James's face and began flailing its limbs with a wild, desperate energy that directed itself at the entire area around its body. It didn't seem to know where he was anymore, and its eyes were either melted or concealed behind the wall of flames that encompassed its whole upper body, so it couldn't look for him, only attack blindly.

James dodged a couple more strikes, and seeing an opening, he threw himself between the creature's legs, tucking in his head and rolling to get away. He wasn't going to risk his life any further as his Stamina dipped into the red. He was now almost certain the Corpse Eater was dying, but he couldn't afford to stay too close and watch what happened to it while it was in this seemingly berserk near-death state. With his Stamina near zero, he needed desperately to get to any safe place before he collapsed.

He began to run away from the Corpse Eater, and his mind returned to the group of people he was running toward. They were still standing there in the same place, apparently ready to provide support from within the trees but unwilling to risk their lives even now by stepping into the clearing. *A damn useless warning they provided*, James thought. But their complete unwillingness to leave the tree line thus far undermined one of his initial half-formed theories about why they had suddenly appeared: to steal his group's kill. *Then why?*

His train of thought was interrupted by a sound behind him. He didn't need to look back to know the Corpse Eater was chasing him. It had taken a little time to figure out which way to go, so James had a small lead, and he was almost caught up to his slow-moving party. The party was just about ten feet from the tree line.

But the question of what it was about the other group that was making him nervous surged up with sudden, overwhelming urgency.

How did they know the Corpse Eater was more dangerous than it seemed, as they said? How did they know it was there at all? It was hiding.

James caught up to his group, and he didn't know what to say to get them to stop moving toward the other humans—or even if it was smart to say anything. The other group looked to be at full Health, and maybe whatever plans they had for James's group would be better than being slaughtered by the panting, still-pursuing Corpse Eater. Almost anything would be.

So James remained silent as his group got within five feet of the tree line, where the ground suddenly fell away. James and the rest of his party found themselves falling down, down, down, quickly sinking into darkness. The last thing he saw before he slipped below ground level was the face of a man from the other group, just beginning to slip into a smile.

CHAPTER THIRTEEN

In the Dark

There were several cries of pain as James's party struck the bottom of the pit. Cliff, who had seemed barely conscious when James caught up to the group, let out a moan and then fell into an eerie silence. Alan's voice cried out as his body struck hard ground with a sickening crack. And in the distant, ground-level air above, the Corpse Eater could be heard letting out a piteous cry of its own as it burned.

James would almost feel sorry for the poor thing, if it hadn't nearly wiped them out.

A female voice from above said, "There, there. I've got you, big guy." A green glow could be seen emanating from the area next to the opening of the pit.

"They're healing it?" Mitzi croaked. She sounded a little bit hurt from the fall, but mostly shocked at what was happening. It was impossible to see her expression in the dark that surrounded the foursome.

"Humans can work with monsters," James said quietly, thinking aloud.

Alan moved, shifting positions, then let out another soft cry as an audible grinding noise came from one of the limbs he'd adjusted.

"Don't move, guys," James said. He had used Pillage to take Healer abilities too, and although he was low on Stamina, he had plenty of Mana left. *Healing Aura.*

A green glow emanated from James's body, and it expanded until it bathed all of them in a healing light.

"Of course," Alan muttered. A moment later, a stronger and overlapping glow burst forth from his body, and there was a gradual, grinding sound of bone as it slowly twisted around and clicked back into place. The old man had to stifle several more cries of pain, but the suffering was over relatively quickly, and his leg, which had snapped upon hitting the rock bottom of the pit, quickly restored itself to working order.

Both James and Alan regained their full Health after a few minutes of this, and they turned their attention to Cliff. From outside the pit, they could hear water splashing, but they ignored the sounds of the enemy humans apparently putting out the fire on the monster's body. They had their own problems to deal with.

Laying on Hands! The more intense green glow surrounded both Alan's and James's hands, and together they massaged the stump of Cliff's arm with their thick healing auras, until slowly—and evidently very painfully—the severed arm began to grow back.

Cliff, who James thought had passed out, moaned like the limb was being chopped off all over again. "Stop! Please, goddammit! You're torturing me!"

Then there was somewhat more profane language.

By a silent agreement, Alan and James ignored him, both his words and his feeble resistance as he slapped at both of them with his good arm and kicked with his legs. Cliff needed to be whole again to be useful in this desperate situation, and that was that. After around a minute of painful regeneration, he passed out.

They continued the healing process for several minutes more until an entire new arm, pink and soft and hairless, had grown out to reach its full length.

Then came the natural questions for James.

"So, when did you get magical powers?" Mitzi asked very bluntly.

"And healing!" Alan added.

"Just recently, as it happens," James said. "I have an upgraded version of Loot that allows me to take abilities from dead bodies."

"So that's why you wanted to come back to the starting point," Mitzi said. It wasn't a question.

James had quickly decided to be more or less transparent about Pillage, given that he'd shown his new Skills outside already. "That was a big reason, yes. Also restocking equipment and hopefully meeting some new people. I wasn't expecting the new people to partner with a monster and ambush us, but sometimes life gives you lemons."

"Some ugly lemons," Mitzi muttered, then said, "I would appreciate a more direct explanation next time."

"I didn't want to disclose my ability," James replied bluntly. "I would advise you to be similarly careful the first time you meet someone new. Fortunately, my new Skills allowed me to distract the monster for a bit longer than I otherwise could have."

"I'm not saying you were wrong to use your advanced Looting Skill on the corpses." Mitzi sounded more annoyed now than she had been before. "But I hope we're now inside of your circle of trust!"

"Well, I definitely trust you and Alan more than those people up there." James pointed straight up for a moment before he realized that his companions probably couldn't tell what he was doing. It was dark in the pit now that the healing glow had faded.

The best distraction from being angry at me is being angry at the real enemy. Persuasion! False Impression!

"You know, the shocking thing to me isn't that we've been trapped by humans," James said, tone thick with feigned outrage. "It's how quickly they decided to throw away their natural in-group loyalty to humanity and side with a creature they met here. It's been less than a day!"

Seriously, how did they even figure out that they could make a deal with the Corpse Eater? James wondered. *Does it talk?* He had jumped to the possibility of a deal between human and apparently semi-intelligent monster extremely quickly. Mostly because none of the basic Classes, which everyone had started with, possessed any beast taming Skill as far as he'd seen—and James had seen the names of *a lot* of different abilities now. *And it would be extremely unbalanced if someone got such a Skill just through their life history.*

Mitzi opened her mouth as if she wanted to say something, but then she let out a sigh instead and shrugged. Alan was the next to speak.

"What are we going to do now?" Alan asked.

"Well, unless we can talk our way out of here, we need to get ready to fight," James replied immediately. "I'm pretty hungry, and I can imagine you must both be famished too. Why don't we have some wolf meat and restore some energy?"

He reached into his bag and pulled out three Wolf Meat Bundles.

"You can really eat at a time like this?" Mitzi asked. "After getting so close to that disgusting *thing* while you were fighting?" She shuddered slightly.

"It's like you really were made for life in the System," Alan quietly agreed. "Or like this place was made for you."

After they had healed the Corpse Eater—that is, extinguished the flames that covered its body like a heavy winter coat and saved it from the brink of death— the party leader, Kurt Royersford, meekly asked if it would go down into the pit with them to finish off the weakened enemy party. The semi-restored creature grunted a refusal in its Gollum-like voice and walked off to try to find some flesh to eat, which Kurt understood would allow it to recover lost Health more quickly than by receiving healing from a human. Though they had only really conversed with the creature a few times, he had gathered from one of these conversations that this was a common ability for monsters.

It seemed unlikely that there would be any dead bodies left nearby, considering the huge number that the enemy had Looted prior to fighting the Corpse Eater and falling into the ground, but no one in the party was terribly committed to keeping the monster close by if it wanted to be somewhere else, so no one raised the point.

Standing near enough to the pit to watch it without being overheard—speaking in tones low enough that they could barely hear each other, let alone being audible to their victims—Kurt Royersford's party discussed how the plan had gone.

"I told you we should never have contracted with *that thing*!" Sierra Rodin complained.

Kurt looked around a little nervously. "That *thing* can probably hear you!" he hissed. "We made a choice as a group. We had a vote!"

"Yes, we voted," David Rodin said with a sniff. He sounded distinctly unimpressed with the democratic process as he'd experienced it.

The Rodin twins were a strong package, a Healer and a Mage, so in the hurried moments when the survivors had been regrouping after the initial wolf-pack attack, Kurt had considered them strong candidates to pull into the group. Unlike the other members, however, the twins had proved constant dissenters in the short time since the party formed. And they seemed to form their opinions as a pair.

"Everything is working the way it's supposed to," insisted Shannon Roth. "The only problem was that they ended up all falling into the pit together, instead of some falling in and others getting picked off outside."

"Yeah. The big problem was that freak leading them," agreed Joel Robinson, the last member of the group and the only other melee warrior besides Kurt.

"If he could be turned, he could be a powerful ally," Kurt said, crossing his arms and deepening his voice. Everyone looked at him askance. He ignored the side-eye and decided to broach the subject with the Corpse Eater. "Hey, what do you think of asking the strong guy to join us?" Kurt raised his voice to make sure he could be heard by the monster still wandering nearby.

They heard the trees nearby shifting and breaking as the monster moved closer to their position. Then a broken, croaking voice responded, "Gets him for a friend if yeh can. If not, make a good meal!" The Corpse Eater's contribution to the discussion was crude but decisive, as was usual in their association with the creature thus far.

"I guess it doesn't do any harm to ask," Sierra said.

"We outnumber him, and he's got to be tired after that show he put on," Joel contributed.

"But makes him gimme the othersss," the Corpse Eater intoned. "Or no deal!"

"Fine, then. We're agreed," Kurt said. "Now let's come up with a battle plan in case we have to fight him."

The group moved even farther away from the pit opening to continue their discussion until it was barely in sight. No one was likely to climb out right now unless they had a death wish anyway.

* * *

In the belly of the pit, the party ate their meat, cooked over Mitzi's magical flame, in a near silent state of anticipation. James perhaps wasn't as nervous as his companions, but the party seemed to be in a tight spot.

Cliff remained unconscious, and although James, Alan, and Mitzi were recovering Mana and Stamina with every passing minute, the group would undeniably be at a disadvantage if they were subject to a renewed attack right now.

As he ate, James reviewed his newly very enhanced Status information, thinking about how he might best use the resources therein to get himself and his party out of this situation.

[Status
Name: James Robard
Race: System-Boosted Human, Lv. 1
Class: Medium Warrior, Lv. 3
Job: Attorney (Pre-System)
Health: 961/961
Mana: 600/884
Stamina: 201/900
Stats
Strength: 40(43)
Agility: 35
Stamina: 30
Fortitude: 26(31)
Dexterity: 31
Perception: 27
Will: 26
Intelligence: 34
Free Points: 0
Skills
Adamant Defense, Lv. 1
Anthropophagy, Lv. 0
Basic Cold Resistance
Basic Elemental Magic: Earth, Lv. 2
Basic Elemental Magic: Electricity, Lv. 0
Basic Elemental Magic: Fire, Lv. 1
Basic Elemental Magic: Gravity, Lv. 0
Basic Elemental Magic: Water, Lv. 2
Basic Elemental Magic: Wind, Lv. 0
Basic Proficiency–Common Weapons
Crushing Bite, Lv. 0
Emotional Control, Lv. 1

Empathic Projection, Lv. 2
Empathy Control, Lv. 2
False Impression, Lv. 1
Hand of Glory, Lv. 0
Healing Aura, Lv. 1
Heavy Strike, Lv. 0
Holy Barrier, Lv. 0
Identify, Lv. 2
Laying on Hands, Lv. 1
Mass Pillage, Lv. 1
Pain Resistance, Lv. 1
Persuasion, Lv. 2
Pillage, Lv. 7
Precision Strike, Lv. 0
Quick Strike, Lv. 1
Silent Spellcasting
Situational Intelligence, Lv. 1
System Interface
Universal Language Comprehension
Wolf's Bite
Talents
Basic Spellcraft, Lv. 0
Cannibalism, Lv. 3
Cool-Headed, Lv. 1
Efficient Magic, Lv. 0
Manipulation, Lv. 1
Selective Empathy, Lv. 2
Titles
Chosen One of Apophis
Devout Beacon
Swiss Army Mage
System Pioneer]

This thing is getting long, he thought. The Status really didn't look like it belonged to a Medium Warrior at level three, considering that he had already been a Medium Warrior level three when that level two wolf broke his arm with its bite. James guessed, though he couldn't be sure, that a similarly low-level creature would not be able to do the same thing to him again.

Hell, he'd taken on that level seven Corpse Eater practically one-on-one less than an hour ago! No, he was in a different bracket of power now. Probably not near the top of the hierarchy, but likewise nowhere close to where he'd been before.

His Status screen had a lot of data he hadn't reviewed yet, including some uniquely named material he'd taken from people who had just seemed to stand out a little more than the other dead. Particularly notable were the Titles of Chosen One of Apophis and Devout Beacon. Hand of Glory he'd taken from a plain enough looking Rogue, though it likewise sounded very cool to him. He wasn't sure about Swiss Army Mage.

But it was time to look more closely at the assets he had available and start powergaming. That was the only way he was going to get the group out of this pit safely.

CHAPTER FOURTEEN

Our Darkest Hour

James began going through his Status sheet like his and his party's lives depended on it. They'd hit a low point in their journey, and it was time to start cheating with his abilities if that was at all possible.

A resigned silence hung over the party as James sat staring into space. Nothing interrupted his focus except for the occasional quiet exchange of words between Mitzi and Alan, who sat watching the opening of the pit for the enemy.

But even James, with his newly superhuman Perception, neither heard nor saw any sign of the other party. Nothing but the wind.

His review of the new abilities was enlightening.

[Adamant Defense: Allows you to put up a more powerful defense against an attack or a series of attacks for a sustained period, whether with weapons, tools, environment, Mana, or body parts, than would normally be possible. Activation cost of 20% of base Stamina. Effect scales with your Strength or Will, depending on whether the defense applied is physical or magical.]

That must be the Heavy Warrior starting Skill. A stronger but more costly version of the Medium Warrior defense Skill. I guess it could be good if I can't dodge an attack, although since my Agility is pretty high, I'm not sure when I would use it. Maybe if a big group attacked me.

There were five different kinds of elemental magic in his repertoire, but James didn't look at specifics for them, because they seemed self-explanatory:

[Basic Elemental Magic: Earth, Lv. 2

Basic Elemental Magic: Electricity, Lv. 0

Basic Elemental Magic: Fire, Lv. 1

Basic Elemental Magic: Gravity, Lv. 0
Basic Elemental Magic: Water, Lv. 2
Basic Elemental Magic: Wind, Lv. 0]

Extra levels in Water and Earth magic because I received duplicates of the Skills from more than one Mage. He decided to review the Gravity Skill just because that was the one he wasn't completely sure he understood.

[Basic Elemental Magic: Gravity: Grants the ability to manipulate the pull of gravity, multiplying or dividing the gravitational pull of a target or the pull of gravity on a target. Costs Mana.]

That sounds much more powerful than most of the other elements, James thought. *Does the System realize that fire, water, air, and earth were only elements according to the ancient Greeks, while gravity is one of the fundamental forces governing the universe?* Hopefully, this would help make him overpowered, although he doubted it would do much good against the Corpse Eater, especially at level zero. He would revisit it.

[Hand of Glory: Generates a magical light source that only you and others selected by you can use to see. Costs 5 Mana per minute to use.]

This could make a big difference if we end up fighting the enemy in this pit. We'd be the only ones able to see. And this was a solution to the darkness of the pit they were currently dealing with, though James wouldn't waste his precious Mana on lighting the area right now.

[Heavy Strike: A stronger than normal attack movement. Activation cost of 20% of base Stamina. Effect scales with your Strength.]

Same deal as Adamant Defense, basically, but for offense. This one might be more useful to me than the defense Skill since I already think of myself as the big damage dealer of the party.

[Holy Barrier: A shield of pure, sacred energy and light specialized to defend against dark, unholy mental and soul-based attacks. Activation cost of 10% of base Mana, plus 5 Mana for every second the barrier remains active. Effect scales with Intelligence, Will, and Holy Power. Effectiveness is enhanced by divine blessing(s).]

That ability would probably come in really handy if I were fighting a zombie invasion. Is the Corpse Eater unholy, or is this barrier specific to unholy magical attacks? I guess this also confirms that the soul exists, according to the System. Cool. So is there an afterlife? He decided not to go down that rabbit hole for now.

[Precision Strike: A more precise and potentially deadlier-than-usual attack movement. Activation cost of 10% of base Stamina. Effect scales with Dexterity and Perception.]

That's got to be a Rogue Skill. Weak-point targeting sort of thing. Useful for attacking the enemy's vital signs. But James was beginning to be impatient that he wasn't finding anything that would actually help him defeat the Corpse Eater.

He had already targeted its center of mass—where its organs should be—in the last fight, and that had done precisely nothing as far as he could see. *Only the fire really messed it up. Need to focus on magical stuff.*

[Silent Spellcasting: Permits the user to cast any magical spells they are capable of using without chanting. This causes a slight loss of efficiency; each spell costs 1% more Mana than it would if chanted. There is a slightly elevated chance of losing control of the spell.]

This is pretty cool. Having to chant spells was something that was new to James, since he'd only just obtained magic Skills, but he could already tell he wasn't into it. Now he could banter while fighting instead of chanting gibberish. Like Spider-Man!

He moved onto the Talents.

[Basic Spellcraft: You have demonstrated a penchant for creative and magical thinking through life. You have shown a deep ability to control your own reality through imagination and willpower. You carry that ability forward into the changed world of the System, where magic will now factor into everyday thinking, whether a person wishes to escape from reality or not. Your adaptable ability with magical thinking will allow you to create new magics and bend existing magical abilities into specific tasks more precisely than others. This Talent may generate many new Skills.]

Frankly, this sounds better than any of the Talents I started with, and with a much more flattering description, James thought, jealous for a moment before he recalled how he had gotten this one—early on in the Pillaging, before he had suppressed the System pop-ups. He remembered a teenage girl, half-eaten by wolves and dressed in a plain white tunic. *Probably a psychiatric patient before this.* Then he felt like shit for envying someone who had been mauled to death by wolves and undoubtedly died in horrible pain. *Rest in peace, wherever your soul is now.*

[Efficient Magic: As a creator who constantly worked to a deadline through life, you were the rarest of things: an artist who turned in their work on time. You have shown the capacity to tame the engine of creativity and force it to submit to efficient processes unconditionally. In the changed world of the System, you will find you can improve upon magic as it is used by others, both by eliminating unnecessary elements and by adding innovations. Generates Skill Silent Spellcasting.]

A bit like Basic Spellcraft, except that this one generated a specific Skill. It's interesting that they both make me better at manipulating magic. Maybe I can do things that are subtler and better than just throwing fireballs or big orbs of water. He wondered how many different Skills and Talents were possible, then instantly decided that was a pointless question.

Now onto the Titles, where things would hopefully become even more interesting than these rather potent Talents.

[Chosen One of Apophis: A Title granted by a god. Apophis has blessed you, so rejoice. Enjoy a 100% boost to all Stats and Skill effects when acting to increase the entropy of your environment. Enjoy a 1000% boost to all Stats and Skill effects when acting to measurably increase the entropy of any universe. The great God of Chaos has plans for you.]

On first read, the whole text of this Title made him uneasy. *I don't like that at all. I assume a god won't be happy that a blessing he gave to someone else ended up with me, and I don't even know when I'm acting to increase entropy.* He thought for a moment. *Really, I do know when I'm acting to increase entropy. It's whenever I'm destroying things and disrupting the ecosystem.*

James was less than eager to serve this god. Assuming that Apophis did not object to someone stealing the Title of Chosen One of Apophis, James could only imagine what sorts of tasks it would want to put him to as its agent on Earth. There was nothing he could do about it for now, though, besides trying to make the best use of the Title that he could.

[Devout Beacon: As the recipient of a Chosen One Title, you are a shining symbol of that deity's presence on Earth. Others who are aligned with that deity will be drawn to you, as well as those with a strong potential for alignment with that deity. Gain affinity at a vastly accelerated rate with those individuals. Enjoy a vastly increased likelihood of those individuals submitting to your authority as the Chosen One and a Devout Beacon. Gain proficiency in Skills related to the competencies of your deity at an increased rate.]

Trying to make me a cult leader. Got it. He would just have to try to deal with the implications of that Title when and if they arose. He tried to suppress the spark of interest he could feel in himself at the idea of having influence over large numbers of people. He already knew how corruptible he was, and he remembered the old saying about power.

[Swiss Army Mage: As a spellcaster who has shown a talent for multiple distinct and usually incompatible magical affinities, you are a rarity who will be sought after and perhaps hunted by many factions in the newly System-infused world. Your nature is that of an adaptable wizard. Enjoy a drastically increased probability of learning new magical disciplines and succeeding in magical experiments.]

An unambiguously positive one. That's nice. He was relieved he didn't get another Title, perhaps one that would make him the voice of another divine being on Earth or something.

James began trying to pull together a strategy for fighting based on the selection of abilities he had. The Chosen One of Apophis Title would have to play a central role, certainly. It was the closest thing he had to an overpowered ability besides Pillage, and Pillage wasn't a fighting Skill.

But he only had one wild idea of how to use the Title in this fight, and he didn't want to resort to attempting that unless he had to. Whether it would succeed or fail was a terrible gamble, dependent on factors that were unknowable to him at the moment. Even if his idea was successful, the consequences of trying it were hard to predict.

He decided to try bringing his team into his thought process. After all, he probably wouldn't be fighting alone here. Having reviewed his new Skills, he was ready to lay at least some cards on the table. He felt he was substantially deadlier than he himself had realized before the Status sheet review. Maybe his comrades would surprise him with something exceptionally powerful of their own.

James broke the silence. "So, I have an ability that lets me get additional power every time I Loot a body. What kind of other unique abilities do we have in the group?"

The group didn't seem to share his optimistic frame of mind.

"I have an ability that helps me to gain a person's trust more quickly," Alan said. "The System said I'd lived my life in a way that gave me a trustworthy aura. Not sure how that's going to be useful in a fight."

With Cliff still unconscious, it was Mitzi's turn to speak.

She shook her head. James was surprised to realize he could see it, as his eyes had adjusted a bit to the darkness.

"I don't think I have anything very useful either," Mitzi said. "I have a Skill for using improvised weapons and an ability that lets me focus more completely on a single task for concentrated effort. It makes my Skills more effective, but I've already been using it."

She looked over in Cliff's direction as if hoping he would chime in with a usable ability, but he remained stubbornly unconscious despite the dialogue going on around him.

"I suppose this is rock bottom," Alan said. "The upside is that there's nowhere to go but up." But his voice sounded a flat, hopeless note.

The three of them were probably all sharing the same thought: *Nowhere to go but up—or death.* Death was a very real possibility. They might already be sitting in their grave.

"Well, with Pillage I have several different kinds of elemental magic," James said. "Fire, Earth, Lightning, Water, Wind, and Gravity." Mitzi looked surprised as James listed off the range of elemental Skills. "I have a precision attack Skill, a heavy attack Skill, and a few Titles that make my abilities generally more dangerous and destructive, but nothing that gets us out of the pit and guarantees victory against superior numbers. I guess that's all we've got for now." He tried to keep the disappointment out of his voice. He didn't want to lower their spirits any further.

In fact, ideally, the group needed more of an inspiring speech. After a long pause, he tried his hand at being inspirational.

"On the whole, I'm proud of how well we've done on our first day here," James said. "Our little group is probably in the top few percentiles of performers so far. And based on the Skills I have, I do have a couple of possible plans for how we could—"

"Hey, you down there!" a voice called down into the pit, interrupting James's train of thought.

CHAPTER FIFTEEN

Collision Course

Hey, you down there!" a voice called down into the pit, interrupting James's train of thought. It wasn't quite as intimidating as the speaker perhaps intended, James thought.

He was actually relieved that someone had interrupted his attempt at an inspiring speech. He would need to rehearse, at least inside his head, before he started reciting another such. But now he had the happy opportunity to model "stiff upper lip" in another way.

"Hello, up there!" James called back. "Ready to surrender? I promise to spare all the humans up there if you do! You haven't done any lasting harm yet."

"You're a joker!" the voice called back. "I like that. Why don't you come up here and negotiate? We can discuss some real terms."

"Sure thing!" James said back. "Care to toss me down a rope? This is a deep hole you've dug us into!"

Alan muttered, "Are you sure you want to go up there alone?"

"I'll be okay," James said. He only realized as he was speaking that there was no bluff, no exaggeration in what he was saying. He felt *good*.

"Do what you have to do to survive, kiddo," Mitzi said quietly.

Alan nodded. James saw the bald outline of his head bobbing up and down. "You clearly have what it takes to keep going in this world, James. Maybe even thrive. Don't go getting yourself killed on our account. If you have to give us up to live, well, we probably weren't getting out of this hole on our own anyway." He looked to the still unconscious Cliff. "I'm sure he would agree, too, if he was awake."

"I highly doubt that," James said, "but I will keep your feelings in mind. I'm not quite ready to give you two up yet, though. And, believe it or not, I have a clever plan." He winked, before he realized that the old man probably couldn't see him in the darkness. His tone had probably conveyed the wink anyway.

A rope suddenly came slapping down against the side of the pit.

And James began to climb. It was surprising how quick and easy it was. They had left him down there long enough to recover a significant chunk of his Stamina and Mana, as well as completely refilling his Health, but the real difference maker was how much his Strength Stat had increased after using Pillage on hundreds of corpses. He was so much stronger than he'd been as a normal human, even at his athletic peak in college, that he was pretty sure he could have used his bare hands to climb out of the pit, carving handholds into the stone with his fingers.

Thankfully, they hadn't forced him to test that supposition. The enemy was seemingly trying to be reasonable. Either they genuinely believed they needed to negotiate with him rather than trying to defeat him directly, or they were planning to ambush the strongest opponent, him, alone in the hopes that they could take him by himself if they fought all together.

James thought that trying to ambush him would be a terrible mistake, but part of him wanted that fight. Even though he was in control of his emotions right now, he could feel a surprising amount of rage boiling under the surface. They had attempted to kill him and separate him from his family forever, to keep him from ever meeting his baby.

What had you ever done to them? a dark voice inside him whispered. *This is why you should do unto others* before *they can do unto you.* He pushed that voice down a little, but not as hard as he would have before. He really felt that these people deserved some terrible punishment, but he wanted to remain capable of civil negotiations.

Perhaps those unexpectedly self-effacing parting words from Mitzi and Alan were also driving him. They seemed so resigned to their fates, almost ready to die if it would help him to save himself. He *had* sworn to protect Alan earlier, and wasn't he a man of his word ever since he turned over his new leaf ten years ago? And he was growing a little bit fond of the old-timers.

James reached the top of the pit with these feelings floating through his mind. He was met with the sight of five people.

This is all of them, he thought. The same people he'd seen as he fell, in the same small group and even arranged the same way, though they weren't standing as close to each other as they had been when James fell into the pit.

Only the male who had smiled as he watched them fall stood within lunging range of James. The rest were standing a bit farther back—afraid of him? They probably didn't have any backup waiting in the wings, he assessed, besides the Corpse Eater standing somewhere he couldn't see right now. He looked the group over.

There was a tall, pale, slender pair who somehow looked alike, but almost perfectly masculine and feminine, respectively—the man enjoying the sort of strong, chiseled features that James used to envy and the woman delicately beautiful. To the side of them was a portly man, otherwise nondescript, who looked nervous at the sight of the man climbing up from the pit. James enjoyed seeing that. He knew that his stature and muscles had grown a bit with the increase to his physical Stats, though he hadn't been given the opportunity to see himself in any reflective surface since the Pillaging in the clearing, thanks to these fools.

Next, a young brunette woman, likewise nervous. *Probably she and that other guy suggested running instead of waiting to possibly fight me, from their pants-soiling expressions.* And then there was the man who stood closest to him: shorter than the first guy, but athletic, with hair the shade of orange rind. Instinctively, James thought this must be the leader.

No other reason to stand closest to the danger. If I killed him, would they just collapse?

He looked from face to face, trying to decide. *Probably not? I think the first two might be related, and they'd at least stick together. The other two might just run for it, though. Might happen that we'll test it out.*

"I'm Kurt," the fellow James had identified as the leader said. He extended his hand, and after only a moment of reflection, James took it and shook. Some of the tension in the air seemed to ease.

"James," James said. "I suppose you're the leader of this motley crew?"

"We, uh, make decisions together," Kurt said, his eyes darting back for a fraction of a second to the two who looked like siblings. James didn't miss the small movement.

Rivalry? Two people he desperately needs to keep on-side? Are they the strongest as well as being closer to each other than to the group, or are they just the most difficult for our would-be leader here to control?

"I think democracy might be over," James said. "It's premised on an equality of standing between people that no longer exists. For instance"—he gestured toward the pit—"those people down there are under my protection." He pointed at his own chest and then leaned in toward Kurt and scowled. "Because I'm the strongest." Establishing dominance was the top diplomatic priority for James.

"Can't deny that you're strong," Kurt said, chuckling nervously. "That's why we invited you up. We wanted to consider whether you might be a good fit for our little group."

"How does it work?" James asked. "Between you and the Corpse Eater, I mean."

"Well, we made a contract," the nervous portly man had begun to speak.

"It's an ability Kurt has," the frightened girl added.

"Um, could you all introduce yourselves, and one of you explain?" James asked.

"Sure thing," the nervous portly guy said. "I'm Joel."

"Shannon," the female speaker added.

James looked to the two in the back.

"Sierra," the woman said after a moment. "And my brother David." She nodded behind her at the statuesque man who shared her general look.

Those two are the psychologically toughest ones to shake, James assessed. *The other two aside from the leader are already scared of me, and the leader is on a tightrope trying to maintain control of his group.*

"Okay, and how did you find yourselves under the sway of the monster?" He pointed at Joel. "You. Go." He singled out Joel not because he was likely to be able to explain the best, but because he was the weakest link James could see. Him and Shannon, but he didn't want to be perceived as picking on the girl. Picking on a guy looked much better, more intimidating.

"Sure," Joel said. "I—"

"Why don't I explain?" Kurt interrupted.

"How about you shut up?" James said. "I'm not talking to you. I know you're the one who probably dragged the rest of them into this."

"We made a decision together, by a vote—"

"There's no democracy at the end of the world," James cut him off. "I know you want to sell me something. *I* want the truth. I'm sure you prepared a speech, but that's the opposite of what I want. Let him do the talking if you want me to listen to you. Otherwise, we can just do this the other way." He put a hand on his knife. "Okay?"

"Sure." Kurt nodded. He looked absolutely livid, but he was also within very close range of James if a fight broke out.

"So, I was the one who wanted to go back to the clearing after the five of us decided to group together," Joel began again. "I figured we could get some extra potions and gear, maybe kill a couple of those wolves, best case. And worst case, if the clearing was still full of wolves, we would be able to see that from far away, and we would just keep back and not go in."

James idly wondered if many other people would start having the same idea that both he and Joel had hit upon. *Or maybe they already have*, the cynical voice in his head said. *Who says you're the first group they targeted? That monster got up to level seven somehow. Was it from eating wolf leftovers?*

"When we got here, the wolves had mostly cleared out," Joel continued. "We killed a couple, and then he appeared. The Corpse Eater. He'd been watching, and he came out and spoke to Kurt, then to the rest of us. Promised us an easy way to get through Orientation. We voted, and in the end, we made a Beast Contract with him. It's a Skill Kurt has. We got a Job to go with our Classes in the Status. So, we get Job levels whenever the Corpse Eater gets levels now, and we don't have to do all our own fighting.

"I don't know if you knew this already, but your Race level is the most important thing in your Status. It's what shows up when you use Identify on someone. It goes up once for every two levels you get in Job or Class. If you're leveling both instead of just one, you can level your Race much faster. You get closer to becoming a stronger being that much more quickly. That's what Race levels are about: transitioning you from a basic human into something more powerful."

Joel stopped talking and sucked in air for a moment, having delivered all that exposition without pausing.

"Nice explanation," James said, nodding. "Sounds like you and your friends got a pretty good deal." *Identify*. He turned the Skill on the person he was speaking to first.

[Joel Robinson, Lv. 3]

Higher level than me—in Race levels, at least. He turned his gaze on the others. A notification popped up for Identify leveling up, but he instantly dismissed it. His heart sank a little. *There goes my faith in humanity.*

[Kurt Royersford, Lv. 3]

[Shannon Roth, Lv. 3]

[Sierra Rodin, Lv. 3]

[David Rodin, Lv. 3]

"How many people did you have to give it so far?" James asked. "And what exactly are the terms of this contract, which I guess you're probably trying to get me to sign on for?" He gave Kurt a sidelong glance as he said this last.

"The nature of this place is no-holds-barred competition!" Kurt interjected. "Don't act like we're guilty of something you weren't going to do yourself in the end."

"Another group before yours," Joel said quietly. "A pair before them. Eight people."

"All right," James said. "I can tell some of you at least feel something about what you've done. That was an important part of what I wanted to find out. Now what are the terms of this contract?"

"Simple, really," Kurt said. "We agree to cooperate with the Corpse Eater in killing groups of unaffiliated humans, we get levels, and neither side intentionally hurts the other, or the contract is broken."

"Interesting. So, you guys could backstab the Corpse Eater, and all you'd lose is the contract. I thought the terms would be more one-sided, more like enslavement. I know what I want to propose now. I'll give your group a choice.

"You can break the contract with your pet monster, and we'll kill him together, in which case you can also join my group, and I'll give you guys plenty of opportunities to get levels. Or I'm willing to let you all—including the Corpse Eater—leave alive, as long as you go soon, so I can bring my people out of your pit trap safely.

"I think the strategy of mooching levels off a monster is pathetic, and slaughtering random humans this early in the competition is a bit disgusting, so I'm certainly not signing on for it, but I also can't bring myself to hate you for it. I can tell some of you are scared, and you just want the same things that we want in the end. If we meet again, we don't have to meet as enemies. What do you say? Oh, I'll let you talk amongst yourselves in case you want to put this to a vote."

James thought he was being very reasonable, considering that if they tried to fight him as a group without the Corpse Eater, he was confident in being able to slaughter the whole group. Almost all of their levels were undoubtedly in Job rather than Class, and they had expressly been relying on someone else to do their fighting for them—and that against ordinary humans probably around level one—while he had been killing his way through Orientation for half the day and had also Pillaged Skills and Stats from those hundreds of bodies.

If they tried to fight alongside the monster, things became more complicated, but he at least still had a plan of action. A crazy plan of action, but wasn't trying to ambush a wolf with a dagger for his first kill a bit crazy too?

The group did huddle up after he stopped talking, walking back some distance from James—perhaps to be out of range of his hearing, perhaps just to be farther off in case he wanted to launch a surprise attack. Just in case he ended up on the wrong side of this situation, he began Silent Spellcasting, deliberately gathering orange Mana so slowly that it was almost invisible. This was the very beginning of his plan.

Even with his recently amplified Perception, he only caught scraps of the quick, quiet, yet seemingly heated exchange taking place almost in the distance.

"—stronger than the Corpse Eater—"

"I think we should consider—"

"—go with our original plan."

He heard only disconnected fragments, and only when they separated slightly did he realize they were actually done talking.

"We've made our decision," Kurt said. He had a foxlike grin on his face as he spoke. "We're sticking with our original plan!"

James felt a heavy thud behind him as the Corpse Eater landed only a few feet away.

Round two, he thought. He wasn't quite sure whether he felt disappointed or glad.

CHAPTER SIXTEEN

With Friends Like These . . .

This is such a bad fucking idea! He might be even stronger than the Corpse Eater!" Sierra objected.

But she was the only one objecting.

"I think we need to consider the long term. Even if he was a little stronger than the Corpse Eater, can he take us as far as it can?" Shannon asked. "We're getting Job levels every time it kills a few people. That's incredible! And we just so happen to be in this Orientation where half the participants have to die, where it's *acceptable* to kill people."

"How about survival?" Joel questioned. "Are we all going to survive a full-frontal attack on this bastard?"

"Hey, it's you and me in the front on our end, brother," Kurt said. "I've got your back, but don't forget that we still have our big gray friend ready to jump in as soon as we give the signal! He's going to do most of the close-up fighting. This guy couldn't beat the Corpse Eater last time. How's he going to do it this time?"

Sierra thought of how the last time had ended, with her healing the creature from the brink of death and Shannon using her water magic to put out the flames it was covered in. She wanted to say something about self-serving memory, but she could see everyone's faces. It was clear that the same coalition that had voted for the contract with the Corpse Eater in the first place was all psyched up for this fight. Just her and her brother again. *Stupid on top of stupid!*

She looked at David, and she could see that, under his stoic expression, he was afraid. Just like her. But they couldn't just leave. A Mage and a Healer alone in this forest wouldn't get far. That was why they had joined this group in the first place. She almost wanted to laugh at the absurdity.

At a glance, she could see that the supposed level-one human they were planning to attack was stronger than any of the members of their party. Orientation had been very good to him. His clothing was beginning to look tight around his body. Muscles bulged under every fiber. Their only prayer was that the Corpse Eater could kill him before he got within close range of the human component of the crew.

She would almost suspect that Kurt was willing to use the other members of the group as human sacrifices and risk everyone dying but himself, just to keep his contract with the monster going. But if he was going to be that kind of coward, he probably wouldn't have chosen a close-combat Class for himself.

"Well, with the general consensus what it is," Kurt said, "let's go with our original plan."

Sierra watched, numb, as their leader turned to the man across from them. It was only now that she noticed the enemy was glowing. A gentle orange aura was forming around him. He had already anticipated what their decision would be, and he was ready. Sierra wanted to grab Kurt and shake him, but she knew that it was too late to stop this now.

"We've made our decision," Kurt said. He had his back turned to Sierra, but she could swear the fool was smiling. "We're sticking with our original plan!"

The Corpse Eater leaped out from the tree line on cue, teeth bared, claws raised for a heavy overhead swing. A perfect ambush.

Or it was supposed to be.

David and Shannon started chanting their spells, and Joel and Kurt positioned themselves at the front of the group, theoretically poised to attack—but what they saw next made them hesitate.

They had witnessed the previous fight between the enemy and the monster, but they had watched from a distance, and there were multiple people in the fray, preventing Kurt's party from observing any individual fighter too closely.

This time, it was obvious that the creature was outmatched.

The enemy dodged without looking, his body a dark blur as a claw swipe that would easily have killed anyone in Kurt's group swept past him. The man was just too quick.

And Joel and Kurt stood frozen. They were supposed to charge in, take advantage of the enemy's confusion at the sudden attack, and strike him from behind while he was turned away, facing his assailant. A simple plan. Instead, they held still, apparently paralyzed, and the enemy advanced, darting away from the Corpse Eater's wide swings toward the much softer human targets.

Not for the first time, Sierra cursed herself for choosing to be a Healer. She just wanted to avoid fighting, but if she had realized the gutless people she would be surrounded by, she would have chosen the Rogue, the Light Warrior—anything that could defend itself.

Instead, she held back, clutching her staff. All she could do now was wait for the carnage to begin and hope there were big enough pieces of her party left for her to heal them.

James had seen his senses increase in acuity over the last day from roughly slightly above average for a human to a level that he suspected was humanly impossible before the System.

He no longer had to turn around to see where the Corpse Eater was striking. Its limbs were so large and heavy that they kicked up a small wind that preceded each aggressive movement.

And James could feel the gentle approach of the wind before either claw could get too close. Even with his eyes closed, he would have had a rough idea of which direction to dodge in.

His focus wasn't so much on the Corpse Eater, deadly but clumsy, or even on the enemy party, though he advanced toward them whenever the creature's strikes left him room to move away. His focus was on shaping his intentions, on *why* he was gathering this Mana around himself, continuing to silently charge an attack as he dodged.

His intention was to increase entropy, create chaos, with the Mana he was gathering.

[Chosen One of Apophis: A Title granted by a god. Apophis has blessed you, so rejoice. Enjoy a 100% boost to all Stats and Skill effects when acting to increase the entropy of your environment. Enjoy a 1000% boost to all Stats and Skill effects when acting to measurably increase the entropy of your universe. The great God of Chaos has plans for you.]

As James dodged another claw strike, he visually scanned the opposing party looking for who the weak points might be.

Only then did he notice that two of their number were quietly chanting to themselves and gathering Mana like himself: David Rodin and Shannon Roth. The spells from those two wouldn't be ready yet because they had been participating in the group huddle discussion, and he could see the halo of Mana around them—clear for David, blue for Shannon—wasn't especially thick yet, but they needed to be stopped. Getting hit with magic when he was in the middle of fighting would be at least as dangerous as getting hit by a Corpse Eater claw, and the magic might come at him with much less warning.

He quickly drew a knife from his belt—one of the starter equipment weapons, not a Wolfbone Dagger—and hurled it at David Rodin's center of mass. With his increased Dexterity and Perception, James felt virtually certain about where and how that throw would land when it hit. But it didn't hit at all.

Joel and Kurt both moved to block the knife. Kurt got there first and swung his sword up to intercept. The blade clanged off of his sword with a hard, sharp metallic sound, and although it annoyed him that Kurt had managed to stop his attack, James was pleased to see the way that Kurt was forced to step back slightly by the impact. *Benefits of increased Strength*, he thought. *It's just like I imagined. I can do this. Just have to avoid getting mangled by the Corpse Eater.* He leaped to the side and landed on all fours as another Corpse Eater claw attack came out of his peripheral vision. *If I can manage that, I can tear them apart.*

He easily dodged a pair of thrown knives from Joel and Kurt just after he landed. *I probably could have caught those. Amazing the differences Stats make.* But he couldn't get cocky and play with them. Their numbers could still be the decisive factor rather than his Stats.

Need to focus on the Mages, get in close before they can fully charge those attacks. If I take too long, the melee fighters will slow me down too much, and they'll hit me with whatever spells they're—

But suddenly the clear aura around David surged and then disappeared completely. *He's done?* James expected to be hit by something, and he started moving sporadically back and forth, avoiding being still for too long or moving predictably. But nothing struck. *An invisible attack?*

The aura had been strangely clear, unlike any other magic he'd seen in his brief time as a fighter, and James realized he had no idea what David's power could do. *Which element is clear?*

There was little time to question. Now the melee fighters charged him. Both warriors joined the Corpse Eater in attacking, but James's superior Perception and Agility showed their power here.

The two warriors were like a pair of turtles next to James, barely able to assist the Corpse Eater at all. Their weapons were by all means dangerous if they could hit, but James was able to move into unexpected places and make them get in each other's and the Corpse Eater's way. It kept having to slow its strikes down and swipe at the ground to avoid hitting Kurt or Joel, and James read its moves as frustrated and increasingly desperate.

James thought he was probably more in control of the fight with Kurt and Joel "helping" the creature than he had been when he was just fighting the monster itself. He kept the trio from surrounding him—it wasn't time for that yet—kept dodging, and kept chanting. The lava lamp glow grew and grew, to the point of forcing his assailants to squint as they looked at him.

Soon I can release it. James had never tested the power of his recently gained magic except against the Corpse Eater, briefly, when he tried to release as much power as he could as quickly as he could to save himself and his party. Now he was counting on magic to win him the fight. Certainly, he could kill the human members of this party with swords and knives if his reading of their capabilities was at all accurate. The monster was another matter.

James found an opening between the slow, almost useless attacks from the humans and the big, broad, clumsy but fast attacks from the Corpse Eater. He stabbed his Wolfbone Dagger through that small weak spot in the enemies' defenses, aiming for the gap in the armor covering Kurt Royersford's neck. A quick, delicate, precise attack that would open up the leader's throat.

One down, he thought, already factoring in this kill before it was accomplished. Only the Corpse Eater would be quick enough to intercept him, but a strike from it would have to go through Joel. *And if Joel doesn't run away, he's next.*

Kurt's eyes widened, his body instinctively stiffened, and he tried to pull back—but he would be too slow. The blade struck something hard, and James froze. The hard thing he'd hit wasn't a bone in Kurt's neck. He hadn't even penetrated the skin yet!

There didn't seem to be anything in the way at all, but James's weapon stopped moving for a key moment, and Kurt was able to pull himself backward in that moment of stillness, crashing into Joel as he frantically avoided the stab. James's arm continued moving once Joel was out of the way.

What stopped me? James questioned. He was so taken aback that the Corpse Eater's next attack managed to graze his forehead, and he only managed to avoid being scalped by contorting his body backward to make it a glancing blow.

But the cut, and its accompanying trickle of blood, did not distract him from the real problem.

Telekinesis? Magic force field? he guessed. *How strong is it? Can I break the defense with brute force?*

Some invisible force had blocked his blade from delivering a fatal wound, he was certain. If this was going to happen again, he had to know how to get around it. Or perhaps he could break through it.

My plan can still work, he thought. He could *feel* it working, as power far beyond what he had unleashed before gathered around him. Surely whatever magical defenses David had given his allies—and James was sure enough that this *was* David's power at work—would be penetrable. *He didn't even take that long charging it.*

James used Quick Strike to both dodge an incoming attack from the monster and to launch himself onto Joel, whose legs were still entangled with Kurt's following their collision seconds before.

Then he plunged the Wolfbone Dagger down, aiming directly for Joel's eye, striking with deadly intent—and this time he saw it. Something stopped the blade, and James saw that a tiny, transparent pentagon shape had appeared an inch above Joel's wide, fearful eye and stopped the blade.

That damned clear aura. James pressed down with more force, putting as much of his body weight behind the stab as he could muster, and he felt two things almost at once.

First, the magic shield gave way, and the Wolfbone Dagger plunged deep into Joel's eye socket and through to his brain. Blood gushed out of the shattered socket and onto James's pants. James felt the man's body writhe once, then go limp beneath him. There was a smell of copper from the blood and a foul undertone as Joel's bowels released. The ugliness of death overtook James for a fraction of a second as he realized he had killed a man for the first time. But he didn't have much time to think about it.

Because, second, the Corpse Eater finally landed a solid hit, slashing deep into James's thigh. Hot, lancing pain ran up the leg, and he could feel that the leg was almost useless. The muscles were shredded. Had he not already been kneeling atop Joel's body, he probably would have collapsed to his knees.

Most importantly, a torrent of blood flowed from the wound.

I think he hit an artery, James realized. He suddenly felt very woozy. *Maybe more than one artery.*

CHAPTER SEVENTEEN

Brothers in Arms

James swayed slightly from side to side before he got a hold of himself.

Still in battle. Can't sleep now. He bit down on his tongue, and the hot, coppery blood taste in his mouth helped keep him rooted in the present, in the conscious world.

He was fairly certain he was close to bleeding to death.

Good trick, James thought. He kept his focus, as much as he could, on his Mana and on his reason for gathering it; the plan remained unchanged. He had somehow maintained his grip on the Mana around his body, which he could feel was something he could have lost hold of.

And now that he had stopped himself from swooning, he could even spend a little mental energy admiring the enemy side's tactics, especially when he could think so much faster than any of the enemy party could move. *There was no way for me to penetrate that defense without a lot of effort. The kind of physical exertion that would make it impossible for me to dodge at the same time. They sacrifice one member of the group, and they all but guarantee a kill on a much stronger opponent. Objectively a strong plan.*

He pulled the rest of his attention away from the dying Joel—the man with the knife in his eye wasn't going anywhere—and looked around himself. The enemy party had closed in, seemingly either less afraid now that he'd taken a real wound or hoping to save their comrade from death.

James strongly suspected the former, especially if his assessment of their strategy was correct.

As its human helpers rushed in to help it secure the kill, the Corpse Eater tried to pull its claw out of James's thigh.

Despite his thigh muscles being partially shredded, James tightened what was left and tried to keep the claw where it was. Even as massive amounts of blood poured out, he wanted to keep the creature as close to him as possible.

The others were moving in all around him of their own accord. Even the Mages, presumably thinking they wouldn't have a good shot at him with their spells if they stayed back.

Fools. The moment had arrived for his big trick. James gritted his teeth in a grim smile.

Nearly surrounded by enemies, a surge of adrenaline pumping through his veins helped James keep from fainting due to blood loss.

As he focused once more, harder and with a sense of finality, on his purpose for gathering energy, the orange Mana around him thickened and grew brighter at a more accelerated pace. To the enemies, he could tell it must be nearly blinding now, like rushing toward the setting sun.

A last moment for them to reconsider rushing toward James. A last moment for them to regret.

I'm trying, he thought, *to burn down this entire forest. Trying to set off a fiery explosion that ignites everything above ground level. Trying to destroy this ecosystem completely and replace it with a waste.* Natural explosions kept going in all directions until and unless something stopped them. But James could direct these magical flames, and he didn't want them going underground, where his party remained alive.

Everywhere else was fair game, though. Everything else as far as James's Mana could reach was fodder for Apophis. James thought that should appeal to a God of Chaos.

As the Corpse Eater raised its other claw to strike him down, James finally released the orange aura that had gathered around him. The Mana took physical shape in the form of a massive pillar of fire surrounding James, which burst outward in all directions, traveling as fast as any explosion in the pre-System world ever had.

Burn all of creation to ash. The thought was almost a prayer.

James could feel that the intense flames he unleashed had used up the vast majority of the obscenely large Mana pool he had for his level, but the resulting inferno was more than he could have hoped for. It struck everything around him in all directions except for the direction of its creator, stopping at ground level as he had wished.

From his vantage point in the center, it was like watching the final explosion of a small-scale action movie on an Imax screen from a front row seat.

Transparent pentagonal shields rose to defend each of the victims, but these feeble protections were instantly overwhelmed and destroyed, and six bodies were suddenly wreathed in flames. The Corpse Eater was worst affected, as it was both naturally weak against fire and in physical contact with James when he unleashed his energy.

Its bloated head flared up into a flaming, gray jack-o'-lantern for a moment, and then it melted like a chocolate in the sun—if melted chocolate stank of sweat and decay. The notifications began to roll in as James's focus wavered for a moment, but James ignored them for now.

Need to heal first. The pain from his leg wasn't nearly as bad as when he'd broken his arm, but he was still bleeding like a stuck pig, and he could feel darkness clawing at the edges of his vision. Pain Resistance was one thing, but blood-loss resistance was a Skill he'd never acquired.

He forced himself to fight the pull of the dark. *Can't pass out here. They'll kill me, if any of them live, and I might die even if they all die too. Laying on Hands!* His left hand was instantly surrounded with deep green light, and he held it next to his left leg where the blood still ran in hot rivulets down his torn thigh, and where he could now observe the muscle was exposed to the naked eye.

James clenched his eyes shut as he focused everything he could on not dying, and as a result, he missed a couple of developments. While everyone outside of the pit besides himself was on fire, only three more figures fell to the ground.

Shannon had failed to activate the water spell she was preparing in time to protect herself, and she lost her focus completely when she was engulfed in flames. She quickly succumbed, collapsing and laying still as the flames slowly spread from her body to the surrounding dry grass.

Kurt, for better or worse, had been the only one fleeing from the scene of battle at the moment that the flames had exploded outward, spooked by the experience of nearly having his throat slit. He was farther away than other members of his party, despite having engaged in close combat with James, and he therefore avoided the brunt of the flames. Only the lower half of his body and his back caught fire.

Even after being ignited, Kurt retained enough presence of mind to frantically stop, drop, and roll, spreading the fire in all directions around him but slowly beginning to weaken the very persistent fire that covered his own body.

His quiet whimpering as he tried to put the fire out was one of only a few sounds James perceived as he healed himself, along with the rush of flames surging outward and Sierra Rodin's screaming.

So, I didn't kill them all, was all James thought. It wasn't as if he had the bandwidth to do anything about it just now, though.

As James had noted on first assessing his opponents, David Rodin had always been athletic. Slender and strong, with a gymnast's build. He was a naturally gifted athlete, but he had never done much with his gifts besides maintain them. Until today.

At the last possible moment, as James set off his explosion, David's incredible natural reflexes kicked in. He found himself able to move surprisingly quickly when thrust into the near-death situation. Perhaps this was something he had always had the ability to do, but now, for the first time, he had a reason.

The world seemed to slow down slightly, just enough that he could have saved himself by throwing himself out of the way of the looming inferno, down into the pit that lay just a leap away. Instead, David successfully threw himself in front of his fraternal twin, Sierra, sacrificing himself in an attempt to save his sister.

By throwing himself in front of her, David absorbed the worst burst of the flames of anyone but the monster. His skin blackened, smoked, charred, and curled, instantly turning the texture *and smell* of burned bacon. The flames invaded his open eyes and mouth with such speed and force that his death was mercifully quick.

His last thought was of his sister.

This was of little comfort to Sierra, who was protected from almost all of the flames through the combined power of her brother's spell, cast to protect the entire party earlier, and his sacrifice. Her clothing and her left arm still caught fire, but in one swift motion she was able to rip her burning blouse off and use the silk to smother the flames on her arm.

Her body operated on autopilot to save herself. Then she saw the charred body of her brother falling to the ground in front of her. His face—no, the blackened remainder of the front of his head—was barely distinguishable from charcoal.

"*Aaaaahhhhhhhh!*" Sierra screamed out. She threw herself onto her brother's body, tears streaming down her face. A moment later, she gathered herself enough to emit the green healing light. It cured the minor burn on her shoulder, but there was nothing healing could do for her brother now. Nevertheless, she persisted, blindly pushing green energy into the blackened corpse and intermittently screaming at the top of her lungs.

As the three survivors of the fight struggled in their respective battles, the area of forest closest to the clearing slowly burned all around them.

You have to go. An echoing voice in Sierra's head. An echo with the voice of her . . . her . . . As she brushed against the edge of panic, her mind blanked out the identity of the voice and its relation to her.

She desperately didn't want to focus on it, so she didn't. Only the voice and the message remained. The voice continued, *You have to leave! Now!*

But it was hard for her to feel the urgency. She had an important task she was doing, although her mind had lost the details of it just now. That was why she was glowing green. That was why she was pushing out so much energy, even though she could feel herself getting weaker and weaker the more power she output. It didn't matter, though. She had to keep going until . . . some task that she absolutely *had* to accomplish, no buts about it—another piece of information that her mind had blanked out.

The hot smell of smoke entered Sierra's nose. *Someone's burning something,* she thought distantly. *Doesn't smell like incense. Who left the oven on?* Sierra was living with two roommates while she tried to get her acting career off the ground. This was so like them, so irresponsible. *Someone turn the stove off!* Sierra wanted to shout. But her mouth wasn't cooperating. Instead of yelling, it just quivered, and then she quietly coughed.

She looked around without really seeing much of anything. The air was just a thick wall of black smoke. How had she not noticed how bad this smoke was until now? *Connie? Anne-Marie? Who left the oven on? I really need to turn the oven off.*

She wanted to get up and find the oven through the thickening smoke cloud, but she couldn't really move. There was something—a weight of some sort—on her lap. Something she refused to look at. Something she couldn't just push away and leave behind.

Sierra breathed in and got a lungful of smoke, then coughed again, choking slightly, eyes watering. She ripped a long strip of fabric off her shirt, which was wrapped around her arm instead of on her body for some reason, and she tied it around her mouth. She thought she remembered that using a mask was a good trick for breathing better in smoky air. That would give her time to figure out her next move. *Why am I only wearing a bra?* The thought entered her brain and then flowed out just as easily. It wasn't important.

Leave my body and get out of here! Another intrusive thought she had trouble blocking out, but she shoved it away, then breathed in and coughed once more. She looked around.

Get out of here, she thought. *That was what the voice said. Why?*

She coughed again and lost her train of thought.

CHAPTER EIGHTEEN

House on Fire

James finished healing his leg injury, and he felt much better, at least physically.

It was amazing what regenerating a pint or two of blood could do for you. His head was clearer. His vision wasn't dark around the edges. He didn't feel dizzy.

Considering that he'd just taken on five people and a monster at once, he was doing very well. He doubted any of his victims could say the same. *Don't mess with Apophis*, he thought.

It was clear, in retrospect, that much of the power that had infused his final attack had come directly from Chosen One of Apophis. If not for that, perhaps he would be one of the bodies on the ground instead.

He sobered a bit at the thought. *I just killed five people, but that could just as easily have been me. I need some way of producing order instead of chaos. Other people aren't going to survive around me if this is what every day is like.* He looked down and finally noticed that he was still on top of Joel's body, only it didn't look like Joel's body.

Bile rose in his throat at the sight of the remains of the semi-cremated body, but he forced it back down. The worst of the flames had passed on to strike targets at James's sides, but Joel hadn't escaped. He'd been so close that his body was mostly ashes and dust.

James looked down at the body. *I make no apologies*, he thought. *I won't regret this. I refuse.* And he didn't feel guilty, exactly. But he was split. Part of him wanted to stay as angry as he'd been when the fight started. But the targets were dead. Where would the anger go?

The other part of him was preoccupied with hoping he would never have to meet this man's family, or any of these people's families.

He reminded himself that if there was any moral order to the universe, it was on his side.

Then James looked away from the blackened shape, and he pulled himself to his feet. *Time to quit wallowing and get my bearings.*

Looking around, he didn't see anything standing close by him. The smoke in the air made it hard to see where anything was, though. *I really did a number on the clearing*, was all his eyes could tell him.

The next thing he checked was his notifications. They would tell him how much experience he'd gotten, who he'd killed, and if there were any Skill or Talent levels in this for him.

[Sufficient experience accrued! Pain Resistance leveled up!]

[Sufficient experience accrued! Emotional Control leveled up!]

[Sufficient experience accrued! Basic Elemental Magic: Fire leveled up!]

[You killed one Corpse Eater, Lv. 7. You gained 120 exp!]

[Medium Warrior leveled up!]

[System-Boosted Human leveled up!]

[Medium Warrior leveled up!]

[Medium Warrior leveled up!]

[System-Boosted Human leveled up!]

[You killed Joel Robinson, Lv. 3. You gained 40 exp!]

[Medium Warrior leveled up!]

[You killed David Rodin, Lv. 3. You gained 60 exp!]

[You killed Shannon Roth, Lv. 3. You gained 40 exp!]

[Medium Warrior leveled up!]

[System-Boosted Human leveled up!]

[Sufficient experience accrued! Laying on Hands leveled up!]

Some diminishing returns on the kills, James noted. *Of course every level would need a little more experience than the last. Same as with video games. I'm honestly surprised this is all, though. They were all higher level than me on paper. No bonus for killing higher-level people and monsters?* The notifications he had received were excellent on the whole, though.

But they did not seem to include everyone he'd thought he had killed. He thought he had slaughtered the whole group, but he was fairly certain he hadn't seen all of the names in the jumble of notifications. Surely if he was mistaken, one would have tried to attack him while he was healing himself.

He reviewed the notifications again while keeping a wary eye out for anyone who might try a sneak attack. Sure enough, there were two still living. For Pete's sake, *the leader's name* wasn't even among the dead!

Another quick glance around his immediate vicinity revealed no humans standing nearby, though there was a lot of smoke that clouded his vision, and it seemed to have grown thicker since he last looked. He had indeed set a chunk of the nearby forest on fire with his magic, it seemed. Probably patches of forest in all directions. It wasn't just something he tried to imagine himself doing for a power boost. Of course, he didn't flatter himself that, even with the boost from Chosen One of Apophis, he had actually burned down the entire massive Orientation forest, but he might have made a dent.

He would need to either go around casting water magic to put the fire out or get to a safer place soon, and it might be too late for the water magic. Even if the flames hadn't had time to get out of control, he had definitely needed the multiplier effect of his Title to exert that level of power.

Would he be able to put out a fire that might be up to ten times the size he could normally create with just his normal quantity of Mana? *Doubtful.*

He briefly reviewed the key aspects of his Status.

[Status
Name: James Robard
Race: System-Boosted Human, Lv. 4
Class: Medium Warrior, Lv. 8
Job: Attorney (Pre-System)
Health: 603/961
Mana: 150/884
Stamina: 61/1225]

Yeah, my Mana's shot, as I would expect. Health isn't great. Stamina looks like rock bottom, but I already know that just a few levels ago, my total Stamina was less than my current level of Stamina. So, I can presumably move around for as long as I need to, as long as I don't try using any heavy Skills.

He activated Mass Pillage to get the remaining goodies, and he faintly glimpsed the glows coming from the various bodies of his victims. The lights originated in four different directions, all within the range of the ability, and the notifications rolled in.

From three of the humans, he got nothing interesting since everyone only had starting equipment. The only unusual detail was that the meat the System kept *insisting* on extracting from the bodies of those he killed was labeled as varying degrees of burned or charred. He picked Stats to take from each body except for those of David Rodin and the Corpse Eater. From David Rodin, he stole a Skill.

[Skill Obtained: Basic Non-Elemental Magic!]

Nice! That must have been how he cast the barriers he used. It was exactly what James would have wished to take from that enemy. The magic was scarily powerful since it was invisible until someone attacked it or vice versa.

From the Corpse Eater, which seemed like a fairly unique creature, he took a chance on trying to obtain a Title, but what he got looked somewhat underwhelming on the surface.

[Title Obtained: Citizen of the Dead Marsh!]

It seemed to just be a clue as to the Corpse Eater's origins, at most. At worst, it might be a complete irrelevancy. He focused in on the Title to check it out.

[Citizen of the Dead Marsh: As a creation of the Lord of the Dead Marsh, albeit the least of his creations, you are a known entity in his domain. As such, you may come and go as you please without being harassed by the security forces, provided you do not break the Lord's laws. And you will always be able to find your way home.]

A little more interesting than I thought. Is the Dead Marsh a setting in the Orientation? A place I could find back on Earth? Just flavor text? It couldn't be that last one, though, or the Title would just be utterly useless. Perhaps James had another piece of the mystery of the Orientation space in his hands. But time to think on that later!

He breathed in and coughed slightly. The smoke was starting to drift closer to where he was now. He needed to go.

He rose, and as he was about to turn and walk back to the pit, he saw the outline of a crouching figure through the smoke. The figure didn't appear to be moving, and he decided to walk over and see why someone was crouching or kneeling there. Perhaps there was an enemy he had failed to finish off who was too badly injured to walk?

Sierra was on the verge of fading back into semi-catatonia when a shadow suddenly fell over her. Sierra was beyond caring whose it was by this point. She was still trying to figure out where the stove was, and all the owner of the shadow was doing was blocking her light.

"Get out of the way," she managed to whine quietly.

The shadow drew closer. Two strong hands gripped her by the shoulders and shook her forcefully.

"Let me go!" she cried.

"Get up!" the voice said. *Get up!* the other voice, the voice in her head—the voice of *her brother*—agreed. It all started to flood back in. *Go with him!* the voice in her head said, beginning to fade. *Live!*

She blinked tears away and returned to reality. The meaning of what she was doing suddenly returned. She looked down at the charred remains of her brother and saw that his body was glowing slightly.

She shuddered and gasped, and fresh tears began to stream down her face.

"My brother—why? What are you doing?"

"I, um, Looted everyone in the area. I have a Skill that lets me do that to enemies as a group. I'm—uh—I'm sorry. Honestly thought you were all dead at first, but looks like you and the leader guy survived, though I don't know where he is."

She remembered who this man was now. The enemy. The one they tried to gang up on. The one who had killed her brother and her whole group, including the monster that was fighting alongside them, with an insane fireball more powerful than anything they could counter. Somehow. Even though she had used Identify, and he was no higher of a level than them. This new world was unfair.

How could this have happened to her and David? They had both been excited about this strange new world. A new start for both of them. They had tried to be so careful.

As she sat lost in thought, she heard the enemy's voice again, "Now, what the hell do I do with you?"

When James discovered who the figure was, the sight gave him pause. The girl was covered in soot, her face streaked with dried tears, coughing at every inhalation. She didn't seem to be able to move from the body of her dead brother—that was who James assumed was lying in her lap, charred beyond recognition, glowing as he began to disappear.

She's an enemy. I really should *kill her.* But he found he was already putting his daggers away. She was clearly out of her head, from the fact that she wasn't moving, hadn't bothered to put her shirt back on, and was cradling her brother's body as if she could save him even as it glowed from being Pillaged.

If she wasn't a threat, he ought to, at the least, leave her to her fate. She would probably die of smoke inhalation since she seemed unable to move, and the fire was only growing more intense in the parts of the clearing that were already burning. James suspected that if the System hadn't made them all superhuman to some extent, she would have already passed out. But he found the idea of leaving her to die in a fire more unpleasant than that of killing her.

The woman was staring right through him now, but he thought she would recover her senses soon enough, and what then? She would probably want him dead. Very, very dead. That's how he would've felt about someone who killed his sister. As he thought that, the dead brother's body vanished from her lap, courtesy of the corpse disposal of Pillage.

Now she was staring daggers at him. *Oh dear. I knew this was a mistake.*

"You did this!" Sierra screamed and leaped at James.

Moving almost without thinking, he took hold of her thin arms—she was really quite delicate and fragile in his hands, he had time to notice—and he tossed her in the direction of the pit. She landed on her ass with such force that she skidded slightly, stopping only a couple of feet away from the edge. *Is that my plan, subconsciously? I'm taking her with me? Saving her from the fire by hiding her with my party? This is so stupid.*

For some reason, he just didn't want her to die. Maybe it was just because she was a pretty girl with a gentle face, and he was used to thinking of women as harmless. The other girl had been pretty enough too, and he'd roasted her with the other members of her party. But that had been in the heat of combat, and this was something different.

Awesome! I'll rescue her, and she can cut our throats in the middle of the night, he grumbled internally. *She'll probably chop off my balls first, and well deserved for being an idiot with no sense of self-preservation.* Nevertheless, he approached the pit and threw her over his shoulder.

"I'm coming back down!" he yelled.

Then James leaped down holding Sierra over his shoulder, ignoring her feeble resistance.

The fall was still rough, but this time he was expecting it, and he landed with bent knees, suffering no real harm despite having an extra human's body weight on top of him.

"James?" Alan said. "What in the world is going on? What happened out there?"

"Hi, Alan," James said. "Could you help me tie this girl up?" He threw out some rope from his magic satchel.

"Uh, sure."

Sierra was secured quickly and with little resistance, though not without protest.

"This isn't necessary," she claimed. "I'm not going to attack you."

"Well, you were doing your best at it out there," James said. That more or less shut her up, and she compliantly held her arms behind her back while Alan tied her up snugly.

Taking a prisoner was a stupid idea, his inner voice told him. *One extra mouth to feed. And this one will stab you in the back the first time you turn around.*

Yeah, I know, he answered himself. *Chivalry dies hard.*

CHAPTER NINETEEN

The Bunker

Going to tell us what exactly happened now?" Alan asked. He was staring upward as he spoke, watching a cloud of smoke drift distantly overhead.

"In just a minute," James said. He was using Silent Spellcasting to charge a wind spell, and what he wanted the wind to do was complicated, so he actually needed to focus. Alan seemed to notice that James was glowing slightly and left him alone for the moment.

When he felt he had enough Mana charged—it was hard to explain how he knew, but perhaps judging such things was inherent to having magical Skills at all, or perhaps it was down to one of the Talents he'd Pillaged—James let loose a wind that swept away any and all carbon dioxide, smoke, and other bad air that might have found its way into the pit. This was tricky enough, but he had also added on a second part to the spell, directing it to suck breathable air down into the pit.

As the second part of the spell activated, a notification popped up.

[Required conditions met! Basic Spellcraft leveled up!]

Well, that's pretty cool, James thought. *I need to actually figure out what that Talent does.*

After a few seconds of the spell working—he could feel the air quality begin to improve and the spell energy begin to dwindle—he started casting earth magic. He didn't do anything fancy with it, though. Just sealed off the roof and closed the bad air out and the good air in.

The pit was plunged into darkness.

"Well," Mitzi said, "now that you're done controlling all the elements and bringing balance to the Force, could you please explain what happened outside, and why we now have a prisoner? It would also be nice to know if we should expect reprisals from the rest of her crew."

"Right," James said. "Well, I went up there to negotiate, but negotiations broke down into hostilities. After I was attacked, I defended myself with a big fireball and lit all of them, the Corpse Eater, and the surrounding area on fire." He pointed at Sierra. "Somehow, she survived, and I wasn't going to leave her to burn to death, even if she was an enemy. She's one of two who survived, so I don't think we have to worry about being hit back."

"So, your spell is why we're hiding from a fire down here like it's a nuclear fallout bunker?" Alan asked wryly.

"Out of all the details in that story, dear, is that really the one that needs further analysis?" Mitzi asked. "Thank you for defending us, James."

Thank you, Mitzi, James thought.

"I am very thankful," Alan agreed. "We don't have to be afraid of that monster and its minions anymore, and it's all thanks to you, James. Did you get hurt at all?"

"Nothing I couldn't recover from," James said.

Gradually the group quieted down, once all the questions that remained to be answered were answered. Alan and Mitzi reported that Cliff had remained unconscious, and there were no other events of consequence in the pit during James's fight. James provided more details on the sequence of events that led up to the fight and tried to downplay the radius of effect from his Apophis-fueled explosion.

He didn't want the group to have the idea that he could blow up all future enemies, since that plan had only worked this time due to his conscious intent to cause as much destruction and chaos in all directions as possible. He also didn't want to explain the reason why this attack was particularly powerful, because being the Chosen One of an evil chaos god would make him sound potentially untrustworthy.

Sierra remained silent, mostly staring straight ahead, apparently lost in her own world. Alan had placed her seated near Cliff, and James went over once just to make sure that her bindings were adequate, both so that she wouldn't lose circulation to her extremities and so that she couldn't get loose and murder her neighbor in the night.

He needn't have worried. The old man tied knots like a boy scout. James filed this away in case he needed to take any more prisoners.

And then, as there was very little else to do in the pit besides talk and rest, they gradually went to sleep. No one bothered standing guard. Sierra was well secured, and it seemed unlikely that anyone or anything else could even figure out where they were. A fire raged outside, and thanks to James's magic, the pit was sealed off like a crypt.

That was how they passed their first evening in Orientation. They all slept, more or less peacefully, on the rock floor of the pit that had been dug to entrap them.

When James awakened, he listened to the sounds of the group breathing for thirty seconds or so to try and figure out if any were awake. It seemed they were all in deep sleep, so instead of moving around, he started fiddling with his Status screen.

The first thing he did was distribute his Free Points. He didn't have much of a program for their use, but he decided to balance his Stats as much as possible for now. They were already going to be higher than those of other people of his same level, so he might as well get the benefit of that by ensuring he didn't have any obvious weak points that would be easily attacked.

For now, that meant boosting Perception, Will, Dexterity, and Fortitude.

With those points disposed of, he was left alone with his thoughts.

Day one of Orientation is in the can, he thought. *Gods help us if day two is at all similar.*

But really, aside from ending up in a deep hole in the ground, and Anthropophagy and Cannibalism reminding him that the System expected him to start munching on humans any day now, the day had gone exceptionally well. And he was slowly resigning himself to consuming human flesh if it proved necessary, since this dog-eat-dog System world had gotten harsher than he had expected more quickly than he could have imagined. He would probably need even more Strength than he had recently acquired if he was to survive the Orientation.

There was the small matter of the prisoner he had taken. Perhaps Sierra could have been integrated into the group but for the fact that he had killed her brother right in front of her. No small thing, and not something that was likely to be easily forgiven. *How could that ever be forgiven?* James questioned.

The dark voice in the back of his mind said, *You should never have saved her after doing that.*

More importantly, he thought, ignoring that voice, *how did she survive, anyway, when her brother was scorched so badly right next to her? He looked like a skeleton coated in coal dust before he disappeared.*

A pause.

That was *a human being once*, he reminded himself. *I've seen so many dead bodies lately that it's easy to pretend he was just an object.* Another moment in which he just inhaled and exhaled, mind a blank.

Then, *I killed three people.* He sat in silence for a few minutes, contemplating his actions. He had rarely felt bad about things he'd done "wrong" in life, except when caught red-handed. This time, he had actually been defending himself and others. Under the law, he was right to act as he had.

And he couldn't find it in himself to feel bad about it.

His regard for human life outside of his own family had always been more conceptual than real, even before the world ended, and society began breaking down. *I can't let myself get completely desensitized to the tragedy of human death either.* But it was a feeble, insincere protest. He hated to admit it to himself, but he was probably already most of the way there.

He tried another angle. He reminded himself, *David Rodin was Sierra's brother. Shannon Roth was someone's daughter. Joel Robinson had someone out there who loved him too, probably. Everyone has a mother.* He thought of his own mother, learning of his death, but his mind rejected the possibility immediately. He would survive Orientation even if he was standing atop a pile of bodies at the end.

I ought to feel something about this, though. He was annoyed at himself for this vacuum where his conscience ought to be.

He pictured the bodies he had seen in his mind. That, at least, produced a feeling of disgust in the pit of his stomach. But any sense of guilt that he had remained stubbornly silent, and at last, he gave up.

Better to set aside the question he had spent many hours pondering in the past, of what exactly was wrong with his moral compass. This Orientation was a survival situation, and such reflection could only hurt him anyway. There would be time later to contemplate the weight of his own actions, as well as the scale and depth of the calamity that was the System's initiation process.

Setting these negatives aside, he felt sure that he must be in the top few percentiles of performers so far, if such things were measured by the System. He had abilities that he was certain no one else had—if only because they seemed to be individualized to some people, and no one else had Pillaged the starting clearing as he had. As long as he could survive for enough time to refine his use of those Skills and Talents, and he invested the time required to level them, he should have a long-run advantage over others whose base Talent pool was more limited.

Given how quickly he had increased his own Stats with Pillage, James couldn't help but suspect that many others would have similar growth-boosting abilities that would put him in an arms race. There was no way the System, as he had experienced it thus far, would unbalance things in favor of one specific guy.

Everyone had some abilities to increase their odds of survival. Some were better than others, but the odds that his power set was the best were low, to say the least.

I need to prepare to run into more predatory groups like this last one, he thought. Part of this would be by getting stronger, which he intended to do anyway. Part of it would be by making it harder to get a good read on himself and his team.

And there was one thing he could try out right now. *False Impression!*

Just in case he met up with someone whose Identify had reached a higher tier of precision than his own—for now, James only received another person's name and level when he used Identify, but he assumed the Skill could upgrade and get more useful information from humans, as it did from monsters—it was time to experiment with his counter-intelligence Skill.

James pulled up his Status screen and fiddled around with it. All he had to do was focus on changing elements on the screen, and if he held the idea in his mind firmly enough, the display changed.

It was a little eerie, like those New Age thinkers who believed the power of the mind could change physical reality around them. The power of James's mind could at least change how others *perceived* reality.

He determined that he shouldn't change his name or level on the Status sheet, at least for now. That would look too suspicious to his own party. He just erased the Talents, Skills, and Titles that would make him look shady or manipulative: Anthropophagy, Empathic Projection, Empathy Control, False Impression, Pillage, Mass Pillage, Persuasion, Situational Intelligence, Cannibalism, Cool-Headed, Manipulation, Selective Empathy, Devout Beacon, and *especially* Chosen One of Apophis.

That last didn't make him look shady or manipulative so much as evil and dangerous, which was of course far from the truth.

James reviewed his amended Status screen.

[Status
Name: James Robard
Race: System-Boosted Human, Lv. 4
Class: Medium Warrior, Lv. 8
Job: Attorney (Pre-System)
Health: 1024/1024
Mana: 1122/1122
Stamina: 1225/1225
Stats
Strength: 50(53)
Agility: 45
Stamina: 35
Fortitude: 27(32)
Dexterity: 32
Perception: 33
Will: 33
Intelligence: 34
Free Points: 0
Skills
Adamant Defense, Lv. 1
Basic Cold Resistance

Basic Elemental Magic: Earth, Lv. 2
Basic Elemental Magic: Electricity, Lv. 0
Basic Elemental Magic: Fire, Lv. 2
Basic Elemental Magic: Gravity, Lv. 0
Basic Elemental Magic: Water, Lv. 2
Basic Elemental Magic: Wind, Lv. 0
Basic Non-Elemental Magic, Lv. 0
Basic Proficiency–Common Weapons
Crushing Bite, Lv. 0
Emotional Control, Lv. 2
Hand of Glory, Lv. 0
Healing Aura, Lv. 1
Heavy Strike, Lv. 0
Holy Barrier, Lv. 0
Identify, Lv. 1
Laying on Hands, Lv. 2
Pain Resistance, Lv. 2
Precision Strike, Lv. 0
Quick Strike, Lv. 1
Silent Spellcasting
System Interface
Universal Language Comprehension
Wolf's Bite
Talents
Basic Spellcraft, Lv. 1
Efficient Magic, Lv. 0
Titles
Swiss Army Mage
System Pioneer]

He shook his head. *Still not right.* The Status sheet now read as a confused mishmash of Skills from different Classes, which would still strongly suggest there was something *off* about James, something that had allowed him to accrue so many different types of abilities despite being a Medium Warrior.

He could erase a few close-combat Skills and pretend to be a Mage, which would explain how he had such a wide variety of spellcasting Skills and Talents, but then he would probably have to keep most of his melee weapons hidden somewhere and avoid being seen using them. As soon as he was seen resorting to those weapons first in a fight, which was still somewhat more natural to him than casting, his cover would be blown.

No, I'm thinking about this wrong. I can still keep myself as a Medium Warrior, and I can explain that my life pre-System got me the Swiss Army Mage Title. No one else I coincidentally run into is likely to have that specific Title, and I can say that's why I have all these other magical Talents and Skills.

For a few final touches, he hid Adamant Defense, Crushing Bite, Hand of Glory, Heavy Strike, Holy Barrier, and Precision Strike from visibility. The Rogue Skills, Heavy Warrior Skills, Crushing Bite, and whatever Holy Barrier was would not be explained by his cover story.

As he finished making adjustments with False Impression, James heard a change in someone's breathing. It was funny how his increased senses allowed him to pick up instantly on someone in the process of waking up. It wasn't exclusive information for long, though.

When Cliff woke up fully, everyone else knew it almost immediately. Those who had been asleep were swiftly awakened.

"Beth, why the hell is the bed so hard?" he slurred the last word groggily, so it came out as "harth" instead. "I had the craziest dream. You'll never believe it. I lost an arm!"

At this point, there was a sound of scrabbling in the dark, as if Cliff were looking for something. Then a hard *smack!* sound.

"Ouch! What the hell?"

CHAPTER TWENTY

A Place at the Table

As soon as he heard the sound of something striking flesh, James jumped into action. *Hand of Glory!*

Sparks of light emanated from his raised left hand, scattering to all corners of the pit within a fairly large radius around James. The pit was large and deep for a human-dug hole, but small enough that the lights lip up the entire lower area. The effect of the light was limited to only those whom James allowed to see it. However, since James tentatively considered all those in the pit as allies, everyone could see everything.

What the light revealed was Alan and Mitzi, startled by the sudden light on one side of the pit, and Sierra on the other side with Cliff next to her, holding one hand over his nose.

"I guess this place is real," Cliff said. He sounded disappointed. "Uh, sorry." He directed this last to Sierra.

"What's going on?" James asked.

"Your friend here grabbed me, and I kicked him," Sierra said bluntly before Cliff could say anything.

"I said sorry," he muttered.

As much as James would normally have enjoyed seeing Cliff humbled, this wasn't how he would have chosen to see it happen. James had not yet decided what to do about Sierra after the party left the pit. But as long as Sierra was alive, James wanted her to feel that she had been treated fairly by him and his party. Cliff's actions here would reflect on James as well as Cliff himself.

"We're getting out of here," James said. "We'll have more elbow room very shortly. You two, try to keep your hands and feet to yourselves while we get out." He tried to give his words a sardonic tone, but it seemed to fall flat, as neither of them was smiling. *Morning is off to a great start.*

"And just how are we going to do that?" Cliff asked. "Is there a rope ladder that I can't see somewhere? Or a cave exit? Is this a pit or a cave anyway?"

Cliff woke up on the wrong side of the pit. James barely kept himself from smirking.

Sierra didn't speak and just looked at James expectantly. James didn't answer verbally. He'd already started Silent Spellcasting while Cliff was talking, but it required focus to give the earth magic the amount of direction he wanted to provide and minimize the risk of hurting anyone.

Alan and Mitzi remained silent as well, and there was around thirty seconds of pure silence while James gathered the brown earth aura around himself.

As Cliff opened his mouth to speak again, the ground began to move beneath them, and he clammed up. The stone floor of the pit rose slowly like an elevator, scraping against the uneven sides of the pit and smoothing them out.

"So, you can do magic now?" Cliff said after a long moment of silence as the steady rise continued. "Even though you were some kind of warrior last time I checked."

"And without chanting," Sierra added quietly.

"Right, and that. What she said," Cliff said.

"I'm a man of many talents," James said quietly. A single bead of sweat ran down the side of his head. The movement of the ground in the pit had been harder than he was trying to let on, mainly because of the combination of complex instructions and great weight being moved. He wanted to tell them both to shut it, but he kept the impulse in check.

"Who is she, by the way?" Cliff asked, pointing at Sierra. "Did we get a new team member while I was unconscious?" He looked her over again. "And why is she tied up?"

James rubbed his temples. "Cliff, this is Sierra. For now, she's our prisoner, okay? Please be quiet a minute. I need to focus on the spell. I'll explain everything once we're on solid ground."

The silence abided until James had raised the floor to almost the height of the ceiling. Then he used the last bit of charged Mana to raise the ceiling and, with a final effort, tossed it aside, leaving them able to hop off of the platform and onto solid ground. Once its passengers had disembarked, the heavy rock crashed down to the bottom of the pit once more with a loud thud.

"So, when did we start taking prisoners, Captain?" Cliff asked. There was a trace of humor in his tone, but also a hint of something James had only rarely observed in Cliff before: deference. He tried to respond with a similar energy of mixed irony and seriousness.

"I made a command decision, Ensign. I went to negotiate with the monster and the party that chopped your arm off and threw us down that pit. Negotiations turned hostile, and I was forced to defend myself."

Through all this talk, Sierra stared down at the ground, avoiding looking at anyone, arms still tied at her sides.

Alan asked, "Can I untie the young lady now, James?"

"Yes," James said after a short pause. "There's no point in restraining her now. I only brought her into the pit with us because the fire was all around us, and I was pretty sure she was going to die of smoke inhalation otherwise. We can go our separate ways now."

Alan walked over to untie Sierra, and James began examining the surroundings. The flames really had scorched the earth, and though a few trees nearby still stood, they were blackened, and some still smoked. Aside from those stubborn stragglers, the tree line had been pushed back for many yards in all directions, until the fire burned itself out, weakening as it got further from the clearing.

James was thinking about the group's next course of action, specifically which direction they should travel in, when he noticed that the unbound Sierra was walking toward him. Having seen this, he pretended not to notice until she was within a few feet of him.

His mind was racing, wondering why she wasn't keeping her distance or even leaving the clearing and getting as far from her brother's killer as she could. There was plenty of daylight for her to travel in before she would need to camp for the night, and she needed to use it.

He had contemplated that she might want some revenge; that was why he had her tied in the first place. But surely she couldn't think she could do any damage in a face-to-face fight in the daylight.

So why?

She reached him.

"Can I talk to you?" Sierra asked quietly, her tone flat. He met her eyes and saw an emotion he knew well there: resentment. There was also something else, but it was something he couldn't recognize.

"All right," he said. Then he stood there, waiting.

"I meant away from the others," she added, clearly a little frustrated.

"Sure, fine." He kept his tone flat.

They stepped away. Alan and Mitzi were engaging Cliff in a quiet conversation about something else, which sounded from a distance like it had to do with how many survivors were left, and it was a topic that seemed likely to keep them busy for some time.

James checked the number quickly himself just to see if he was missing anything interesting.

[2789/3468 Survivors]

The change didn't seem significant to him. He already knew that half must die. Less than a quarter had died despite the System's dirty tactics.

The weakest had been culled, and presumably that process was largely done. Those who had wounds from the initial ambush had either been healed or succumbed to them. The struggle that remained now was which of the still-living, stronger survivors would make it out of Orientation and which would not.

Of course, if he hadn't run into me, and I had just reviewed people's attributes on a sheet of paper, I would have given David Rodin very good odds of surviving. James glanced at Sierra Rodin. He wasn't afraid of fighting her here, when and where he could see her—she was a Healer, after all—but it struck him that he wouldn't want her cooking his food.

She stopped walking abruptly some way into the trees. Apparently, she had decided that they were far enough from the group to talk because she opened her mouth to speak immediately. *She's commanding the tempo of the interaction,* he noted as she began. *Controlling when and where we talk, whether she does it consciously or otherwise. She's probably used to getting her way. I already have one headache in the group, and she'll be troublesome for whoever has to deal with her—*

"Do you want me to die?" she asked flatly, interrupting his whole train of thought. Instantly, he thought he knew where she was going. *Oh. She intends to be a lot of trouble for* me *specifically.* "Because that would seem to be your plan."

"How so?" James deliberately kept his answer short. He knew what she was driving at, with ninety percent certainty, but he wanted to make her say it herself. Take some control of the interaction back.

"By sending me off on my own! I'm a fucking Healer, man! And I only picked that Class because I assumed I'd be with—" She bit her lip and shut up.

Does she recognize she's only reminding me of why I need to get her away from us?

"You're a Healer, so you'll be valuable to any party that gets you," James said. "Do you want me and the members of my party to die?"

"What are you talking about?" Sierra presented what James read as a feigned affront.

"It's one of the logical ways to read you complaining about separating from my party. Maybe you want revenge. You didn't get it last night, but you were restrained. If you stick close to us, you'll have a lot of opportunities. God knows you have good enough reason." He leaned in close to her, trying to provoke something. "Don't tell me it hasn't crossed your mind."

"I—I don't—I—" She paused and took a deep breath, then seemed to take a moment to collect herself.

"Okay," she began again. "I'm not going to say I'm not angry or *upset* about what happened. That would be a lie. I'm probably going to be hearing his voice in my head for the rest of my life. I miss him. And I resent that you killed him. I admit it. I was up half the night thinking about it. Wishing I could strangle you." She took another deep breath. "But that wouldn't bring my brother back. And I also know you were defending yourself, not on some kind of killing spree. My group attacked you—against my arguments, by the way—you retaliated, and in the end, my brother died protecting me. He wouldn't want me to get myself killed trying to murder you while you're surrounded by your friends. Revenge isn't worth it."

She was speaking the language of logic, which was James's native tongue. And he did recall that he'd heard someone's voice, although he wasn't sure whose, seemingly arguing against attacking him. There was just one problem.

"That argument fits the situation right now. Who knows if Lady Luck will continue to favor me?" He held up his left hand, with his wedding band on it, next to his face. "I have a wife and a baby on the way that I have to survive and get home to, setting aside the wellbeing of my group, which also seems to be my responsibility for now. Why should we keep you around? It seems like a bad bet."

He had come to the conclusion there was no good answer before they had even started talking, which was why he had said she was going her own way in the first place. He had half turned away to go before she began her reply.

"Because I'm desperate!" She grabbed his arm between his hand and his elbow and kept him from moving away. "I'll make myself useful, I swear! I haven't done anything to hurt you, just thought about it, and I admitted that much! Plus, you already saved my life. I owe you. I know that. And you know I'm a Healer. So, if you keep me around, one of these days I just might save your life." She gave him steady eye contact as she spoke, and he couldn't detect any signs of deception. Only desperation.

"We have a Healer already," James said.

"What, the old man?" Sierra asked. She looked as if she were about to argue something related to that, possibly something about Alan's likelihood of survival if James's instincts were correct, but he gave her a look that cut that line of argument off before it began. Instead, she looked at the ground and exhaled slowly, as if trying to compose herself.

"Fine," she resumed, still staring down. "What do you need? There has to be something I can do for you that the others can't." James felt her hand shaking on his arm. She was more than desperate, he realized; she was afraid. He sighed. He already knew what he was going to do, and he didn't like it.

"What did you do before the System?" he asked.

"Acting," she said.

"Jesus Christ!" he hissed to himself. To her, he said, "Sorry, I just had the thought that I can't even trust your facial expressions." She let out a little nervous laugh at that.

He continued, "I was hoping you'd say you were studying medicine or something when I asked that, so I would know you have some useful non-System skills."

"I know basic survival stuff. I used to go camping a lot with my dad," she offered. "I remember how to start a fire, pitch a tent, tie knots—"

"How long ago was that?" he interrupted.

"Um, it was fifteen years ago. My parents separated. Divorced. After that, I was with my mom. She didn't like the outdoors so much."

"All right, I'm never going to be able to justify this logically. Go ahead and stay, against my better judgment." She seemed stunned. He continued, "Now let's go back before they think we've been eaten by wolves."

Her hand released his arm, and he was able to turn and begin walking away. After a moment, she caught up to him.

"At the risk of looking a gift horse in the mouth," she said, "I do have one, um, request."

"Oh, you do." He chuckled. "Go ahead, shoot."

"I don't know if there's anything you can do about this, but I'd like to learn how to fight."

"That's smart. But why did you pick the Healer Class in the first place?" he asked.

"So I wouldn't have to fight," she said, "but that was naïve." She locked eyes with him. "The fight comes whether you want it to or not. Next time, I want to know how."

"That's very sensible," James replied. "If there's some chance for you to learn something about fighting, we'll take it if it's reasonably practical. I'm not some martial arts master, though. I just have higher Stats than is normal for people right now. There's probably not much I can teach you myself yet."

"Fair. Thank you for letting me stay. I, uh, won't forget this." She seemed happy, almost smiling for a moment.

"And for what it's worth, I'm sorry I killed your brother."

She just gave him a slight nod in acknowledgement. They walked the rest of the way in slightly uncomfortable silence, each acclimatizing themselves to the new status quo in their own ways. James had several notifications waiting, but he ignored them, going over his decision again and again like he would go over a cavity with his tongue.

Already, James doubted his decision. He probably should have made a clean break. He was doing her a favor by not killing her, frankly. Having her near him was like keeping a ticking time bomb in his backpack.

But it would have been slightly painful to send her off to die on her own. A woman in need of protection. That had always been one of his weaknesses.

It probably would've been controversial within his group to send her away too, though he didn't intend to acknowledge that to Sierra. James wasn't a dictator. Certainly not yet. *Baby steps.*

In that vein, it was a good thing for him to keep increasing the number of people who placed themselves under his command, in his care. After his victory over the Corpse Eater and repeatedly being treated as the leader of his small band, James was starting to think that perhaps he could become someone of importance in this new world. He'd already proved himself a great fighter, and every follower he acquired would be walking proof of his fitness to lead.

In that sense, Sierra might be useful whether she wanted to be or not.

CHAPTER TWENTY-ONE

The Hunt

When James and Sierra returned, he asked the others if they'd come up with anything regarding the group's next moves.

"As it happens," Alan said, "we have." He pointed off into the distance within the forest. Far beyond the realm of gently smoking trees that surrounded the burned clearing, almost on the horizon, rose a thick black column of smoke.

Someone's started a fire, James thought immediately. *But why?*

"That's very interesting," he said, gesturing at the column of smoke in the distance. "Any thoughts on what it means?"

"Probably humans," Cliff said.

"Yes," Mitzi said. "We were hoping it means a group is trying to reunite the people in the Orientation who were separated in the first attack."

"Yeah, that seems likely," James said. "At least I hope it's humans. I don't think the System would throw a fire-breathing dragon into Orientation, but you never know. Maybe it's really committed to seeing us fail. Hopefully, they lit the fire for the reason you mentioned, as opposed to just getting themselves into a big fight that caused a chunk of the forest to catch fire. Or using the smoke to call for help. Anyway, I think it's worth checking out. Strength in numbers and all that."

Alan nodded, smiling as if pleased that James had come to the same conclusion as him.

"What's the plan if we run into trouble?" Cliff asked.

"Let's try out the formation you came up with earlier. You and me in the front, Healers and Mage in the back."

"So, she's staying, then?" Alan asked, pointing his thumb at Sierra.

"Correct," James said. "It can't hurt to have two Healers."

"Okay," Alan said.

Mitzi looked like she had questions, but she said nothing, just watched James thoughtfully. Cliff stared off into the distance at the smoke as if he didn't care about what was being discussed.

James wondered, *What exactly is the dynamic in my group? Are they afraid of me? Is that why Mitzi isn't saying whatever she wants to say here? And Cliff too?*

It didn't matter for now, but he wondered how they would behave once they were in the company of another group. *I don't think leading by fear—if that was what I was doing—would be sustainable long term, nor do I really want to sustain a state of terror in the people around me.* Then he remembered something.

"Oh, Cliff," James said, placing a hand on the older man's shoulder. "Earlier, the group was sharing abilities in the pit. We each have Talents or Skills that aren't explained by our Class. You were unconscious, so I was wondering if you had any abilities that might help us in a fight."

"Me? Oh, uh, I just have the normal Medium Warrior abilities, I think," Cliff said. "Guess I wasn't as special as you guys."

There was a strained silence as everyone stared at him. More than one set of eyebrows rose. James didn't want to openly accuse Cliff of lying, but the group seemed to be doing that for him. He waited, and then Cliff spoke again.

"Oh, no, wait. I just remembered," Cliff resumed, pressing his palm against his forehead. "I do have, uh, a thing. I have a Skill where I can draw away the attention of enemies. That's probably not something everyone has, right?"

"Good to know, Cliff," Alan said. "No, we don't all have that."

That really fits Cliff perfectly, James thought. *I wonder what else he has hidden up his sleeve.*

"How about you?" Mitzi asked. James saw she was turned to Sierra.

"Oh, I had a thing, but it was about being a twin. Since my twin is dead, I'm not sure it would do anything anymore."

"I'm sorry for your loss," Mitzi said.

"Yes," Alan agreed.

Cliff looked a little annoyed to be saying anything, but he added, "Sorry for your loss."

Then Cliff turned to James. "Hey, man, did you kill everyone but her"—he gestured to Sierra—"or did someone else survive? Alan was filling me in on what happened, but I'm a little hazy on that."

"There was another survivor," James said.

"The leader of the band. Right, James?" Alan asked.

James nodded. He felt a small headache coming on. He didn't really want to waste more time dealing with Kurt Royersford when they could be looking for allies, but Cliff was right to bring him up.

"Do we need to do something about this?" Cliff asked.

"What do you think?" James turned to Sierra. "Is he going to hold a grudge and come after us again in the future?"

She hesitated a moment, then seemed to come to a decision. "Yes, he probably will. He'll wait until he's strong enough, so he might not feel confident enough to do it now. But he'll absolutely want to get revenge if he thinks he can manage it. In the short time we were in a group together, he was always overly aggressive, overconfident, and overcommitted. I've known people like that before. They don't know when to let go."

James nodded. "Thanks for the honest answer. Next question." He turned away from Sierra to look at the other members of the group. "Does anyone have any tracking Skills?"

Mitzi and Alan shook their heads.

"Didn't you serve in the war, Alan?" Cliff asked. "They teach you how to track people in the army, right?"

Which war? James wondered. But it didn't matter.

"They taught me lots of things in the army, but I'm not Rambo or a Green Beret. Even if I were an amazing tracker, look around us." He gestured to the burned-out area they were standing in. "The evidence of where this guy went is probably burnt to a crisp. Not that I'm sure we would want to hunt down a fellow human being anyway. We could probably go through the remaining eighty-nine days without seeing him."

Alan looked to James. James nodded.

"We'll deal with Kurt Royersford if we see him again, then," James said. *Hopefully, he's wise enough to let sleeping dogs lie. If not, I'll deal with him when he rears his head again.*

After this, Cliff changed the subject to food. The group took a few minutes to check on their collective supplies of food, pooling them in a pile in the center. This led James to remember and contribute the canned items he'd packed pre-Orientation. The group rationed the supplies and then divided the items up among themselves, so everyone would have something to eat if they separated.

While the food was out, they had a quick and very carnivorous breakfast of tuna and bacon, splitting some of James's and Alan's rations.

There was a little more back and forth regarding the logistics of travel, and then the group walked off in their agreed formation in the direction of the distant smoke.

As they walked, James finally reviewed his notifications from the conversation with Sierra. More levels in his social Skills, unsurprisingly: Empathic Projection, Empathy Control, False Impression, Persuasion, Situational Awareness. *I wasn't aware I was using any of those in that conversation.*

They hadn't gotten far into the woods before James raised a fist to bring the group to a halt. He could see rustling in the low branches ahead, and it wasn't subtle. A lot of something was coming.

It was almost a relief when the first head peeked out and revealed itself in front of them, and he saw that it was just a wolf. *We've handled those before. We're stronger now.*

Still, he used Identify on this wolf, and he was surprised by what he found.

[Feral Forest Wolf, Lv. 4: A wolf cultivated for the Orientation by the System. Part of a pack, this specimen is one of the weaker members. Inferior to the average System-Enhanced Human in Stamina and Dexterity, but superior in Agility and Strength. Stronger when under the command of a higher-level life-form.]

This random beast was of a higher level than everyone in the group except him. *The beasts are getting stronger just like we are*, he guessed. The average wolf might have gotten noticeably stronger in just a day. And there were at least a few more moving through the bushes around them.

He got a bad feeling as the other bushes rustled. *They might not be ready for this yet.* He began silently casting, colorless Mana gathering around his body.

"Everyone get behind me!" James yelled. And, as if they had practiced it, they huddled in a small semicircle behind James, facing outward, weapons drawn. James held a shortsword in one hand and a Wolfbone Dagger in the other. Mitzi had begun chanting quietly behind him. They were almost as prepared as they could be. Almost. He continued gathering Mana for his spell.

A total of five wolves emerged, and he Identified them all. Most of them were level three, but his bad feeling proved justified when the last wolf appeared on the left. A monster very noticeably bigger than his fellows, with two heads and fiery yellow eyes. Literally fiery—they seemed to be rimmed with living flame.

[Command Forest Wolf, Lv. 7: A wolf cultivated for the Orientation by the System. Part of a pack, this specimen is one of the upper-tier members, a beta. Equal to the average System-Enhanced Human in Stamina and Dexterity, vastly superior in Agility and Strength. Stronger when under the command of a higher-level life-form.]

This one is the beta, James thought. *Maybe I can take it. Probably. I'm at a higher level now than when I fought the Corpse Eater. But there's an alpha out there somewhere, unless System wolf packs work very differently. What level is that?*

He found his heartbeat racing with a potent blend of nerves and excitement. He wanted to get past this beta command wolf thing and take on the big one that was undoubtedly waiting somewhere deeper in the forest. But he couldn't be totally sure the group would survive this attack yet.

The spell gathering around James reached completion, and the aura around him disappeared suddenly. He grinned. Hopefully, that would take care of the survivability of his group.

"Did you just—is that my brother's ability?" Sierra asked.

"Yes," James said. He lowered his voice. "I have a different version of the Loot Skill, and I can take an ability from a dead enemy. Your brother had the most useful ability out of your group."

Sierra seemed to be processing this for a few seconds before she spoke again.

"You don't have, um, all of his abilities?" she asked finally.

James just shook his head. Most of his focus was on the enemy now, as the wolves had shifted to surround the party as best they could.

"Ready to attack, Cliff?" James asked. A major benefit of getting into this fight now would be leveling Cliff up after the fighting he'd missed yesterday, and the rather weak performance in his last fight.

"Let's roll!" Cliff moved up alongside James to the right, clearly preparing to take on the wolves on that flank—the ones that were not two-headed monstrosities. *Good plan. The big guy is mine anyway.*

James silently chanted another spell, this one in an element he hadn't tried yet. He could sense Mitzi was charging her usual fire Mana behind him, and he wanted to try something different.

As the group stood waiting, spells charging, the lead wolf seemed to realize that waiting for James's group to move would leave the pack at a disadvantage. One head barked, apparently issuing an order, and the wolves leaped at the humans. The level four beast in front of them pounced at James, and he swung down his shortsword with as much strength as he could—plus some Skill-based reinforcement. *Heavy Strike!*

The strike cleaved the wolf almost in two, and it instantly collapsed to the ground unmoving, a smattering of red and purple guts exposed. But in the moment that it had taken his full attention, the beta wolf had drawn in close, unopposed.

Cliff was sticking one of the wolves to the right with the end of his shortsword, while Alan and Sierra protected Mitzi from wolves approaching on either side using their staves. No one seemed like they could move quickly enough to stop the big two-headed wolf as it approached from out of James's peripheral vision. Mitzi chanted even faster, and at the last moment, as the wolf was about to leap on James, she threw out a hasty, half-charged fireball.

It was small and weak, compared to what she'd thrown against the Corpse Eater earlier, because she'd rushed it, but that didn't matter. The command wolf turned one fearsome head toward the fireball, opened its jaws wide, and sucked the attack up like a meatball. The only sign of an effect was a single puff of smoke from one nostril. The creature seemed to grin.

The command wolf's other set of jaws moved around James's neck as he was turning to face it, pulling his sword out of the first wolf's body. The teeth closed in around the top part of James's spinal column over his armor—and suddenly stopped. If someone could get an impossibly close look at James and the wolf, that spectator would have seen a number of tiny, barely visible clear shields of Mana individually blocking the wolf's teeth.

James smiled. *I poured a ton of Mana into those shields. They won't give way easily.* He whirled around and swung his sword down at the beast's side. It pierced the fur and skin, but the cut wasn't very deep, he noticed. *This could take a while.*

The beast let loose a painfully loud roar from one head, and with the other, it snapped at James's neck again. This time he sidestepped. He knew the shields he'd placed around himself and the party would absorb some damage, but he didn't want to learn their limits today. Assessing the wolf's Agility, he thought he was a little bit faster, but it wasn't as comfortable of a gap as he'd have hoped.

The two began a deadly dance of sword and dagger against fangs and claws. The two heads snapped at him again and again. The biting heads—along with occasional howls that threw him off balance so consistently that he thought they must be a Skill—kept him from landing a serious blow. The translucent shields appeared and blocked the few claw swipes that came close to doing damage, while he completely dodged the clearly deadlier jaws.

James had no attention to spare for the larger fight that was happening away from himself and the command wolf, aside from trying to lead the creature away from its companions so that his group would have a better chance. He was already splitting his mind between silently gathering Mana and continuing to hold the beast off in melee.

Another bite came closer to James's body than he'd have liked, and he blocked with his sword on instinct. The wolf bit onto the blade, though, and it aimed its other head at him while he was stuck in the same place. The beast opened its jaws wide, and James saw what looked to be the same fireball it had swallowed earlier come flying back out.

He didn't even try to dodge; he just let the weak ball of fire burst against his magical shield, which remained active for the moment. With the beast fixed to his sword by its own bite, he stabbed the Wolfbone Dagger into the side of that head's neck. The blade only penetrated a short way into the thick flesh, but a gratifying trickle of blood made its way slowly down the neck. He tried again, this time Skill-enhanced. *Heavy Strike!*

The other wolf head tried to intercept by biting down on his arm, but the magic shield protected him again, what felt like one last time—he could sense the shielding waver underneath the bite. The blade penetrated deep into the target head's gullet, unleashing a small geyser of blood.

The wolf head that had been stabbed released its grip on the shortsword immediately. The wolf clawed at the ground with both front paws, the bleeding head apparently seizing complete control of the body for a moment. The other head continued snapping at James furiously but seemed unable to move within biting range. James had slipped a few feet back as the wolf released his sword. The beast seemed unable to move effectively while the head James had stabbed continued writhing in its apparent death throes.

This was the opening James had been waiting for. He unleashed the spell he had been charging in the form of a large orb of water, which swallowed up the two-headed wolf entirely along with a big chunk of the surrounding area. *Sure, they could swallow fireballs, but how about the opposite element? In pond quantity?*

The beast continued to struggle with its one dying head for long, precious seconds, and then the remaining brain seemed to secure its control over the body once more. It began to swim toward James.

CHAPTER TWENTY-TWO

Submerged

It was slightly disappointing to James that the water magic didn't seem to have done any direct damage to the wolf.

All the chunk of Mana he'd spent had done was make an obstacle for the monster to navigate through.

He could feel that it was seething mad, from both the intensity of its expression and the fury with which it swam. But it hadn't slowed down at all; he could sense that, if anything, the wolf had sped up as it tried to escape from the big glob of water encircling it.

And then, for a moment, James became less worried about the beast swimming toward him and more *surprised* to realize that he could feel—what seemed to be, at least—*everything* that was going on inside the water. It was as if the wolf was a ladybug walking along his skin. He could feel the motion of the orb like it was part of his own body—not painful, just an awareness of movement.

He had a sudden idea stemming from that sensation, and he focused on the water and tried to move it with his mind. If he could sense it like it was part of his body, maybe he could maneuver it like that too. The feeling was like trying to move a limb that had fallen asleep. There was clearly a connection there, but a lack of use had left it clumsy and dull.

But as with a numb, half-aware limb, James thought the connection just needed to be exercised a little. He reached out with his mind. He felt vaguely like a Jedi, reaching out for the Force, but unlike every time he'd imagined doing that as a kid, this time, he felt *something there*.

It took a moment, but the water responded.

The liquid stirred in answer to his thoughts. A single unnatural ripple formed in response to no motion but the motion of James's mind. Such a small thing, but it meant everything right at that moment.

As the beast was now getting very close to swimming out of the body of water and reaching James, he applied his efforts to making the water protect him. He ordered the liquid directly surrounding the wolf to move farther back toward the center of the pool and the water that was farther from the wolf to come forward toward James and cut off the beast's path.

The result was that, although the wolf's paw broke the surface for a moment, its body was quickly sucked back into the middle of the water. As the wolf began to struggle more frantically to get out, to *breathe*, James continued manipulating the water, and his control was strong enough, at least so far, to keep the beast where it was.

I wonder if I could infuse other water with my Mana and manipulate it too, or if it's only water that I've created myself. So far, this was noticeably easier than controlling the fire Mana had been, and there were no signs of the wolf breaking free from his control. The mad burst of speed toward him before had seemingly been the fastest it could swim, and that wasn't fast enough.

As the beast's movements began to slow, James relaxed a little, drawing in deep breaths, adrenaline slowly draining from his system.

I really thought you might have had me for a second there. The wolf let out a small spurt of fire from its remaining jaws, but—given its position in the middle of the water—the flame was instantly snuffed out. It tried swimming to the bottom next, but James again pulled it back to the middle of the orb. *No funny business. I won't give you the chance to try anything.*

The monster didn't give up but only became more frantic, now swimming straight up. But every effort at escape ended the same way, with the beast pulled back toward the middle of the water, a little weaker, a little slower than it had been before. *What a terrible way to die*, James thought. He wasn't conscious of it, but he wore a satisfied smile on his face, like a cat playing with a mouse.

Gradually, the wolf's paws stopped trying to tread water, and its jaws stopped emitting little puffs of fire. The body convulsed and writhed as the monster drowned. All the while, with only a small mental effort, James held the water in place until he got the notification. He felt *powerful*.

[You killed Command Forest Wolf, Lv. 7. You gained 110 exp!]

[Medium Warrior leveled up!]

[Sufficient experience accrued. Basic Elemental Magic: Water leveled up!]

[Required conditions met. Latent Talent, Water Affinity, discovered!]

He again felt the Strength and Agility surge through his body. *These levels could get addictive. It feels like I'm a little closer to being invincible with each one. A latent Talent, eh? Nice bonuses this time. Just more reason to keep killing everything I can! And speaking of which, lest we forget. Pillage!*

[Command Forest Wolf's body processed.]

[You obtained Flame Resistant Wolfskin Pelt, 5x Superior Wolf Meat Bundle, and a Wolfspine Whip!]

Some very cool loot. Straight into the satchel.

[Designate a target for Pillaging: Stats, Skills, Talents, or Titles.]

He chose Talent this time.

[Talent Obtained: Flame Affinity!]

So, the beast had the Flame Affinity, and I seem to have naturally had the Water Affinity. He had wondered why it felt like manipulating the conjured water was noticeably easier than controlling the fire he'd unleashed before. It had also taken relatively less Mana, though that was just based on James's rough calculation. He had to assume that the big fire spell he'd used on the Corpse Eater was equivalent to the big water spell he'd used here, and he factored in the Chosen One of Apophis Title's multiplier effect on the fire spell.

He walked back to the group. They had killed two wolves, which he could see had both scorch and stab wounds, and they had the last one surrounded. It would try to snap at them, and they would counter by shoving it with staves or poking it with a sword. He could see Cliff was bleeding from a bite or two, the Mana for the shield around him having run out. But between him and the two Healers using their staves, they were keeping the surviving wolf from either doing serious harm or escaping, while Mitzi chanted a spell.

James decided to just let them finish their side of the fight. No one was in trouble, and this collaborative fighting practice would only help their teamwork and get them more levels. He took his time walking back, watching the fight with a critical eye and looking for flaws that he could help the group remedy.

The main things he noticed were that Cliff remained seemingly afraid to commit too much against any opponent—he always seemed to hold back a little, apparently trying not to be off-balance—and Sierra wielded her stave like a broom, which was pretty funny to watch but nearly harmless. *Possibly acceptable if she's only supposed to be helping keep the wolf in the killing space, but then why is Cliff striking so weakly and wasting her efforts?* Alan was doing the same as Sierra but with a more practiced appearance, holding the stave like a weapon and swinging with what looked like more force.

It seemed like the three non-Mages were really just keeping the wolf in place while Mitzi chanted. Since they had no real way of knowing when she would finish chanting, it was a big waste of Stamina to do this and not try to land killing blows. *That really describes what Cliff lacks*, James thought. *Killing force.*

While he waited, James Pillaged the wolf corpse that he'd chopped in half earlier, obtaining the same basic rewards he'd received with every other low-level wolf he'd killed, including two points of Agility.

After another thirty seconds of the same holding pattern they'd been in when he started watching, Mitzi finished chanting and threw what looked like a smaller, somehow concentrated fireball at the wolf's head. James was gratified to see Mitzi seemed to be growing more powerful, even if Cliff had underwhelmed him thus far. The wolf's head melted like a candle under the intense fire, and James imagined the three must have instantly received the kill notification because they all noticeably relaxed.

"Well done, team," James said. He gave a cheerful thumbs up.

"We survived!" Cliff exclaimed.

Mitzi just smiled wearily. James noticed she was breathing heavily.

"I have just a couple of suggestions," James said. "Let's discuss over a meal. I'll cook."

He silently charged a wind spell and used it to chop down a tree with an invisible blade of wind. As he began to prepare a fire spell to cook with, he noticed the others divide up the three wolves they had killed and Loot them. James just smiled.

He could take a break from what he was doing and make sure to cast Pillage on each of those creatures before the bodies faded. But he preferred to get the meal cooking and to let the team enjoy their victory without adding a "leader tax" to their gains. Even though it would cost them nothing for him to Pillage those same monsters, it would probably feel like he was one-sidedly benefiting from their work. Which he would be.

The Mana finished charging, and James started the fire. From there, he took his emergency bag from within the magic satchel, and he brought out a cast iron skillet and some canned tomatoes and canned beans. He put the skillet in the middle of the fire and waited for it to get sizzling hot before he added all of the Superior Wolf Meat—which, as if he needed any more reason to hunt down stronger wolves, smelled much tastier than the ordinary wolves' flesh had when they'd cooked it the other night. He gave it a sear on both sides, then opened up two of his cans and dumped the canned tomatoes and beans haphazardly on top of the meat, hoping to give the whole thing a bit of flavor. *If only I had thought to pack seasoning, this would be perfect.*

When the meal was cooked to his satisfaction, James cast a small-scale water spell to extinguish the fire.

"You're certainly becoming very comfortable with using magic," Mitzi remarked.

"I think water magic is going to be my specialty," James replied. "I've noticed I can be a lot more precise and controlled."

"Well, thank you for protecting us all with your other magic," Mitzi said, as if suddenly remembering. "One of those wolves almost managed to grab Alan by the ankle, and I don't know what would have happened if he'd been pulled to the ground."

He waved everyone over, and they gathered around the food and began to eat, using twigs and weapons as eating tools. James himself used his buckler as a bowl. But no one complained about having to eat like animals or about the lack of seasoning. They were all glad enough to have something to eat, beyond just meat.

"It's so much better than last night," Alan said under his breath. He sounded surprised.

Mitzi, who had cooked the previous night's meal with her fire magic, furrowed her brow, as if playfully considering how to take that comment.

"The meat from the two-headed wolf is better," James said. "The item description referred to it as Superior Wolf Meat."

"Ah, that explains it," said Cliff. "We need to kill more of those things, then! What level was it?"

"Seven," James said.

"Just like the Corpse Eater," Sierra said.

James silently nodded. The mood in the air was different after Sierra spoke. He felt from her tone as if it wasn't the Corpse Eater or the Command Forest Wolf she was thinking about.

"Well, we'll have to hope we don't run into any more than one at a time, then!" Cliff clapped James on the shoulder and chuckled, ignoring the somber undertone in Sierra's voice. Or perhaps it was only in James's head.

"I doubt we'll see any in a group together," James said. "Its name has the word 'Command' in it, and in a given group, it would be strange to have more than one leader. The only way there should be more than one is if we're fighting the wolf pack rather than just these little groups. Just my interpretation, of course."

"If we do, we should run," Alan said firmly.

"I agree," James said. "You all run, and I'll cover the retreat."

"Hmm," Sierra said. An expression of doubt, as James interpreted it, but he didn't have the time to guess at what she was thinking. The conversation had moved on.

"What were those tips you had for our fighting, James?" Mitzi asked.

"Not much for you specifically, Mitzi. I'm just concerned the group might be relying too heavily on you to finish fights. I'm guessing you were out of Mana or close to it by the end of that last fight?" He waited for her to nod, which she did, before he continued. "Yeah, we want to avoid that if at all possible. But as for everyone else, there are a couple of things. Cliff, I think you're able to do a lot more damage than you actually are, especially when you have Alan and Sierra keeping the enemy from escaping or dodging by hitting it with their staves." He acted out some of the changes he thought would make Cliff's fighting deadlier. More committed stabbing and heavy downswing moves, mainly.

"Okay, okay," Cliff said, appearing to study James's moves and nodding along. James thought it probably wasn't sinking in very well, but he'd just look for an opportunity to improve Cliff's melee combat Skills in the middle of the next fight if he didn't see improvement.

"As for Sierra, you're using the stave a little too much like it's a broom," James said. He reenacted his perspective on her style to much laughter from the two lawyers and Mitzi, and a slightly chagrined chuckle from Sierra.

"Fine, but I'm pretty sure I don't wiggle my ass like that," she said, reddening slightly.

"Of course not," James said, deadpan. "It's a fight, not a dance floor. I'm just exaggerating for effect. Isn't it sinking in better?"

"Oh, I'm learning so much more, teacher." She rolled her eyes and smiled. The first genuine smile he'd produced in her, James thought.

"Don't you have anything for me, James?" Alan asked.

"Nothing but admiration, Alan. Did you do any martial arts classes to learn to wield a stick that way?"

This provoked a fresh round of laughter in the group, and the banter continued for a few minutes before they decided to get up and start moving.

By now they were all done eating, and the area was filled with the smell of food, so Alan suggested that they move on before the aroma attracted more beasts, and the rest of the group agreed.

They continued to march toward the column of smoke, and after a short time, unbeknownst to them, they crossed over an invisible boundary as they walked. They left the wolves' territory, and they entered the territory of another type of enemy.

Immediately, eyes fell upon them. The five continued chattering among themselves, oblivious.

TWENTY-THREE

Machismo

It seemed as if the group hadn't gotten far into the new area of forest they'd entered before they saw the Orientation sun creeping down close to the horizon.

The smoke they were using as their North Star was still far away, and James thought they had a few more days of walking to go. *This forest is bigger than I realized*, James thought. *I guess the Orientation space would have to be pretty large. Maybe this place is its own dimension.* It would explain how much of a boost Chosen One of Apophis had given him in the fight with Kurt Royersford's party.

"We'd better make camp," Alan said. "Pretty soon we won't be able to see our hands in front of our faces."

"I wonder if it gets this dark every night," James wondered aloud.

"Only every night the forest isn't on fire," came an unfamiliar lightly accented voice from nowhere, deep and smooth.

Everyone instantly tensed at the sound of someone or *something* talking to them—apparently, someone who knew that James had burned down a small part of the Orientation forest.

"Who are you, friend?" James asked, keeping his voice steady while his eyes shifted around the rapidly darkening scene. He couldn't get too nervous about this voice in the dark. Only an idiot would reveal himself by talking from a position of surprise if he wanted to start a fight.

"We're just some unlucky campers, friend," said the voice. "Same as you."

"Not the same as me, then, pal." James smiled and showed as many of his big, gleaming white teeth as he could. "I was born lucky. Why don't you show yourself?"

He fixed his eyes on the direction he was pretty sure the voice was coming from now, and sure enough, a shape moved in the darkness.

"I'm impressed you could see through my Stealth Skill," the man said as he emerged from a gap in the trees. He was a dark-skinned Hispanic man, around six feet tall and well-built with prominent cheekbones. Around twenty by James's reckoning. He and James were able to look each other more or less directly in the eyes. James had grown about an inch since he started leveling and taking Stats from bodies.

"If you hadn't been talking, I'm sure I never would have noticed you," James replied. "You must be a Rogue?" He wasn't really asking. The stranger's clothes were the standard Rogue starting gear that James had seen on so many corpses he'd Looted. *Perhaps I should have taken some more Skills instead of just Stats from them.*

"As it so happens, I am," the man said. "Every group needs a scout, right?"

"All too true," James said. "Hopefully, our scout wouldn't just walk up and introduce himself to a group he was following, though. It seems like a hazardous decision for someone with that role."

"Are you trying to convince me that you have a scout out there somewhere, or that I'm in some danger?" the man asked. "Because I followed you folks a ways—"

"You could at least give us your name before you start trying to get us to tell you details about our group," Cliff interjected.

James smiled. "You know perfectly well how dangerous your situation is. Even the person who's pointing that bow at me couldn't shoot fast enough to save you when you're this close."

The stranger and Cliff both turned to stare at James.

"How did you know?" the stranger asked, visibly perturbed.

"I think my colleague here was correct. It's only good manners to introduce ourselves before we start asking questions. I'm James."

"Ramon," the man said. He still looked disquieted. "So, how did you know?"

"I have sharp ears, and the archer confirmed my guess by moving again when I mentioned that I knew there was someone else," James said. "But generally, when someone with a Stealth-based Class comes out and starts talking, I know you're not likely to be alone. If you want to grow as a Rogue, you have to work on a poker face and act a little more consistently with the cliches that people expect. It's only by playing with people's expectations that you can really catch them off guard."

Ramon snorted. "So that's how it is." He looked amused.

"Could you tell your friend to come out now?" Cliff asked. He had his hands reflexively raised slightly as he spoke, as if he were expecting to have to deflect a blow. "We don't like being in the crosshairs of someone we can't even see."

"Yes. If you come in peace, you shouldn't have a hidden archer waiting to shoot us," Mitzi said.

"Forgive my rudeness," Ramon said. "The Orientation has been a little rough for my family so far. If we had misjudged you, your group wouldn't have been the first to try and kill us." He gestured toward the trees. "Felicia, let's talk to them face to face!"

A small, athletic-looking Hispanic woman emerged from the tree line, finger still on a bow string, but the weapon and arrow pointed toward the ground.

She snapped something at Ramon in rapid-fire Spanish, and he responded, "*Calmate! Vienen en paz.*" James's mind somehow translated this as "Calm down! They come in peace!"

"My cousin," Ramon said by way of explanation.

I know Spanish now! It was an astonishing realization. *But of course Universal Language Comprehension had to mean* something.

"*Mucho gusto,*" Alan said, going over to her and extending his hand. This too translated itself automatically for James, "It's a pleasure."

Alan doesn't seem to have noticed the language translation from the System. He must have already known Spanish.

After a moment, the young woman lifted the arrow off the bow string and shook the old man's hand. The two began chattering quietly together, a conversation which James chose not to listen to. He instead returned his attention to the Rogue.

"You mentioned the Orientation has been rough on your family," James said to Ramon. "How many of you are left?"

"We only lost two, but that feels heavy enough," he said. *Still trying to keep things vague*, James noted. *How do I earn his trust?*

"We've been working hard just to stay alive," James said. "I've noticed there is a fair amount of strength in numbers."

"That's true," Ramon said. "Maybe you should meet my uncle."

Was that the slightest hint of unease as he mentioned his uncle? James questioned.

"Her father?" James asked, nodding his head at Felicia.

"Yeah."

"Sounds good. Lead the way."

"We don't need to wait for your scout?" Ramon asked, grinning.

"You know there's no scout coming," James said, returning his smile.

Ramon and Felicia led them through the darkening forest for ten minutes until Ramon brought them to a small makeshift camp.

The family had apparently cleared away a small portion of forest in setting up camp. The scrawny stumps of dead trees stood in a ring encircling the perimeter. *A bit like a fence, if you only needed to keep out small animals*, James thought.

In the camp proper, the family had set up tents made from System-provided robes as well as from tarps that one of the family members must have thought to bring with them.

James estimated a total population of around two dozen people from the number and size of tents. A dozen camp members stood outside, not counting Ramon and Felicia, apparently having heard someone coming. Most of them openly stared at the newcomers, while a few pretended to perform chores and *covertly* stared at the strangers. People gradually stared less as the group approached closer and Ramon said a few quiet words to put them at ease.

There was no doubt that they were a family. Setting aside the similarities in appearance between some of the camp members, James also recalled seeing several of them back when he first arrived in the Orientation. He had even Identified a few.

They were the Rodriguez family, who had been sucked into this place together. He couldn't help but be a bit jealous as he thought of Mina and Yulia fending for themselves somewhere without him.

The mood here was a bit subdued, though, despite the fact that they were all together. Perhaps it was because of the two members of the family they'd apparently lost. Or maybe it was because they were worried about their children or grandchildren.

James saw three generations present: an older generation that ranged from late middle age to shriveled up prunes, a parent-aged generation from mid-twenties to early forties, and a much smaller cohort of teenagers. He had noticed the lack of children before in the first minutes of the Orientation, but it was more striking when he walked among a large extended family group. There were no children below thirteen years of age.

Take away people's children, he thought. *I suppose that must be pretty depressing.* He did not allow his mind to go to his and Mina's unborn child.

James made these observations as the group slowly made their way through the camp. His mind was almost unoccupied by any actual social interactions. Ramon didn't introduce the group to individual family members yet, but he briefly assured people that they weren't hostile and led them through the campsite toward a tent that was located near the center of the cleared area.

"You guys should wait here just a minute," Ramon said. He smiled, but he looked a bit nervous again as he walked away from them, leaving them about fifteen feet away from the central tent. As Ramon lifted a flap and crouched to enter, James smelled something originating from within the makeshift structure: the nauseating, sickly sweet odor of decay.

He wrinkled his nose and then looked around at the others, but no one else had visibly reacted.

"Anyone have any theories on why the Rodriguez family had someone following us the last few hours?" James asked in a hushed tone.

"Well, if they know you burned down the starting clearing, they have some idea of how dangerous you are," Mitzi said. "For some groups, that would be reason enough."

Alan shook his head. "No, I don't think that's it. The young woman told me there was someone sick in the camp. Someone almost dead. She seemed very upset about it. Maybe someone closely related to her. I didn't want to pry too much. I think they were hoping we could help. They could see Sierra and I were dressed in Healers' clothing."

James stared back at the tent. "Interesting." *Almost dead? That smell stinks of almost dead to me. I had begun to wonder if we were unwittingly close to the Dead Marsh.*

There was a sound of arguing, raised voices clashing from within the tent. It sounded like old versus young to James's recently improved ears. This went on for a few minutes.

You should just go in and settle the dispute for them, came an irritable voice in James's head. Then the countervailing thought: *That wouldn't be very diplomatic, though*.

James thought for a moment. *Or maybe it would. I think Hispanic cultures place a premium on strength. Maybe a show of machismo would go over well.* And with that thought, James let his bias toward action carry the day.

"Alan, Sierra," James said. They both perked up. "Let's go into the tent."

"Are you sure, James?" Alan asked. "They seem to be dealing with some personal matters."

There was a sound of something smashing against the ground inside the tent.

"Yes, I'm sure," James said. "Someone in there needs medical help." Sierra shrugged, Alan seemed to resign himself, and the two followed James as he pushed his way through the tent flap.

Inside, they saw a Hispanic man in late middle age. He was frozen in surprise at their sudden entry with his index finger sticking in Ramon's chest like he wanted to stab the younger man. In the back of the tent, James spied a small figure buried under blankets. The entire tent was suffused with a putrid odor of corruption.

"Please pardon my interruption," James said. "I couldn't help but overhear you arguing about me, and I thought I could help settle it."

"Hello," the older man began. "I think Ramon here was just telling me about you, ah, James? It's a pleasure to meet you, but you shouldn't be in here. My sister-in-law is recovering from—"

"My friends and I can heal whoever is sick, as long as they're not dead," James interrupted. "We can start immediately."

"Thank you!" Ramon said. "Thank you so much! The woman who's ill is my *abuelita*; she was our only Healer—"

"*You* heal?" the old man interrupted. "Really? Do you mean you were some kind of doctor before this?" He looked skeptical, and James realized that in his Medium Warrior armor, he looked far from the *de facto* Healer that he was.

He activated his Healing Aura just so the old man could see the green energy gathered around him. He nodded, waiting for approval.

The old man stepped back, pulling Ramon with him. There was a short, frenzied conversation between them.

James only caught snippets despite his superhuman senses.

"—trust them?"

"No choice—"

"—Warrior alone with your *abuela*—"

"She'll die—"

That last exchange came through very loud and clear. Ramon looked unmistakably angry, with tears in the corners of his eyes.

The old man turned away from Ramon and walked back over to James, who was almost ready to make this decision for him.

The two looked into each other's eyes for a long moment, and then the old man's face took on a look of resignation.

"Please help my sister," he said. The old man grabbed Ramon's arm and led him from the tent, leaving James, Sierra, and Alan alone with the tiny body wrapped in blankets.

"No pressure, guys," James said. "They might all attack us if this lady dies, though."

He knelt down and began unwrapping the body, the smell growing ever stronger as some of the old woman's blackened flesh came into view.

Alan gave him a withering look. "No pressure. Thanks."

James drew his starting dagger and leaned down over the body as if looking for a place to cut. "Come on, Alan. Since this thing started, have I ever gotten you into anything I couldn't cut my way out of?"

CHAPTER TWENTY-FOUR

Persuasion

You seem in way too good of a mood about this," Sierra commented as she watched James hover over the woman with dagger in hand.

"Why shouldn't I be happy?" James asked, looking up at her and Alan for a moment. "We're about to save a life. Really, between the three of us, we should be able to save pretty much anyone who's not already dead. We're already performing feats of healing that Jesus never did in the Bible—"

"Fine, fine," Alan interrupted, seemingly becoming impatient. "How do you want to do this? Now that you've started unwrapping her from her cocoon there"—he gestured at the covers that James had begun pulling away from the old woman—"I'm sure it would be best for her if we move quickly."

"I'm going to try cutting some of the really diseased flesh off, like a surgeon," James said. He gestured down with the knife at the woman's bare arms, the only visible flesh below her face, which were mostly blackened with rot. "The two of you use Laying on Hands wherever I cut, and hopefully, that will be the most efficient and effective way to use our collective resources. If she still needs more healing, we just keep Laying on Hands until she's all the way done."

"Just like a real doctor," Alan said. He seemed to be in a sarcastic mood this evening, James noted. *Perhaps I was a little too flippant about this whole thing for him.* "Do you watch a lot of medical TV shows or something?"

"Just *House, M.D.*, I'm afraid," James said.

"Oh, great, the most unrealistic one. Great. Fine. Go ahead and cut away, *Doctor.*"

Again, Alan sounded almost angry at James, for the first time in their acquaintanceship. James wanted to ask about it or say something to smooth things over, but he knew now was far from the time.

So, he began cutting into black flesh, dropping it off to the side in a bucket Sierra found. It was much more nauseating than simply smelling the corruption in the air had been. He occasionally had to pause just to focus on keeping the nausea down. Still, his hand was remarkably steady.

I could have been a surgeon, he thought. *If this wasn't absolutely horrifying.* But he didn't stop to congratulate himself. He kept cutting away rotten meat—and there was *a lot* of it—only pausing when he occasionally needed to move out of the way so that Sierra and Alan could cast Laying on Hands on the recently cut, pus-oozing wounds that James had made.

James had become fairly efficient with a blade, and the rot was thankfully contained to the old woman's upper body, specifically her upper left torso, so the whole procedure was fairly quick. Perhaps fifteen minutes elapsed, and he was done cutting. He joined the two actual Healers in performing Laying on Hands, and the three covered every region of the patient's body more than once, giving her as much attention as they could to ensure that they saved her from death.

James saw Sierra smiling slightly as she could see the magic beginning to work, while Alan retained a professional, stoic demeanor throughout the procedure. It was almost as if he'd done this before.

James's Laying on Hands leveled up twice during the procedure, which was gratifying. He was getting both political capital and Skill levels out of this, which somewhat helped make up for ticking Alan off.

Finally, after they had applied a little more Healing Aura, a healthy pallor returned to the old woman's face. Her wounds were all closed, and as they dressed her in a fresh set of clothes and covered her in a—less overwhelming—layer of blankets again, the three could hear her beginning to peacefully snore. When they'd begun, her breathing had been shallow and unsteady, fading gasps.

"We did it," James said. *We're literal miracle-workers*, he thought. *Praise me, Rodriguez family!*

"Yeah, I didn't even know that was possible," Sierra agreed.

Neither did I, really, James thought.

"Thank fucking God," Alan said. He wiped sweat from his forehead.

James was quietly alarmed. *I've never heard Alan swear before*, he realized. *I really need to talk to him after I deal with the Rodriguezes.*

The three emerged to a crowd that had gathered around the tent. Just over twenty minutes had passed since they went in, enough time for word to spread to the whole Rodriguez clan that someone was healing the old woman. Mitzi and Cliff stood at the periphery of the crowd, and Alan gave Mitzi a quick nod with a small smile, to her visible relief.

"We finished the work," James said. He flashed a bright smile at the crowd.

The old man rushed past him and into the tent. James tucked his head back under the flap and watched. The old man started off by checking the old woman's temperature and then her pulse. Then he embraced her and began murmuring something in her ear that James couldn't make out.

"Thank you." Ramon's voice came from behind James, muffled by the tent flap.

James pulled out from within the tent, and he saw Ramon tightly embracing Alan. The tall, lanky old man awkwardly returned the embrace, looking unsure how to feel. James smiled.

False alarm, maybe. Alan certainly wouldn't end up regretting this.

Ramon hugged Sierra and then James in turn, and as he moved from person to person, some hesitation within the crowd seemed to break, and the other Rodriguez family members clamored to thank the strangers too. Some offered hugs, some words of gratitude, others simply smiles.

In the ensuing chatter, James learned the basics about the group. They were a close-knit family, it seemed, and they all lived in close proximity to each other in their homes on Earth. This also gave him an idea of the significance of what he and the actual Healers had just done. The woman they had healed was Mama Camila, and the old man was her brother-in-law, Papa Salvador—Chava for short—who had been very close with Mama Camila ever since his brother, her husband, died some twenty years past. Between their respective marriages, they were parent or grandparent to almost every Rodriguez here.

When James asked Ramon what exactly had happened to Mama Camila, the Rogue shuddered, and his face took on a look of mingled disgust, fear, and loathing.

"They came from the trees," he said. "That's why we stopped here and cleared the trees." He gestured at the miniature clearing that the Rodriguez family had formed; James looked again at the stumps lining the little camp—trees they had chopped down to prepare the site.

Apparently, they didn't just want firewood.

"What came from the trees?" he pressed.

"Some creatures with many legs and a poisonous bite," Ramon answered. "Spider-like monsters as big as pit bulls. Mama Camila already wasn't in good shape, but when they started biting her, she started to rot from the inside."

James had already seen the wounds, so he didn't wince at the description. A little part of him wanted to correct Ramon that the creatures had a *venomous* bite, not a poisonous one, but that seemed like a poor point to stick on at the moment. *The damage to Mama Camila's flesh was no joke. I need more information.*

As he was about to ask for further clarification, though, he felt the tent shake behind him. He looked back, and Papa Chava was stepping out of the flap.

The old Hispanic man's eyes were red from crying, but his face was dry, and he wore a smile that communicated everything that the rest of the family needed to know about the condition of the woman inside the tent.

Papa Chava spoke. "Thank you all so much for saving Camila's life. After the attack coming from the clearing and the monster attack, we didn't think there was anything more we could do for her. Please ask us for anything we can give you, and we'll help however we can." The effect of the old man making this statement in front of the whole family was obvious; he was speaking in the name of them all, offering the help of anyone and everyone there.

"All we really want is to get more people together and move further through the forest," James said. "There is strength in numbers, and we can do more damage to monsters in this Orientation as a group than any of us could alone. We believe the smoke over in that direction means there are more of us humans over there." He gestured toward the black smoke, still easily visible from their position even in the dying evening light. "Once I understood that your family was here, I had the idea that you might go with us."

As he spoke, James already had an idea in mind of how his words would be perceived. *Only a few possible responses from Chava: enthusiastic acceptance, questions about our future plans, or refusal with excuses.*

"Well, we really want to find more people to gather with, but you see, there are some challenges." *Refusal with excuses it is. So much for "anything we can give you" or "anything we can do."*

But he didn't intend to let this little bit of resistance derail his larger plans.

He launched into his already thought-out response, making sure to keep his voice slightly raised, loud enough for everyone to hear. *Persuasion!*

"I understand your fears for your family, and I share them. The monsters that attacked your sister-in-law are a problem, and I wouldn't expect you to travel while worrying about a renewed attack. However, we are in an Orientation. The name implies that this experience is meant to prepare us for greater challenges and dangers to come. I believe that if you stay here, you will be safe for a little while, but you'll be completely unprepared to face larger dangers that will inevitably show up. I believe we need to form a large group and hunt many more monsters together. It is the only way we can collectively grow stronger while maximizing our safety. This is a horrifying and dangerous place, but we also have to face it as an opportunity to prepare for the future.

"If we don't make the most of the Orientation, even if we're lucky enough to survive it, we won't make it far after that. To make a stronger group, I would like to join forces with you all and possibly others. Together, we can defeat whatever pack of monsters that stand in our way. If your family is willing to follow us on our path through this forest, I'm all but certain that our chances of survival will significantly increase. We can become stronger together, and we can make a place for ourselves that's safer than this clearing in the middle of giant spider territory."

Volume, tone, phrasing. All chosen with careful attention to the intended effect, different constituencies present, and likely future consequences. Looking over the faces of the small crowd, James could tell he had won most of these people over. They would not only follow him willingly, but they had also developed the beginnings of trust. After all, he had already accomplished something that the entire family had seemingly given up on by saving Camila's life. *They're almost there.*

The other result of his short speech was a big increase in experience for his social Skills.

[Sufficient experience accrued. Persuasion leveled up!]

[Sufficient experience accrued. Empathy Control leveled up!]

[Sufficient experience accrued. Situational Intelligence leveled up!]

[Required conditions met. Cool-Headed leveled up!]

And there was the last reward, a final notification that appeared as he was examining the faces in the crowd:

[Required conditions met. Job unlocked. Job Politician is available to you. Accept?]

Something to review in more detail a little later when he was on his own.

For now, he was still in the mood of the crowd. There were murmurs of agreement and interest from all corners. Several people were looking to Papa Chava for his approval, though James was pleased to notice that others were already looking directly to him as their savior.

James glanced over to his original crew. His offer had a different impact on them, as he had known it would. Cliff looked excited. Alan was annoyed. Mitzi wore a calm expression, as if she had expected exactly this. Sierra's expression was more guarded, as if she were still deciding what to think, or she was simply better at concealing her emotions than the others. As he looked at the group, she even met his eyes for a few seconds, and he thought he caught a trace of a smirk before she turned away.

Don't know what that means. But he didn't allow it to unnerve him. His party would only benefit from the strength of this enlarged group, so they would all come to accept it sooner or later.

Papa Chava cleared his throat and prepared to speak, and a silence fell over the rest of the family.

CHAPTER TWENTY-FIVE

Minimal Loss

We can become stronger together, and we can make a place for ourselves that's safer than this clearing in the middle of giant spider territory," James finished.

Well done, Sierra thought. *He's already got this whole family ready to follow wherever he leads, and I'm sure his ambitions won't end there.*

She couldn't help but smile a little. The speech was a little heavy-handed, but there was no arguing its effectiveness. *Stick with me, and you'll never go hungry again!*

But now the ball was in the old guy's court again.

He cleared his throat and began to speak.

"Thank you, young man." *I wonder if he'd call him "kid" back in the old world.* "I can't say I completely disagree with you." *But he* mostly *disagrees with you.* She felt her lips turning up in a smirk again, but she controlled it and reminded herself that James's failure here would be bad for all of them.

"Why don't you and I discuss how we can best ensure a safe migration, since you believe so strongly that this is necessary?" he finished. The old man gestured back at the tent that Sierra, Alan, and James had just left.

"Sure," James said. "It would be my pleasure."

Well, that was a mistake if the old dude wanted to talk James out of this. As soon as they're alone, James will use whatever Skill he has to make his words more effective on the old guy at full blast. There had to be such a Skill in James's arsenal, she had no doubt. She'd been tracking his abilities—difficult, when he seemed to have so many—and this little speech confirmed to her that he must have something that made him more persuasive than was natural.

His actual arguments were compelling, but not "staring at the speaker in admiration" compelling, which was the result he'd actually achieved with several of these otherwise seemingly ordinary, sensible people. One of her own Skills was similar in effect, so she assumed he must have acquired something from a theater person or a politician in the starting clearing.

James and the old Latino entered the tent together, standing close together as if they were old chums, both seemingly putting on an act for the Rodriguez family.

How many abilities of his does this make? He had an advanced Looting Skill, all the Medium Warrior Skills, that Rogue Skill that generated light, and at least two flavors of elemental magic. *Especially fire.* And now add some form of mental manipulation to the list.

She wondered for a moment if he'd used it on her or others in the party. *Not on me,* she thought. *I still don't like him. He'd at least do the bare minimum to make sure I liked him and had no desire to harm him if he was going to manipulate my mind. But the others? Maybe. And if I had to, I could definitely persuade them to think that he had.* Public opinion within his original group seemed like it would be a weak spot for James while he tried to play politics with these new people.

Sierra wanted to go and eavesdrop on James and the old man to better understand the politics of their new situation as it developed, but the young man who had brought them there approached her.

"Ramon, I had no idea your family was so big," she said. She had nothing in particular to say to him, so she just mentioned the first thing that came to mind. "Do you have any siblings here?"

"My little brother is over there"—he pointed to a teenager who was about a foot shorter than Ramon—"and my sister, she, ah . . ." He hesitated for a long moment.

"Was she hurt or something?" Sierra asked.

Ramon shook his head. "No. At least, I don't think so. She just isn't here."

How is that possible?

"When did she go missing?"

"We were sitting around the kitchen table before Orientation started, holding hands and praying. When we arrived at Orientation, my brother and my parents were here, but she—" He shook his head.

Sierra thought of something she'd noticed earlier when she and Kurt's party were staking out the starting clearing.

"How old is she?"

"Just eleven."

"Are there any other kids you saw that age or younger who made it here?" she asked.

Ramon was about to respond when there was a rustling at the central tent flaps. Both she and Ramon turned toward the tent, which was only a short jump away from where they stood. James and the old man were stepping out.

Already? I thought James would be twisting his arm in there for at least twenty minutes. This was less than ten.

"Everyone, great news!" the old man said.

"What was his name?" Sierra asked Ramon quietly, pointing at the speaker.

"He's my Uncle Chava," Ramon replied.

Chava continued, "Mr. Robard here has kindly agreed to solve our security problem. He says he'll wipe out the spiders as a group, *singlehandedly!* To ensure minimal possible loss of life, he proposed that he would fight them alone."

James silently nodded from the side.

"Thank you kindly for the offer," Chava went on. "We can only accept with our thanks. You're an incredibly brave young man, and this is a dangerous task, so I hope you will allow my family to tell you everything we have observed about the creatures and wait until morning before you set out."

It was almost pitch black outside now, the sun a distant glow. With the camp lit mainly by firelight, Sierra questioned whether doing anything other than waiting until morning was even a reasonable option. Unless James had a night vision Skill she didn't yet know about, which was entirely possible, he'd be suicidal to leave now. *Not that agreeing to fight the spiders alone is anything less than potentially suicidal.* But at least it didn't seem entirely out of character.

James nodded. "I wouldn't think of doing anything else. Thank you for your support."

Chava smiled at him. It was a thoughtful smile in a wizened face. The old man clearly thought he was getting the better end of this deal, and Sierra would have had to agree with him. *Did he twist James's arm instead of the other way around?*

"We will make ourselves available to you, then," Chava said.

"Excellent. I will go around and continue to gather information," James said.

"Let me know if you need anything else from me, and you'll have it. And thank you again for the miracle you've already performed." Chava ducked backward and returned to his sister-in-law's bedside.

Something is very wrong here, Sierra thought. *This whole picture is very strange.* There were two things she couldn't reconcile with the James she thought she was slowly beginning to understand. She was so lost in thought that she barely noticed as Alan walked back over to Cliff and Mitzi.

First, would he really agree to go fight an enemy he knows nothing about, all alone? He's definitely confident, maybe a little overconfident, but there's a big difference between confidence and recklessness. All of the risks she'd ever seen James take had been calculated. *He ran from the Corpse Eater the first time he fought it rather than continuing the fight with his resources apparently running low. That's how he wound up in the pit. In his next fight, he obviously had a plan, and he found the perfect moment to execute it, and he basically blew us all to smithereens. Then the next time, he fought the lead wolf in that little group, but he only fought that one. And he even had a plan to protect the party from the rest of the wolves.*

Using my ability, chimed a voice in her mind.

Yes, she answered, *but the point is, he hasn't been just rushing headlong into danger. This feels out of character.*

Unless he has more abilities that you don't know about that give him a massive advantage, the voice answered back. *Maybe he has insecticide magic, or something like that.*

She rolled her eyes at the suggestion. *Fine, maybe he thinks he's a match for any spiders in the world. Maybe he's willing to go after them even though all he knows is that they nearly killed the woman in that tent.* But she still had a second reason why she didn't think this was James's plan.

The second thing was simpler, more of a body language read than anything else. James stood to the side and slightly behind Chava as the old man announced James's plan to exterminate the monsters that had the family trapped in this camp. *If this was James's idea, he would have stood up in front of everyone and announced it himself. There's no way he would let anyone upstage him when he's acting the part of hero.* Instead, he stood off to the side, nodding like a schoolboy being given an assignment.

If this wasn't James's plan, that means it was Chava's, and James agreed to it. How did that conversation play out?

She put a pin in that for the moment. James was slowly approaching Alan, Mitzi, and Cliff, and she moved toward them. She wanted to hear what he was going to say to the party.

James's approach was slow because he was suddenly extremely popular. People swarmed around him, clapping him on the back, reaching in for forceful handshakes, pulling him in for hugs—everyone was very excited about what he was offering to do, and people were talking over themselves trying to give him their advice or offer their help.

James spoke up above the hum of the small crowd. "Thank you, everyone. I'll do my best. I can't really hear all of you right now, but I'll come around a little later and get everyone's advice on handling the monsters."

People slowly made way for him after that, some of them seemingly remembering tasks they had to do for the camp and wandering off, while others just moved out of the way and hovered in the vicinity.

Finally, James made it to his original group.

"So, we're going into the jaws of death, eh, man?" Cliff tried to sound flippant, but he came off as nervous.

"You don't have to worry about that, Cliff," James said. "It's my intention to go out and deal with the problem myself."

He sounds like himself, but what's different about him? He's a little more dismissive, a little more arrogant, but is that it?

Mitzi interjected, "Alone? Who do you think you are, Superman?"

"There are a lot of situations where you guys would be very helpful to me—especially when I expect to be outnumbered. But this time, when it's an enemy that—from what little I've heard—is insect-like, hard to target, and uses venom, I think having too many people would just mean everyone else would get in my way. I couldn't guarantee your safety."

"I hope you know what you're doing, James," Alan said. He looked like he wanted to say something else, but he restrained himself.

"Seriously, man," Cliff said. "If you need help, you should be willing to accept it. This is bigger than a one-man job."

"Cliff," James said, "in the unlikely event that I die, I hope you'll take the cautious approach to getting our group the rest of the way through this Orientation. Minimal losses are probably the best we can hope for if I can't deal with a relatively small infestation like this by myself."

Cliff shook his head and looked annoyed, but he didn't say anything back to that. Perhaps he didn't want to say anything too negative in case James actually died.

James turned to Alan and Mitzi.

"I'm sorry that I have been making command decisions recently and haven't been consulting with all of you. I'll try to do a better job of taking group opinions into account moving forward. In this case, though, I don't see anything that anyone could say that would change my mind. I'm the man for the job. This needs to be done to get the family to come with us."

It looked like him, sounded like him, but something was definitely off. She just couldn't figure out what it was. There was more back and forth, but it was mostly in the same vein. James either won the others over slowly or simply wore them down as their expressions shifted to accept the necessity of his plan. Everyone agreed that the overall goal was reasonable, even if they had been initially reluctant to let James go and hunt alone.

She kept watching James's face as he spoke, as if whatever was off about him right now were written there in code.

Sierra was the last to speak. "I think you're crazy, but I've already seen how much damage you can do by yourself. Come back with your shield, or on it!" She gave a small, bittersweet smile.

This just feels wrong.

CHAPTER TWENTY-SIX

Elephant's Memory

James finished talking to his group, and he finally had time to consider the Job he'd been offered.

He walked to the very edge of the camp so he could sit down cross-legged with his back to a tree and just focus on his Status screen. He pulled up the Politician Job description.

[Politician: Having shown a knack for manipulation and persuasion, and a commensurate hunger for power, you angle for a leadership position within any group around you. A Politician makes the life-forms around them into their power, bending them to their will and feeding off of those who obey them, by whatever means. The Politician drives their underlings to salvation or ruin, depending on their preference. With each level, gain +3 Charisma, +2 Will, +2 Perception, +2 Intelligence, +2 Free Points.]

Whatever, James thought, regarding the actual substantive text of the description. *I don't mind the judgment so much now. Just keep giving me good shit like this Job.* The Politician position would give him more Stats per level than his basic Medium Warrior Class, which was impressive enough to win him over, though the Stats provided were mainly mental ones—Charisma, which he didn't even have yet, along with Will, Intelligence, and Perception. The fact that it might not help him punch better did not sway him at all. *I have the feeling that different Stats balance each other out, anyway. Intelligence and Will contribute to magic, and Perception will actually help me in a fight.* It wasn't really a hard choice.

[Accept the Job Politician? Y/N]

He selected "Y," and several new notifications jumped into view.

[You obtained the Job Politician!]

[You unlocked the Charisma Stat!]

[You acquired the Talent Manipulation!]

[Existing Manipulation Talent detected! Existing Manipulation Talent and associated Skills leveled up!]

[You acquired the Talent Mass Manipulation!]

[You acquired the Talent Leadership!]

Oh, yes! This Job and its associated abilities sounded like exactly what he needed to build security and strength in the new world.

The new features that came with his Job were interesting.

[Charisma: A Stat that measures your innate charm and attractiveness to others, which directly affects your ability to inspire devotion in them. Allows you to sometimes obtain another being's loyalty even against their own self-interest.]

Sounds very useful for a Politician. Probably absolutely broken at higher levels.

He had two new talents:

[Leadership: As a Politician, you are more effective than most at bending others to your will. You sell others convincingly on your ideas, and you make them feel more comfortable following you than operating according to a plan of their own devising. In the changed world of the System, the leaders have a heightened chance to change the structure of the social hierarchy using the power of their ideas, words, and presence. Generates Skills Inspiration and Organization.]

[Mass Manipulation: You have spent a lifetime developing the competency of Manipulation. You have a deep ability to influence and deceive, which tends to succeed with some even when others are aware of your motives and methodology. Now you're capable of exerting influence on a large scale. In the changed world of the System, the greatest mass manipulators rule. Generates Skills Loyal Following and Public Speaking.]

And the new associated Skills:

[Inspiration: The ability to inspire your followers to achieve great things while working in your name or interests. Boosts Stats of those who accept your Leadership while they fight for you. Effects scale with Charisma and Will.]

[Loyal Following: The ability to inspire irrational devotion in your followers and other beings who spend sustained periods of time around you. Effects scale with Charisma and Will. Effects greatly increased with larger audiences.]

[Organization: The ability to comprehend and manipulate the structures of human-crafted systems, from planning an order of battle to managing groups of humans more generally. Effects scale with Will and Intelligence.]

[Public Speaking: A specialized form of Persuasion. Boosts your ability

to convince groups of intelligent life-forms to think as you wish and do your bidding, even at great personal cost. Effects scale with Will, Intelligence, and Charisma. Effects greatly increased with larger audiences.]

He also noted he had three Free Points from the last level-up that he hadn't yet allocated. *Well, since I don't intend to charm the monsters, I won't put my Free Points into Charisma.* He decided to throw them into Fortitude, since he was about to willingly throw himself into a position where a death by a thousand cuts was a real possibility.

Then James went around and began asking Rodriguezes for advice. Earlier, he had assured various people that he would come around and ask them for their thoughts later. He wanted to start things off on a good foot with his new group members, and keeping his word even in small things was an important part of making a good first impression.

So, he walked through the camp, shook hands, returned embraces, and kept a big, confident, friendly smile on his face until it felt like the edges of his mouth would crack open into a Joker-esque parody of a smile. He pressed the flesh and made everyone feel as if they were his close personal friends and the center of his attention.

Just short, little interactions. After the first few, they were hardly informative anymore. Each new family member's testimonial largely underscored what he had already heard about the monsters he would be fighting.

But James wanted to make sure he had all the details, and more importantly, he wanted every single member of this band to feel as if they had some stake in his victory, so that his triumph would be their triumph. So, he kept going.

I'm deliberately regressing the Orientation to primitive social dynamics, he thought. *Strong chief go out, hunt big game, bring back trophies and meat. And the crowd goes wild!* Hopefully, the spiders did drop meat, although James couldn't easily imagine eating one of the creatures that he'd heard described.

A strong composite picture of the creatures that had driven the Rodriguez family into taking shelter emerged.

The monsters were giant mostly black spiders. Roughly the height and weight of a mid-sized dog. Thick exoskeletons that were hard to pierce with starting equipment, coupled with sharp fangs that penetrated through armor with little resistance. They had a habit of hiding in trees and descending to attack the base of the human neck, aiming for that natural blind spot that almost all life-forms had in common.

The Rodriguezes weren't sure how many of the creatures there were, but they hadn't killed many, and somewhere in the neighborhood of a dozen had attacked.

The only lucky thing was that they didn't seem to be very intelligent. They had little in the way of self-preservation instinct. The pattern of behavior was that they bit a few people and tried to drag them off across the ground, which made it relatively easy for those who were not bitten to start fighting them as a group, beating away the ones dragging their friends off.

Mama Camila had also successfully healed almost all the injured before the creatures had targeted her. The monsters had given her so much leeway to heal people before attacking her that only one family member ultimately died.

From that, it seemed clear that the spider monsters weren't actually going after her because she was healing people, but because she was one of the many humans in their territory.

Either that, or they were taking direction from elsewhere, and it was taking some time for the commands to reach the front lines. James doubted that, though. Spiders in the pre-System world weren't big collaborators like eusocial insects, as far as he could recall. They probably wouldn't be working together effectively here either.

Still a high difficulty. An unknown—but high!—number of enemies. Penetrating fangs that can pierce through armor. About as big as a bulldog. Venomous bite that erodes your flesh. And they aren't fearful of humans. A lot of unknowns, and much of what he did know was scary.

A daunting challenge, but he quietly relished the idea of putting himself through such an ordeal and coming out on top.

No, wait, why did I agree to do this alone? James questioned. *A daunting challenge? This really does sound a lot like a suicide mission. Even if it would be exciting, why would I agree to fight the monsters by myself? I have a family too. I can't sacrifice myself for these strangers.*

He had asked himself the same thing when his group was questioning his decision, but every time he tried to recall the conversation with Chava, his memory went slightly foggy, and he found himself inventing reasons why only he could accomplish this task, and no one else could help.

And since James was fairly persuasive, the reasons seemed to be enough to convince his group, so he himself didn't have to dig too far. As he tried to recall the conversation with Chava in more detail, his mind forcefully slipped off the subject and looked for a distraction.

As if on cue, a distraction appeared.

"Hi, Cliff," James said.

They exchanged a few pleasantries, Cliff telling James he was a real prick for volunteering himself for what could be a suicide mission without discussing it with anyone first, and James agreeing with Cliff but adding that if anyone could protect the group in the event that something happened to him, it was surely Cliff.

Flattery had always been key in his dealings with the law firm partner.

"As for your strategy in the event of my death, I would stay with the Rodriguezes," James added. "If the monsters are still out there and have killed me, then it's only the strength of numbers that will keep you safe. In that case, maybe staying here is the most viable approach."

"That's what I've been talking about from the beginning, man," Cliff said. "Strength in numbers. It's still not too late for you to take me and the rest of the crew with you. I think Ramon would help us too, if we just ask. He strikes me as a brave young man."

"I appreciate that line of thinking, Cliff," James said, smiling genuinely. There were times, like now, when he liked Cliff despite how difficult the man could be to work with. "I'll do my best to retreat and get help if I feel overwhelmed. My plan remains the same, though. Minimize casualties by minimizing the number of people deployed."

"Whatever you say, Captain!" Cliff shook his head but smiled.

After that conversation, James couldn't remember what he'd been thinking so hard about before Cliff turned up. *Couldn't have been too important, then.*

He turned his attention to his Status menu. His new Job and associated abilities had leveled up a few times through his conversations with the Rodriguezes, so it seemed like a good time to check on what he had available for the battles to come.

He looked at the Status screen for a moment, then shook his head, smiled to himself, and erased the False Impression version. *Okay.*

[Status
Name: James Robard
Race: System-Boosted Human, Lv. 6
Class: Medium Warrior, Lv. 9
Job: Politician, Lv. 3
Health: 1225/1225
Mana: 1560/1560
Stamina: 1296/1296
Stats
Strength: 52(55)
Agility: 47
Stamina: 36
Fortitude: 30(35)
Dexterity: 32
Perception: 39
Will: 39
Intelligence: 40
Charisma: 16
Free Points: 6
Skills
Adamant Defense, Lv. 1

Anthropophagy, Lv. 0
Basic Cold Resistance
Basic Elemental Magic: Earth, Lv. 2
Basic Elemental Magic: Electricity, Lv. 0
Basic Elemental Magic: Fire, Lv. 2
Basic Elemental Magic: Gravity, Lv. 0
Basic Elemental Magic: Water, Lv. 3
Basic Elemental Magic: Wind, Lv. 1
Basic Non-Elemental Magic, Lv. 1
Basic Proficiency–Common Weapons
Crushing Bite, Lv. 0
Emotional Control, Lv. 2
Empathic Projection, Lv. 3
Empathy Control, Lv. 4
False Impression, Lv. 3
Hand of Glory, Lv. 1
Healing Aura, Lv. 1
Heavy Strike, Lv. 0
Holy Barrier, Lv. 0
Identify, Lv. 2
Inspiration, Lv. 2
Laying on Hands, Lv. 4
Loyal Following, Lv. 2
Mass Pillage, Lv. 1
Organization, Lv. 1
Pain Resistance, Lv. 2
Persuasion, Lv. 5
Pillage, Lv. 7
Precision Strike, Lv. 0
Public Speaking, Lv. 0
Quick Strike, Lv. 1
Silent Spellcasting
Situational Intelligence, Lv. 3
System Interface
Universal Language Comprehension
Wolf's Bite
Talents
Basic Spellcraft, Lv. 0
Cannibalism, Lv. 3
Cool-Headed, Lv. 2
Flame Affinity

Efficient Magic, Lv. 0
Leadership, Lv. 1
Manipulation, Lv. 1
Mass Manipulation, Lv. 1
Selective Empathy, Lv. 2
Water Affinity
Titles
Chosen One of Apophis
Citizen of the Dead Marsh
Devout Beacon
Swiss Army Mage
System Pioneer]

Looks good and strong. Politician is really working well with my personality so far. Now, what to do with those extra points?

James's review was interrupted when he saw a teenager approaching from the other side of the Status screen. He dismissed it with a thought, and the teenager moved closer.

"Hey, there," he said. "Jessica, right?"

She nodded. "Good memory. Do you remember the names of everyone you met today?"

"Just about," he said. "I never had a perfect memory before, but ever since I've been able to increase my Intelligence with an investment of points from the System, I have a memory like an elephant."

"So, you're an Intelligence-based build?" Jessica looked gobsmacked. "How does that work for killing things?"

"Um, it's complicated, and Intelligence isn't the only Stat I have in abundance," James said. He hadn't expected a teenager to start asking him questions, and he realized he was doing a rather poor job of veiling his answers and keeping his abilities as secret as possible.

"Was there something specific you wanted to know?" he asked. *Or a specific reason why you're interrupting my battle prep time?*

"Oh, my mother wanted to know if you wanted to have dinner. She says she has too much food for just us, and it would be a shame to waste it."

James caught both the phrasing of the sentence and a slight eye roll as the teenager spoke.

"Your mother says that, huh? But it's not quite accurate?" he asked.

"Oh! Uh, I didn't say that."

He waited.

"It's just, we don't actually have a lot of food in the camp, you know?" Jessica continued. "She feels like she has to be hospitable, which I get, and you did something that was super important for all of us, so I definitely support it—"

"But you guys really don't have enough food for guests," James finished for her.

"No, we really don't," she said. "I appreciate your understanding."

James got up. "That settles it. I'm coming to dinner!"

She stared slack-jawed at him for a full thirty seconds before she narrowed her eyes and led the way for him.

When they made it to the family's tent, he reintroduced himself to Maria, the mother; Hector, the father; and Jaime, the brother. Then James brought out his small offering. He still had some wolf meat from the earlier fights, and he put it all on their makeshift table, which consisted of a piece of whiteboard propped up on tree branches.

"How generous of you!" Hector commented, eyes fixed on the packages of meat.

"We have to share with the rest of the family," Maria said immediately. "Thank you very much, James. You're a life saver in more ways than one!" She gave her husband a look that was all but indecipherable to James at that moment, but which he later recognized as "I told you so" regarding the decision to invite the stranger to dinner.

After Maria had distributed the meat around the camp, she cooked the one parcel left of those James had brought, to add it to the meal. Then the family, plus James, gathered around the campfire, Hector Rodriguez said grace, and they tucked into a meal.

As James sat to eat, his mind was elsewhere. There was a bittersweet joy in helping feed the Rodriguez family, who felt essentially trapped in this small corner of the forest with little means of getting supplies in. But he wished he could be feeding his own family right now, and the fear that they might be going hungry at this very moment tasted bitter in his mouth.

"Look! It's the words in the fire again!" Jaime Rodriguez's words jolted James back to the present.

"Hey, don't look at that," Hector rebuked immediately. "You don't know who it is that's talking in there!"

James was transfixed. Words had appeared in the fire in the form of blank spaces in the flames, where the blackness of the night shone through.

The flames read, "Follow the smoke to safety."

"You said it's the words *again*?" James asked.

"They appeared last night too," Jessica said.

"By some magic, they seem to appear for a while in every fire in the camp when night falls," Maria said.

"Well, maybe it supports your plan," Hector acknowledged, his tone grudging. "In this household, though, we don't trust words that appear in flames." The note in his voice changed to something James didn't recognize at first. "If you and Chava weren't suggesting it, there's no way we'd go walking toward that column of smoke. Probably just the opposite direction." He looked at James warmly. "But after what you've done, we'd follow you to the gates of hell."

Oh, of course. That note in his voice is trust.

They were all looking at James then, and all he could do was smile and thank them for the meal.

After dinner was over, Cliff came to tell James where the party was sleeping that night. Chava had ordered a place cleared and a tent raised for them very close to his own.

As he laid his head to sleep that night, though, he wondered, *Who is it that's putting that message in the campfire? Are they friend or foe? What will we find if we navigate toward that column of smoke?*

CHAPTER TWENTY-SEVEN

Natural Born Killer

The day broke, and the camp awakened. James had his gear packed and his equipment ready for use before the camp was even fully roused.

He stayed only long enough to eat the eggs that the Rodriguezes prepared before leaving. They had rationed themselves to one egg per person, he noticed, so he thought the food problem might become quite dire very soon. It seemed clear that how they had planned to wait out the Orientation without going through monster territory again had not been fully thought through.

It was more of a blessing than he had initially realized that he had come along to solve their "being quietly besieged by monsters" problem, and he resolved not to ask for any supplies from them, despite the fact that they had eaten all of his stock of wolf meat. *If it's absolutely necessary*, he thought, regarding possibly resorting to the *other* meat he had in abundant supply.

Before he set out, Ramon came to fetch James from where he was saying his goodbyes to his own group.

"Mama Camila is awake," Ramon said, voice heavy with emotion. "She wants to see you."

"Thank you for letting me know," James said.

"Of course," Ramon said, clapping his hand on James's shoulder. "You saved her!"

That was what Mama Camila wanted to say to him too, it turned out.

"Thank you so much for everything you're doing for my family, James," she said in gushing Spanish. "Such a strong, kind young man. I'm sure you and Ramon will keep us very safe. I see you're married—" she glanced at his wedding band—"or I would introduce you to my granddaughters."

James couldn't help being touched by the effusive praise from this woman who was still bedridden, staring warmly up at him from the makeshift bed the family had prepared for her.

"It was my pleasure to be of help in whatever small way I could," James said. "I look forward to working with your family to survive this place. I hope we can continue to help each other for a long time to come." He gave his best smile. He expected that Camila and Chava were the two people essentially running this camp, and winning either or both over would mean he would have the whole family beside him in future endeavors. He couldn't quite recall how well the conversation with Chava had gone, so this was an important diplomatic moment in his mind.

The small group of people here wasn't the whole family, either, based on his conversation with Maria and Hector last night. Even setting aside the children who had been separated from the group by the System, there were numerous cousins and half-siblings who had different last names, and even relatives with the same last name who lived farther away and had therefore presumably been swept away to a different Orientation with the onset of the System. It was a sizable group of friends to make.

James reached out to take her hand, and Camila grabbed on and pulled him in for a hug.

"You're the first friendly person we met here," she said quietly in accented English. "So glad we find you."

As they released each other, she squinted her eyes through her thick lenses and asked, "Dominican?"

"No, but I get that a lot," James said. "Just Black and White." *Maybe that will burn whatever political capital I've earned saving her life*, he thought. But she didn't seem to change the way she was looking at him. Maybe the in-group loyalty didn't matter, or maybe she actually *didn't like* Dominicans.

He had found it surprising in the past how prejudiced some Hispanics were against Hispanics of other nationalities. Then again, his own Black grandfather would complain loudly about Haitians who couldn't speak English working at McDonald's, so clearly race wasn't a powerful enough unifier to avoid dislike between different nationalities.

James said his farewells to the Rodriguezes and his group once again, and he headed off.

When he had initially intended to set out, the sun had barely risen. Now it was much higher in the sky—around ten in the morning from its positioning if James had to guess. He didn't have any other way of gauging the time, as he didn't wear a watch, he hadn't brought his smart phone, and even if he had either of those items, he had no reason to believe the Orientation space was located in the same dimension as Earth—or that his own time-keeping devices would work here. The System had implied more than once that there were multiple universes, after all, and with the power-up he'd received when he invoked Chosen One of Apophis the one time he'd used it, he was pretty sure Orientation was in its own small universe.

He walked aimlessly at first, wearing the Flame Resistant Wolfskin Pelt he'd acquired from the Command Forest Wolf wrapped around his head and neck like a hood. The fur should be one of his strongest pieces of armor, and his main concern was a sneak attack like those the Rodriguezes had repeatedly described. At least this way his vitals would have some protection, and as long as he wasn't killed instantly in a fight, he felt that he would find some way to come out all right.

He had been walking for some time before he felt something was off. He wasn't sure what it was that set off his alarm bells, so he kept walking, albeit a little more slowly. Situational Awareness leveled up as he moved, but he spent no time reading notifications at this strange and deadly moment.

A few minutes later, there it was again. Now he knew what it was: tree branches shaking when there was no apparent wind. *Something is up there.* He began charging Mana. If nothing came down from the tree, he would flush whatever it was out.

But, as if it could sense what he was doing, the thing chose that moment to strike. The tree rattled gently once more, and then a big, black, multi-limbed *shape* descended. He jumped away as soon as the creature dropped, landing five feet from it.

It wasn't so different from what he had imagined: an almost pure black spider the size of a pit bull. Long, hairy limbs. Fierce-looking fangs that dripped a dark liquid onto the ground. It was smaller than the wolves had been. Despite that, James felt a far more ominous sense of threat from the creature. He remained calm, but there was a tinge of fear pulsing in the back of his mind, under control but clearly present.

[Sufficient experience accrued. Emotional Control leveled up!]

[Required conditions met. Cool-Headed leveled up!]

James angrily ordered the notifications out of view and put on the focused mindset that banished all such distractions from his field of vision, but he felt marginally better about the situation already.

The difference of the levels for Emotional Control and Cool-Headed was already kicking in. His emotions had receded further into the darkness of his mind. He could be more objective. The situation was manageable. *Only one enemy, even if it looks like Shelob made a baby.* Not much to be afraid of.

And the spider hadn't moved since landing. Perhaps it was afraid of him. Its fangs were still dripping venom, and where the liquid dripped, the grass blackened and withered away. *Just have to avoid those fangs.* Hopefully, it had no other method of attack.

The creature made a move, and James tensed. It was just one limb inching forward, but his hand went right to one of his Wolfbone Daggers. He was ready to chop that leg off in an instant if the creature moved within range. The traces of fear receded from his mind. Action erased them.

Then he noticed, almost directly behind and above him, a faint vibration of leaves in another tree. It was a delicate sound, barely there but present. James's senses alerted him just a fraction of a second before the second spider launched itself at the back of his neck. He had time to duck down, draw his daggers, and turn, all at superhuman speeds—and then this second creature was upon him.

In an instant, the weight of the falling spider combined with the upward thrust he gave his dagger pushed the weapon up to the hilt into the center of the spider's body. James saw the tip barely pierce through the other side, and the creature twisted and writhed on his blade, inadvertently doing more damage to itself. Despite the injury, the spider kept trying to snap its fangs at him, jerking its body in the direction of his throat. James just focused on keeping the fangs far away from his flesh.

There was a quick movement from behind him now; the first spider leaped at him, but again he reacted quickly. He was able to twirl around and throw the impaled spider's body directly into the lunging spider's maw. He realized as he watched the spiders collide in midair that it felt almost like it was happening in slow motion. He could not only react in time to the spiders' quick movements, but he seemed to be a lot more agile than them. *All those Stat points*, he had time to think.

Then he saw the lunging spider's venom-tipped fangs penetrate deeply into its brethren's carapace, and the victim's body begin to spasm visibly almost at the instant of contact. As the attacking spider pulled its fangs out, James jumped in, his remaining dagger raised high above his head in both hands. The spider recognized the danger, tried to pull back, and pushed off the ground with all eight of its feet—too slow, too late.

James plunged the Wolfbone Dagger all the way through the spider's torso, into the joint between the head and body. Some combat intuition told him that the spot he'd chosen to strike was a vital point, and the results confirmed it. The spider spasmed twice before it stopped moving.

So easy.

The notification dinged.

[You killed Feral Wood Spider, Lv. 6. You gained 80 exp!]

[Sufficient experience accrued. Basic Proficiency–Common Weapons leveled up!]

James used Pillage on the first creature, and he chose Skills as the target. He was hoping to get the power to produce that strange black venom.

[Feral Wood Spider's body processed.]

[You obtained Small Exoshield, Venom Sac, and a Small Spiderknife!]
[Skill Obtained: Shed Skin!]

James turned his attention to the remaining dying spider. It was almost completely dead, just twitching a little, and James could see through the holes from the other spider's bite that its flesh had melted away underneath the exoskeleton where the venom had gone.

Almost dead already, but just for fun . . . He stomped his left foot down onto the spider's head. It made a very satisfying *crunch. Yeah, I'm not afraid of these things. They crunch too well for that.*

[You killed Feral Wood Spider, Lv. 5. You gained 67 exp!]
[Medium Warrior leveled up!]

Pillage! He targeted Skills again. *Surely, this time.*

[Feral Wood Spider's body processed.]
[You obtained Small Exoshield, Venom Sac, and a Small Spiderknife!]
[Skill Obtained: Shed Skin!]
[Existing Skill Shed Skin detected! Additional Skill Shed Skin merged into existing Skill Shed Skin.]
[Sufficient experience accrued. Shed Skin leveled up!]

Goddammit! Let me at least check what that Skill does. It'd better be good.

[Shed Skin: A healing Skill that allows the user to heal shallow wounds by shedding and rapidly regenerating your outer layers of flesh and skin. Activation cost of 10% of base Stamina. Consumes caloric energy.]

Ridiculous bullshit! Another healing Skill? I should have known, I guess. Some bugs can do that stuff. Maybe it will be useful later if I level it up now.

"For now, I need to find more bugs to kill," James said to himself. He was not ugly, but he smiled hideously now. Despite being annoyed about not getting the Skill he wanted, he was internally quite pleased.

The spiders were very killable. He could get the Skill if he killed enough of them, he felt sure enough of that. A fun and simple problem to solve, killing things. There was something in him that felt very relaxed at the thought. No politics, no ass-kissing, no mercy, just blood and guts. Even if he didn't get the venom production Skill, the process would be its own reward.

James was looking forward to continuing this break from other people.

A Thousand Words

The month was August 2031.

Nikolai Rostov stared over his young girlfriend's shoulder at the campus computer screen.

"How long is this going to take?" he asked, exasperation seeping into his voice. "You said it's just a thousand-word statement, right?"

"Like I told you earlier, Nicky, it's a thousand words, but I have to choose them carefully, or I'll never get my transfer. You know how hard it is for me to express myself. I'm not like you!" Her words carried just the right notes of pleading and flattering, and with her slight southern accent, he found her highly persuasive.

Rostov sat down beside her, all right as rain again. "That's why you're one of my favorites, Carrie-Ann. You always know what to say to me." That, and the fact that the waifish girl could get him into community college buildings, where he could make more new friends.

She reddened like a summer strawberry from her face down to her neck, and Rostov smiled, foxlike, from behind her. He also liked knowing exactly which buttons to push. Some girls were complicated and difficult to manage, but Carrie-Ann Moore had been easy for him since the day they met.

As with so many other girls her age, she just wanted someone to love her and give her direction.

He had accompanied her to the library on the transfer application errand hoping to meet some new recruits for his group, to make up for a few who hadn't come back from one of Rostov's errands, but it was unnervingly quiet here today. Much too quiet for his liking.

There had been a few students in the library when Rostov and Carrie-Ann arrived, but they had almost all seemed to clear out within half an hour. Now there were just a couple of older students left: two guys Rostov took to be returning to school after some years in the workforce.

Neither of them was in one of his target demographics. They were focused on their work, clean-cut, completely serious. A little boring. Worst of all, they looked like they knew what they wanted out of this place—and out of life.

Which meant he couldn't give them something they thought they needed.

In fact, they looked so strait-laced—Rostov abruptly got up again. Carrie-Ann looked up at him anxiously. He shook his head and forced a smile.

"Just going to use the facilities, sweetling."

And she was back focusing on her transfer document.

She wouldn't react well to being abandoned here, Rostov knew. But he was willing to gamble that Carrie-Ann would return to him. He had to follow his instincts.

Through years of petty crimes, to beginning to gather his followers, to committing more serious offenses, those sharp, foxlike instincts had only very rarely steered him wrong. Instincts for people. Their strengths and weaknesses, psychological vulnerabilities, their susceptibility to his influence.

And, more relevant right now, instincts for situations. The quiet library, with only a few people in it, was setting off alarm bells. He snuck a couple more sidelong glances at the other students in the library as he marched off into the stacks. Those few inhabitants were too apparently studious, a shade too old on average, and far too male. On average, the times he'd been here, the library had been mostly female with lots of quiet conversation, and they were all what he would describe as student age. Too many anomalies to be a coincidence.

I wanted to have Carrie-Ann print more of my flyers out, but that's not important now. He could go by the public library later and do it himself, assuming the authorities didn't have some sort of monitoring for his library card. Or he could forget about recruiting more members for the Church of the Awakened Sun, and he could get out of Dodge.

Maybe he was being crazy. He didn't even know for sure if the cops had his name. But, as Rostov's father, Oleg, had described more than once, his son was usually crazy like a fox.

Even when Rostov behaved impulsively, the impulse usually turned out to have a good reason his conscious mind wasn't aware of at the time.

If I have to, I'll abandon this name and this whole state. It wouldn't be the first time he'd left a place where he'd started to feel police closing in. This would be the place he'd had the most investment, true, but it was also the place where he felt the most heat around him. He had bodies here.

He slunk around the end of the stacks, beelining past the restrooms, toward the back door.

Yeah, I need to get out of town. This was hubris. Showing my face here after last week.

A shadow fell across Rostov's planned escape path, and he looked up, immediately conscious of how furtive his movements looked.

"Nikolai Rostov?" the man in front of him asked, looking him right in the face.

Rostov self-consciously straightened himself out and then tilted his head to the side in the perfect pantomime of puzzlement.

"Rostov?" he echoed back, shaking his head slightly, a hint of feigned confusion in his voice. He took a good look at the figure in front of him. Tall, lantern-jawed, with sandy brown hair that Rostov idly noticed would be receding in a few years.

For now, this man looked like a walking advertisement for police officers. He wasn't in uniform, no, but he didn't need to be. If Rostov had gotten a better look at this occupant of the library earlier, if he had really examined him, he would have seen that this man *screamed* cop from every pore. And Rostov would have bolted even faster.

There was the crew cut hair that made him look like a military wannabe. The muscles, which did not look terribly imposing, but which the officer had clearly trained with an emphasis on function over form. The cargo pants and tight polo shirt, which looked less like a community college student's outfit and more like a cop's street clothes. And he was clean cut like a boy scout, no hint of the stubble that a college student might have allowed to grow.

If this was supposed to be any kind of undercover operation, the disguise is really lazy, Rostov decided.

"Officer Jeffrey Ross," the man introduced himself. He was holding his badge at Rostov's eye level and smiling now.

Cocky prick.

"Ross. Officer Jeffrey Ross," Rostov repeated, throwing his best Russian accent onto his pronunciation of the syllables. He only knew a few scattered words of Russian from the years before he'd turned thirteen, before Oleg abandoned Nikolai and his mother, but he could still put on his father's accent when he needed to.

Nikolai Rostov was nothing if not a performer, and this moment seemed to call for the performance of a lifetime.

"I, ah, English not so good," Rostov said. He was hoping that perhaps these people did not know what he looked like, that whoever had dimed him out had not given a description of his distinctive physical features: a lean, foxlike face, dark hair, and a pointed salt-and-pepper beard.

If anyone were to describe him at all, he was certain they would not describe him with an accent. It was an affectation he could throw on or erase at will, a gift from his father. He hadn't used it since he'd migrated to Florida. Rostov could do Southern just as well as he could do Russian, or Brooklyn, or California surfer. When he was young, he'd spent years in each of those regions, at first with his parents, and then kicked around between relatives and foster homes until he came of age.

The whole broad pattern of his life could be described as preparation for his current circumstances.

If he could just fool this oaf of a policeman for two minutes, perhaps he could sneak out, buy a bus ticket, and be halfway to Georgia before the police put two and two together.

There was a long, tense moment where the officer looked at Rostov. There seemed to be a flicker of doubt in the policeman's eyes.

Then the stalemate was broken.

"Nicky!" Carrie-Ann's voice rang out.

Rostov didn't react at all. He was certain he kept perfect control of his expression at the critical moment. But the tiny flash of uncertainty in the policeman's bearing had disappeared, if it was ever really there.

Was he just playing with me? Rostov thought.

"Aren't you going to go see how your little girlfriend's doing?" Officer Ross asked, triumphant.

"I'm sure your associate is taking good care of her," Rostov replied dismissively, not allowing the officer the pleasure of seeing him sweat. But Rostov also dropped all traces of a Russian accent. He wasn't going to fight against the certainty of what was happening now.

They wouldn't have approached Carrie-Ann if they had any doubts left about who he was. She was a real-deal student here, despite how her extracurricular activities with Rostov might have distracted her over the past couple of semesters.

She would break while in police custody, Rostov decided. It was an offhand thought, not something he deliberated very long on, but he felt sure of it.

"Are you going to arrest me or something?" Rostov asked. The officer had been looking, distractedly, off in the direction of Carrie-Ann and whoever was dealing with her. Rostov did not like to cede the spotlight, especially not when control of his situation had otherwise already been ripped away from him.

"Oh, yes," Officer Ross said, turning back to him. "Here." He held up a pair of cuffs, and Rostov extended his arms obediently.

Then Ross cuffed him from the front. *Amateur*, Rostov thought. *Isn't it standard procedure to put my hands behind my back?* He had a slightly more than casual interest in police and their procedures.

But he noticed the policeman had said something now that Rostov had his full attention again.

"Did you really think I'd let you get away?" Ross was asking.

"Oh, Officer. If you and I were alone, I would show you such signs and wonders, I wouldn't be concerned about getting away." Rostov slipped instantly back into cult leader mode.

Ross looked at him strangely.

"I see you read your Bible," the policeman said at last. "Exodus, right?"

"We aren't so different, Officer, except that my mind has been opened to a higher truth."

"That, and the murders," Ross replied.

"People always assume the worst about those they don't understand. I've never hurt a fly."

"I guess that's what the trial's for." Officer Ross seemed tired of talking now. Perhaps he lacked the intellectual equipment to continue the discussion.

Rostov heard three sets of footsteps approaching: one in heavy boots, one in normal nondescript shoes, and one set that made him turn and look. Carrie-Ann's soft footsteps gave her away as the other person approaching.

Rostov saw that she was handcuffed behind her back. She met his gaze and gave him her weakest smile, and he could see water pooling at the corners of her eyes.

He returned her smile with his usual confident air, and said, "It's going to be all right, Carrie-Ann!"

He knew it wouldn't be all right, but perhaps a little infusion of bravado would make her that little bit harder for the police to crack.

The footfalls stopped. Rostov noticed the other two plainclothesmen escorting her. One was a tall Latino with a short mustache. The other, the man in the boots, was a heavyset middle-aged White man with a walrus mustache. Rostov was certain that fellow, at least, hadn't been in the library when he looked around earlier. *Otherwise, I'd have left much sooner.*

Walrus mustache seemed to be in charge. He muttered a few words to the tall officer, and the tall man began leading Carrie-Ann out via another door.

"I love you, Nicky!" Carrie-Ann called out at the last moment.

"Love you, Carrie-Ann!" Rostov called back without hesitation. It was nothing to him to say it, nothing but inflating her confidence a little more. And like he'd said earlier, she *was* one of his favorites.

Walrus mustache approached, looking like he was conflicted between righteous anger and a sense of victory. Rostov knew immediately that he was the brains of the operation.

"Nice to meet you, Nikolai. I'm Detective Harrison Fromme." The words were controlled, but Rostov could feel the seething cauldron of rage beneath.

"A pleasure, Harrison," he said lightly, returning the unearned familiarity.

Officer Ross placed a heavy hand on Rostov's shoulder as if in warning.

"You've really done a number on that girl. You know that, Nicky?" Detective Fromme said.

"So you say," Rostov said. He shrugged. "People always hate and fear and judge what they don't understand."

It would remain a core of his defense even at trial.

CHAPTER TWENTY-EIGHT

Target Rich

James continued to enjoy himself.

Pest control was fun! Another spider ambushed him, this one all by its lonesome.

This time, he didn't bother drawing his daggers at all. It was just one little bug.

He smashed its head into its body with a single punch and killed the creature nearly instantly, inadvertently basting his fist up to the elbow in a greasy mess of white and green spider innards. The corpse twitched twice, and then the notification sounded and confirmed his kill. He grinned despite the gross liquid coating his lower arm. *All too easy.*

But he realized this could be a very slow method of killing these things. Relying on them to ambush him would leave him at the mercy of their pace, and it certainly wouldn't assure he cleared all of them out by the end—though, what would?

Exterminating bugs was tricky even in the pre-System world. That was why there were companies specialized in the task. Killing all of the spiders or termites or ants even in a small, discrete region was more like a wish than a goal one could logically and systematically work toward.

Plus, despite being invertebrates, these creatures surely had a certain level of primitive survival instincts. Eventually, they would probably stop throwing themselves at him, especially if they noticed that he was covered in the internal organs of other spiders he'd killed.

At that thought, he began silently casting water magic to clean his arm off. He wouldn't want to scare the other spiders away.

Once he'd finished washing up, James decided to try another method of hunting. Having observed the spiders flinging themselves down at him from positions in the trees every time they attacked, he figured the trees were their primary habitat. And having examined the trees—they were almost all some kind of deciduous tree he didn't recognize—he thought that the same branches the spiders liked to jump from might be able to support his weight.

He decided to try leaping into the trees and went hunting for spiders at their own level.

James was strong and agile enough to move quickly and efficiently among the branches, though his lack of practice made precision a bit difficult. More than once, he fell from the trees as he made a misstep among the branches. The challenge made it fun, though. It added spice to the otherwise dull process of searching for prey.

He played around and made it a game of seeing if he could hit the correct targets when hopping from tree to tree, whether he could tell just by looking if a branch could support his weight or not, and how high he could get with a single jump. The targeted jumping was surprisingly difficult because branches moved, and they didn't have a lot of friction, meaning he could easily slide off if he didn't correctly gauge the distance and force needed.

Figuring out how strong a branch was likely to be was also more difficult than he expected. Perhaps it was because his body was more densely packed with muscle than he was used to, but many branches he expected to carry his weight splintered into pieces and sent him flailing for a handhold so he wouldn't fall all the way to the ground.

However, jumping as high as he could with a single jump was a great and immediate success. James found he was strong enough to jump halfway up the height of a fairly tall tree in a single bound. He hadn't had so much fun outdoors since he was a kid, and he lost himself for a while trying to outdo his own high jump records.

It was a beautiful day outside, perfect for play. Then again, every day James had spent in the Orientation space had been gorgeous except for that one day some jerk had ruined by lighting the forest on fire and filling the sky with smoke.

Once he got back to business, James flitted through trees for roughly a quarter of an hour, looking for targets, but they were surprisingly hard to find. Their dark-colored bodies blended in well with the shadows that the thick tree cover provided, and more than once, James contemplated burning the tops of the trees to make his search easier. But this would just deplete his Mana, probably result in no actual direct kills, and draw the attention of a larger number of enemies than he would be prepared to fight single-handedly. So, he restrained himself and continued his stealthy search tactics.

He eventually found two big spiders this way. After a prolonged struggle, including diving through the trees onto the ground, breaking one of the spiders on a massive rock that happened to be beneath them, and disemboweling the other with a dagger, he concluded that this was not the right way to go about his task.

I even caught them napping, he thought, because the two creatures had seemed sluggish when he first stumbled upon them. *So why was it so difficult?* He sat down beside the bodies, and after he cast Pillage—he obtained two more copies of the Shed Skin Skill, leveling up the existing Skill—he reviewed his approach. There had to be something wrong with it.

Although he had successfully found his targets and gained some experience, he was more hurt and exhausted from having ambushed the spiders than he'd been after *being ambushed* before. Part of that was down to him not being used to moving around in the foliage, which was the spiders' natural habitat, not his. It was only natural that running and jumping in the trees would tire him out more than walking or running on the ground would. Another part of the problem was that he had chosen to take the fight to the ground by crashing his body down through the branches to put the spiders at more of a disadvantage. But if he hadn't, how much more difficult would it have been to kill them up in the trees, where his own movements were still clumsy and awkward?

Regardless of whether the scraped elbows and bruises were something he could avoid next time he went looking for spiders in the treetops, it didn't make much sense to go waltzing into the creatures' homes to fight them where they likely preferred to fight. The search method wasn't efficient for whatever reason, and when he fought them, it didn't benefit him to do it up in the trees.

Even if he tried forcing the spiders out of the trees down to the forest floor, the fall did just as much damage to him as to them. Relatively more damage, really, since he was otherwise good at avoiding their attacks.

Speaking of which: Healing Aura. His body immediately began to mend its minor scrapes and bruises under the healing green glow. He had no serious injuries, so he didn't even focus much on the healing process and just let his aura do the work.

I guess it's back to walking around and letting them ambush me for now, James decided. He had no better ideas, but he hoped that further trial and error would give him some inspiration. He walked around aimlessly for another twenty minutes or so, by his estimate, before something interrupted his wandering. He tried to pay close attention to his surroundings and observe anything that might help him hunt the next monster.

When the spiders next ambushed him, he noted that he was beneath a thick covering of trees, creating such a cover of darkness that he could barely see all the little hairs on his hand—yes, that was how good his vision had become—but still, the creatures failed to take the element of surprise.

Just like in the first attack, there was a telltale shaking of the tree branches each time one was about to launch itself at him.

What they need is some kind of Stealth Skill, he thought. He counted the movements of the trees and decided there were five spiders coming down at him now from three trees in two different directions. The next moment they fell upon him and proved his assessment correct.

He had time to shift his body before they landed, putting the closest two creatures between himself and the next three. Then he swung down on them with two Wolfbone Daggers, embedding them in the backs of the two nearest spiders.

Two down. One strike each was all it took now, but the others threw themselves at him— absolutely fearless—while his daggers were embedded in the bodies, and he was forced to fight the next one that came barehanded. He brought two fists together and smashed down on its head, producing a squashed bit of exoskeleton and a thick, gray-white liquid that coated his hands. The next one almost managed to close its fangs around his bicep while he was dealing with its comrade, but he managed to pull away in time.

Then he was dealing with two, one on each side, both closing in, fangs snapping. He launched a kick at one as hard as he could and flung it away—he heard it distantly thud and crack against a tree—and he grabbed the other by its fangs and ripped it in half lengthwise with a mighty jerk of his fists. James let out a satisfied grunt as the spider's head split in half.

He tried to ignore the viscera that splattered in his face, but it did keep him from smiling even though he was otherwise enjoying himself quite a bit.

The last spider, exoskeleton visibly broken with spiderweb cracks—*ha!*— running across its back, staggered toward him with what seemed like a drunken cadence. *Brain damage with that crash into the tree,* James guessed. *Or damage to the nervous system. I wonder if I could figure out which if I dissected it.* He easily danced out of its range and controlled the distance between himself and the creature.

Since this last one was slow and clumsy, he took a few seconds to look for a heavy tree branch. Then he broke it off from the tree it hung on and used that to finish the spider off.

Really a mercy, he thought. *I'm sure it wouldn't have survived this forest with those injuries anyway.*

Then the notifications came streaming in.

[You killed Feral Wood Spider, Lv. 4. You gained 52 exp!]

[You killed Feral Wood Spider, Lv. 5. You gained 65 exp!]

[You killed Feral Wood Spider Lv. 6. You gained 80 exp!]

[You killed Feral Wood Spider, Lv. 7. You gained 100 exp!]

[You killed Feral Wood Spider, Lv. 4. You gained 52 exp!]

[Medium Warrior leveled up!]

[A Class Evolution is available. Review? Y/N]

Finally, my chance to get some new powers that will set me apart from everyone else!

But he didn't know how long the Evolution process would take. So, first of all, he used Mass Pillage. He selected Skills to steal once again.

[5x Feral Wood Spider's body processed.]

[You obtained 5x Small Exoshield, 5x Venom Sac, and 5x Small Spiderknife!]

[Skill Obtained: Shed Skin!]

[Existing Skill Shed Skin detected! Additional Skill Shed Skin merged into existing Skill Shed Skin.]

[Skill Obtained: Shed Skin!]

[Existing Skill Shed Skin detected! Additional Skill Shed Skin merged into existing Skill Shed Skin.]

[Skill Obtained: Shed Skin!]

[Existing Skill Shed Skin detected! Additional Skill Shed Skin merged into existing Skill Shed Skin.]

[Sufficient experience accrued. Shed Skin leveled up!]

[Skill Obtained: Shed Skin!]

[Existing Skill Shed Skin detected! Additional Skill Shed Skin merged into existing Skill Shed Skin.]

[Skill Obtained: Shed Skin!]

[Existing Skill Shed Skin detected! Additional Skill Shed Skin merged into existing Skill Shed Skin.]

Well, at least now Shed Skin was up to level three, and James had obtained more of those Venom Sacs that he imagined would be useful in the future. All tucked away in his magic satchel, naturally. No point in wasting them on the spiders when the creatures died so quickly and easily without any assistance.

James wasn't even mad about not getting a venom production Skill this time, even though he was positive that every single creature he'd killed today must have one.

Nope. I don't even care anymore. Who cares if I never get one, he thought. There may have been the slightest trace of sour grapes in this thought pattern.

In any case, nothing could tarnish James's excitement about undergoing Class Evolution.

At last, James selected "Y," and the options displayed themselves.

Riding the Lightning

The first trial was a farce.

Their first mistake was trying Rostov next to his people. They hadn't had much choice, of course.

No one was willing to plead guilty. They were still in the headspace Rostov had made for them.

Kelsey Woodward and Wanda De Vries sat next to Rostov, close enough that he could hold their hands under the table, with the lawyers relegated to grouping up on either side of the girls. Jimmy Wainwright was at one end of the table with his counselor, and Roy Hauer sat at the other end.

Rostov could shoot each of them reassuring eye contact whenever he wanted to. And, of course, no one in the Church of the Awakened Sun wanted to be the loser who looked weak in front of their leader or in the sight of the cameras and the world.

Then the show began. Some slow opening acts. A sheriff's deputy testified about responding to a fire.

Shocker: the firefighters had found some bodies in a burned-out schoolhouse. Someone had made a statement by burning a few schoolteachers in their school. There were pictures, showing that the bodies left behind were blackened and crispy.

A medical examiner testified that smoke inhalation showed that the bodies were still alive when the fire started.

Well, duh. Otherwise, it wouldn't make much of a statement, Rostov thought.

Then the real performances started.

There were a few witnesses who had turned state's evidence and promised to testify against Rostov and his wicked, bad, no-good cult.

And the suckers working for the state believed it!

First, Carrie-Ann took the stand. She was showing slightly, her belly noticeably round, and Rostov was surprised to realize it had been a full three months since he'd been arrested and since she had seen him last.

"I'm pregnant, Nicky!" she announced to the world before she'd even been sworn in. "You gonna marry me?"

"Sure thing, babe!" he called back. He chuckled to himself. He'd had the thought that she might be getting in the family way before now, but it was sweet of her to come here just to confirm it.

The judge gaveled and screeched for "Order in the courtroom!" but Rostov knew the truth. There wouldn't be any order as long as they kept putting on *his* witnesses and thinking they were theirs.

The prosecution made a limp attempt to get some real answers out of Carrie-Ann. Instead of answering any of them, she rambled on about possible baby names, tried to directly question the jurors about how handsome her fiancé was, and sang "You Are My Sunshine," which the Church of the Awakened Sun had treated as a hymn.

Rostov had several good laughs before the prosecutor gave up on Carrie-Ann and called his next witness. Defense counsel did not bother cross examining Carrie-Ann, but Rostov did blow her a kiss on her way out of court.

Holy shit, Rostov thought as he heard the name of the next witness. He was still a little stunned when the bailiff led Nikki Peeples in. *I can't believe she talked them into this.*

Nikki was the closest thing the Church of the Awakened Sun had to a spokesperson besides Rostov himself. At first she played it straight. She answered the questions about her name, where she was from, and how she met Rostov honestly. Then he sat back and enjoyed her ten-minute monologue about their religious beliefs, which she had clearly prepared in advance.

She spoke on how all life came from the Sun and fire, and all life must return to it, and the prosecution struggled to get a word in edgewise. The prosecution seemed to give up for a little while, perhaps thinking if he just let her speak, she'd answer his questions afterward. She was giving some background narrative as she told the story of the Church, so at least that much was on the record. As she continued to monologue about the need to share the Sun's love with each other, Rostov scanned the jury box to see how they were taking it.

Several of them were clearly bored, but a few looked riveted.

Well, I'll be damned. I think her public speaking has improved a bit. We might convert one or two of the jurors!

The prosecution ultimately dismissed the witness after it became obvious that she wasn't going to give them any more information besides religious dogma. One of the attorneys looked like he wanted to ask her a question, but all five defendants glared him down until he sank back into his chair. Rostov gave Nikki "fuck me" eyes as she sidled out of the courtroom, and she winked back at him in response.

Teddy Ranco took the stand, swore to tell the truth, the whole truth, and nothing but the truth, and then pledged his personal loyalty to Nikolai Rostov, one true Prophet of the Church of the Awakened Sun. His responses to the prosecution's actual questions were profane, descriptive, and far from helpful to the prosecution's case—though, to judge from the Public Defender's expression, they didn't help Rostov either.

Probably none of the testimony from the church members had helped, if the atmosphere around the defense attorneys was any indication.

Rostov didn't mind, though. He liked it, and in his subtle ways, he encouraged it.

If the trial became a joke, it turned from their way of hanging him into another way for him to say "fuck you" to the prosecutors and police, the sleazebags and liars who wanted to put his neck into the noose.

Rostov was pleased to see the public defenders looked just as uncomfortable as the prosecutors. They were all part of the same thing as the prosecution, both members of the same club. The same club, as far as Rostov was concerned, that they liked to beat people like him up with.

Your whole system's a joke. I'm just holding up the mirror.

After Ranco, the prosecution asked for mercy.

Well, technically, they asked the court to adjourn for the day so that they could prepare different witnesses. It seemed their remaining witnesses were also members of the church, and they had learned their lesson about putting loyal churchgoers up on the stand.

All defense counsel vigorously protested. Their clients' rights to be speedily tried were being injured, and they wanted it noted for the record that the defense was prejudiced by any delay. And Rostov just wished for some popcorn.

The media retained its interest in the trial even when days were taken up mainly with testimony that was boring—or, in the case of the church members, testimony that wasn't fit to air or print. The real circus, Rostov's attorney informed him on one of the later days, was taking place outside.

Nearly every one of the dozens of members of the Church of the Awakened Sun who were not called as witnesses or brought up on charges alongside their leader was out there protesting.

Women walked the streets wearing nothing but sunflowers, tape, and booty shorts. Men strolled up and down the courthouse steps bare chested with slogans written in blood on their skin.

Exercising their First Amendment, like good Americans.

All through the trial, they chanted slogans.

"Let our Prophet go!"

"The First Amendment stands for religious freedom!"

"Different is not evil!"

Perhaps that last was not the most applicable to the present situation, but Rostov enjoyed the irony, nevertheless.

And he enjoyed how, when the prosecutorial witnesses were at their most preachy, the slogans would sometimes seep into the courtroom.

Ultimately, the state could only keep up the filibustering of its witnesses for so long. Then the defense had to have its turn.

Rostov himself took the stand. He and his counsel had agreed with the judge that he would testify in the narrative.

"Dear friends, I stand before you today a man accused of great wrongs. Wrongs that I vehemently deny!" His voice was warm and honeyed, thick and rich with feeling. "I grew up not far from here, and I discovered my faith in the beauty of the Sunshine State." He made eye contact with each individual member of the jury in turn as he spoke. "Praise our lord, the Sun! But I have never killed or ordered dark deeds done in the name of that fiery lord of light. Nor do I believe that any of my friends and coreligionists would harm anyone."

Rostov went into his whereabouts on the evening of the massacre, the tenets of his religion—which he now falsely claimed included non-violence—and the character of his fellow defendants. All phenomenal human beings, naturally.

He genuinely believed that he connected with a few of the jurors on a human level. Rostov had always had powerful eye contact, and he thought that he could feel some of these people tilting toward him.

Cross-examination was a verbal battle between Rostov and the state, which ended in mild embarrassment for the prosecution.

"So, you mean to tell me that your friends here weren't near the fire, but they had ashes all over their clothing, and they weren't involved in the crime, but there was blood on that fellow's shoes—"

"No," Rostov interrupted.

"No, you don't mean to deny their guilt, or no, you know they are guilty, or—"

"No," Rostov said calmly. He knew the prosecutor was trying to get him riled up. "I cannot prove a negative, sir. You can't ask me to prove someone else's innocence. But we're living an outdoorsy life, and it's easy when you're setting bonfires all the time to get ash on your clothes. And although you're trying to provoke me into saying something out of emotion, I'm not our forensic witness. It's not my job to disprove your phony baloney forensics."

For a few seconds the prosecutor, standing there red-faced, was speechless.

Then he sat down, looked through his notes, and popped back up with his next question.

It was a small moment, but the optics were terrible. A cool, composed defendant versus the beetroot-red, emotional prosecutor. The cross-examination never recovered from that.

There were other defense witnesses, but none of the other defendants themselves testified, per advice of counsel.

The defense forensic witness spread around appropriate amounts of doubt and uncertainty about the blood on Roy's shoes. Unfortunately, despite the defense's best efforts, the fact that the non-Rostov defendants had forensic evidence directly linking them to the murders remained a very stubborn impediment to acquittal.

Despite Rostov's best charm, and his attorneys' good, honest hard work, the first jury deadlocked, resulting in a mistrial.

Almost a year passed before the case came up in court again. A year in which Rostov and his followers were locked up. A year for the reality to hit them, each in their own ways, that despite everything they'd done, they weren't getting out of this.

The second trial was a very different affair.

The first judge retired, and he was replaced by a judge of a different generation, who banned all cameras from the courtroom and instructed his bailiffs to arrest anyone who made a peep out of turn in court.

Instead of assigning one of her top deputies, the state attorney handled the case directly.

And Kelsey Woodward and Jimmy Wainwright cut deals. They went from defendants in the case to friendly witnesses for the prosecution.

They came out and cried and whined about how big bad Nikolai Rostov made them do murder, influenced them, controlled their minds. *A pair of big crybabies*, Rostov thought. Wanda and Roy stayed faithful, but the value of their fidelity was limited.

The jury ate up the co-conspirator testimony. The verdict was obvious to Rostov long before the jury came back from deliberations, and he pulled back from the whole trial. Nested deep inside himself, he could ignore it. He didn't bother rising when the jury came in, despite the court's admonitions. He was done with this place.

Rostov was elsewhere when the jury declared him guilty as an accessory to murder.

On August 4, 2042, the police car drove past the protesters and pulled into the parking lot of the maximum security prison.

A man with crew-cut hair, receding noticeably, stepped out. He was out of uniform today, but his police bearing was unmistakable.

He approached the booth to enter the prison.

"Officer Jeffrey Ross here to witness the execution of Nikolai Rostov," he said.

"We're expecting you," the woman sitting behind the bulletproof glass said, barely looking up at him as she spoke. She tapped a name on a list.

He waited for her to buzz him in, but she seemed to be in a chatty mood.

"Any more of the victims' family members coming?" she asked.

"I don't know how many are already here," Officer Ross said. Then he shook his head. "Actually, I don't know generally."

"Oh. Well, how about Detective Fromme?" she followed up.

"Detective Fromme is in the hospital." Ross's voice broke slightly as he spoke.

"Well, I hope he feels better!" the woman said, picking up on the emotion in Ross's voice. She pushed a button, and a loud buzzer sounded.

"I don't think it's very likely," Ross muttered to himself as he advanced. The last years had fallen hard on Detective Fromme. Ross's mentor had slipped into a coma following a devastating stroke. His prognosis wasn't good. Ross planned to head to the hospital after he finished witnessing Rostov's execution. He was doing what Fromme would have wanted.

A few more attendants buzzed Ross through more doors until, finally, he arrived in a waiting room with a clear glass window. Ross could see the electric chair. He shuddered slightly. Despite having spent the last ten years in law enforcement, he had only rarely had to shoot someone, and never fatally. Witnessing an execution seemed like a grisly way to spend his afternoon.

If anyone deserves it, though, it's Nikolai Rostov. I'm going to finish it for you, Harry. I'll see the bastard dead.

Nikolai Rostov was bored with death row.

For the first few years, there had been a fear of death, which led him to launch frantic appeal after appeal. He was largely self-represented because he had only been entitled to a public defender for his trials, and the non-profits that tended to help people on death row did not wish to be associated with his case.

It was obvious to anyone who read his case file that he must be guilty of something. The phrase "the twenty-first century Charles Manson" was uttered in more than one legal organization's offices, Rostov knew.

The fact that it was true did not make it less galling.

The only distraction from his fear of death was Carrie-Ann and their new baby, which provided some limited comfort. *I've done as much as my own father did*, Rostov thought after one visit. *Made another little Rostov to cause trouble, without being around to raise him.*

Any sense of regret was faint. It was more of a sense of irony that gripped him.

The next few years were spent in painful isolation. Rostov was mostly isolated because death row was an isolating place, deliberately separated from the general population of the prison. And the few other people he spoke to, fellow murderers, were boring folk.

Conjugal visits with Carrie-Ann had been nice periodic breaks in the boring prison routine, but gradually, somehow without him knowing it, she had drifted away from him. From Rostov's perspective, she had stopped appearing one day, and eventually she had sent him divorce papers.

He signed them without thinking too much about it. There were dozens of women writing letters to him every day, hoping to become the next Mrs. Rostov, and Carrie-Ann had started to let herself go.

If he regretted anything, it was that she took their son, Vladimir, with her. But it wasn't as if he was going to be a good father anyway, so no great loss there.

Rostov was concluding a last visit with the second Mrs. Rostov—really Mrs. Filbert, since she hadn't taken his last name for her own safety—when Barry, the corrections officer, came to get him.

"Ready to ride the lightning, Nikolai?" Barry asked as he snapped the cuffs back on.

"Niko, you didn't request the lethal injection?" his wife asked. She looked stricken with horror.

"You really don't have to attend, my dear," Rostov said. He didn't want to be rude, but since he was about to die, the usefulness of company in general was rapidly disappearing.

He had chosen electrocution because, despite his initial squeamishness, it was at least a more interesting way to die. He was a man who'd lived his life by symbolism and violent public statements, even when he had refused to acknowledge responsibility for those statements as in the case of the killings he was convicted of ordering.

By choosing electrocution rather than lethal injection, he would die consistent with that.

Turning his back on his wife, Rostov walked down death row one last time. He occasionally rapped his hand against a door, and people who knew him on the row would call out to him.

"Yo, Niko!"

"You 'bout to ride that lightning, bro?"

There was a weird camaraderie about this place leading up to an execution.

Finally, Rostov walked through that last door. He saw a big glass window, and through it he could see a couple dozen people he halfway recognized. He gave Officer Ross a little wave before the guards strapped him in.

It's still never hit him, Jeffrey Ross thought. *It's still nothing to that son of a bitch. He doesn't even care that he's about to die.*

Looking back, Ross didn't think he'd noticed Rostov show any emotion besides amusement and sadistic glee at either of his trials. Maybe feelings other than anger and amusement didn't register for someone like him.

At least now it finally comes to an end—

[Greetings, heroes!]

CHAPTER TWENTY-NINE

If the Shoe Fits

The Class Evolution options were all interesting.

[Assassin]

[Gladiator]

[Gray Magician]

[Jack of All]

[Magic Swordsman]

[Predator in Human Skin]

Some very fierce options. That last one in particular sounds chilling; a Class to strike fear into the hearts of enemies. But it's not as if my enemies get to see my Class before we fight. Now, let's review in order.

[Assassin: An evolved Class. Proficient with a variety of killing methods and stealth techniques, emphasizing precise strikes with deadly force, poison, and pointed or bladed weapons. This Class is specialized in killing, skilled at stealth, disguise, subterfuge, subtlety, and all of the armed and unarmed physical killing arts. With each level, gain +3 Agility, +1 Strength, +1 Stamina, +4 Dexterity, +1 Perception, +4 Stealth, +3 Free Points.]

Interesting that my experience using magic doesn't seem to have affected this one and what it offers. I guess if you could make an Assassin who also used magic, that would probably be too broken. Next!

[Gladiator: An evolved Class. Proficient with a vast array of weapons and armor. Physically strong with an emphasis on brute force mixed with cunning over stealth or magic. Skilled at unarmed combat as well as armed combat, with a proficiency in flashy, arena-specialized martial arts, albeit with less proficiency than that possessed by Classes specialized in martial arts. With each level, gain +2 Agility, +4 Strength, +3 Stamina, +1 Dexterity, +2 Charisma, +2 Fortitude, +3 Free Points.]

In almost all ways inferior to the Assassin Class for what I'm looking for. The flashy martial arts will never come in handy unless I decide to engage in all of my fights in front of an audience, and reading between the lines, I won't even be the most skilled at martial arts. That's probably fair. The way I've been fighting doesn't emphasize technique as much as just getting the job done. But in every aspect except for the Charisma boost, the Assassin Class is better. Next!

[Gray Magician: An evolved Class. Proficient with small arms as well as with various forms of magic. Physically tough and quick but with an emphasis on cunning, stealth, and magic over brute force. Skilled in the subtle ways of magic, which they mainly focus on destruction and to a lesser extent on healing, utility, and protection. Modestly skilled with weapons and unarmed combat, but treats these as a last resort, a hidden trick to play when spells fail. With each level, gain +1 Agility, +1 Strength, +1 Stamina, +1 Dexterity, +1 Perception, +4 Will, +5 Intelligence, +3 Free Points.]

Something of an opposite to Gladiator. An emphasis on magic is convenient in some ways, but contradictory to my existing plans. I still want to party with Mina and Yulia, who will probably have magic covered. Maybe I'll revisit later if there's really nothing better than this and Assassin.

[Jack of All: An evolved Class. Specialized as a generalist, these individuals are good at anything they try their hand at. Skilled wherever they focus and capable of using any approach they choose to train to solve a problem. With each level, gain +2 Agility, +2 Strength, +2 Stamina, +2 Dexterity, +2 Perception, +2 Charisma, +2 Fortitude, +2 Will, +2 Intelligence, +2 Free Points.]

Almost reads as a filler Class for someone who's indecisive. Specialized as a generalist? Sounds like a contradiction in terms! I wonder if that's a flaw in the Class. Can you ever really be specialized in generalization? The good thing about this, however, is the way the Stat points are distributed. There is a little added to everything with a total of twenty Stat points per level given, which makes it the strongest Class on paper so far. If the last two aren't better, I think I'll take this one. It's probably flexible enough that I could make it into whatever I want, as the Jack of All name would seem to indicate. And three extra Stat points is nothing to sneeze at.

[Magic Swordsman: An evolved Class. A swordsman equally skilled with the blade and with magic, specialized in these two areas of combat but less skilled than an expert specialized in one. Modestly skilled in unarmed combat, but much less so than with sword or spell. This Class is adaptable to different battle situations and capable of effectively functioning as a one-person fighting party. With each level, gain +3 Agility, +3 Strength, +2 Stamina, +1 Dexterity, +1 Fortitude, +3 Will, +3 Intelligence, +1 Free Points.]

A version of the Jack of All specialized in fighting, whereas Jack of All could become good at anything, James assessed. *Not superior to Jack of All, even if I find it more appealing than most of the other Classes on an intuitive level. It's so easy to imagine myself swinging a sword while throwing a spell. It's more or less how I've been fighting ever since I got magic, after all, and it feels very anime.*

But he moved onto the final option.

[Predator in Human Skin: A unique evolved Class. Skilled in every killing art. In the grip of a predator, every available resource becomes a weapon. Capable with brute strength, weapons, magic, traps, poison, acid, environmental manipulation, lures, stealth, invention, and all of the methods of the predator, they also maintain a robust self-healing capability and deep reserves of power to continue the fight until its conclusion. With each level, gain +3 Agility, +2 Strength, +2 Stamina, +2 Dexterity, +2 Perception, +3 Charisma, +2 Fortitude, +2 Will, +3 Intelligence, +3 Stealth.]

He immediately thought that this option sounded very cool, a description to match the label. But he had some reservations.

A Class that doesn't give me any Free Points, James noted. *It's even more of a jack-of-all-trades than Jack of All, in that sense. Though it invests more in a few specific categories than Jack of All does. Does that mean I'll gradually become unbalanced?* A counter to that occurred to him. *Does the fact that the Class that's constructed most powerfully on paper doesn't provide the possibility of balance indicate that balance is not a desirable result in constructing your build? Specialization is necessary?*

It seemed like a plausible enough explanation. The System was inadvertently communicating to him that he'd been making a mistake by thinking about having a balanced Stat build at all. *That's the problem with the Jack of All build. If you're too balanced, you'll always be mediocre at the things that matter. You have to make tradeoffs.*

He returned to the description for Predator in Human Skin and read through it again. Something jumped out at him from the first line. *A unique evolved Class? None of the other descriptions said that, did they?* He confirmed it was the case.

Is it something specialized or created just for me? The System had seemingly done that before with some of his initial Talents—at least, so far as he knew, he hadn't met anyone with the Talent Cannibalism or the Skill Pillage yet, and he seemed to be gaining Strength and commensurate confidence in his powers at a noticeably faster rate than those around him, which wouldn't be true if they had the same gifts as him.

A unique evolved Class, eh? I'll take it! He had already almost decided on that option, but just thinking about how well the System had specialized itself to him thus far, the decision became much easier.

He selected the Predator in Human Skin Class, and his body shivered as knowledge poured into his mind. Not knowledge of any specific fighting discipline or magical technique so much as a fuller awareness of the capabilities of his body and his resource pool. For instance, he knew now how far someone would have to twist his neck backward to break it, and he also knew roughly how much force each of his arms could apply in a particular position, the combination of which gave him a pretty good idea of how he could apply the proper amount of force to snap someone else's neck. He knew how large of an explosion he could make or how large of a pool of water he could make if he spent his entire Mana pool at once. He knew that he would now be able to tell how much air someone had left inside their body if he began strangling them.

These felt like they should be bits of knowledge only the Assassin would have, but James could tell, just from the way he felt right now, that if the Predator in Human Skin and the Assassin met on a level playing field, both aiming to kill each other, the predator would eat the Assassin for breakfast.

Someone whose job is to hide and kill from a position of stealth doesn't have to be as strong and fierce as the predator. Or maybe the Predator in Human Skin Class just reflected someone whose natural gifts in the art of killing exceeded those of an Assassin.

This is what it means to be a Predator in Human Skin. He shivered again. The surge of knowledge, the power hidden just beneath it, and the sensation of a new depth of sensory perception all felt immensely pleasurable.

James forced himself to pull back on reveling in the new sensations for a moment, and a series of pop-ups appeared immediately.

[**Congratulations! You have become a Predator in Human Skin!**]
[**You unlocked the Stealth Stat!**]
[**You acquired the upgraded Skill Basic Proficiency–All Weapons!**]
[**You acquired the Skill Basic Proficiency–Unarmed Combat!**]
[**You acquired the upgraded Skill Predator's Strike!**]
[**You acquired the Skill Predator's Armaments!**]
[**You acquired the Skill Predator's Armor!**]
[**You acquired the Skill Predator's Missile!**]
[**You acquired the Skill Predator's Insight!**]
[**You acquired the Skill Predator's Instincts!**]
[**You acquired the Skill Predator's Intuition!**]
[**You acquired the Skill Predator's Senses!**]
[**You acquired the Skill Natural Camouflage!**]
[**You acquired the Skill Parallel Minds!**]

I made the right choice. He knew it in his bones. *I got so much from accepting this option.* And now he felt that he knew, as if by instinct, the best way to progress more rapidly in his task.

It was time to resume his good work.

James opened his magic satchel and took out a few of the bundles of human meat that Pillage had repeatedly given him. He hadn't known what to do with it, until now.

These spiders were predators, and they had tried to drag the people they attacked away from the location of the fighting. It stood to reason they were looking for fresh meat, perhaps to feed their young, perhaps to feed themselves. They ambushed humans that walked nearby. But if they smelled fresh meat—and James felt intuitively that spiders probably could smell, even though he hadn't seen a nose on any of them—then wouldn't they be drawn to that enticing aroma?

He gathered a little brush from the fallen twigs nearby to use as tinder and then used magic to start a small fire beside the meat. He wasn't really trying to cook it, just to spread the smell of human flesh on the wind. As the fire grew, and the bundles of meat began to glisten and sweat next to the fire, James could smell his plan beginning to succeed: there was a meaty smell coming from the bundles.

It was a lot like the smell of roasting pork, and he became aware he was getting hungry. He would not think about that now, though. Instead, he charged his Mana again—he noticed it seemed a little quicker than before his Evolution—and cast a wind spell to spread the meaty smoke farther and wider than it would naturally float.

Then he stepped backward, retreating into the bushes. He drew his crossbow from the satchel, loaded it with bolts, and laid it down beside him. Then he laid down in a position with the best vantage point and angle he could find and made his body as still as he could. He wasn't sure which Skill he was using, but he could feel his body growing unnaturally quieter. So still and quiet that it felt as if he were closer to death.

His heartbeat had slowed down, and his body had arranged itself as flat against the surrounding soil as it could. He could feel it gradually stiffening like a corpse as he lay in place with slowed circulation. He even felt his Mana pull back into his core from the general surface area around his skin. Everything was stillness.

And he waited.

He waited in silence and stillness, completely content and relaxed.

He waited for an amount of time that would have frustrated him once, even though he had considered himself fairly patient in his pre-System life.

It was strange that he didn't feel restless or bored, he thought. He could never have imagined that he would be sitting like this, calm and unmoving, waiting for something that might not happen for what felt like half an hour without feeling restless.

But he felt as if he could lie in wait forever.

Even his mind was still and calm, focused on the enemy he waited for.

Although part of him was thinking about the changes happening to his body, he could feel another separate part of his mind remaining on high alert, ready to take up the crossbow in a flash and begin an ambush attack.

That must be Parallel Minds, he thought. *It stands to reason that a predator should have something like that.*

At last, the spiders came.

CHAPTER THIRTY

The Gathering

The spiders descended one by one, in quick order.

Like eight-legged rottweilers dropping down from the trees with ugly, beady eyes. At first, James contemplated getting to his feet and charging in after a half dozen had appeared, but some instinct stayed him.

The instinct was wiser than his conscious mind, it seemed, because the parade was only halfway done. The half dozen increased to a full dozen over the next few minutes. Included among this number was an unusually large specimen with white and gray bands around its long black legs. James instinctively pegged this as the clear leader around which the others maneuvered.

He used Identify on it.

[Command Wood Spider, Lv. 9: A mutant spider cultivated for the Orientation by the System. Part of a cluster of spiders, this specimen is one of the superior members, second in status only to the Queen Mother. Controls lesser spiders. Superior to the average System-Enhanced Human in all attributes other than Will and Fortitude. Stronger when under the command of a higher-level life-form.]

Almost the same level as me. As he read the description, James noticed that the spiders were drawing gradually closer to the fire, the meat, and James's hiding place.

The small space around the fire where the creatures had descended fairly crawled with the giant spiders now, and James was beginning to doubt the wisdom of this course of action. He felt a real sense of the risk he had decided to take in the name of hunting more of the monsters at once. Somewhere in his mind a pair of numbers emerged, which he immediately associated with two concepts: 87 percent chance of survival, 64 percent chance of victory.

Are those real? James wondered, but he was already fairly certain he knew the answer.

Everything he'd seen in the System was real. Any new senses or knowledge that he perceived proved immediately useful. There was little point in questioning it. Something about his new powers—about his new Class, to be specific— allowed him to gauge his odds of victory in a given fight. It wasn't any stranger than other things he'd experienced thus far. He felt ready to leap into action, but he wanted to gather a little more information first, and he had at least a few seconds before they discovered him. Having reviewed his new abilities while he was waiting for the creatures to come, he activated the most appropriate one.

Predator's Insight!

Instantly he felt his gaze drawn to particular parts on the big spider's body. Weak points, it seemed, included the eyes, major joints on its body, and the joints on the limbs. Points of danger were the fangs—*duh!*—and a part of the rear underside of the spider, which his senses indicated was both a danger area and a weak point.

That must be where it generates silk from, James thought. It was the only really unique thing about spiders, after all.

He looked over the other spiders, and they appeared much the same under his predatory gaze, though with more weak spots and fewer threatening fangs and spinnerets. James decided that he would tackle the leader first. He began Silent Spellcasting, quietly pulling Mana out of his core, and the spiders jumped into action. The big one reared up on its back pair of legs, made a strange piercing screech, and gestured with its two front legs at James.

Looks like I broke my stealth, James thought. Then two spiders leaped upon him.

James had to let go of his crossbow, but he managed to keep the spellcasting going while pushing off from the ground with all four limbs and jumping onto a low-hanging branch. The limb lasted only a second, however, before it broke under his weight, sending him plummeting into the thick of the spiders. Three surrounded the area where he was about to fall, while the others crouched, poised to leap onto him as soon as he landed.

Shit. The moment after the branch broke, James unleashed his flame spell prematurely, aiming a half-dozen little bursts of flame into the eyes of the spiders that waited around where he was about to fall, hoping to at least distract the spiders a bit and perhaps blind them. As he descended, he charged another attack in both arms.

Heavy Strike! As he landed, he smashed the two closest spiders into greasy smears on his fists. The instant kill move cost him a lot in terms of Stamina, but it was well worth it. The spiders that had been poised to leap at him hesitated now, and James thought he detected something different in the air. An odor faintly reminiscent of ammonia. His senses were all amped since the System and especially since the Class Evolution. He wondered if this was the smell of fear.

He had little time to consider the question. The third spider that was closest to him did not share the more distant spiders' hesitation. It rushed in while his hands were still embedded in spider guts, and it tried to snap its fangs shut on one of his legs. James lifted his hands, stuck-on spider bits and all, and closed them around this spider's head, holding it in place only a few inches away from his shin. Then he slowly but surely crushed its head between his powerful hands. No Skill required, so very little Stamina expenditure.

As he did this, James raised his eyes to look at the other spiders. With one firmly contained in his grip, the remaining nine were the real threat. Especially the big one. And then the big spider moved. It reared up on its back legs again, raised its head, and screeched once more.

The other spiders, hearing their leader's apparent order and seeing James so occupied with one of their brethren, seemed to lose their fear and began scurrying at James *en masse*.

He used another Heavy Strike to finish crushing the spider's head in an instant, and then he drew his sword from his side. He had just a moment to reassess the situation before the remainder of the spiders were upon him. *More than anything else*, he thought, *I need to take out that leader*. If he burned through all his Stamina, and the leader was still alive, that 87 percent chance of survival was sure to drop precipitously.

As the eight subordinate spiders closed in, James moved. *Predator's Strike!* With his sword pointed straight at the leader, James struck with inhuman speed, lunging across the six feet that separated him from the creature in a flash. His lunge carried him over the other spiders to the leader. He embedded the sword deep in the spider's center of mass, and gray fluid slowly oozed out.

But the leader remained alive and seemingly strong. It screeched. It raised its front four legs and tried to grapple with James—fangs snapping open and closed as it drew closer—and he was forced to let go of the sword and throw himself off to the side to avoid the deadly embrace.

Three of the remaining spiders leaped upon him, and as James tried to pull away again, he felt something soft and sticky grip his arm. He looked down and saw a silken thread stuck fast to his left arm. The other end was attached to the lead spider's abdomen. *That thread is a threat*, James thought. *But also a vulnerability.*

He didn't try to shake it loose right now. Instead, he began focusing on the three spiders closest to him. He dodged between snapping fangs and attempted full-body tackles. He drew a Wolfbone Dagger and embedded it in one's back. And as he weaved between the three spiders, he entangled them in the thread that bound him to the lead spider. Now they were all tied together. The command spider, seeming to recognize the hazard of what was happening, disconnected the thread from its abdomen, and not a moment too soon.

James raised the arm the thread was stuck to, and with all his strength, he whipped his arm forward in another Heavy Strike. The three spiders attached to the thread went flying with the full force of his fist pulling them. The thread, whip-like, smashed the spiders against two conveniently placed trees, and there was a loud, violent sound of smashed exoskeletons. Only then did James rip the remaining thread from where it was stuck to his arm, taking a chunk of his skin with it. The spiders that had struck the trees weren't dead, but they were wounded, suffering broken exoskeletons or missing limbs, moving feebly and slowly, and he didn't have time for them right now.

The remaining half dozen were charging him. They seemed to sense that if they worked together, they could not lose, even against someone who had killed so many of their brethren. And it was true that James was slowing down. He had less than half of his Stamina remaining, with fewer than half of the spiders killed.

Still, he liked his chances!

He used Silent Spellcasting again as he attempted to dodge among the various spiders' snapping fangs and keep them from attacking him from too many sides at once. If worse came to worst, he needed to at least kill the leader and avoid being bitten by that spider. Its venom would undoubtedly be more potent than that of its subordinates, and James wasn't certain he could heal himself before the venom would kill him.

A disemboweling slash here, a heavy blow to the head there, a stomp to the body of another. James whittled down the group's numbers until there were only three of the smaller spiders left, plus one of the broken spiders still twitching and the Command Wood Spider hanging back. The leader seemed wary; James's sword was still sticking out of its cephalothorax like a warning of what might happen if it closed the distance again.

Cowardly, James thought. *If it would be a little braver, I could end this for sure.* His Silent Spellcasting was almost fully charged.

Then it happened. As he danced away from one strike, one of the spiders near to his left leg finally succeeded in snapping its fangs closed and penetrating the outermost layer of skin. James pulled away, but he already felt that the area of skin and flesh had been injected with venom.

Shed Skin! The outermost layers of skin and flesh separated themselves from his body, and James thought that he had avoided the venom with this trick. But the Stamina expenditure to shed the skin, and the extra layer of flesh hanging off of his body now, slowed him down even more. The other two spiders nipped at his flesh as well, though they only caught onto the loose bits of skin he was shedding.

And James felt hunger growing as his Stamina continued to drop.

No choice now. Have to use it. James released the fire spell he had been silently charging, and flames burst from his body outward in all directions. He could feel that all the little spiders had been hit, their lives snuffed out instantly, and at last, even the more distant Command Wood Spider was caught in the flames. James enjoyed a small surge of strength that he guessed was from a level up—he was still focused on the fight, so his notifications were suppressed for now.

But the Command Wood Spider had been farther away, hanging back from the fight. Far enough to throw its body backward and escape the more intense blast radius.

James had avoided invoking Chosen One of Apophis so he wouldn't make too large of an explosion and potentially create a fire large enough to endanger the Rodriguez camp. Although he could tell that the flames had struck his last target—and he felt sure enough that the power he had invested would scorch the spider's exoskeleton—he had a bad feeling that it wasn't enough.

He collapsed to his knees, nearly exhausted. Even with the level up, almost everything he had was spent, the lead spider was still alive, and he felt so damned hungry!

CHAPTER THIRTY-ONE

Under the Skin

James knelt, trying to move as little as possible so that he could recover his Stamina more quickly. With his focus weakened, the notifications began rolling in.

[Sufficient experience accrued. Natural Camouflage leveled up!]

[Sufficient experience accrued. Parallel Minds leveled up!]

[Sufficient experience accrued. Predator's Insight leveled up!]

[You killed Feral Wood Spider, Lv. 8. You gained 122 exp!]

[You killed Feral Wood Spider, Lv. 7. You gained 100 exp!]

[Sufficient experience accrued. Predator's Strike leveled up!]

[Sufficient experience accrued. Heavy Strike leveled up!]

[You killed Feral Wood Spider, Lv. 6. You gained 80 exp!]

[You killed Feral Wood Spider, Lv. 7. You gained 100 exp!]

[Sufficient experience accrued. Heavy Strike leveled up!]

[You killed Feral Wood Spider, Lv. 6. You gained 80 exp!]

[You killed Feral Wood Spider, Lv. 7. You gained 100 exp!]

[You killed Feral Wood Spider, Lv. 8. You gained 122 exp!]

[Predator in Human Skin leveled up!]

[System-Boosted Human leveled up!]

[Sufficient experience accrued. Shed Skin leveled up!]

[You killed Feral Wood Spider, Lv. 6. You gained 80 exp!]

[You killed Feral Wood Spider, Lv. 7. You gained 100 exp!]

[You killed Feral Wood Spider, Lv. 6. You gained 80 exp!]

[Sufficient experience accrued. Basic Elemental Magic: Fire leveled up!]

[You killed Feral Wood Spider, Lv. 7. You gained 100 exp!]
[Required conditions met. Flame Affinity leveled up!]

Good stuff, James thought. *If I wasn't so tired, I'd be overjoyed.* More than tired, there was something else: a sense of apprehension hanging over him.

He was surrounded, though not too closely, by a smokescreen. He detected something moving through the smoke. There was no doubt in his mind of what it was. That damned Command Wood Spider was still alive, and it was now actively looking for him.

Now it decides to be brave, James thought. *While I can barely muster the energy to move. Smart.* He was slowly but steadily recovering his Stamina, but it was slowed down even further by smoke inhalation, and certainly the creature had more Stamina remaining than he did. The lead spider had hardly done any fighting. If this became a battle of attrition, James had no confidence he could hold his own.

He let his body collapse to the ground completely and lay prone. If he couldn't win a straight fight right now, that left the obvious option. Cheat.

He ordered his body to do the same things it had done before when he had camouflaged himself. He wasn't trying to hide this time, though. He was playing dead.

Boris, the spider, crawled on all six of his remaining legs through the smoke. Two of his legs had been burned off at the first joint, but that was all right. They had been shielding Boris's delicate eyes, and if the fire that human had unleashed as a last-ditch attack had been enough to incinerate part of his front two legs, it surely would have at least partially blinded him. And now was the time when he could least afford to be blinded.

Boris needed to quickly locate and recover that human's high-quality meat for the Queen. That would excuse the failure of losing eleven of her lesser children to ambush.

Surely the strong human's body was exactly the food she was searching the forest for!

He felt a spark of joy in his core at the thought that he was the one to find it. *I'll bring it to you soon, Mother!*

The human was obviously at death's door when it unleashed that desperate attack. The other spiders had injected their venom in several areas. All Boris had to do was figure out where the body had fallen.

He wandered through the smoke a little ways. It was hard to find his path back since he had thrown himself as far out of the way of the fire as he could.

Still, better a slightly annoying search than getting roasted. Or more roasted. Parts of his upper body were brittle and ready to shatter, but he would shed this skin and heal most of his wounds once he had accomplished the mission.

He needed to find and drag the body away from here before predators could be drawn from the neighboring territories so that they wouldn't try to poach Boris's offering.

Boris's eyes scanned through the smoke as he advanced. He had upgraded them when he had his Evolution, the better to scout enemies and prey with. Now, the eyes finally paid off.

At last, there was the human! Boris approached slowly, cautiously, the way he had been trained his whole life—the last fourteen days since the Queen had spawned him. He valued his life more highly than he did those of his brethren because he was special to the Queen.

He looked for any signs of life in the human. The dark-skinned figure was lying on his back, completely still. There was no movement of the chest that Boris could see, which he had learned from experience meant the human was not breathing. No sound of a heartbeat that Boris could detect from far away, but that might just mean the human's body was slowing down.

Despite the lack of life signs, Boris was cautious.

He had learned his lesson from fighting this human up close once—he still had a sword hilt sticking out of his chest, nestled between two vital organs but thankfully missing both.

This human was dangerous, and he didn't want to try to drag away a still-living human, like some of his less intelligent brethren might. That was a good way to get one of those vital organs perforated and die before he could return to the Queen.

Boris decided on a good security measure that would allow him to transport the human body safely, living or dead, and that did not require him to enter stabbing range. Boris began spinning thread onto the human, first a few strands to bind the arms together, then the legs. Then Boris got within closer range of the human so that he could turn the body over, and he began binding the human's whole body below the neck in a cocoon of strong spider silk.

Finally, Boris's body released a tension he hadn't realized he'd been holding. At last, he could relax. The human was wrapped up thoroughly. Even if he wanted to fight now, it would be impossible.

Boris gripped the cocoon in two mighty legs and threw the human's body onto his back. He began walking up the side of a tree with his prize—then felt a sharp pain in the back of his head. Then another.

Then Boris felt nothing. His body turned limp, lost its grip on the side of the tree, and fell to the ground.

[You killed Command Wood Spider, Lv. 9. You gained 180 exp!]

[Predator in Human Skin leveled up!]

[Sufficient experience accrued. Predator's Armaments leveled up!]

[Sufficient experience accrued. Predator's Strike leveled up!]

James growled quietly to himself. Then he spat the remaining pieces of spider brains and exoskeleton out of his mouth. As soon as he'd swallowed a single piece of the dead Command Wood Spider, he had noticed his Health begin to decrease.

I guess I can't restore my Stamina more quickly by eating dead spiders, he thought. *No wonder Pillage didn't give me any meat when I killed the other ones.* He needed something else to restore his energy, which was almost at bottom after he killed the last enemy. That spider was a devious creature. James had not expected that it would wrap him in silk before trying to drag him away. After all, he had nearly brought his pulse to a stop.

The spider couldn't have detected any signs of life, he thought. *But I was so much of a threat that it secured every part of the body that it imagined could be a threat.* The spider's mistake had been leaving his head uncovered.

With Predator's Armaments, which allowed him to temporarily make any weapon—including parts of his body, such as his teeth—deadlier, and Predator's Strike, which gave his attack a speed and damage boost, the spider had never seen James's finishing blow coming. Literally, since James sank his teeth into the back of the spider's head and kept biting until its brains were reduced to mush. The spider never had the chance to see James make his move, never had an opportunity to defend itself. Better that way since he didn't have another attack like that in him.

Now, with the spider having dropped dead, falling to the ground on top of James, the only problem he foresaw was getting out of this spider silk binding with no Stamina left. A problem he solved by Silent Spellcasting a flame on all sides of his body. The spider silk burned like it was made for the purpose, and, as a bonus, it took with it the extra layer of loose skin that James had shed as it burned. The new layer of skin that remained was initially as moist as the gooey flesh of a newborn baby, and the slowly dying flame dried it off pleasantly.

With the cocoon wrapped around him gone, and the spiders all dead, James could finally sit up and relax a little. *That was far too close. I hope it won't always look that bad when I have a 64 percent chance of victory.* But maybe two-to-one odds were far from the near guarantee he had perceived. Would he really have bet his life on anything with an 87 percent chance of survival in his previous life? Bet his ability to return home to Mina and Yulia and his and Mina's child?

No. Absolutely not. What is this place doing to me? Am I losing my sense of self-preservation? Turning arrogant?

He decided he probably was, after a moment's reflection; turning arrogant and losing his instinct for self-preservation. Maybe it was tied into how his body felt. *I feel young again.* Not young as in the early thirties age that he was in real time, but young like the twenty-year-old with a perfect body that he had been ten years earlier. Young enough to be invincible. The fittest he'd ever been. Even his mind felt like it was moving more quickly. His senses were certainly sharper than they'd ever been.

As *Dragon Ball Z* might have described it: it felt like he was in his perfect form. It was exhilarating just to be alive as he was now. *Like all my lost potential suddenly rushed back and realized itself or something.* There was a certain heady satisfaction there. *All the people who believed I was meant for greatness were right . . .*

Before he lost himself in self-congratulation, he pulled himself back to the present situation.

I can't believe I threw myself into such a risky position. It felt weirdly inconsistent with his own previous character, almost enough to produce cognitive dissonance. And no, he wasn't injured, but he'd had a whole group of people ready to fight next to him.

It hurt his head a little to try and think about why he'd done this, and he gave up on the self-examination after around thirty seconds. *Next time, I'll use my allies*, he thought finally. *A general is only as good as his army.*

But for now: Mass Pillage! A little self-reflection would not be enough to put him off collecting the rewards of this fight, at least. Even if the whole endeavor of offering to fight off a whole colony of giant spiders by himself had been an act of massive and puzzling hubris on his part, he still wanted to get all the rewards that would inevitably accompany the result.

He just needed a safer plan to do that. And he needed to get out of this place while he made that plan. The smell of burning spider flesh was disgusting to his nostrils—probably something to do with why they also tasted disgusting and why it actually decreased his Health slightly when he swallowed a piece of spider—but surely something in these horrible woods would find it appetizing. He didn't want to be here when that creature arrived.

[5x Feral Wood Spider's body processed.]

[You obtained 5x Small Exoshield, 5x Venom Sac, and 5x Small Spiderknife!]

[Skill Obtained: Shed Skin!]

[Existing Skill Shed Skin detected! Additional Skill Shed Skin merged into existing Skill Shed Skin.]

He smiled this time. He was never going to complain about accumulating more experience for the Shed Skin Skill again. It had saved him from probably succumbing to necrotic venom in this fight, and he didn't mind if he leveled it up to one hundred.

[Command Wood Spider's body processed.]

[You obtained Medium Exoshield, Superior Venom Sac, and Medium Spiderknife!]

[Skill Obtained: Venom Fangs!]

Just at the moment when I accustom myself to disappointment, James thought. *The gods seem to have a sense of humor. I'll pick up my things and then review the Skill.*

All of the items generated by Mass Pillage had been pulled by his will into his magic satchel, but there were still the weapons he'd used in the fighting.

James had very little Stamina left for fighting purposes but enough to walk over to collect his crossbow, daggers, and shortsword, which were scattered in different areas of the fighting ground. Then he walked off through the trees, aiming to get as far as he could from the site of his slaughter before the other denizens of the forest could make their way to him. Already he heard the trees behind him moving with renewed bestial activity, which he was not adequately prepared to deal with at the moment.

He would have to sneak away quietly and hope the rumbling of his stomach and the crunching of the underbrush didn't draw their attention.

What Fresh Hell?

As the text filled his view, and the voice recited absurd information into his ears, Officer Ross looked around. His training and experience had taught him that in an emergency situation he needed to account for what everyone around him was doing. He wanted to confirm that everyone else had frozen in reaction to the same thing he was seeing and hearing.

He saw that everyone else had frozen in shock—all except one.

Through the glass, he saw that Nikolai Rostov was sitting with eyes clenched tightly closed, seemingly trying to ignore the announcements. But the stranger thing was the expression on his face. The cultist was smiling.

"What fresh hell is this?" Rostov demanded with a boldness he did not feel. Hallucinations always brought out a poetic mood in him. But he felt the cold grip of terror in his guts. Despite the impossibility of what his senses presented, he wasn't sure this was a hallucination.

As soon as the words had come, he'd felt a sudden heat around him, and a second voice completely drowned out the first in his ears.

"These announcements are always annoying. You don't need to listen to much of this. All you need to know is that you only have to survive for an hour and a half to make it to the Orientation. Not an easy task for a man strapped to the electric chair."

Then Rostov felt himself pulled through space and time. He stood in a place of sweltering heat and encircling flames. Now, as he looked around after making his pronouncement, he questioned where in the world he could be. Everywhere around him was nothing but seething fire. Above him was just a deep blackness. He swallowed slowly.

Am I dead already? Rostov questioned. *Receiving my eternal reward?* Even for a man like him, the prospect of burning forever was nothing to laugh at.

"Hello, my dear Nikolai!" the voice that had pulled him away said. "Welcome to my home."

The voice let out a throaty chuckle, and Rostov shuddered. It wasn't anything the voice had said, though that comment about his execution had felt like a taunt. He'd long ago accepted the reality of his impending death, and it would not be the first time he'd been taunted about his fate. It was just the sound of that voice.

A demonic sound—that was what it felt like. A monstrous sound like nothing he'd heard before.

The quality of the voice permeated his body. A deep, croaky timbre that seemed to seep right into his bones and rattle them.

He could feel that the voice was not of the Earth, and that painful knowledge made him weak at the knees.

Perhaps this was the beginning of his torments.

Rostov couldn't resist asking, "Uh, am—am I in H-Hell?"

Another bone-rattling chuckle.

"Heh. Heh. Heh."

Rostov could feel the source of the voice make an effort to restrain its mirth at the last of those chuckles.

"My friend," the voice said, "you are still alive. How could you be in the afterlife? No, you are in my realm. In spirit, at least. Your body is still right where you left it. Reach out with your mind and touch it if you don't believe me."

Rostov closed his eyes and tried to imagine himself back in the electric chair, and he instantly felt his body there. Trapped in place. His legs hung down the front of the chair, strapped into their restraints. His wrists remained locked tightly to his sides. He could feel the ugly metal cap secured to his skull. And his back slumped against the uncomfortable chair.

Then he opened his eyes again. He was still in the place of heat and flame.

"Is this a visit to Hell, then? I would think that would at least wait until after I was actually dead, but I don't really know how these things work. Who are you?"

The voice sounded playful as it replied. "Do you not remember me? You, who led men and women in prayer to me? You, who, alone of all the humans currently living in your world, ordered burnt offerings made to garner my favor? I'm almost hurt, Nikolai! I had grown quite fond of you."

"You're the Sun?" Rostov exclaimed. He'd thought that he was preaching bullshit all those years. Surely, he had been. It was just a way to grasp hold of a little power.

But now he had drawn the attention of something beyond his comprehension.

"I am the Sun God, yes. Be honored, human. I have chosen you from among all humanity to bear the responsibility of preaching my word and offering sacrifices in my name."

Rostov stood speechless. *What the fuck is going on here? I was supposed to die. Why are you even talking to me? You must have the wrong guy.* All of these words ran through his head, but he didn't speak them. The pressure and heat in the god's realm had increased, and Rostov had the idea firmly in his mind that if he once said the wrong thing to this being, he would be turned to cinders in an instant.

"As my Chosen, you should have the distinct honor of beholding my true face."

There was a swirling of fire and smoke from all around Rostov, forming a tornado of flames in front of him. He raised an arm to shield his eyes from the heat and brightness that threatened to blind him. An absurd idea since his physical body was in another place, and yet the feeling persisted.

After a few seconds of squinting at the column of fire, Rostov saw the shape change. It condensed and turned opaque.

Finally, it coalesced into a nude humanoid figure with the head and horns of a bull and the wings of an eagle. The monstrous *thing* was dozens of feet high. Its flesh was wreathed in flame, and it breathed fire in and out of its nostrils. Rostov had to tilt his head back to take in the entirety of the figure.

What are you?! Rostov thought.

"I am called Moloch," the being said, as if in response to his unspoken question. **"I sense that you will serve me very well indeed."**

Rostov's mouth gaped. The former cult leader was only dimly aware that he had fallen to his knees.

[Take the remaining time to make your careful preparations for Orientation. The task we set before you is not easy, but whether you believe it or not now, it is necessary. In time, those of you who live may come to agree with us. We hope for the best of you to succeed.]

"Christ on a cracker!" Officer Ross exclaimed. He had let the announcement finish what it apparently had to say since it seemed important and possibly urgent. But now he sprang into action.

"Did everyone else hear the same shit I just heard?" he asked, standing.

The other people in the pre-execution waiting area provided affirming noises or gestures, mostly grunted "Yeahs" and nods.

"Good, I'm not crazy, then," Ross muttered.

He turned to the viewing window. Rostov was still there, still seated in his chair with his eyes clenched shut, and still apparently weirdly happy at the announcement.

Maybe it's not weird, Ross thought. *If he thinks this System will save him somehow . . .*

He turned back to face the room. A guard stood by the door, visibly still stunned, lips moving as he muttered to himself. Officer Ross thought he vaguely recognized the lip movements. It took him a moment to place, but the guard appeared to be praying.

Ross approached and looked down at the man's name tag. It read, "Underwood."

"Corrections Officer Underwood!" Ross said.

The man came out of his trance and straightened his posture.

"Yes, sir, what is it?"

"I'm Officer Jeffrey Ross. I worked on that man's case." He gestured at the viewing window. "And I need to know: what is the procedure for this situation?"

"P-procedure?" the man asked.

"Yes. What's procedure if something happens to interrupt an execution? An act of God, or some kind of emergency?"

"Mm, ah, we don't have a procedure for this—"

"Procedure is that any act of nature or God that would prevent the execution requires that it be rescheduled," a voice said from behind Ross.

Both officers turned their heads to see the prison chaplain, dressed all in black except for the typical white collar. The man was tightly clutching a cross that hung from his neck. He looked anxious to Officer Ross, but he was clearly more together right now than the guard.

Ross turned his body fully toward the man of God.

"Preacher, do you know what this man's in for?" he asked.

"I am vaguely aware," the chaplain said.

"Well, let's not be vague," Ross said. "He led a depraved pagan cult. He sent his followers to burn innocent people to death. Teachers. He had them burned in the schoolhouse! They didn't even give them a proper burial, just left them there."

"I don't know what you're telling me this for, sir," the chaplain said stiffly. "If you're asking me to pass judgment on this man, that's for the Lord—"

"I want to know how I make sure that his sentence is carried out!" Ross interjected.

"Why the urgency, Officer?" Underwood asked, his tone curious but guarded.

"The urgency is that something is going on." Ross gestured at the space where he could see the timer still ticking down. "I'm concerned that we're about to face a prison break or something like that on a massive scale. Reality is being altered. This man"—he flailed his arm in Rostov's direction—"cannot be allowed to walk free ever again."

A pit was forming in Ross's stomach as he checked the time remaining. **[01:05:22]**.

* * *

"**I will always be with you,**" Moloch said, his voice surprisingly soothing and penetrating at the same time. "**I will hold your hand through the Orientation and into the new world to come. You will enjoy power and pleasures beyond those you have previously tasted. All you must do is serve me in all things and feed me sacrifices.**"

"Master, I pledge myself to your service," Rostov said. All his life, the only thing he had ever truly been able to respect was power. At last, he encountered supreme power, and he felt an unfamiliar emotion: devotion.

"**Go now. Inhabit your body again,**" Moloch said. "**Do whatever you must to survive these remaining moments. I cannot interfere directly to protect you here and now. I cannot grant you access to your Skills until the System's timer finishes.**"

"Yes, Lord," Rostov said simply, bowing deeply.

He closed his eyes, and when he opened them again, he sat in the electric chair as before. But somehow everything seemed to have changed.

A figure stood in the room with him who shouldn't have been there, while everyone else manning the execution chamber was gone. A single obstacle to Rostov's sweet release and a return to power—no, an improvement of his prior circumstances and an elevation to the greatest power he had ever known! He felt the adrenaline coursing through his veins, but also a twinge of fear.

"Officer Ross," Rostov said, "what are you doing here?"

"You know what I'm doing here, you son of a bitch," Ross growled back. "I'm here to put an end to you."

"Are you so confident that this is the end of the world that you're willing to ignore the law?" Rostov asked, both stalling for time and genuinely curious. [00:49:38].

There was more than a little time left, but perhaps he could keep the Officer from executing him long enough for someone still interested in following procedures to delay the execution. With other people here, Rostov had a lot of faith in his ability to talk his way out of dying within the next hour. He had all the motivation in the world, after all.

"Everyone in the next room is hearing voices and seeing things," Ross said. "I assume you did too. If it's not the end of something, it's damn close! It's that, or you've doped us all up somehow, and this is when you make your prison break. Either way, you die before that timer runs down!"

"And if the timer means nothing?" Rostov said.

"Then I'll claim temporary insanity!"

Officer Ross grabbed the lever that would power up the chair, and Rostov realized that Ross was neither bluffing nor amenable to persuasion. What had turned him so desperate to see Rostov dead, the death row inmate had no way of knowing. But he couldn't let himself die like this, not with freedom and life and *so much power* right around the corner.

"Help!" he screamed at the top of his lungs. "Officer Ross has lost his mind! He's about to flip the switch! Help! Murder! Help!"

Ross hesitated for a moment at the surprisingly shrill sound of Rostov's shrieking, and Rostov heard the sound of some movement in the distance, somewhere off down the hall. But wherever help was, and whatever help there was, it was far away now, and Ross's hand was on the switch.

A moment later, Rostov heard nothing. He only *felt*. Fifteen hundred volts of electricity surged through his head and legs, and he briefly faded into unconsciousness.

When the darkness passed, Rostov felt a damp cloth on his face.

"W-where am I?" he asked, voice hoarse. "What happened?"

"Oy, he's awake!" called the familiar voice of Barry the corrections officer. The soothing damp cloth pulled away from Rostov's face, and in its place, he was hit with bright, head-splitting light.

He groaned and reached to shield his eyes from the blinding whiteness. Or rather, he tried to raise his hands and shield his eyes, but he found them still bound in wrist restraints.

As his reaction to the sudden burst of light faded, Rostov's vision recovered, and he quickly assessed the room. Its previous occupants were back: two guards and the doctor. One of the guards had restrained Officer Ross, the other was standing near Rostov with the damp cloth, and the doctor was striding toward Rostov.

Rostov immediately checked the timer. [**00:29:56**].

Almost there, almost there, he thought desperately. *Just need them to hold off on executing me for another half hour.* It seemed implausible even as a proposition, considering how eager Officer Ross had been to take the matter into his own hands. Surely these brutal, hard men who brought people here every few months to be killed wouldn't bat an eye at making sure his sentence was carried out, no matter what he said.

Rostov had felt confident in his ability to talk his way out of this before Officer Ross had ignored him and pulled the lever anyway. Now his brain was fried, and he wasn't certain he could even speak coherently.

"We have to put him down *now*! Now, dammit!" Ross's voice cut through the haze in Rostov's brain.

The guard was speaking more quietly, but Rostov could make out the word "procedure." Two more guards appeared in the doorway.

At least they'll keep that madman away from me, Rostov thought. *It would be something to have someone like that on my side, but as an enemy, he's practically feral!*

"The Governor is on the line," one of the new guards pronounced loudly.

He was clutching a small phone, which the guard who had been restraining Ross took. The other two guards now stood carefully between Ross and the electrical equipment. But Rostov was staring at the phone. What was the Governor going to do here?

"Governor Doyle says to go ahead with the execution as scheduled," the guard with the phone said. "We're not to let anything disrupt it."

Fuckfuckfuckfuckfuckfuckfuckfuck!

"Yes!" Ross said. He practically cackled with glee. "You're gonna get everything that's coming to you, you smug son of a bitch!"

The doctor had reached Rostov, and he leaned over him now, pressing his stethoscope to Rostov's chest. The doctor looked to Barry and shrugged.

"He's as ready to be executed as they ever are. Let's not keep Governor Doyle waiting."

Barry looked at Rostov. "Sorry, man. Your time's come. Luck's run out. Any last words, you'd better say 'em now."

Rostov sat numb, exhausted, brains scattered. His ingenuity had completely deserted him.

Barry looked to Ross. "Procedure is fucked anyway. You want to pull the lever?"

Ross just nodded.

"Everything ready?" Barry asked another guard.

A nod from him too.

Ross walked over and put his hands on the lever. He made eye contact with Rostov. His face took on a bittersweet expression, then a look of resigned sobriety. He was about to take a man's life. Then he began to pull the lever—and the lights flickered. And went out.

It took Rostov a moment to realize what was going on.

Praise Moloch, I'm saved! This had to be a literal act of the god. Was Florida's electric grid running off of solar power, perhaps?

His attention was pulled away from the sudden burst of gratitude by the sound of Officer Ross swearing in the dark.

"Shit!" Ross exclaimed.

The lights came back on then.

Ross yanked the lever back up and pulled it down again, but nothing happened.

"Power's out," one of the guards said. "We're running on the generator now. It doesn't produce enough power to run the chair."

"Shit!" Officer Ross repeated. "What can we do?"

"Nothing but wait for the power to come back online," Barry said.

[Ten of your minutes remain!]

Ross sat in stunned defeat. Rostov also sat, strapped in as he was to the chair. He was burned wherever the electrodes touched him and half-mad with relief and joy and incredulity.

He had to restrain the urge to gloat.

He'd been shocked once today already by Ross's desperation to see his sentence carried out. There was no need to add any more tension to the room in these last moments.

And what remained of the timer ticked by in a surreal silence.

CHAPTER THIRTY-TWO

Conflicted

James rushed through the forest as quickly as he reasonably could while retaining some semblance of stealth.

His progress felt unnervingly slow, while the sounds of movement in the trees seemed to be gaining on him. Whenever the branches closer to him began to shake with movement, he headed off in another direction, but the shaking would only return again, more quickly and closer than the previous time.

Eventually, he resolved that he would have to make a stand. His Stamina was scraping the bottom now, and soon he wouldn't be able to so much as move if he kept allowing himself to be chased this way.

James sat down in the middle of a small clearing, as far as he could from any tree cover. He sat cross-legged, and he waited, trying to recover as much Stamina as he could while keeping his senses open. His Mana had been much less devastated by the fighting than his Stamina, so he decided his defensive tactics would have to be purely magical this time until his Stamina could recover. He began Silent Spellcasting, gathering non-elemental Mana.

Even if he couldn't move well right now, he could defend himself with a powerful Mana shield around his body. It felt a bit desperate, hiding behind a barrier, but it would give him room to recover more Stamina and prepare his next spell.

As the Mana built up, he saw the branches ahead of him move. Then the branches to the side moved. Then it seemed as if all the trees around James shook with the weight of the monsters preparing to ambush him.

He swallowed. He wasn't afraid—he wouldn't let some brainless monsters do that to him—but the situation had him on edge. He needed at least another thirty seconds to charge his shield to full power, though ten seconds would do for purposes of having a defense. But it didn't seem as if the enemy was going to give him that.

As if on cue, a half-dozen spiders flung themselves down from the trees in front of James's eyes, and he let his spell loose. The Mana vanished from around him, and he prepared mentally to receive hits to his shield without flinching. He had no intention of moving from this spot before he had to; as long as he sat still, he would slowly recover precious Stamina.

Need more killing techniques that don't burn off a percentage of Stamina every use. It was absurd that someone who had his ridiculous pool of Stamina might die as a result of running out. But it did seem like a credible possibility at the moment.

The spiders moved in on all sides, initially wary of someone who was still coated in the semi-dried blood and guts of their fallen comrades. But they looked like they were gaining confidence with every step.

Should I pray to Apophis? James thought wryly. *Or would that god just squish me for stealing the Chosen One title from whoever he* really *chose? It's not my fault, Apophis. I didn't kill him!*

James winced as a loud noise rang out, and one of the spiders in front of him collapsed. *Oh, that was a good noise!* The other spiders seemed to think that James was the source, and they charged him all at once when the first of them fell. More noises rang out, and two more spiders fell. The remaining three spiders bounced off of James's shield and readied themselves to try again.

James belatedly realized the sound he was hearing was gunfire. And the shots continued. Two more ringing booms, and another spider dropped. The other two continued moving undaunted, indicating the shooter had missed. *Pretty good accuracy so far, though*, James assessed.

And now he moved too. No big motions or techniques. He just drew his crossbow and fired off a shot of his own at one of the surviving spiders, which had turned away from him and was looking off into the woods, trying to locate the source of the shots. The bolt penetrated deep into the hide of the target spi-der. A moment later, a shot rang out, and a chunk of its head exploded.

[Feral Wood Spider, Lv. 5 killed. You gained 8 exp, based on your contri-bution to the fight!]

Some very nice shooting, James thought. *I'll have to thank this person, whoever it is.* It struck him as a little odd that the first person he was running into who was armed with modern weaponry was rescuing him from these monsters. Then again, given how hapless most of the people he'd met thus far seemed in the face of Orientation dangers, it wasn't surprising that one of the more capable people would have a gun. Grabbing a firearm had been James's first reaction to the System informing him of its presence. *Maybe bringing a gun to this place is going to be the giveaway sign of a reliable person in future.*

The last spider died from a final gunshot while James was thinking about how he would thank his savior. He didn't have much in the way of material goods that might be of value unless this person was missing some of the starting equipment. James had multiple sets of that, thanks to his Pillaging of most of the earliest fatalities of the Orientation.

Wait a minute! James realized he had multiple Stamina Potions in his satchel, and he growled quietly to himself. *Ridiculous. I was almost ready to get myself killed over lacking Stamina.*

Without giving the matter any further thought, he took one out and drank it.

[You consumed one Stamina Potion. You restored 50 Stamina!]

That's really not much. They must have been made under the assumption that we would consume all of our starting potions before we had the chance to level up too much. Compared to my total Stamina now, that's pitiful.

A shape emerged through the trees now, and James refocused on that. He knew the person he could see approaching was his savior. The figure looked male. As he got closer, more details became apparent.

White guy, thick glasses, and sandy brown hair that someone cut using a bowl, he assessed. *He looks so goddamn young!* James judged from his attire that the shooter had chosen the Light Warrior Class when he arrived.

As the figure of the stranger became clearer, James realized that the shooter, the man who'd saved him, was just a teenager. *Probably seventeen? Hardly older than Yulia . . .* He had left Yulia and Mina with the guns, but as he saw this teenager striding confidently through the underbrush, he couldn't imagine Yulia having quite the same success as this boy. She was so meek. And yet he was probably only two or three years older than her.

There was something different about him that James couldn't quite define. The teenager was hunting alone, just like James. *I know why I'm out here by myself,* James thought. *But what gives him that boldness? I wonder what kinds of abilities the System gave him.*

The teenager drew close enough for James to see more details of his equipment. He had the starting sword and dagger sheathed at his waist. Over his light armor, the teenager wore a backpack, a rifle on a strap over one shoulder, and in his left hand he held a dark-colored pistol. James was no gun expert. He could not identify it from sight. More importantly, he wondered if this teenager's parents were here and how he had ended up in possession of two guns.

"Hi, there," James said as the young man approached.

The teenager waved awkwardly. "Hello, I'm Tim."

"James," James said. "It's good to meet you. I really appreciate you showing up when you did."

"Oh, I'm glad I could be here when you needed a little help," Tim said. He was in the clearing now, and James wondered when he was going to put away the pistol that he still held in his left hand. Tim seemed to be very conscious of the weapon's presence. Instead of putting it away, he toyed with it, stroking his index finger up and down the slide, as if it excited him to be holding it.

"Not as glad as I am," James said, trying to keep his tone level and ordinary. "I guess you've been faring pretty well in the Orientation, seeing as you've got bullets left."

"Oh, those," Tim said. "Yeah, I'd say I'm doing okay. I actually know how to make my own bullets, though. My father taught me before he passed." Hard to read the emotions in the teen's voice when he said that. Upset? Happy? It was a mystery that James wanted an answer to immediately.

"You know, I almost brought my own gun," James said.

"You should have. This is definitely the place for it! So fucking exciting!" The teenager grinned.

I've been enjoying myself, but I think this guy might have a screw loose. He's way too excited to be here.

"Yeah," James said. "It is kind of exciting. I gave my gun to a family member to take. Probably for the best, really. We didn't have the same last name, so we ended up in different places. Is your family here?"

"Family?" Tim asked. He paused as if trying to remember what that word meant. Then he smiled, just slightly; the corners of his lips turned up for a second before he forcefully repressed it. But James saw.

He might be a problem.

"No, my family's not here," Tim finally managed.

James thought he could guess why.

"Well, maybe there's something I could do to help you," James said.

A surprised look appeared on Tim's face.

"What do you mean?" he asked.

"You're here all on your own," James said. "Surely there are resources you're missing or running low on, and I owe you one. It's okay to ask for help. No one can make it in this place on their own."

"I've been doing just fine all—"

Tim's reply was interrupted by a loud rumbling gastrointestinal noise.

He and James looked at each other awkwardly for a moment before James chuckled.

"So, I guess you're pretty hungry," James said.

"I haven't eaten since around lunchtime yesterday," Tim said, frowning down at his stomach.

They sat around the fire in an uneasy quiet. The sun was setting in the distance, and the temperature was growing correspondingly milder around them. James had coaxed Tim into at least putting away the gun, but it sat within easy reach in the oversized left pocket of Tim's cargo pants. Far enough from his finger on the trigger for James's comfort and close enough to give Tim the sense of security that he needed to relax a little.

Tim had allowed James to "Loot"—really Pillage, but since James didn't speak the Skill name out loud, no one could know that—the bodies of the spiders Tim had killed, saying there was "nothing decent" to get off the spiders anyway. The result was another level in Shed Skin for James.

Over the fire, twigs held four portions of meat on skewers—human meat, since that was all James had and since the offer of food had seemingly pacified his guest. Four portions rather than two, because as soon as James offered to feed Tim, the teenager had insisted that James eat too. A wild look in his eyes convinced James that this was not a request.

The idea of eating human flesh was still disgusting to contemplate, and there was something almost equally horrifying about feeding it to someone else without his knowledge. *But I've crossed worse lines than this already*, he thought. James still remembered the names and the faces of the handful of people he'd killed, as well as those still living who'd tried to kill him.

And be honest, the dark voice in his head chimed in. *You have no intention of stopping. You're not going to back off. You're going to press your foot to the gas if it keeps you alive and makes you stronger.*

James acknowledged that was true. He was ready to spill far more blood than just those few people if it would benefit him and the people he cared about. If he could snap his fingers right then and kill half the people in his Orientation at random, and in return be reunited with his family, he had no doubt in his mind that he would do it.

The System seemed determined to have him eating human meat eventually, just from the abilities it had granted him. *"In for a penny, in for a pound," I think the saying goes? What is it they say human flesh tastes like? Chicken? Pork?*

He was not quite convinced it would taste like anything other than bile in his mouth, but he went on arguing with himself.

The only justification for this taboo, this hesitation, is that humans evolved not to eat other humans, James reasoned. *That was because of social cohesion and because there are diseases that you can get only through cannibalism.* James had researched this after he read the Hannibal Lecter novels as a teenager. *But I'm not hurting anyone, so there's no threat to the strength of my group from me doing this. And the System made me immune to any diseases or other negatives from eating human flesh with the Anthropophagy Skill. So there's no reason to hesitate. I'm just being squeamish. Being a wimp.* Which seemed absurd.

If there's one thing I'm not, it's squeamish.

And eating would help James recover his Stamina more quickly, which was important since low Stamina was the only factor besides the gun that forced

James to consider what Tim thought at all. Tim was not, he guessed, anywhere near as versatile as James was. Tim might be of a similarly high level if he'd been killing things regularly since his arrival, which he probably had been. But even then, he surely wouldn't have the same diverse set of abilities that James had stolen.

It was also possible that James was completely bulletproof now, with his Stats as high as they were, but he didn't believe it—nor did he have any desire right now to test that at close range.

So, the two males sat across from each other in a strained silence, waiting for the meat to cook.

James's Stamina had recovered enough now that if he needed to fight, he could, but he hoped this situation might resolve itself without devolving into violence.

"So, how did you end up in that situation?" Tim asked, suddenly breaking the silence.

"Sorry?" James asked politely. He had been sort of in his own world, conflicted over whether he should try to kill Tim in case he posed a threat in the future or spare him in consideration of the fact that the teenager had arguably saved James's life. He was leaning toward the latter, but he was also keenly aware that Tim might not give him that choice.

CHAPTER THIRTY-THREE

Charm and Harm

How'd you end up being hunted by that gaggle of monsters?" Tim asked. He sounded slightly annoyed at having to repeat himself.

"Oh, *that!*" James chuckled as if it was the funniest story in the world. "I killed a dozen or so of them, and I think the others were attracted by the same smell of burning meat that I used to lure in the first group."

"You were luring them in and hunting?" Tim asked.

James thought he heard a new note in the teenager's voice. Respect?

"Sure," James said. "You have to bring a strategy to these things, after all."

"That does make sense," Tim said. He looked thoughtful. "I guess this place isn't just about strength and superior weapons. The monsters here are a lot like real animals."

James wanted to ask, "What did you think they were?" But he resisted the temptation.

Instead, he said, "The most important game in this place isn't hunting the monsters at all. It's the human factor."

Tim's left hand seemed to inch indecisively toward the gun in his pocket.

"You mean like hunting humans?" he asked. The tone answered James's remaining question. This kid would never be a poker player. It was obvious that this young man was at least interested in hunting humans, whether he had done so already or not.

"No, Tim. I told you, in the long run, you won't be able to survive in this place, in *this world*, on your own. You need to find your tribe. Find your people."

Tim looked a bit downcast at that thought. *I guessed right. He's a real loner, probably can't function easily in a group. Doesn't seem to like eye contact, can't read other people's feelings, has trouble hiding his own emotions. I wonder if he's on the spectrum. Or he's a total psycho, and I'm reading him the exact wrong way. Impossible to be sure.*

"Meat's ready!" James decided. He pulled the skewers away from the fire and handed two to Tim. *Last chance to avoid doing this*, James thought. *Maybe I could pretend to take a bite?* But it wasn't a serious possibility. He looked sideways at Tim, and he saw Tim's eyes staring back at him, waiting for James to take the first bite.

Last chance, and no chance at all, James thought. *Not unless I want to fight him.* And he really didn't. His resources were still only partially restored, but James still thought he could win. He had resources that couldn't be measured by any Stats screen, and Skills and Talents that Tim wouldn't believe.

But with James relatively weak, he didn't feel assured of victory over Tim. The young man was still a somewhat unknown quantity, after all. And for James to be certain, he'd be forced to fight in a way that would ensure that one of them would die. Whatever Tim's faults, and James had his ideas about what those might be, Tim had been nothing but helpful to James so far. He didn't want to kill the kid, even if Tim might be out here hunting humans.

No one had been killed, as far as James knew. He thought of Sierra. *Maybe I'm collecting strays, leaving people alive willy-nilly like this. Strays that might fight beside me one day, and just as well bite me the next, depending on the circumstances. Useful strays so far, I think, but still.*

James took a big bite of the meat on the skewer. *No point in doing things by halves.*

The meat tasted disturbingly *good*. It really was like pork. Fattier, juicier, and more tender than the wolf meat had been. On some level, James realized that this was another possibility he had been quietly afraid of. *I could get used to this.* He chewed the food slowly and finally swallowed the bite.

[Consumed the flesh of Mage Rachel Roper!]
[Resources will be restored more quickly while you absorb the flesh.]
[Sufficient experience accrued. Anthropophagy leveled up!]

Of course it did. Since he had never used it before, it had been at level zero, where he'd hoped to leave it.

Beside him, Tim began biting into his share of the meat as soon as he saw that James had swallowed the portion he bit.

"This is delicious," Tim said. James saw the meat juice dripping down Tim's chin and knew he meant it. "What kind of meat is it, anyway?"

"Oh, it's pork," James said. *More specifically, long pig.*

"Could we have some more?" Tim asked after finishing one portion.

"Sure, why not?" James said, shrugging. *I've already crossed the line once. What's a few more portions?* He prepared and threw another few skewers on the fire.

"Hey, if you don't manage to find your tribe," James said, "you can look for me after we get back from this place. I'm going to get as many people together as I can."

"Why?" Tim asked.

"You mean, why am I doing that, or why you?"

"Both!"

James thought about all his knowledge of the System so far, his half-finished theories and partially baked plans, before answering. He hadn't needed to articulate much about why he was pursuing his course of action to anyone yet. Not that his group wasn't interested, but they were normal people, and he knew his line of thought was somewhat outlandish compared to the normal mode of thinking. He decided to share a little of where his mind was at with Tim, just to bounce ideas off of someone.

"The world order is going to collapse completely," James said. "The descent of the System onto Earth is going to destroy every government. A complete breakdown of law and order." The next part of his explanation hinged on his understanding of Tim's character. "For people like you and me, people who are good at surviving and keeping our heads together in an emergency, this breakdown is a big opportunity. New countries will probably be carved out in the aftermath. New countries means new leaders. There will be wars, chaos, hunger, brutal behavior. But for the survivors, for the winners, it's a chance to remake the world their way. But no one can do that by themselves. You really need people. As for why I like you, specifically? I think I see something in you that would make you a good addition to the group. You're a good shot with those guns. You clearly have some survival skills. It would be good to add someone to my team who carries his own weight consistently. And you almost definitely have Skills and Talents I don't even know about yet." He delivered that last with a friendly grin.

"If you don't think the other members of your team can carry their weight, why bother with them?" Tim asked. "You said individuals can't make it on their own, but you think you can make it carrying other people?"

"They're pretty good most of the time, even if I'm ragging on them a bit to you. They're definitely more beneficial than troublesome, or at least most of them are."

"Fair enough, I guess." Tim looked like he was thinking hard about James's prediction of the future.

He probably hasn't thought much beyond the next meal since he got here, James assessed. *If as far as that.*

"And you were saying you'd like me to join?" Tim finally asked.

"You're an ideal candidate in many ways. If not for one problem, I would be actively pursuing you to join me right now."

"What problem?" Tim asked. It didn't escape James that now, as with every time they seemed to hit a snag in the conversation, Tim's hand seemed to slip, of its own accord, a bit closer to the gun in his pocket.

"Be honest with me, Tim," James said. "You've been out here on your own the last few days. Have you been hunting just monsters? Or also people?"

Tim's body visibly tensed at the question.

"I'm not accusing you," James reassured. "Just asking. I've killed a few people here myself." *In self-defense, but that's not an important detail right now.*

"What if I have?" Tim replied.

"Well, I recently met up with a nice Hispanic family," James said. "Lovely people. They seem to like me well enough, and they're the reason why I decided to clear the forest of its spider problem. But if you're a human hunter, I can't help but wonder if you might pose any kind of a threat to them, either because you like hunting people or because you'll have made enemies who will eventually associate us with whatever you've been up to for the last couple of days. As much as I'd like to work with you in the future, I don't want to create risks for my people."

"I see. So, you're not interested. You're more concerned with keeping the group happy." Tim sounded disappointed and frustrated. Then his tone shifted. "And if I did happen to accidentally go after someone from your group going forward? Like, say, a member of this family?"

James used a Predator's Strike movement to get within touch range of Tim faster than the teenager could possibly have reacted, and he grabbed the teenager by the area between shoulder and neck that wasn't covered by armor. Predator's Armaments made his nails temporarily into knives, and James grabbed the unprotected skin tightly in his blade-nails.

"Tim, I might take that kind of thing personally, especially seeing as I fed you and treated you so hospitably," James said, squeezing with his hand until he drew little rivulets of blood from the pale skin. "If someone is one of my people, I protect them. I'm sure you can understand. In the event that I fail to protect them, I would at the very least *avenge* whatever is done to them. That would also apply to you, should you and I establish some similar relationship in the future.

"That possibility is part of why I've been fairly friendly to you. But please don't mistake my friendliness for weakness. I could have killed you anytime I wanted since we've been sitting together, including while you were holding that pistol you like so well. I didn't because I appreciated your help, and I like you and might want you to join up with me when it's more practical. Not because you pose a threat to me. You don't."

"Right. My m-m-mistake," Tim stammered, face contorted in pain. His hand—the one that he might have used to go for his gun—was stuck in midair, frozen in indecision between his desire to clutch at his shoulder and his fear that any movement might be perceived as resistance by James.

He's a big pussycat, James thought. *Scary hunter from range but can't take being squeezed a little bit from close up. I bet he hasn't been injured since he got here. Has he even allowed any of his prey to see him up close?*

This gave James another idea. He released Tim's shoulder and stepped back.

"Say, do you know if any of these people you may have hunted would have seen you before, when you were hypothetically hunting them? Or were you too far away for that?"

"Can't be sure," Tim said, hand clasped to his little shoulder wounds now. "I try not to be seen when I'm PKing, but when people seem helpless, and I think I have the edge, sometimes I get a little overexcited and wind up a little too close."

"PKing?"

"Oh, player killing."

James struggled mightily and mostly succeeded in keeping a look of intense annoyance from coming across on his face. Fortunately, Tim seemed to be distracted by his shoulder pain for the microsecond before James contained the emotion. *Does this moron really think this place is some kind of game? Player killing, my ass! These people have families.* He had to remind himself that Tim could prove useful precisely because he was the kind of person who would willingly do these things to people. While James himself might suffer some minor pangs of conscience, here he had a sociopath who he could perhaps use as his assassin; a knife in the darkness for when James himself needed some fellow human dead. *It would be a waste to kill him now. Right?*

As he relaxed to consider the question for a moment, a wave of notifications hit.

[Sufficient experience accrued. Emotional Control leveled up!]

[Sufficient experience accrued. Persuasion leveled up!]

[Required conditions met. Skill unlocked: Intimidation!]

[Sufficient experience accrued. Politician leveled up!]

[Sufficient experience accrued. System-Boosted Human leveled up!]

He felt a sense of satisfaction as the alerts appeared before he sent them away. *Yes, he's worth it*, James decided.

He stretched out a hand toward Tim. The teenager's eyes widened, and he raised the hand not clasped to his shoulder as if to fend off an attack. Before Tim could do anything else to defend himself, though, Healing Aura bathed him in its gentle green glow.

"Oh, you can heal," Tim said. He sounded confused.

"Yeah, I know it's weird. I have a few different special abilities." James kept it vague. The less Tim understood James's powers, the more impressive they would seem. So James wouldn't give too much information. Tim would be tough enough to manage—Politician leveling up was proof enough of that—and controlling the information he could obtain on James's strengths and weaknesses was just a basic precaution when handling an untrustworthy prospective ally. "I figured since I made those little cuts to prove a point, I should also erase them myself." James tried to smile benevolently, though he suspected he looked like a cat eyeing a canary.

"Thanks," Tim said. He smiled tightly in return.

"I really do hope you and I run into each other again at a more appropriate time," James added.

"Right," Tim said, rising. He could tell he was being dismissed, and in truth, he felt lucky to be allowed to leave. He could feel the truth of what James had said. *I wasn't a threat at all.*

If those nails—those *claws*—of his had aimed just a few inches the other way, James could have just as easily torn Tim's throat out.

Although the sun was below the horizon, and he would have to find his own place to camp alone now as he had the previous night, Tim was happy just to stay alive. If James really meant all that he'd said, then he had assessed Tim, decided that Tim was a potential threat to James's group, *and* concluded that he could kill Tim. But then James had, by some logic alien to Tim, determined that Tim was worth sparing. That sounded like astronomical luck to Tim.

I need to be a lot stronger, Tim thought as he walked away. *Next time I see him, there won't be any possibility that he could casually kill me.*

After all, this new world was meant to be a playground for special people like Tim. That was what the Keres who'd blessed him had said, and Tim believed it.

CHAPTER THIRTY-FOUR

Open Season

*W*ell, *I'm sure the decision to spare him won't have any consequences later,* James thought a little uneasily.

He had weighed whether to mention his wife and sister-in-law to the probable murderer as people who were under his protection, but ultimately decided against it. Tim's future course of action was just too unpredictable. The teenager seemed just as likely to go after James with a grudge later as to become a useful asset one day, and he really didn't want to bring that possibility home to his family.

You're being too nice, his dark inner voice chided. But James thought he'd handled the situation as well as possible.

If he goes after my group, that's unfortunate, but I'll just make an example of him so that it doesn't happen again. Put his head on a spike or something. At some point, violent interhuman conflict is inevitable, and it won't be any worse if he's the perpetrator versus someone else. He did feel a little guilty about letting the potential threat live, but killing off all possible threats to the group wasn't a mission he'd taken on. *I at least put the fear of God into him.*

For now, he needed to make camp. His Stamina should be fully restored after a good night's sleep. But first, he needed to make sure he could sleep safely. This was his first night sleeping alone in the Orientation and also his first night sleeping in what he considered enemy territory. He had been underground the first time. An idea suddenly struck him.

Underground! That's where I should camp out!

He had spent the first night in a pit, and he had easily gotten out of that. And while his Stamina was relatively dear since he spent huge chunks of it at a time whenever he fought, his Mana pool was very nearly full at the moment.

James began Silent Spellcasting.

Once an extravagant amount of Mana was charged, he began excavating. He dug out a deep hole, and he chose to direct the digging almost straight down, just like the pit he'd slept in on that first night. The dirt he scattered as widely as he could, to disguise what he had done. The forest floor for around a twenty-foot radius was dusted with a thin powder of dirt, little enough that he felt neither humans nor intelligent beasts were likely to be tipped off as to what had happened.

Then he began tearing thin branches off of nearby trees until he had a pile big enough to thinly cover and disguise the pit. He charged wind Mana briefly, then leaped into the hole and used the wind to pull the branches over it, covering the pit over almost completely. With the darkness above, James could hardly see from the bottom of the pit whether there were any gaps in the pile, but that was fine. Looking down at the pile, any predator looking to see if any prey lived beneath it would have the same problem he was having. It was pitch dark inside the pit. Perfect for concealment and for sleep.

James charged earth Mana again, and he made a series of pointed spikes emerge diagonally from the walls of the pit, long and thin, sharp enough to violently deter anything that might want to come down looking for him. After he had made a half-dozen rows of what amounted to earthen pikes sticking out of the walls, he got a notification.

[Required conditions met. Innate Talent unlocked: Earth Affinity!]

Neat. So, water and earth came naturally, and I acquired fire. It probably said something deep about his nature, which elements he had affinity for naturally, but for now, he was just sleepy. *I think I've done everything I reasonably can to defend against home invaders.*

With that last comforting thought, James trusted in his plan, made himself as comfortable as he could at the bottom of the pit, and went to sleep.

He was out in no time at all. He'd always been good at conking out as soon as his head hit the pillow, but lately, he was impressing himself with his ability to fall asleep peacefully on cold, hard, inhospitable ground.

However he managed it, James slept peacefully for some hours. He wasn't sure how many, but he could tell from the light when he woke that it must be early morning. He wondered what had awakened him. He felt tense, as if he'd been awakened by some sort of fight or flight response. As he questioned why he was awake and what was giving him that feeling, a droplet of liquid plopped against his cheek. The droplet felt thick and trickled slowly down the side of his face, and James immediately intuited that it was not the morning dew.

He smelled the air and confirmed that the droplet—or something else very close to his head—smelled like blood. He looked up, and he saw a large shape impaled upon the spikes he'd made. It was moving faintly against the dim morning light, and he gradually made out its features as he stared.

It was a large deer. Maybe not large for the System-altered world, but large given James's experience. It groaned quietly in pain, but it seemed to be too weak to try and extricate itself from its situation. It also lacked the necessary limbs to pull against gravity and free itself.

James quickly decided to mercy kill this creature. He drew his Wolfbone Dagger, and in one smooth motion, he slashed the beast's throat. Blood spurted all over James's face, and he wished for a moment that he had thought to climb out of the pit and approach the beast from above. The damage was done now, though, and the buck stopped bleeding surprisingly quickly. It turned out that Tarantino movies did not accurately represent what arterial blood spatter looked like.

An alert appeared.

[You killed Big Buck Reindeer, Lv. 9. You gained 200 exp!]

Nice! More than the spider of the same level, without nearly the same level of trouble. Pillage!

The buck's body glowed, and the familiar notifications began appearing. He selected Stats to steal.

[Big Buck Reindeer's body processed.]

[You obtained Reindeer Leggings, 5x Reindeer Meat Bundle, and a Big Antler Spear!]

[2 Points of Agility gained!]

James found himself in possession of a pair of smooth deerskin pants, which he immediately put on. They were almost criminally comfortable. He now had more—and probably better quality—meat than any wolf had ever given him. And the weapon took the form of a long, multi-pronged spear made of beautiful, smooth cream-colored bone.

Holy crap, that loot's amazing! Plus, I don't have to eat more human flesh if I get hungry! And I did literally no work for it besides digging this pit. That last was the lesson James took from this random act of the System. The deer falling into his hole and impaling itself was not only a lucky stumble into a better class of prey. It was a revelation. It was time for James to embrace a new way of hunting.

He spent the remaining hour before the sun came up the rest of the way, along with the next few hours afterward, chopping down trees and transforming them into weapons. He magically dug a trench and then filled it with sharpened stakes pointing straight up. He covered the trench with a thin layer of dirt and grass, strong enough to support itself but weak enough that any impact would cave it in. He used twigs from one tree to cover his sleeping pit back up as if nothing had stumbled into it yet, and he re-sharpened the spikes that had dulled slightly from impaling the deer.

The move he was proudest of was when he embedded a dozen Spiderknives into a log, tied that log to a tree with rope, and stuck the log in another tree, such that the log would swing toward the tree it was tied to as soon as James gave it a push. He chose trees positioned so that the log would swing toward enemies who had avoided the other traps.

The log was so heavy that James had to use his gravity magic for the first time. After a few failed attempts, he was able to make the log light enough to be secured in the branches of the tree where he wanted to set his trap. James had to cast the gravity magic over the log again periodically, to avoid any accidents, but the sheer difficulty level of making this trap made him all the prouder. He was also pleased to level up his gravity magic Skill twice.

Basically, James did everything he remembered ever seeing in a *Predator* or *Rambo* movie, in his own way and with his own equipment and Skills. With magic and superhuman Strength and Agility assisting him, it was done by midday.

The next step was to supply the trap with real bait. Remembering how he had lured in the spiders, he placed multiple bundles of human meat on the ground beside the pit trap with brush nearby, and he lit the brush on fire.

Finally, James positioned himself in the tree the big log sat in, and he charged wind Mana. Just like before, he used the wind as subtly as he could to spread the smell of the slowly cooking meat all around the clearing, gradually spreading outward. Then he drew his crossbow again, prepared it, and waited.

And waited.

Waited some more.

Waited with his body as still as he could make it—unnaturally, impossibly quiet. Pulse slowed down to an impossible degree. Almost dead, or so he would have seemed to anything that happened to look.

Waited flat as a board, pressed against the tree until he felt as if it were a part of him.

Waited until the elapsed time seemed to fade into a single, endless moment, the only notable movement the sun in the sky.

Until the first creatures came.

It seemed he was still in spider country because the first movements his senses picked up were the telltale signs of them that he had grown used to: spiders shaking the branches of distant trees.

James remained unmoving, watched for them to grow closer. Finally, as they approached the bait, he saw two spiders fling themselves from the trees into the clearing. As they fell through the air, James sighted, aimed, and fired once from the crossbow. He had just enough time to reload before they landed. The targeted spider curled in on itself, writhing in apparent pain, pierced through the first joint, between head and body. The other spider turned to look at the first, and in that moment, as it turned away, James dropped the crossbow and threw himself upon it.

He drew his dagger as he fell, and he landed right on top of the creature. There was a rapid flurry of stabbing and biting, and the spider fell down dead. No special techniques this time. Hardly any Stamina used. And as for the biting, James used Shed Skin and recovered instantly from the surface wounds.

Pillaging the two spiders' bodies gave him more of the same equipment the other spiders had furnished, plus more experience for Shed Skin. Then James returned to the tree and perched himself in the same spot once more.

The next time the wait wasn't nearly as long.

James sensed ground-level creatures coming, approaching from a direction that would cause them to pass right over the covered trench. He began charging Mana.

As the creatures came into view—a half-dozen wolves—James unleashed his earth Mana and pulled the thin covering of earth off of the trench. The wolves, unable to stop their forward momentum in time, found themselves careening into the ditch full of sharpened stakes.

Not all were impaled, but as the two survivors came over the lip of the trench, looking mad as hell, James ended them with crossbow bolts to the eye and throat, respectively.

James Pillaged the wolves, reset the earth atop the trench, and returned to his tree to wait again.

The pattern continued for the full afternoon; James slaughtered dozens more creatures by the time the sun began to draw near the horizon. It was the most productive day of hunting he'd ever had, by far. Although no further spiders appeared after the first pair, James killed more wolves, some big green monkeys with pink faces that Identify labeled as Monster Macaques, and some ugly giant birds that Identify called Riot Roosters. He gained a level in Predator in Human Skin, though it was extremely notable how much more slowly the levels were coming. It took a different quantity of the same level of beasts to see an increase now.

James was thinking he should probably make a different plan to hunt down the remainder of the spiders at this point, when the ground began to shake. It was clear another creature was coming, and James returned to his hiding place, prepared his crossbow with another bolt, and waited again for the prey to come to him.

Shortly, he saw a pair of great antlers followed by a massive, fur-covered body.

CHAPTER THIRTY-FIVE

A Family Affair

The Orientation sun cast its warm glow over the leaves above Sierra's head. She found the yellow-green glow to be surprisingly beautiful for such a deadly place. There was peace in it.

But maybe it seemed more beautiful than ordinary sunlight simply because, for once, she had time to stop and reflect. She wasn't rushing toward anything, she wasn't hiding from anyone, and she certainly wasn't getting ready for a fight.

How many days have I been here now? she questioned, still a bit sleepy. *I thought I'd probably be dead by now, honestly. Not outliving*—but she refused to complete the thought. She refused to let her mind dwell on her brother.

I'm still here, a little voice in her mind asserted. David's voice.

Not like you're supposed to be. Not in the flesh, next to—I mean—I can't right now, okay? she replied in her thoughts. There had been times when she'd answered back to the sound of her brother's voice inside her head, instead of ignoring it or pushing it off. But today she wanted to try quieting it.

"It's okay to talk to yourself, as long as you don't answer back," their mother used to say. Once upon a time, that line had been funny. Now Sierra actually had a voice in her head. A semi-wanted voice, but she was ambivalent about it.

There had been moments, particularly right after James annihilated her first group, when David's voice had been a lifeline in her head. And then there were long periods, hours at a stretch, when his presence went dormant. But now, when she heard David talking in her head, it made Sierra feel a little crazy. It was hard to be sure if it was real or just something she wanted to believe in. She hoped it was the Talent that she and David shared.

Sierra pulled the ability's description up again, just to make sure it was still there.

[Conjoined Souls: As you were twins in the womb, sharing blood and vital matter, so your twin souls are joined in life. Your Mana pools, abilities, and souls are linked to your twin's forever.]

It's the same. Exactly the same. Not just in my head.

She sighed and shook her head. *There are a million things I should be doing right now instead of worrying about my sanity. While James is away, this is my opportunity to endear myself to his group. If I can't find a way to ingratiate myself with them, I can at least make myself useful to the Rodriguezes.*

She didn't relish the possibility of parting ways with James's group in favor of staying with the Rodriguez family in the future. There were too many unknowns.

To start with, she had slept on what had happened between James and Chava Rodriguez, and she now firmly suspected that Chava had used a Skill of some sort to get James to agree to go and hunt the spider colony alone in the woods. James's behavior following their conversation felt too inconsistent with the person she had observed over the previous days.

For anyone but him, the hunt would be a suicide mission. Sierra had seen him fight, so she had no reason to expect that he would be defeated. But she didn't think he would have taken on a task so large alone. It presented too great a risk of death, and he had plenty of people who would gladly fight alongside him. He didn't strike her as the selfless hero type.

Therefore, the answer had to be that Chava possessed some kind of mental influence Skill. It wasn't so far-fetched with everything else she'd seen thus far; she had already reached the conclusion that James had such a Skill himself.

Having reached this conclusion, she didn't like the idea of belonging to a camp led by someone who had used mental manipulation to send someone to what he surely believed was his likely demise. So, she found herself in the strange position of hoping sincerely for James's safe return.

In case he didn't survive, she would do her best to prepare for her survival in the post-James world, but the best thing for her would be a triumphant return that would hopefully knock Chava on his ass. The next best option would be to stick with the party after James's death and persuade them that Chava was bad news. And third best would be sticking with the Rodriguezes and hoping she didn't draw Chava's negative attention.

Sierra rose from her sitting position. She had a tentative plan for the day: begin to weave herself into the Cliff-Alan-Mitzi circle of trust.

She walked around the camp for a few minutes, exchanging waves and smiles with Rodriguez family members, until she figured out where the three had gone. They were all better morning people than her, and they had apparently decided not to waste the daylight.

Sierra found them all standing at one of the very edges of camp. They were training, and she stood at a distance, watching them, for a short while.

Mitzi was throwing her usual fireballs, aiming them into the ground, the tree stumps the Rodriguezes had left when they cleared part of the forest to make their camp, and occasionally the air. Based on what Sierra observed, it looked like she was trying to increase her casting speed.

Alan and Cliff were sparring, embarrassing though it looked to Sierra. Cliff wasn't as old as Alan, but she still saw two old men slowly swinging sticks back and forth at each other. Cliff was a bit quicker and stronger, but he seemed to moderate his attacks for Alan's benefit.

It was interesting, Sierra noticed, that Alan seemed to be taking the spar so seriously.

Is he trying to get some kind of combat Skill? Sierra questioned. Not for the first time, she wondered if it was possible for Healers like her and Alan to obtain close combat Skills. It wasn't something she had necessarily needed to worry about, ever since she realized that she retained David's magic after his death.

But since she didn't want to use that right now—and didn't want to answer the inevitable questions that her unique Skill would raise—learning how to fight up close could be very valuable.

At the least, it would bring her a step closer to catching up to James.

Then Sierra's eyes widened.

In the short time she had been with James's party, she had only ever seen Mitzi use fire magic. But now she saw the older woman glow a pale-yellow color and then throw a small bolt of lightning from her hand.

Maybe Mitzi has a second elemental affinity, she thought. *Did she just realize, or has she been keeping it a secret?*

But Alan and Cliff's reactions told the story.

"My goodness! You did it!" Alan cried.

"Congratulations, Mitzi!" Cliff said, grinning.

Their reactions made Sierra feel less like she was an interloper kept out of the loop on these issues, but she still noticed a hollow sensation in the pit of her stomach.

It wasn't hunger, although the food had been sparse enough in the camp that morning. No, she missed that kind of closeness, the camaraderie that the three elders shared. Her own group hadn't been particularly close, but at least she'd had her brother.

The only way out is through, she told herself. *Make your community here, among these people.* They all seemed good enough. Better than Kurt. Even James cleared that low bar.

Sierra stepped out of the line of tents and walked toward the trio.

"Hey, guys, can I train with you?" she asked.

"Of course you can!" Mitzi said.

Alan nodded and smiled.

Cliff looked the least pleased of the three of them, a bit like he'd swallowed a lemon. But he covered it quickly and then smiled and nodded too.

And once Sierra ignored Cliff's reaction, she had a surprisingly good time.

The old people were surprisingly able to endure a long period of sustained exercise, and Sierra, who hadn't done anything strenuous that morning up until the sparring session, found herself drenched with sweat in no time. And yet they continued for hours!

It was like that one time she'd joined David for hot yoga, and by the end, she felt almost ready to pass out. Except that these people weren't her fit brother. They were senior citizens!

"How?" she managed toward the end, when the four were taking a breather.

Alan and Mitzi looked at her curiously. Cliff had gone off through the tree line to relieve himself in the woods.

"How can you guys do that?" Sierra asked once she'd caught her breath a bit more. "Continue exercising like that with only short breaks for so long?"

The old couple exchanged glances, and then Alan smiled.

"Well, the Tutorial was very useful," he said. "Learned all about the impact of the different Stats. Stamina helps a lot. It's like a second lease on life." He sounded proud of having figured it all out.

"You mean, it was mostly useful to me," Mitzi corrected, grinning.

"I have asked my wife for a few tips since we got here," Alan amended, crossing his arms slightly.

"The System Homunculus spent a lot of time working with me, explaining how the different Stats and abilities work," Mitzi went on. "He was very patient about answering all of my questions."

"Yes, I probably should have asked some more," Alan said. He sounded slightly embarrassed now.

"Well, you did the most important thing and got him to explain how to use your healing," Mitzi said, mollifyingly. "Where would we be without that?"

They have such a cute dynamic, Sierra thought. *I want that someday.* But there was something specific Mitzi had said that caught her attention.

"That's weird," Sierra said. "How long did the Homunculus spend with you guys?"

"Oh, hours and hours," Mitzi said.

Alan looked at her strangely.

"Wait, I had assumed you just used your time more efficiently than me when you were telling me about it," he said. "I only got an hour, tops."

Sierra's lip curled in annoyance. "That's still longer than David and I got." Her mind ran back over the events of the Tutorial, which had been shared between the twins.

It had been shorter than either Alan or Mitzi's, and she realized now why that was. *It was my fault. Who else would be dumb enough to piss off the stupid Homunculus?*

Alan and Mitzi turned to Sierra, and their expressions morphed into ones of concern. Sierra realized that her face was conveying far more emotion than she'd intended to show as her thoughts wandered away from the topic she'd asked about. There was a rising heat and pressure in her forehead, and she forced herself to turn away from the old couple.

"Thanks for training with me, guys!" she called over her shoulder. "Let's do it again soon. I've got to go help the Rodriguezes with something!"

She almost ran from the spot, and once she was out of sight, she returned to the tent, curled up inside her sleeping bag, and lay holding herself until the wave of regret had subsided.

In the darkness of the tent and sleeping bag, Sierra lay alone with her thoughts. David's voice trying to reassure her that it wasn't her fault. Her wish that this horrible Orientation could turn out to be just a dream. She eventually pulled herself out of her funk by reminding herself of the purpose she had set for herself that morning.

I've already made some progress befriending Alan and Mitzi, she thought. *Now I'll try and make myself useful to the Rodriguez camp.* It would at least make a good distraction from her own thoughts.

She walked back out into the common space of the camp. The sun was already drawing low in the sky. *I sulked for a long time.* It would feel like she had wasted those hours, but it wasn't as if there were a lot of chores for her to perform.

Then again, there were a number of people performing work outside of the tents. She observed the same sorts of daily household maintenance tasks that she'd seen them working at when she and the others had first arrived at the Rodriguez camp. Something felt slightly different about it, but it took Sierra a moment to put her finger on what it was.

It's mostly women doing chores this time, she realized. *In fact*—she studied the faces of the figures at work—*it's only women and teenagers!*

Sierra approached the nearest person, a short thirty-something woman with a prominent nose.

"Hey, um—"

"Karla," the woman supplied.

"Karla," Sierra repeated. "Nice to meet you. I'm Sierra." She smiled tentatively.

Karla gave her a winning smile in return.

"Nice to meet you too," Karla said. "What's up?"

"I was just wondering, where did all the men go?" Sierra asked glancing around the campsite.

Karla frowned, though it didn't feel like it was directed at Sierra. "They're out hunting. Chava sent them to look for meat."

"None of the women?" Sierra asked. She barely kept herself from rolling her eyes.

Before Karla could answer, both women heard a rustling sound in the trees. They turned their heads, and they saw the hunters returning from the forest. The result of the hunting expedition was obvious from their downcast expressions. Four of the men carried one of their fellows between them. One of the four was Ramon, Sierra noticed. She felt vaguely glad that the person whose name she knew wasn't hurt. The last two men walked closely together, one clearly leaning heavily on the other.

Jesus, that *clearly didn't go well.*

As Sierra watched, she realized Karla had disappeared from next to her. The woman was rushing forward, flinging herself into the midst of the hunters, and finally clutching at the arm of the man who lay prone suspended between the other four.

"Javier!" she cried. "What happened to him?"

Sierra approached close behind, aware she might be able to lend some help.

She was close enough to hear what Ramon said, though he muttered it almost under his breath.

"The spiders got him."

If they didn't get beyond spider territory, Sierra thought, *there's no chance they actually got any of the meat Chava sent them for.*

Pushing that idea aside, she pushed past the men and Karla and activated her ability. She could see from the rise and fall of his chest that the badly wounded Javier was still alive. Perhaps she could save him.

Laying on Hands!

CHAPTER THIRTY-SIX

Fear and Loathing

The last big beast to appear was another huge buck reindeer like the first James had seen that day. As it approached, it periodically sniffed the air as if it were pulled in by a smell.

James recalled the meat smell he'd magically spread earlier. *Et tu, Rudolph? Do even herbivores eat meat now?*

After a moment, he thought, *Probably. Our world is thoroughly screwed. We're probably going to need to bring back walled cities when we return to Earth.*

He continued watching the reindeer, which kept slowly approaching his position. It wasn't entirely clear at first, but gradually, as it drew closer, James realized that this buck was even larger than the one he had slain early that morning.

Unlike that buck, which had fallen into his pit unexpectedly, James was able to spy on this one and try to make some headway toward figuring out why its fellow had come near his pit in the first place. This buck leaned down and appeared to be eating the fallen twigs that James had used to cover his pit. *So, not a carnivore?* James thought. He would still like to keep giant reindeer out of his future community, but at least he probably didn't need to worry about deer trying to eat people. *But if it doesn't eat meat, why did it come here in particular? Maybe it's an omnivore?*

James couldn't really see much because the sheer bulk of the reindeer's body was in his line of sight, so he couldn't even tell if the reindeer was actually munching on vegetation or just standing still, body bent low, for some reason.

From what he could see, though, it seemed the creature must be enjoying those twigs quite a bit, as it stayed in that position with its head pointed down toward the pit for a relatively long while. Unfortunately, unlike its predecessor, it seemed to understand that there was a drop-off there, and this reindeer avoided falling into the pit. *Smarter than your friend.*

That was all right, though, because moving around the pit put the buck right in the path of the suspended log trap that James had not yet had the chance to use.

As the reindeer moved into the ideal target position, James pushed the log, dispelled the gravity magic that had made it lighter, and activated the Skill Wolf's Bite, which he had only rarely had the chance to use before.

[Wolf's Bite: A fierce attack with any pointed, penetrating weapon(s). If more than one pointed object strikes, attack may deal crush damage as well as penetration damage. Activation cost of 20% of maximum Stamina. Cooldown of 30 seconds. Effect scales with Strength and Will. If more than one penetrating point strikes the target, damage also scales with number of penetrating points.]

This was the sort of abuse of that Skill that James had always imagined implementing. He was using pointed, penetrating weapons; there were a dozen knives embedded in the log. If the log did some kind of enhanced crush damage as a result of having all those blades embedded in it, James could imagine the huge piece of wood turning that reindeer into a furry, red smear on the trunk of the opposite tree. He eagerly watched to see what would happen as the log impacted.

The attack hit right in the reindeer's flank and absolutely pulverized the buck, slamming it into the other tree and pinning it with seemingly all but two of the many knives penetrating its body. James hopped down for a closer look and saw that the buck's ribs had been mostly caved in on one side by the log. Blood dripped from the side of its mouth, and the creature looked half-dead to James's eyes.

But as he stepped closer, and the beast saw him, the buck's eyes changed. The dull, half-dead stare turned wild. Then the buck made a loud roaring noise, and its legs pushed off the ground, pushing its body against the log, trying to get free. Pushing in James's direction.

"Good luck, pal," James said. "That was the biggest tree I could find. I couldn't get that thing up into the branches without using gravity magic, and my Strength Stat is probably higher than any other human out here. Even if you were a magical, flying reindeer, you couldn't escape."

As if in response to James's taunting, the reindeer gritted its teeth and seemed to push even harder. Before James's disbelieving eyes, the heavy weight slowly moved off of the massive body, and then, with a sudden forceful push, it moved back toward James.

"What the f—"

The creature roared, cutting him off. Then it turned its head, ignoring its bleeding wounds, and used its antlers to shove the log toward James.

"Crap!" James ducked and darted away, slipping underneath the log and crab walking, his back to the ground, toward the once-more-covered trench.

Then a bloody hoof came down on his right arm. At once, the reindeer stopped him fleeing and began crushing the arm under its full weight. His vambrace shattered instantly under the pressure.

James cried out in pain. The agony was exquisite, even through Pain Resistance. He was impossibly strong and durable for a human of his level. Otherwise, his arm would have snapped like a twig already, as it had days before.

But he still couldn't move the arm away, struggle though he did. As the reindeer slowly pressed more and more weight down, James could feel the bone inch closer and closer to breaking. He gritted his teeth, endured the pain, and scrambled with his left hand for the Wolfbone Dagger that was sheathed on his left side.

He was focused on drawing that weapon when the other front hoof came down on his chest, right above his heart. James felt a sudden horrible *pop*, and his chest armor shattered under the mighty hoof. A rib cracked instantly as the hoof directly struck his chest, and he coughed and wheezed, his lungs violently compressed under the pressure. His heart didn't feel so good either. He could feel his pulse race and slow, bouncing back and forth between speeding up and slowing down unsteadily.

Still, James maintained his deadly focus. His left hand pulled the dagger out of its sheath, then rose up and shoved the dagger with all the force he could muster into the leg that was crushing his chest. He stabbed the reindeer mechanically, over and over, unable to direct his movements very precisely in his current condition. He was painfully aware that the situation had turned deadly and that he couldn't stop stabbing if he wanted to live.

With every second he endured the beast's crushing weight on his chest, his breath became feebler, shallower, more ragged, and more of a struggle.

What the hell is this reindeer? What did I do to provoke this level of rage?

Suddenly, a droplet of red liquid hit James's face. The deer was still bleeding from its wounds. His sense of smell pulled him away from the present moment, as he recalled how he'd woken up that morning. Woken by being drizzled with blood that smelled just like the blood that was dripping on him now. Was it possible that this stupid beast could tell he had killed one of its brethren? He thought of how much bigger this one was, how fierce it was.

Was that deer I killed earlier its kid or something? I should've taken a bath between kills and got rid of the smell! Part of him wanted to laugh, though perhaps that was his brain's low-oxygen way of softening the likelihood of imminent death.

Although he had begun reflecting on the reasons for the reindeer's ferocity, James never stopped stabbing and slashing at the leg that was crushing his rib cage. There was no way this conflict would be settled by dialogue after all, even if he understood the beast's motivations.

Finally, with a mighty swing fueled by adrenaline and desperation, he severed the targeted leg below the knee. He sucked in a deep breath reflexively with the pressure finally mostly gone, only for the air to be forcefully pushed out of his lungs again as the full weight of the reindeer collapsed on top of him. The open hole in the reindeer's stump of a leg gushed blood all over him.

The reindeer moaned in pain from atop James, and it tried unsuccessfully to sweep down on James with its antlers, but it lacked the flexibility to reach the human who was pinned under its chest.

James managed to land a couple of decent stabs into its guts despite being pinned down, but he lacked the space to move and launch a really significant blow.

He tried to use Pillage, thinking the reindeer was already technically dying, but the Skill failed. *Not close enough to death?* It seemed the monster might have enough power left in its body to take James with it.

For a painful length of time, man and beast seemed to be at an impasse as the beast slowly bled out from the severed limb and an ever-increasing number of abdominal perforations, while James drew in less and less air with each breath as the reindeer's literal tons of weight slowly crushed the life out of him.

Against his will, James saw the image of his family in his mind's eye, receding out of reach as the blackness clawed at the edges of his vision.

But James would not let this creature take him from them. And he had an edge over any brutish monster. He was more than crude physical matter.

Using all his mental energy, he began Silent Spellcasting, charging as much Mana as he could as quickly as he could in an effort to save himself from possible suffocation.

The reindeer, apparently sensing the dangerous activity beneath it, tried to flail at James with its remaining legs but couldn't adequately reach him—it tried to rise, but didn't succeed. The beast was on its last legs. One way or another, it was dying. The only question was whether it would take James with it through sheer spite.

After a minute of charging Mana, James unleashed the spell. It felt like his last chance before he would suffer more cracked ribs and possible internal organ damage from the sheer weight bearing down on him.

A giant fist of stone rose from the earth James was casting on, and it slammed into the reindeer with all its weight. The reindeer instantly flew off of James, and he was able to turn his head and see the fist slam the reindeer into a tree. The fist landed in the undamaged ribs of the side that had not been hit with the log, smashing every bone in that part of the buck's body and, James imagined, finally turning its vital organs into a dark red paste as he had imagined the log trap would.

Pink and red matter streamed from the deer's mouth, and the light went out of its eyes almost instantly.

[You killed an Alpha Buck Reindeer, Lv. 18. You gained 800 exp!]
[Predator in Human Skin leveled up!]
[System-Boosted Human leveled up!]
[Predator in Human Skin leveled up!]

The adrenaline and battle focus dissipated in a rush, and James felt the full brunt of his injuries hit him all at once. He gasped and shuddered with the beating of his heart. Every inch of him hurt, but especially his right arm and his chest. He knew that if he looked in a mirror right now, he would see an ugly vision. A human with a badly smashed up, bruised, swollen, and probably fractured right arm. There was also a massive hoof-shaped dent in his rib cage right above his heart.

If I were still low level, that dent in my rib cage probably would have killed me by itself. Everything about that fight was goddammed lucky, James thought. *Too lucky. Too close. If not for the Class Evolution I just had . . . I can't ever let myself get that close to death again. How would anyone weaker than me even survive this place for ninety days?* He didn't need to check his Health pool to know how close it was to the bottom.

He quickly took out a Health Potion and drank it.

[You consumed one Health Potion. You restored 50 Health!]

It wasn't much, but it felt warm going down, to the point that James wondered if it might contain alcohol, though he didn't taste any. It was good to swallow something that eased the pain, if only slightly.

Healing Aura! Laying on Hands!

For the first time, James activated both of his healing Skills at once. Why not? He had the Mana for it, and that reindeer had royally messed him up.

Mana for days! James thought, then winced as his chuckle at the thought shifted his broken ribs.

James focused his Laying on Hands on his shattered ribs first because, despite the pain of his arm, those gave him the most discomfort when he moved. The broken structure of his chest also made him feel uncomfortably close to death.

He lay almost unmoving, healing from the damage, staring at the dead reindeer. Even in death, even with its body pulped by James's spell, its massive form looked majestic and powerful. *I'll never forget you,* James thought. *The beast that almost killed me.*

"Rest with pride," he muttered.

He used Pillage on the body of the reindeer and selected Skill to take, almost as an afterthought.

As he slowly healed, James felt a sense of euphoria. Part of it was relief at the realization that he had survived. Part of it was joy at the knowledge that this was the strongest opponent he had ever fought, and he had won. Part of it was the renewed hope that he would see his family again. But the biggest source of energy and excitement was a growing awareness of his body.

He could sense somehow that he was almost ready to break through to a new level of power. This fight had brought him close to some further stage, or at least that was how he felt. There was a tension throughout his frame, a feeling of overflowing vitality despite how battered and broken his body was.

And by now he had learned to trust the signals his body sent him. *What will I become next?*

But he didn't want to think too much about that now. He knew that he had been so thoroughly wrecked by the reindeer's mauling that he shouldn't spare any attention or thought just now for anything outside his self-healing process.

James was so focused on using his combination of healing Skills to get back into top condition that he didn't notice the many spiders crawling from the forest floor and descending from the trees. He didn't spot them until they had him surrounded, and it was too late.

CHAPTER THIRTY-SEVEN

Zugzwang

Alpha Buck Reindeer's body processed.]
[You obtained Alpha Reindeer Leggings, 6x Reindeer Meat Bundle, and an Ego Antler Spear!]
[Skill Obtained: Berserk Mode!]

That's nice, James thought vaguely, distracted as he directed the items as usual into his magic satchel. He winced a little as he continued trying to iron out his broken ribs into their normal shape. It was painful but ultimately no big problem for him. He would happily spend the ten or fifteen minutes suffering a little pain to return to top condition. His chest being cracked like an egg had been scary, but soon he would be at a hundred percent again.

Suddenly, there was a gentle tug at his hands where he was holding his satchel, and he was forced to divert his attention. He looked down and saw the Ego Antler Spear was not entering the Small Bag of Deceptive Dimensions alongside his other loot. He touched the spear and tried to shove it further in, and he realized that either the bag was full—at long last too packed with equipment to handle another item—or the spear was actively resisting his push.

The name was Ego Antler Spear, right? Does that mean it has its own will?

He let go, and the spear floated out, clearly under its own power. James took its physical details in for a moment. The tip was a two-pronged twist of antlers that had been braided together into incredibly sharp points. The whole haft was the same color as the antler tips, clearly made of the creature's bones or even just excess material from the horns.

James half-expected the spear to float into an attack position and impale him now. *Rudolph's revenge!* Instead, the spear floated in a semicircle around James, then turned into what looked like an attack position aimed away from him. It was almost like it was trying to point.

James looked in the direction the spear was pointing, and he saw them. The creatures had been hidden from him—partially by the approaching darkness coupled with their dark-colored chitin, partially perhaps by some Stealth Skill, and partially by his near-complete focus on healing himself. His Predator Senses weren't really doing much right now.

But now he could see, and he opened his senses wide to get a good idea of the threat all around him. He saw now that there were hundreds of spiders. Black, shiny, chitinous shapes great and small. There was at least one of the Command Wood Spiders like the one he'd killed before and scores of the smaller Feral Wood Spider specimens that he had encountered previously. And something new: there were countless miniscule Baby Wood Spiders, per his Identify.

James turned his head and verified what he expected: the hundreds of spiders included an even larger group arrayed behind him. There were several Command Wood Spiders, scores more Feral Wood Spiders, and countless Baby Wood Spiders crawling around on all sides of him. He was surrounded on the ground. He looked up into the tree above him and immediately wished he hadn't. There were a half-dozen spiders slowly making their way down toward him from the treetops. They must have climbed up from the other side of the tree, where he had no visibility, to come in from behind.

Back of the neck is their favorite blind spot to attack, James thought. *This attack pattern makes sense, except for one thing. When did they start hunting in such massive packs?* The only answer that made sense was that after several smaller groups of spiders had gone missing, the spider colony had made a decision somehow. A decision to go after their predator with maximum force.

He could use Chosen One of Apophis and try to blow them all up with fire magic, but that would start a larger conflagration that would reach the Rodriguez camp for sure. And depending on how well the spiders had organized and distributed themselves—not to mention how intelligent they were—there might be some positioned out of range of any magical attack.

James envisioned himself surrounded and overwhelmed by surviving spiders. *Well, what if I don't do that?*

His Predator Instincts generated a pair of numbers in his head. They were ugly numbers. Twelve percent chance of victory and 50 percent chance of survival.

So my odds of living through this would come down to a coin flip, James thought. *They definitely picked their moment well. I'm already beaten half to death. They even made sure to wait until the buck was dead so he wouldn't trample any of the babies. I'm almost in checkmate. With the ones above me, I have to move quickly, or I'll be surrounded from all angles. But where? Any movement takes me right into the middle of them and makes my immediate situation worse.*

What's the term for that in chess? A position where you only have bad options? James's mind flitted away from that digression and back to breaking down the situation he was in.

How will they attack? The ones above will probably jump down first, right?

He noticed something he hadn't before: how quickly he seemed to be thinking in this emergency. The spiders he sensed above him were hardly any closer since he'd noticed them. It was as if time had slowed down while he was focusing on solving this problem.

Maybe it's all the points in Intelligence?

But then his many points of Intelligence made themselves known in a much more useful way. *I have an idea.* The idea unfurled itself into a plan with three stages, incorporating everything he knew about the spiders and their behavior from across multiple encounters.

James moved decisively now.

He grasped the Ego Antler Spear by the haft and held it menacingly, ready for use. He had to cancel Laying on Hands in his dominant hand to use it to grip the spear, but his wounds were already much less severe than they had been.

Intimidation!

"Come and get some, you sons of bitches!" he yelled out loud. "You can only die once. Who wants to be first?" He gave his new spear a practice thrust as if eager to use it. There wasn't much chance the spiders would back down, but if he didn't give them an exaggerated idea of his own condition, there was no chance at all.

There was a moment of stillness after James made his Intimidation attempt. Then he felt a sudden grip on his hand. He looked down and saw a tiny string of web leading from his hand up into the tree. He yanked his hand free only to feel a half-dozen tiny pulls on his legs.

He looked and saw three strings fixed to each of his calves. As he moved to rip them loose, he felt an unknown number of threads attach to his back. Then more on his arms, face, and feet.

In just a few short seconds, James was so covered in threads that he could not see anything but silk thread. He tried to move, but every inch of him was increasingly bound up in the silken casing. The best he could do was to suck in air and expand his body a bit so that he would have space around him. The spiders were spinning a cocoon around him, like the Command Wood Spider from before, but this time they were covering every inch of his body, and the sheer quantity of tightly wound threads was incomparable.

James fell to the ground, unable to move his legs properly within the silk casing. But he had retained his grip on the spear, so it was in the cocoon with him, along with his other remaining equipment. He didn't think he could move it much, though. The silk was heavier than he remembered from last time he'd been wrapped up, as if they had a special version that was meant for imprisoning their harder to kill prey. He could feel he wouldn't be able to easily escape using physical force.

Then he heard the rustling movements of a half-dozen spiders rushing at him.

A second later he felt their bites, which penetrated through the silk into his skin in a half-dozen different areas of his body. Left hand, right thigh, back of the neck, left calf, right bicep, left buttock. The bites were all shallow, since the silk got in the way, but there was easily enough venom involved to put him in the same condition that Camila Rodriguez had been in after the spiders got her. It was easier to believe the Rodriguezes had been so intimidated by them now that he was confronted by so many.

But for James, this was all according to plan.

Shed Skin! The layer of punctured flesh separated itself from James's body. He carefully remained completely still besides using Shed Skin. This hunting technique would probably serve him well for a long time to come, he imagined. *Playing possum.* He used the same Skill he had applied before, slowing his heart down, bringing his vital signs closer to death. Making his body almost as quiet as a corpse. And he waited, still as the grave.

Sure enough, the spiders seemed unafraid of him now, as if they believed he was already dead. They approached close enough that he sensed he could crush some of the smaller ones now just by rolling over—a movement he could still make. But he didn't waste the element of surprise he had gained that way. He remained still.

He wasn't interested in reengaging with the small army of spiders given the 12 percent chance of victory and the 50 percent chance of survival. No, he wanted to wait for them to fall into their pattern.

A few of the smaller ones began pulling at the cocoon from the outside, and he felt himself lifted onto a slightly elevated object. Then the elevated object began to move, carrying his limp cocoon-covered body through the forest. It must be one of the Command Wood Spiders again.

Success! Now James just needed to wait, and they would carry him home so that the whole community could feed on him, as he imagined was their plan. Or so that the Queen that he recalled one of the Identify descriptions mentioning could eat him. Either way, the chances of him dying shouldn't increase too much by being in the more dangerous setting, since they would believe he was already dead or near dead, and the chances of him destroying the entire spider colony should increase exponentially.

I had no idea how to find the larger group until they found me, James thought. *Thanks, guys!*

While they carried him through the forest, James reviewed his notifications and examined the Ego Antler Spear with Identify.

[Sufficient experience accrued. Intimidation leveled up!]

[Sufficient experience accrued. Natural Camouflage leveled up!]

[Ego Antler Spear: A spear crafted from an Alpha Buck Reindeer that James viciously slaughtered. Contains the residual survival instinct and ferocity of the reindeer, now bent to the service of its killer. The weapon is intelligent and will protect its owner and move independently when danger looms nearby. Boosts Strength and Agility by 20 each when wielded. Grants access to the Skills Deep Antler Penetration and Weak Passive Regeneration.]

James noticed that his body was still slowly recovering from his injuries, despite the fact that he wasn't charging any Mana or consuming any potions. He had thought he might simply have enhanced natural healing as a result of some of his Stat increases, which might be true. But now that he saw what the description for the Skill said, he recognized that it was probably mostly the Weak Passive Regeneration Skill.

It was a bit weaker and slower compared to when he was using his healing abilities, but he didn't need that much. With this spear, he didn't have to risk provoking the spiders by charging Mana to complete his recovery. He just had to wait.

And he would wait until he was in a complete condition, with full Mana, Stamina, and Health. Only then would the predator strike again.

It was a long walk to wherever the spiders carried him, and James finally took a few minutes to do something he hadn't done in a relatively long time, considering how much it must have changed: review his Status.

[Status

Name: James Robard

Race: System-Boosted Human, Lv. 9

Class: Predator in Human Skin, Lv. 15

Job: Politician, Lv. 4

Health: 2202/3844

Mana: 2888/3465

Stamina: 1096/2601

Wrath Meter: 2%

Stats

Strength: 64(88)

Agility: 66(86)

Stamina: 47

Fortitude: 53(58)

Dexterity: 44

Perception: 51

Will: 51

Intelligence: 57

Charisma: 34

Stealth: 18

Free Points: 0

Skills

Adamant Defense, Lv. 1

Anthropophagy, Lv. 1

Basic Cold Resistance

Basic Elemental Magic: Earth, Lv. 2

Basic Elemental Magic: Electricity, Lv. 0

Basic Elemental Magic: Fire, Lv. 3

Basic Elemental Magic: Gravity, Lv. 2

Basic Elemental Magic: Water, Lv. 3

Basic Elemental Magic: Wind, Lv. 1

Basic Non-Elemental Magic, Lv. 1

Basic Proficiency–All Weapons

Basic Proficiency–Unarmed Combat

Berserk Mode, Lv. 0

Crushing Bite, Lv. 1

Deep Antler Penetration

Empathic Projection, Lv. 3

Emotional Control, Lv. 4

Empathy Control, Lv. 4

False Impression, Lv. 3

Hand of Glory, Lv. 1

Healing Aura, Lv. 1

Heavy Strike, Lv. 2

Holy Barrier, Lv. 0

Identify, Lv. 2

Inspiration, Lv. 2

Intimidation, Lv. 1

Laying on Hands, Lv. 4

Loyal Following, Lv. 2

Mass Pillage, Lv. 1

Natural Camouflage, Lv. 2

Organization, Lv. 1

Pain Resistance, Lv. 2

Parallel Minds, Lv. 1

Persuasion, Lv. 6

Pillage, Lv. 7

Precision Strike, Lv. 0

Predator's Armaments, Lv. 1

Predator's Armor, Lv. 0
Predator's Insight, Lv. 1
Predator's Instincts, Lv. 0
Predator's Intuition, Lv. 0
Predator's Missile, Lv. 0
Predator's Senses, Lv. 0
Predator's Strike, Lv. 2
Public Speaking, Lv. 0
Quick Strike, Lv. 1
Shed Skin, Lv. 5
Silent Spellcasting
Situational Intelligence, Lv. 4
System Interface
Universal Language Comprehension
Venom Fangs, Lv. 0
Weak Passive Regeneration
Wolf's Bite
Talents
Basic Spellcraft, Lv. 1
Cannibalism, Lv. 3
Cool-Headed, Lv. 3
Earth Affinity
Efficient Magic, Lv. 0
Flame Affinity
Leadership, Lv. 0
Manipulation, Lv. 1
Pain Resistance, Lv. 2
Selective Empathy, Lv. 0
Water Affinity
Titles
Chosen One of Apophis
Citizen of the Dead Marsh
Devout Beacon
Swiss Army Mage
System Pioneer]

Well, that's a mouthful!

It had certainly grown since he'd last seen it. And maybe he was only alive after that recent fight because of how high these Stats had gotten and the long list of Skills he'd acquired. He made sure to distribute his new Free Points into Fortitude since he suspected he would need all the Health he could get to survive this experience.

Not sure how I feel about the Berserk Mode Skill. He only vaguely recalled taking it from the reindeer. *I'm guessing the "Wrath Meter" is related?*

But the most notable thing for him was at the very top. As he had retreated into the stillness of his body, James had again felt something unusual about it, as if he were ready for a change, ready to move to a new state. Reviewing the Status screen, James thought that he now knew why.

CHAPTER THIRTY-EIGHT

Burn

Just as his Class Evolution had happened when he hit level ten, James felt that his body would be ready for a new stage once his Race hit level ten.

And he just needed one more level in Job or Class to do that.

If Race was anything like Class, he would have a choice of Races, and part of that selection would be based on his experiences and choices thus far. Perhaps Race Evolution would give him the opportunity to become a more perfect predator or a more effective Politician.

Hopefully, it would not mean losing any more of his humanity than he had already chosen to give up. The memory of consuming human flesh—and enjoying it—still sat uneasily with James.

But the Race Evolution that he was anticipating just gave him another reason to look forward to confronting the remaining members of the spider colony. A reward to anticipate.

After uncounted minutes of walking, the spiders seemed to have arrived at their destination. James's cocoon was removed from the back of the big spider that had been carrying him and was hoisted up, higher and higher, above the ground. He could feel many different spiders lending their strength, deftly carrying him somewhere. At last, he was suspended somewhere in midair. He could visualize generally where he must be: in some massive web, strung from multiple trees across a large area, dozens of feet above the ground.

Probably one of many meals on wheels for the Queen. He waited for long, alert minutes, every nerve tense, anticipating the moment when he would be grabbed by the spiders again and would have to make his move.

At first, he tried to use his five senses to learn something of where he was.

But his sight couldn't penetrate the thick walls of silk. The space was so dark that it was almost a sensory deprivation chamber. His hearing captured only dull footfall vibrations from spiders walking on silk, a bit like the motion of knitting needles. He sniffed the silk, which smelled of mingled glue and unidentifiable musk, but that was useless information. And he wasn't quite hungry or desperate for information enough to try tasting it. Before he knew it, the wait had stretched into hours.

James gradually calmed as he realized that he was probably being stored for later consumption. Now he waited only for the spiders to settle down for the night so that he could make his move. Still, for an interminable period, they kept moving around—probably arranging more food for their Queen.

James gradually learned to tell from the movement of the web he was attached to whether there were any spiders close to him or not. Unfortunately, all he could tell was whether there was any weight on the web. If there was something in the trees nearby him, he probably wouldn't have known it through the thick layer of silk that surrounded him.

Eventually, the spiders seemed to settle down into a much lower level of activity. Most of them had apparently stopped moving, while a few may have been making small adjustments and repairs to the web. *Or patrolling.*

In any case, detectable vibrations were minimal. According to James's biological clock, this should be the middle of the night. By now, his resources were all completely restored. Even his pulverized ribs had merged into their normal shape again, thanks to the Ego Antler Spear.

There was a period when there was nothing to sense, nothing for his predator's mind to focus on. Nothing but the sweat on his skin and the stuffy cocoon atmosphere. Nothing but thinking what to do next and wondering when the time would be just right to act.

As he decided the time had come to *do something* at last, he had a moment of cowardice, despite his fully restored power. He imagined what it would be like if he escaped now instead of executing his plan.

He could use Predator's Armaments to turn his fingernails into tiny knives, slit open the cocoon, drop to the ground, and run away. The half-asleep spiders wouldn't be able to catch him. They'd been slower than he was before, and now that he had leveled up repeatedly, he was certainly much faster than they were.

Maybe he should get out before they tried to eat him. He had no way of knowing their full numbers, or whether they were even all sleeping. The only thing he was sure of was that he had been carried high up from ground level, which he assumed meant he was in the big home spider nest. He'd had plenty of time to speculate about the army of spiders he might be facing while he rested in the cocoon. And if he tried to destroy the colony and failed, there would be no second chances. He could be up against thousands.

He would never be able to save himself if he made the attempt now and failed.

James thought about cutting tiny eyeholes so that he could see out, but he dismissed the idea. He didn't need more information; he needed to make a decision. Run or fight. Abandon killing the spiders or burn the whole nest.

He decided.

Instead of fleeing, James began Silent Spellcasting, gathering as much fire Mana as he could as quickly as he could. It was an easy decision, really. He wasn't going to become the person he wanted to become in this new world by running away from fights. He wanted to be someone who could be relied upon to overcome bad odds, defeat superior numbers, and always win by any means necessary. Tonight would be the first time—the birth of his legend.

James poured his all into charging this spell. He needed to blow up as many spiders as possible in one blast if he were to have any chance of escaping this situation in the aftermath of his spell. Ideally, he would kill the entire colony, but that seemed unrealistic to him without any enhancement.

Maybe I can harness just a bit of Apophis's power, he thought. The idea of grasping that strength right now was extremely tempting. A lifeline. He still remembered the surge of energy from the last time. When he'd fought Kurt Royersford's party, James had made his target the destruction of the forest. If he was correct in his personal theory that the Orientation took place in its own small pocket universe, that target had shown the potential to measurably increase the entropy in the universe.

He read the description again, just to make sure he was remembering what it did correctly.

[Chosen One of Apophis: A Title granted by a god. Apophis has blessed you, so rejoice. Enjoy a 100% boost to all Stats and Skill effects when acting to increase the entropy of your environment. Enjoy a 1000% boost to all Stats and Skill effects when acting to measurably increase the entropy of your universe. The great God of Chaos has plans for you.]

Per the Title, attempting to measurably increase the entropy in the universe caused an eleven-times multiplier effect to Stats and Skill effects.

If he now specifically targeted only this environment, only the spiders' nest, it should only result in a doubling of his attack's power. James was just going off of the Title's description, but the situation was nerve-racking enough that he was willing to take the risk of creating a somewhat larger fire than he intended.

He focused on the plan to destroy the spider colony completely and continued charging Mana. As he picked up the pace of gathering Mana, however, he felt a stirring in the web. Something was moving that hadn't been. He ignored the ominous vibrations and continued gathering power, accelerating to as heated a pace as he could manage.

The vibrations raced up to James, and he braced a moment before the impact came. Several body weights slammed into him, but that was not the threat. The spiders were only roughly the size and weight of large dogs, and most of them were running up toward him, against gravity. The real threat hit right afterward. Multiple sets of spider fangs ripped through the spider silk, aiming for James's vital organs. Some of the fangs ripped into James's discarded layer of skin, but none of them reached his real body.

The ripping went on, growing more furious as Mana continued gathering, making James glow like a small sun in the night, and the spiders shredded the layer of shed skin surrounding James.

Finally, as the fangs were getting too close to his living skin, he unleashed it: a huge wave of power, radiating out in all directions around his body. James felt the spiders blasted off of him, and what was left of the cocoon and shed skin that had encased him burned to ashes instantly. With nothing holding him up, James fell through the air, straight down toward the forest floor. A blazing orange glow behind him lit the ground.

James turned his head and saw that the web—which had been elephantine— had turned instantly into a towering inferno. He couldn't see the shapes of individual spiders on the web, only flames, but he could hear the sounds of bodies cracking and splitting in the heat coming from all around.

James activated Silent Spellcasting again as he fell, this time gathering non-elemental Mana to make a shield around his body.

However, before he could finish charging his Mana, or hit the ground, a heavy impact thudded against his side and sent him flying. The blow didn't hurt much, since he was in midair rather than pressed against any kind of surface, but the sheer power behind it was reminiscent of the Alpha Buck Reindeer he'd fought earlier that day. James saw what had struck him out of the corner of his eye. It was a spider the height of a man and a half, standing up on its back legs like an angry bear. He couldn't get a lot of visual details with the creature in his peripheral vision, but he could see it well enough to target it for Identify.

[Wood Spider Queen, Lv. 20: An evolved version of a mutant spider cultivated for the Orientation by the System. Spawns lesser spiders and builds a nest to perpetuate her species. Controls lesser spiders. Endowed with vastly superior Strength and Fortitude compared to an average System-Enhanced Human and with equal Intelligence and Will as an average System-Enhanced Human. Enjoys the blessing of a divine being. Weak against fire.]

Is this thing blessed by Apophis too? James wondered.

As he flew backward toward a tree, he continued Silent Spellcasting. He hit just before the spell was ready, so he took the full brunt of the impact to his back. It wasn't so bad. No broken bones. Then the giant spider appeared right in front of his field of vision. *She's quick!*

Another mighty limb came down and smashed him through the tree he'd hit.

The spear flew from his hand, and James felt splinters tear into his upper back where it was partly uncovered from his armor breaking earlier.

The giant head of the spider came down on the hollow in the tree that James's body had made. He saw the giant fangs pressing in closer, inches away, only blocked from reaching him by the thick wood that encircled James. The fangs slowly advanced, breaking through the tree trunk, seemingly *en route* to chopping James in half.

As the fangs were about to finish cutting through the tree, he finished charging his spell. The wood gave way to the spider's fangs, only for James's magic shield to appear and block their progress. The spider snapped its fangs open and shut over and over in frustration, the magic shield shaking noticeably under the pressure.

James thought that he could use this opportunity to escape from the spider's grasp, but instead, he drew his daggers and lunged at the Queen's eyes, aiming to cut them out. He felt a growing sense of excitement rather than fear.

A limb as thick as a baseball bat swung toward his head and knocked him off target, striking against his magic shield and throwing his body sideways into the shrubbery. James noticed the Ego Antler Spear hover into view, as if it had been waiting for him.

Weird to have a levitating, independently thinking weapon, he thought. But he put his daggers away and grabbed it. Clearly it wanted to be used, and it came from a much better Class of creature, and with much better Stat boosts, than any of his other weapons. It was clearly his best chance at winning this fight.

"Human, why did you come to destroy my nest? Why have you murdered so many of my children?!" the Wood Spider Queen intoned, her voice deep and echoing yet unmistakably female.

"I think you got the order of events wrong," James replied loudly. "Your children captured me to eat me, and I defended myself by setting them on fire!"

Now that he was a bit farther from the Wood Spider Queen, he could see her body a bit better. It gave him a better idea of her real condition. It was apparent that she had already taken some fire damage herself. Doubtless she'd been resting in the nest when James ignited it. The other trait that was obvious was just how *big* she was. The size of a small car, with strength disproportionate to her size.

"You are the one who entered our territory and began slaughtering us!"

Instead of answering, James began silently charging Mana once again. He already knew what he wanted to try against the Queen. This time, it would be gravity Mana.

"I won't let you finish charging another attack!" the Spider Queen said.

Stop me if you can, James thought.

She dashed in again, just as she had after punching James through that tree. This time she was moving within his line of sight, though, and James found that he could maintain the distance between his smaller form and her bulk. Although she was fast, he was faster, especially with the Agility boost from the Ego Antler Spear.

Outpacing Her Highness, he pulled farther and farther back from the fire, consciously expanding the distance between the Queen and any possible backup from surviving spiders. He ran away for several minutes while charging his spell, continuing to move farther from the burning spiders' nest.

This was a fight that would be difficult to win at close range as things stood, and he'd learned his lesson about entering close range when he wasn't ready from the reindeer.

"Stand still and fight, you coward!" the Spider Queen hissed at him.

She punched a small tree down and threw it at him. James sidestepped easily enough, and the tree whizzed past harmlessly. *Outside of melee range, she isn't nearly so dangerous*, he thought. *She needs her minions. Fortunately, I've fricasseed most of her little family.*

"Did I hear you ask me to stand still and let you hit me?" he taunted. "Do I look stupid to you?"

"Yessssss!" she hissed.

She flung one of her limbs backward, and a long thread that James hadn't noticed before suddenly became visible floating above his head.

"What the hell is that?" he wondered aloud.

And then the tree he'd dodged came flying back at him from behind. James didn't try to step out of the way. The tree wasn't moving fast enough to hurt him this time. She was just trying to reel in her prey, and he deliberately let the tree carry him toward her.

"Got you!" the Queen exclaimed as she raised her forelimbs in the air to smash down on the rapidly approaching human.

"I needed to be closer anyway," James said. He jumped forward, pushing off of the tree branch with both feet and leaping between her down-swinging arms. He grasped one of her limbs, and he unleashed the charged Mana.

A single limb struck him from his left side before the magic took effect, breaking through the magic shield, and he smashed into the ground, rolling until he struck a tree. The casual strike didn't do much real damage, just perhaps a cracked rib, and James quickly hopped to his feet, ignoring the pain in his left side.

The Queen had fallen from her tall, angry-bear posture to a horizontal position, relying on all eight legs to hold her weight up. And those eight legs shook as she stumbled from side to side, unbalanced and unsteady.

"What did you do, accursed human?" the Queen screamed.

James remained silent. He didn't want to give an intelligent enemy any clues about how best to deal with what he'd done. The gravity Mana he'd applied should have increased her weight by four or five times, though it was hard to be exact with his current level of magical skill. Probably, if she knew exactly what was wrong with her, she'd come up with some ways to partly compensate.

"Everything hurtsssss," the Spider Queen moaned. "What have you done?"

James chose this moment to dart in with his spear. *Quick Strike!* He darted into the Queen's blind spot, directly behind her head.

The monster tried to turn to face her predator, but her movements remained clumsy and sluggish as James launched the attack that he hoped would end their fight.

Deep Antler Penetration!

CHAPTER THIRTY-NINE

Ashes and Dust

The Ego Antler Spear took on a warm golden glow as James activated Deep Antler Penetration.

To James, it felt like a literal aura of invincibility, as if nothing could stop his weapon from piercing whatever he struck. Striking the body of the enemy from behind, he felt sure it could deal a lethal blow. *If only I understood spider anatomy better, I'm sure I could guarantee it.*

Deep Antler Penetration landed almost where James had aimed it, but just a bit to the right. He'd been aiming straight for the Spider Queen's center of mass. As he jumped back away from the Queen, he could see the sharp tips of the spear had drilled two deep holes through her body.

At least one green organ was visible through the holes in the exoskeleton, and it looked like it had been deeply penetrated, possibly through and through. The Skill the spear came with had done exactly what it promised. Gray and green goo gushed out from the holes it had made.

It seems possible that the spear actually guided me to a better target than what I initially had in mind, James thought. He remembered the first time he'd tried to thrust a spear through one of these spiders, before he acquired the present, clearly sentient, weapon. He had aimed at the exact center of mass, and the spear had gone all the way through—and done very little to slow that particular spider down.

This spider, by contrast, looked very debilitated by the blow.

"Thanks, Buck," James said quietly, spontaneously naming the spear. It seemed to give off a little more of that warm aura feeling in response. *I guess being able to talk is expecting too much from a weapon.*

"Bastard human!" the Spider Queen groaned. "How did you know—"

The words cut off as green and gray fluid leaked from her mouth.

I'd better finish this now while she's struggling to adapt to the weight and her injury. James charged toward her for another strike, but then the Spider Queen raised her forelegs and slammed them down on the ground, and the earth seemed to shake beneath her feet. James stopped trying to charge her and focused on stabilizing his footing instead as the previously level ground beneath him cracked. In the background, he noticed some smoke rising in the distance, and he realized they had gotten quite far from the spiders' nest.

Nevertheless, he considered running away again. Even if it was fueled by a Skill, the Queen's earth-shaking move seemed to show more Strength than he'd previously thought she was capable of. If she was going to go full throttle until she ran out of steam, it was best for him to avoid and evade rather than to fight directly.

Then the Spider Queen's body took on a strange glow. Cracks appeared all over it, and James thought he knew what was coming. He jumped backward to give her a wide berth. For a moment he wasn't certain if she was using Shed Skin or some sort of transformation into what would be her final form. He had assumed the former, but this looked much flashier than his version.

But then, sure enough, the outer layer of the Queen's carapace began to fall away in pieces, and he saw a fresh, shiny new body peeking out from beneath. Not a new form, just a healing move.

I hope she hasn't completely recovered. She'd be unstoppable if she can shake off injuries like the one I just gave her with some kind of advanced version of Shed Skin.

The body that emerged no longer had the burn marks he'd noticed before. It looked more solid, harder, and stronger, as well as slightly smaller and slimmer—but there was still a meaningful-looking hole through the near-center-of-mass region that James's attack had penetrated. In fact, the puncture looked even worse than before. Since the damage had been mostly internal, shedding an outer layer of skin and flesh just made it more obvious how deep the wound was. *Another few inches*, James thought, *and I would have penetrated all the way through the body.*

The Spider Queen tried to move, stepping out of the skin and testing her legs out, and James watched carefully as well. But her movements looked just as heavy and clumsy as before.

"I don't understand. What affliction is this?" the Queen exclaimed.

"Nothing you can do anything about, it seems," James replied.

He readied his spear for another charge, but before he did, the Spider Queen lunged at him with surprising speed. It was a clumsy attack, but he could sense the power behind it, and James evaded. Her leg struck a tree instead and pushed through it like it wasn't there.

She swung around, trying to strike the just-out-of-reach human, but she was still noticeably slower than before. Her speed and precision were still substantially diminished by the gravity magic, and James guessed she must be using some form of boosting Skill to be able to move as quickly as she was.

As he dodged backward again, the Queen paused in her assault. She pressed two of her forelimbs to her head as if struggling with a migraine. James began Silent Spellcasting again, taking advantage of the gap in the action to more easily focus on charging up fire Mana. He would try to make this next fire spell the final attack if he could, though he had no expectation that she would die easily.

But he had a deep well of resources to draw upon now. As long as he didn't use his heavy Stamina-consuming moves, he could continue this duel with the Queen for hours until she finally perished. Death by a thousand cuts was just as dead as death from a single blow.

"The last of my children has just perished." The Queen's voice was mournful, dark. Hollow.

James had an initial impulse to taunt her. To say something like, *Wow! It took that long for all of your babies to burn? I guess you could have saved them if you hadn't chased after me.* But he suppressed this ugly desire. The taunt was obviously ill-advised. Her children were horrendous monsters to him, but to her, they were probably as beautiful as any baby was to its parents. James thought of the child he was expecting with his own wife, and he felt a small pull of empathy. *Now's really not the time*, he told himself. *The taunting would actually help win the fight.*

Still, the words that came out were a quiet and sincere, "I'm sorry for your loss."

"Graaaaahhh!" The Queen roared with rage. She began lunging and swinging her long legs at James again, flailing blindly now. He returned instantly to cold warrior mode. He analyzed and observed that she must be burning through Stamina more quickly as she launched these frenzied attacks. It was growing ever easier to dodge her strikes, and she was hitting more trees and taking bigger and wilder swings each time.

She'll be completely tuckered out soon enough, he thought. No need to launch his final attack before she tired herself out. That way, she wouldn't be able to dodge.

The two danced around in circles for several minutes—the Queen swinging away like a drunken boxer, James sidestepping and increasing his distance with every dodge.

He stepped back once more, getting farther out of her reach after yet another big swing. But something was different. He found that he had stumbled into something that stopped his right arm from moving back—and cut into the skin. The cut was only slight, but James looked down. It wasn't just any random object that could cut his skin now.

There was a long, thin, taut thread suspended in the air next to his arm, barely visible. In addition to having a little bit of his blood on it, the thread appeared to be a deep burgundy color as far as the eye could see, as if it were a different material than the spider silk he had encountered before.

James looked all around him quickly, and it was immediately apparent that circumstances had changed. On all sides of him now, except for the ground and the angle he had just retreated from on his left, he was surrounded by the deep burgundy threads. They were so thin that it was clear they were spun so as to be nearly invisible.

"Oh, you noticed them already," the Queen said. She sounded a bit calmer now, and James wondered how much of her rage had been affected to try to lure him into this trap.

"What are these threads?" James asked. Every second he stalled, the fire Mana was continuing to charge, so he was happy to talk to the Spider Queen as much as she wanted, given that dodging was no longer an option.

"They're my life threads," the Queen said, voice reverent. "I expend life force as well as Stamina to make them, but the consequence is that they're very special. Razor sharp, incredibly strong, and invisible to the human eye." She narrowed her eyes. "Or so I thought. I assumed you had only noticed that something cut you. But how can you see them?" He noticed that she was sidling closer as she spoke, perhaps believing she was being subtle in her movements. It was fine, though. When he incinerated her, close range would be better than long.

"My Class Evolution gave me superhuman senses," James said truthfully. He didn't see how giving her information like that would help her win this fight, especially when he was only confirming what she must already know.

"Something to remember when I fight my next high-level human, although it didn't help you avoid being trapped by my threads," she mused. "You have given me excellent sport, human, but now it ends. Now you join my children."

She loomed over him, fangs dripping with deadly black venom.

"It's your fault they died!" James yelled. Drawing on his empathy, these were the words he felt would stun him most effectively in her position.

"What? How dare you, you little shit!" His words had clearly stung the Spider Queen, and she was holding off attacking for these critical seconds while he finished charging as much Mana as he could.

James continued. "You sent them out to hunt something that they couldn't handle. When they brought back a predator, instead of protecting them from me, from the fire I started, you wanted to chase me for your own ego. And *then* they died. Who else's fault would it be? I was doing what I needed to do to survive. What's your excuse?"

The Queen paused as if reflecting. Some part of her seemed to recognize the truth in what he'd said. Then she spoke again, wrath and grief intermingled in her voice, her tone low. "Perhaps you're right. Perhaps it is my fault as their mother. Surely, I could have saved some of them if I hadn't chased you." Her volume rose to a near howl. "But you are the instrument of their destruction! You have turned my flesh and blood into ashes and dust! You are a monster! All I can do for them now is avenge them and continue our line."

Her voice slowed and dropped in volume again as she seemed to relish her next words. "When I liquefy your insides. When your flesh brings me to the next stage of my Evolution. When I give birth to my next brood of offspring and feed them on your bone marrow. *Then* I will remember the children you slaughtered. I will offer a prayer to our god that they will live on in the story he constantly weaves. And I will eradicate all those like you in this forest! Goodbye, human!"

The Spider Queen leaned down to bite James's head off, and he finally unleashed his attack. He directed the flames in a flamethrower burst from his hands, turning all the firepower he could muster directly onto the Queen. She took the flames face-first and screamed in agony.

"*Aaaarrgghh!!!*" Even as she burned in mortal peril, her limbs still reached out for him. They rapidly turned into kindling for the growing fire whenever one got close.

The Queen's body shuddered and shrank back under the continued flame-thrower attack, limbs curling and twitching visibly before James's eyes. He recognized those as the involuntary movements that a normal arachnid made as it was dying.

Then there was a change in the air. The atmosphere became heavy. James didn't know what this could be except an even more powerful predator somewhere he couldn't sense, projecting its aura down onto the fight that had drawn its attention.

The little hairs on the back of his neck stood up. He was not afraid yet. He had overcome incredible odds here. He had defeated an apex predator in her own environment.

But he felt a cold chill creeping up his spine. His body seemed to recognize that there was something superior to him in this place.

No, it can't be, he rationalized. *But I should be careful. I'm not in perfect condition anymore. No serious wounds, but if whatever this thing is decides to jump in, I'll have to retreat—*

"Please, no! Lord, I—I can win. I can beat him!" the Spider Queen shrieked as the flames continued to lick her slowly cracking and melting body.

There was something above her in the spider food chain? Maybe a Spider King? James became immediately alarmed. Whatever this was, he knew he wasn't prepared to fight it. *I could burn through her life threads and then—*

"*Ahhhhhhh!*" The Spider Queen's voice grew ever shriller as she screamed. Her burning body glowed ever brighter as if an invisible source of light was approaching her from above. James was reminded of alien abduction scenes in movies, specifically the moment right before the flying saucer gets to the ground and swoops the helpless abductee up.

The wind picked up as if there were some massive object flying down, tearing the leaves off of trees and blowing the brush backward away from the scene of battle. Only James remained standing, almost unaffected. It was as if he was deliberately exempted from the pull of this wind, as if there was a magical shield, more powerful than those he could conjure, around him.

James stood in awe, frozen in place. He had stopped seriously considering running, in part because of a notification that had appeared as soon as the light began to cover the Queen.

It immediately explained why he felt the presence of a crushing life force that could snuff him out as easily as a candle.

[A god has descended . . .]

CHAPTER FORTY

Blood Relations

As a result of saving Javier Rodriguez's life and healing the man with the limp, Sierra leveled up her Laying on Hands Skill once again. She now faced a choice between two new Skills derived from that basic Healer ability.

Given her suspicions about Chava, there were factors pushing her toward both sides. Rather than making an impulse decision, she decided to sleep on it.

But the next morning, she had no more clarity. If anything, her mind was murkier than it had been. She had slept poorly, uneasy in her sleeping bag, her mind semi-consciously fixating on the possibility that the camp might be attacked by spider monsters at any moment.

As dawn broke, she decided that rather than continue to keep her own counsel on this and other matters, she would confide in Alan, the other Healer who she knew had accumulated a lot of experience.

But she wanted to think carefully about what she would say. How to frame the question. What information to pass along.

She spent the first part of the morning walking around the camp, talking to Rodriguezes, trying to gather facts that might confirm or dispel her theory of what was going on in the camp. One detail she gleaned was that no one had seen Mama Camila since the healing.

Another detail, really more of an observation, was that few people seemed concerned about anything Chava was doing. They weren't angry, or even annoyed, about his authoritarian decision-making. They weren't worried about the scarce food. They weren't even scared that the camp might be attacked by the spiders after the last incident.

Karla had been concerned about her husband's recovery, but everyone else reacted to mention of the hunting fiasco as if it were a distant memory.

Sierra found most of the Rodriguezes to be disturbingly apathetic. It was almost like they'd been doped up. She decided to go back and speak with Karla. To her relief, the other woman privately aired some grievances.

"Yeah, Chava is a bit of a *machista*," she said with very little prompting. "You know, my husband loves him, though."

"Your husband is his son?" Sierra asked.

"No, his nephew. It's a little weird, being in this place, away from almost all the members of the family who aren't blood relatives. Everyone here loves Chava. It's like I have nobody to talk to if I want to complain!"

"Well, you can talk to me," Sierra said, smiling. Her mind was racing. *I think I found another piece of the puzzle here.* She discussed the politics of the situation with Karla a little more. Finally, she learned that there were two more Rodriguezes, also women who married into the family and surname, who Karla liked to talk to when she felt like an outsider in this family.

Sierra found the two women outside doing chores, cleaning pots and pans, a few minutes later.

Speaking in hushed tones, they basically corroborated what Karla had told her. Chava was essentially a tyrant with a perfect approval rating among the family, with the exception of those few people who weren't blood relations. Although a lot had gone wrong in the camp, most of the Rodriguez family would quickly process and react to the bad, and then consistently return to thinking and speaking nothing ill of Chava. Any momentary discomfort or discontent was quickly forgotten.

Sierra learned that the currently secluded Mama Camila had also married into the family decades ago, but no one had any idea what she might be thinking. The blood-related Rodriguezes had showed a surprising lack of curiosity about her wellbeing aside from the pronouncements Chava had made that she was "Getting stronger each day" and that she "needs her rest."

After that conversation, Sierra knew that she wanted to speak to Alan and make her Skill decision right away.

She observed that Cliff was engaged in conversation with a few of the Rodriguez men, standing around and cracking jokes. *I guess Alan will probably be with Mitzi,* she thought. She preferred talking to the couple outside of Cliff's presence anyway.

She walked around for a few minutes until she saw them near the outskirts of the camp, alone. She slowly and quietly approached the area of cleared ground where they sat on a blanket. They were eating their breakfast ration for the day—someone had found some oatmeal and shared it around with the whole camp—and Sierra heard them talking.

Instinctively, she stopped, dropped, and concealed herself behind a tent rather than continue to walk toward them. *I don't think they saw me.* They had been looking at each other. In the brief time Sierra had known them, the two seemed to focus squarely on each other when they weren't speaking with others. She was curious about the conversation Alan and Mitzi shared when they were alone. *Could they be under Chava's spell too, or is it only family members?* She told herself that if it became too personal, she would simply get back up and walk over as normal.

To her surprise, the conversation wasn't personal at all.

"Do you think James is doing all right?" Mitzi asked.

Alan sighed loudly.

"I noticed you didn't mention him at all yesterday, but you seem to be lost in thought a lot lately," Mitzi went on.

"Is that unlike me?" he asked.

"Hm, how should I answer that?" Mitzi replied.

Sierra heard them both chuckle. *They're really cute*, she thought. *I hope they live through this place.*

"I am a bit worried about him," Alan said. "He's been gone for a while, and those young men who went out hunting yesterday came back with their tails between their legs even though they went out in force. James is all on his lonesome."

Mitzi must have made a face because Alan asked, "What?"

"The other day, I could have sworn you were going to strangle him yourself, the way you were looking at him!" Mitzi said. "Now you're worrying after him like he's our own son."

"He's too young to be our son," Alan retorted. "And that was then. This is now. The truth is, half the frustration is that I just can't figure the kid out. He has moments of extreme heroism alternating with moments of lust for glory or power, or both. I just don't get what motivates him! I thought I knew him once, before all this. I was angry at him before specifically because he started promising that we could perform miracles before knowing for sure we could execute them. He was inserting us into this family's affairs. I've known men like that before. Guys who take charge and think they know all the answers." His tone became grave. "Sometimes they get people killed. But then James turned out to be right, and we saved a human life. Any delay I may have caused by disagreeing certainly wouldn't have helped Camila. Maybe that would've killed her. He who hesitates is lost, and so forth. So, I can't argue with his results, at least. How can I be mad?"

"Well, there are lots of positives and negatives to James." She sounded chipper. "For what it's worth, I think you crystallized his motivations in a single sentence."

"Thinks he knows it all? Wait. Oh. Heh." He chuckled for a few seconds.

"You think he wants to be a big, heroic leader *and* get all the glory and power, eh? Yeah, I guess that's about it. In the military, we had a different model of leadership."

"And he's in one of his heroic moments now," she replied. "I just wish he didn't try to do everything by himself. First, that hideous gray monster in the starting area. Then, the two-headed wolf. Now, a whole army of giant spiders! Always fighting *alone*, like the rest of us aren't here."

"Now you're the one who sounds frustrated," Alan observed.

"I am! Why shouldn't I be? I command two of the elements. I can literally rain down fire and lightning on our enemies! Why would the leader of our group go off into the forest to die alone when he could have asked me to go fight with him? I bet my magic's stronger than his by now!"

"Yes, dear," Alan said, his tone placating. Then, "It was your idea to focus on him as a leader, remember?"

"And it was a good idea! He's kept us safe. Most importantly, he's kept my sweet husband safe." A pause, and then Sierra heard the sound of a kiss.

"But he does seem to like to bite off more than he can chew," Mitzi finished.

"Amen," Alan said.

Sierra decided that this was the perfect moment to insert herself into the discussion.

She moved around to the side of the tent she'd been hiding behind to get a little farther out of the view of the Rogets, and she stood. Then she rounded the side of the tent as if she hadn't been sitting there listening the whole time.

"Hey, Alan, Mitzi!" she said, her tone full of faux innocence.

Not my best acting, she thought. *But 'twill serve!*

"Hello, young lady!" Alan said.

"How are you feeling today, Sierra?" Mitzi asked.

"I'm all right. I've been mulling over a decision, and I wanted to get your advice," Sierra said.

"Oh, we're all ears!" Alan said. He and Mitzi looked quite pleased that someone was consulting them about something.

Sierra first looked around and made sure that there were no family members nearby. Then, dissatisfied with that precaution—she'd just been eavesdropping on them herself, after all—she led them away a short distance into the woods.

Once she was satisfied that they were far enough away, she began by explaining her theory that James had been influenced to go into the forest and fight the spiders alone by some form of Skill that Chava had.

"I'm sure James would happily have gone to exterminate the spiders with or without any mental influence, but I think he would have asked for volunteers to join him first," she finished.

Sierra thought they were primed already to believe her theory, based on the conversation she had just overheard. *For most people, the most important factor in deciding what to think is what they want to be true, after all.*

"It does feel like he made a very rash decision," Alan said slowly, processing.

"I think you're probably right, Sierra," Mitzi said briskly. "The question is, what do we do about it, and what does this have to do with the decision you're making?"

"I was thinking that maybe Chava also has some Skill that lets him influence his family specifically," Sierra said. "He's kind of running things with an iron fist here, and I realized that it's only the non-blood relatives who seem unaffected. No one is doing anything crazy-irrational, like what we were just saying with James, but they're all content to sit here, near starving, following his orders. And I think he's keeping the, ah, grandmother"—Sierra had just barely stopped herself from saying "old lady"—"away from the rest of the family."

"Sounds plausible enough," Alan said thoughtfully.

"The question I'm wondering about is whether you have the Purification Skill. I leveled up my Laying on Hands Skill a fair amount, and I was trying to decide if I should get Purification or Rapid Healing."

"What's the difference between these two Skills?" Mitzi asked.

"Purification is a Skill that helps you remove Status effects—uh, impurities—from a person. It includes being able to remove things ranging from poisoning to foreign mental influences. Rapid Healing is a Skill that works like a better version of Laying on Hands; it just helps you heal the person faster."

I didn't really want the Purification Skill. It seems too specialized, whereas I imagine that Rapid Healing probably could have saved my brother or anyone who has a breath of life remaining in their body. But the way things are now, it's like the System's screaming at me to get Purification. Maybe it's fate. I can't ignore the reality around me.

"The System didn't even offer me a choice when I leveled up Laying on Hands," Alan said. "There must be something different about your Talents stack that affected it. I have Rapid Healing, following our joint healing effort with Camila."

Wow. Did the System give me early access to a Skill that Alan won't get until later, just so I could address this situation? Or is it like Alan said and just a result of different Talents? I do have David's abilities . . .

"Well, that settles it," Sierra said. "We don't need to both get Rapid Healing right now. I bet I'll be able to get it later anyway, and Laying on Hands is a great Skill in itself. I'm going to get Purification, and I'm going to test my suspicion that people's minds are being clouded."

"That sounds like a good idea. None of us likes the idea of this undue influence in our midst. But, just to play devil's advocate for a moment, what happens if you remove it, and Chava notices immediately?" Mitzi asked.

"Let's wait for James," Alan and Sierra said simultaneously. The three of them grinned.

Sierra sighed. *Frustrating, but I guess there's no one else who can handle crowd control if Chava has a way of tracking who's under his influence and who isn't. If he decides that his family should get violent because we're breaking his control, I don't want to imagine how that would go. I just don't like living in* Invasion of the Body Snatchers *for a second longer than I have to.*

"It's agreed, then, I think," Mitzi said.

Alan nodded, and Sierra reluctantly followed suit.

Sierra split up with the couple, and all three went about their days as if the conversation had never happened. She selected Purification over Rapid Healing.

Another night passed. A new day dawned.

Sierra sat uneasily, eating her bowl of oatmeal. It was noticeably smaller than the previous day's serving, which confirmed her beliefs about the trajectory of the camp's situation. She kept an eye on her surroundings as she ate. Since the theory-affirming conversation with Alan and Mitzi the previous day, she couldn't shake the feeling that she was effectively surrounded by the walking dead. Any moment now, if she didn't keep her guard up, one of them might take a bite out of her. *Never thought I'd be wishing for James to come back.*

It was while she was surreptitiously looking out of the corner of her eye for any sign of disturbance that she noticed movement from within the trees.

Her head immediately swiveled to get a better look. The shape seemed too large to be human, yet it held the shape of a man. It moved, slowly but definitely, toward the camp.

Sierra couldn't make out any features, but she hesitated to raise the alarm. There was something familiar about the figure.

CHAPTER FORTY-ONE

The Aftermath

A god has descended to Orientation 0284715.]
There was a sound of instruments, playing a song that James could only recognize as originating from a long time ago, in a faraway country.

He did note a rain stick among the instruments, as well as unidentified percussion and string instruments. James dimly remembered visits to the Orlando Public Library with his mother as a child, where the librarians would sometimes play music from various countries to accompany stories representing different cultures.

They had instruments like this. What cultures did they use them for? He landed on "vaguely African" for his identification of the music's origin before the god spoke.

"Congratulations on living through all of that, human!" The booming voice reverberated through the air and into James's head and body. The jovial sound hurt James's eardrums badly, and he felt a pain in his head worse than any injury he had taken in the battle with the Queen. He reflexively covered his ears with his hands, but he could tell he had already taken damage from the soundwaves alone. James felt a liquid dripping down the sides of his ears. He only hoped he didn't have a serious brain injury.

"I see my voice was not properly modulated for your level." The voice had abruptly shifted to something bearable, albeit still booming. The tone sounded slightly teasing now, and not entirely directed at James, as if the god were chiding someone who wasn't present. James was just glad that he no longer felt the beginnings of a migraine.

James removed his hands from his ears. They came away bloody, as he had expected.

Surreal, James thought. *I guess he doesn't* want *to kill me, though. Since he could clearly do it with just his voice.*

"It's an honor to meet you, um, god," James said haltingly. Before the System, he had been agnostic leaning toward atheist. This was a conversation he felt very unprepared for. "Uh, my name is—"

"You can relax, human," the god interrupted. **"Don't even bother introducing yourself. I have only a limited time in this vessel before her death will force me out."**

You could save her, James thought. The Spider Queen's body was continuing to slowly crack and melt under James's magical flames, and the god had done nothing to stop that since seizing control. *Couldn't you? You're a* god, *for gods' sake.* But perhaps the god could not directly interfere in Orientation matters. James was hazy on what the relationship was between divine beings and the System. *Or he doesn't really care.*

"I was impressed by your performance against my children, both now and earlier," the god continued. **"I always appreciate someone who uses his brains in a fight and not just his fangs and claws. You seem like my kind of warrior."**

The body the voice emerged from was almost a blackened crisp now, but the eyes glowed gently and appeared very lively despite the swift destruction of the body around them. It would've been captivating to see something that was clearly dying calmly holding a conversation, even if the one inside the body hadn't been a god.

"I wanted to encourage you to seek me out later on. That's all I came for. I think you and I would get along. If you want to find me, you should look off the edge of the map. If you find me, I'll test you. If you pass, I can tell you a story, a story." Those last words were almost a croak.

"Off the edge of the map. Got it," James said. "I think the Queen is just about dead. Is there anything else you wanted to tell me, O Mighty One?"

The god emitted a rumbling chuckle.

"Heh. Heh. The spirit is willing, but the flesh is weak; yes. We'll talk again soon, I hope. If you're the man I think you are, then you should seek me out. Seek me out if you yearn for power and wisdom. I could teach you many things. *Many things.*"

"You're not going to take it personally that I was killing your, um, children, then?" James asked.

"The spider bears many young," the god replied. James could hear a shrug in its tone, though the posture of the body remained unchanged. **"Their lives are their own, and I know you have your reasons.** *I just hope you won't make a habit of it.*" A note of warning there.

"May I ask what your name is?" James had an idea of which god he was speaking to, but he wanted confirmation before he decided if he would actually go and seek this god out.

"I think you know it already," the god said. **"If not, consider that your first test. To enter my web, you will have to speak my name."**

James was silent, but he thought it was as good as confirmed. He knew who it was he was speaking with: Anansi, the Spider. Anansi, God of Knowledge, Stories, Trickery, and Wisdom. *My favorite god from mythology.* James found himself surprisingly pleased to receive the god's approval and attention.

"My time is up," the god broke the silence. **"Good luck, human. Farewell, until I see you again!"**

James awkwardly raised a hand and waved goodbye.

The flames burned the Spider Queen's body down the rest of the way, and James heard the vaguely African instrumental music playing again. The great weight of the presence eased off, and the light pulled out of the Spider Queen's body. The weight and the light floated off into the sky somewhere.

Into the heavens, James thought involuntarily. He needed to integrate these new revelations into his worldview when he had some free time. For now, though, he wanted to find somewhere safe and get some rest. As he relaxed a bit, the notifications came flooding in.

[You killed Baby Wood Spider, Lv. 1. You gained 1 exp!]

James was reminded of a certain hero-turned-villain in a galaxy far, far away: "I killed them. I killed them all. They're dead. Every single one of them. And not just the men, but the women and the children too!" He cringed a little inside at the memory as the notifications continued on for a long time. *Really, though, it is kind of fucked up. Hopefully, this doesn't just reinforce the System's perception of me as some kind of monster.*

[You killed Baby Wood Spider, Lv. 1. You gained 1 exp!]

Well, maybe I am a little bit of a monster, farming all the babies for experience.

A list of notifications unfolded that went on for an uncomfortably long time.

[You killed Feral Wood Spider, Lv. 6. You gained 80 exp!]

[. . .]

Okay, maybe I'm a lot like a monster.

[You killed Wood Spider Queen, Lv. 20. You gained 1000 exp!]

[Predator in Human Skin leveled up!]

There had been somewhere over two hundred spider fatalities before the Spider Queen's popped up—James had lost count and only really noted the level up before this last one, which had brought Predator in Human Skin to level eighteen and System-Boosted Human to level ten. Disturbingly, a huge chunk of the fatalities had in fact been baby spiders. The vast majority of them. The Queen was quite a breeder. *Probably best that I did this, before all those spiders fanned out over the forest, killing and eating everything in sight. Spiders were all carnivores, after all.*

[Conditions met! New Title obtained: Xenocide!]

This shit's getting dark, James thought. He examined the Title.

[Xenocide: As an entity responsible for causing an extinction event for another species that had over a hundred members, your nature is truly that of a monster to be feared. Your enemies will find their names erased from the history books. As such, enjoy a 10% bonus to all Stats when facing an enemy of another Race. Enjoy a 20% bonus when facing an enemy who is the last or only member of their Race.]

So, the System is pegging me as a brutal monster again. Confirmed. Well, at this point, maybe that's fair. But they were spiders. So it was really more of an extermination than anything else . . . Then again, the Queen at least was intelligent. And capable of human speech. That was unexpected. Unpleasant. Can they all become increasingly intelligent at the higher levels or something?

Whatever. Best not to think too hard about this. It's counterproductive at best. As long as monsters start fights, I'll be fighting them whether I like it or not. The Title will end up being useful. Hopefully, I won't end up committing too many more xenocides . . . Time to collect loot!

"Pillage!" He selected Talent; surely a Talent from the Queen would be good.

[Wood Spider Queen's body processed.]

[You obtained Royal Exoarmor, Deadly Necrotic Venom Sac, and Ego Spidersword!]

[Talent Obtained: Monster Matriarch!]

Hm? Do I look like a woman to you, System?

[Talent adapting to you . . . Talent Obtained: Monster Patriarch!]

Better. He examined his new Talent.

[Monster Patriarch: You were born into this world the first of your kind, but not the last. You have a natural capacity to create life from your own organic matter. Generates Skills Monster Generation and Monster Control.]

He tried to contain his excitement. This sounded quite good, maybe even overpowered, although it was clearly very specifically written for someone other than James. But he did question whether the System would really let it work as intended for him, considering he lacked the reproductive organs of a female spider. Or any female reproductive organs at all, actually.

I wonder what I can actually spawn, considering that despite some of my Skills, I'm not actually a monster. The individual Skill descriptions would probably give him more of an idea of how it worked.

[Monster Generation: Create new monsters from parts of yourself. Designate biomass within or recently connected to your body, hold the design of your monster and which of your Skills you wish it to inherit firmly

in your mind, and inject sufficient Mana to give it life. Effectiveness scales with all aspects of your personal power.]

[Monster Control: Dominate the minds of monsters created from your biomass. No cost. Effectiveness is uniformly high but scales with all aspects of your personal power and inversely scales with power and Intelligence of a monster if it surpasses the creator.]

Interesting that those are two separate Skills. And what, do I have to chop off a hand to use Monster Generation? James desperately wanted to experiment with these new abilities. There was an excitement building in him at the idea that he might one day have an army like the spiders' colony at his beck and call.

And there had also been an alert in the midst of the long stream of notifications that had him even more intrigued.

[A Race Evolution is available. Review? Y/N]

At last! he thought when it first appeared. Just what he'd been hoping for and expecting. A new step forward for him. Maybe a new tier of power. But he had set it aside just as quickly as it appeared since there were a number of pop-ups to be examined, and this seemed like something that would take up some time.

But before he could sit down and deal with either the new Skills or the Race Evolution, there was a mountain of spider corpses in the forest to be Looted before other predators could get at the bodies. That would probably further develop his powers in any case. So, experimentation now could wind up being redundant, as well as burn some of his limited window of time.

James set off to claim what was his.

Fortunately, when he returned to the still-smoking husk of the spider's den, there were no signs of any living entities. It was a silent spider graveyard. They were territorial creatures, he recalled from what the Queen had said. *I guess no rival has noticed their disappearance yet.*

Mass Pillage yielded a virtual mountain of redundant spider-related equipment, as well as multiple levels for previously gained Skills and two new Skills, which he examined.

[Silk Production: Develops a set of organs that can be used to naturally produce silk of great tensile strength. Silk can be manipulated via Mana. Silk quality can be improved by the infusion of Mana or other energies. Consumes caloric energy. Consumes additional forms of energy if the user attempts to produce silk beyond a certain threshold without a break.]

That first Skill seemed useful, but it was the second that he found fascinating.

[Stem Cell Production: Generates cells that can replicate indefinitely, permitting enhanced active and passive regeneration, including prevention or reversal of the natural aging process.]

When he examined this one, another notification appeared.

[Quest unlocked: Path to Immortality!]

This immediately interested James, and he examined it further.

[Path to Immortality: You have touched upon one of the paths to immortality. Continue to develop along this path to ultimately transcend death. Reward for Quest Success: True Immortality. Penalty for Failure: Death.]

James chuckled at the penalty. *Sure. You'll kill me if I don't figure out immortality. And there's no time limit given. Funny, System!* He read it again, suppressing any skepticism. *Very brief description. Tantalizing, nevertheless. Imagine if Mina and our family and I could live forever.* Some people, James knew, thought that immortality sounded boring. But he'd noticed that most of them were not immortal, and he was interested in trying the experiment for himself. *I'll do whatever I can to pursue this path.*

For the first time, James thought he could see the System offering something up besides sheer freedom. Something that would make up for everything that it had taken away from countless people already. If it made immortality possible, all the means required would be justified by the ends.

Hell, that's half of why people have kids of their own in the first place. It's the closest—in a humble and insufficient way—that most of us could ever get to approaching immortality. Not that I would ever pursue it at the expense of taking care of my family. He thought of his family and felt that his desire to be reunited with them was undiminished by this discovery. *But it is a lot like a map to the Holy Grail just fell into my lap!*

For decades, scientists had speculated that stem cells could be the secret to the fountain of youth. They destroyed countless embryos, experimented on animals, and in some places secretly experimented on full-grown humans, all to inch closer to something that was now, suddenly and without prelude, falling into James's hands. Eternal youth.

Time enough at last.

As he reflected, James walked slowly back toward the Rodriguez camp. Even with a possible future path to immortality in his back pocket, he still fancied sleeping back among people and completing his Race Evolution near humans too. Even if he was strong enough to slaughter the lot of them singlehandedly, there was safety in numbers. It would take time for him to tame the world enough, or grow strong enough, to feel completely safe sleeping entirely alone.

And he had accomplished all that he'd promised.

CHAPTER FORTY-TWO

Children of the Dark

As James walked, he kept his senses open to his surroundings.

He had fought the Spider Queen in the dark of night. But after that long battle, his conversation with a god that he was ninety percent certain was Anansi, and the trek back to the spider nest to Pillage all the bodies, hours had passed. As he navigated his way back to camp, the veil of night seemed almost ready to lift.

The first rays of daylight were creeping up just below the horizon.

He followed the only nearby source of smoke besides the still-smoking spider nest ruins: the camp fires that the Rodriguez camp kept lit at night.

James remembered reading somewhere that the hours around sunrise and sunset were particularly bad for car accidents. Visibility was poor, the ambiguous lighting making it difficult to distinguish obstacles on the road from the glare off of nearby reflective objects. Deer tended to be active around those times as well.

And James was guessing that this would also be when predatory animals were most active, especially now. Nocturnal predators wouldn't have returned to their dens to sleep just yet, while diurnal predators were just beginning to look for breakfast.

It's a good thing I'm a predator myself, he thought. But he still felt the need for caution.

As he advanced, he sensed movement in the trees around twenty feet to his right. James didn't want to fight right now. Though he was back at full resources after some time walking—a fair bit faster than he'd gotten used to!—he was also fairly certain he had a significant power boost coming. It made no sense to him to do more fighting when he wasn't in his best possible condition.

But some creature was moving toward him, and he thought he heard something else moving after it. Getting into a fight might be unavoidable. He slowed down to listen.

Is this thing being hunted? he wondered.

James finally decided to leap into a tree. He jumped up through several layers of branches until he thought he would be adequately concealed. He generated spider silk—like Sam Raimi's Spider-Man, he had developed spinneret-like organs on his wrists as well as near his ankles—and he secured himself to the tree.

Then he sat still, and with his previously used technique, he minimized all the auditory indicators of his presence. His heart rate decreased, and his breathing slowed and dropped to the minimum necessary.

He stared down, body stiff and unmoving as a corpse, as the first of the creatures below finally came into view.

There was a two-headed wolf of the kind he'd seen before: a Command Forest Wolf. He remembered how the one he had seen before had breathed fire and been fairly formidable back when he was at a lower level. *But why does it appear to be running away from something else?*

Identify!

[Command Forest Wolf, Lv. 12: A wolf cultivated for the Orientation by the System. Part of a pack, this specimen is one of the upper-tier members, a beta. Equal to the average System-Enhanced Human in Stamina and Dexterity, vastly superior in Agility and Strength. Stronger when under the command of a higher-level life-form.]

Well, it's not low level. I could certainly take it, but how many other creatures or humans are there in this forest that it would need to run from? Then again, the non-human population of the Orientation seemed stronger and stronger the more time James spent here.

James found himself slightly nervous waiting for whatever was coming out of the trees after the Command Forest Wolf.

For its part, the wolf looked as panicked as James could imagine a wolf looking. It darted its heads in different directions, as if it wasn't sure which way to run next. It sniffed the air and kept turning its heads from side to side, apparently expecting an attack at any moment. Finally, it raised both muzzles to the sky and let out a single long, shared howl.

"Awooooo!!!" Even that sounded desperate to James's ears. A cry for help.

Kind of glad I'm up here, he thought. *What the hell is chasing it?*

And then he got his answer.

A condensed missile of fur and rippling muscle burst from the trees.

It seized the Command Forest Wolf in its jaws and claws, and James got his first good look at this monster.

It was a wolf too, to the naked eye. At least if you'd only seen wolves before in nature documentaries, and not in old movies starring Lon Chaney. Even then, though, you would have to think that this was a wolf on steroids.

The Command Forest Wolf tried to breathe lightning out of the head that wasn't being mauled in the monster's jaws. James saw electric sparks coalescing into a ball in the Command Forest Wolf's maw. The bigger wolf reacted too quickly for it, though. It grabbed its opponent with its claws and slammed the Command Forest Wolf's muzzle shut. The big thing was clearly something of a tactical fighter as well as a muscular, hulking monstrosity. But James was less interested in which would win and more curious about what the larger monster really was.

Where did that thing come from? Is every myth true? he wondered.

Because he had no doubt about what he was seeing, even before using Identify. The eight-foot-tall, hulking brute of fur and fang that stood beneath the tree, ripping into the smaller, inferior wolf with its jaws could only be a wolf-man. Werewolf. Rougarou. Whatever the culture, the concept was the same.

Maybe I'll actually meet a dragon one of these days, he thought.

Recovering a bit from his surprise, he finally used Identify to confirm his suspicion.

[Damien Rousseau, Lv. 10]

He is *human!* Otherwise, Identify would have given James more information. *I really need to get more experience with that Skill so it will confirm things like "This is a werewolf." Just basic stuff. It's not like knowing whether he has a vulnerability to silver bullets would really help me at a time like this. But not even confirming that he's a werewolf is absurd!*

The apparent werewolf below was now eating the very dead and dismembered Command Forest Wolf, and James found it gruesome even by his standards. It was hard to just sit there as the smell of shit and ruptured organs drifted up into his nostrils. It was even more difficult to watch the werewolf slurp up the steaming entrails like soft spaghetti noodles. With James's heightened senses, he almost wanted to vomit.

Yet he didn't want to take his eyes off of this supernatural apex predator. That took priority.

A thought occurred to him. *Rousseau is at Race level ten.* Race was the level that actually showed under Identify, he had learned through discussion with his comrades previously. Which meant that Rousseau might have already undergone the Evolution that James was about to embark on. *Did Race Evolution turn him into that?*

It was a disconcerting thought. Would James become a monster? *Surely it would at least give him a choice. Right?* James had been given a choice of Classes when he went through the Tutorial, then again when he experienced Class Evolution. *But then, I was only offered one choice of Job.*

James hadn't quite worked out a general theory of how the System worked, so whether he'd have options seemed to be almost a coin toss.

That left him with two opposite impulses. The first was to put off Race Evolution. He hoped he wouldn't need any extra power, anyway. Even now, as he watched this monstrous creature tearing into its prey beneath him, James thought he could probably defeat it in combat if he had to fight it now. *Right?*

If the werewolf was indeed the result of Race Evolution, James didn't think he really needed to go through it.

On the other hand, there was the impulse to forget about his previous plan to return to camp first and do the Evolution here and now.

The forest was clearly dangerous at this hour. Although James could conceal himself—the werewolf was now marking its territory at the bottom of his tree without apparently noticing him—the concealment would be much less effective while James was moving.

But now that he had seen the werewolf, there was another thought preying on his mind. Knowing himself, he was definitely going to say yes to Race Evolution at some point in the future. *I still want much more power.*

And in the event that the initial transformation looked monstrous in some way, James thought it might be a bad idea to be around other humans when he made the change. If he had randomly come across the werewolf and not had his super senses give an advance warning, he'd have attacked it without hesitation. James didn't want to wind up fighting his allies.

Maybe just Cliff. Only if it was strictly necessary, of course.

James decided to do the Evolution right here as soon as the werewolf went on its way.

Whether fortunately or otherwise, he didn't have long to wait.

There was a howling of multiple wolves somewhere in the distance. Then a repeat howl, around twenty seconds later. Closer.

The werewolf didn't respond either time, and James guessed that it was a lone creature. This pack was the one that its prey had belonged to.

His prey, James reminded himself. *Somewhere in there, despite his appearance, there's a human, an intelligent being. If the pack comes here, maybe I should fight alongside him.*

The idea didn't need to be considered for very long, though. The werewolf raised his snout, scented the wind, and fled, running in the opposite direction from the sounds of howling.

James decided to forego attempting to Pillage the remains of the Command Forest Wolf, which were strewn about the ground around his tree. Instead, he climbed a bit higher up into the branches, in case the wolf pack might get the crazy idea that he was the one who'd turned their brother into bratwurst.

If they're dangerous enough for him to run from, I'll trust the werewolf's judgment!

He secured himself to the highest branch that he was sure would support his weight, and he wrapped himself around the tree with a tight cocoon of spider silk.

He'd never done anything so extensive with the thread in the brief time he'd had it, but the multiple levels in the Skill from Pillaging over a hundred spiders seemed to help. He was surprised how practiced he felt at silk spinning, doing it almost for the first time. It was as natural as typing had been pre-System. But then, he supposed the spiders didn't have to think much about it when they were doing it either.

He pulled the Race Evolution prompt back up.

[A Race Evolution is available. Review? Y/N]

James selected "Y," and the world around him instantly faded to black.

There was a feeling of vast emptiness all around James. He didn't know if he had been physically sucked away to another plane of existence, or whether this was a journey into the center of his mind or some such vision quest.

As he tried to interact with the blackness, a few features appeared in the dim void. Twinkling stars shimmered in the vast distance. And several glowing points began to burn bright in the much nearer vicinity. One was red, another blue, one green, one yellow, one purple, and the last was orange.

These are my Evolution choices, James knew immediately.

He moved toward the two nearest floating lights. He didn't know if he walked or floated there himself; there was no feeling of his legs being present at all, no pressure of a limb touching a surface, no awareness of the position of any part of his body.

It didn't matter anyway. This was the place of Evolution. He felt instinctively that it wasn't a place where he could fight or be attacked. *I didn't need to worry about securing myself anywhere*, he thought. *I doubt my body is in the Orientation anymore at all.*

He reached out toward the nearest light, purple, with his mind.

[Dhampir], it said. He wasn't sure if he wanted to read the description or not.

Dhampir, as in half-vampire? James thought. He was well-read enough in fantasy to recognize the obscure term. *First I see a werewolf, and now the System heavily implies the existence of vampires. Starting to feel like I'm in a bad young adult novel.*

But the next closest light, green, erased that impression.

[Reptilian] was the name that appeared. Far from the stuff of romantic fantasies.

I guess I'd better start reading these descriptions, James thought glumly. *Seems as if I'm going to be stuck with one of these for a while.*

CHAPTER FORTY-THREE

And in the End . . .

guess I'll start with the description for Reptilian. Somewhere inside his seemingly non-material form, James thought he might have sighed.

Then he focused on the green light, and the description materialized in the darkness.

[Reptilian: You have fought literally tooth and nail, showing thick skin and a cool head while seizing your opportunities. You have reached elite levels of combat ferocity, predatory stealth, and cold-blooded manipulation among the Orientation populations. Your next step is the form of a Reptilian, a life-form with adaptations suitable for doubling down on all of these outstanding traits. Lose some human-specific abilities in exchange for Reptilian traits, such as enhanced camouflage, cold blood, improved regeneration, and an additional limb in the form of a tail. Gain 2 points for each Stat you have unlocked up to this point for each level in Race.]

That's an interesting choice . . . I'd be a little more powerful, sure, but who would give up being human just for enhanced camouflage, cold blood, improved regeneration—okay, the tail would be pretty cool. But still!

He imagined how Mina would look at him if he showed up at the apartment with the body of a super-sized lizard. The image that popped up in his mind was of a green-skinned Bangaa from Final Fantasy. He could practically hear her shriek. He felt the urge to shudder at the thought himself, but with no body, the shudder just manifested as intense revulsion. *No. No, thank you. Next!*

Now he read the Dhampir description, since he was already close to the purple light associated with that Race.

[Dhampir: You have shown a capacity for secrecy, charisma, and an affinity with the mystic arts. You have achieved incredible results as a stealthy hunter and demonstrated promise as a cold-blooded and manipulative leader of humans. Your next stage is the form of the Dhampir, a step on the vampiric evolutionary tree. Part vampire, part human, you can choose between preying upon humanity or living as a daywalker who defends humans from your vampire cousins. Accept a weakness to sunlight in exchange for enhanced attributes across the board at night. Gain Shadow Affinity, Basic Shadow Magic, Basic Soul Magic, and 3 points to each Stat you have unlocked up to this point with every new level in Race.]

Well, at least vampires and part-vampires are known for being attractive to humans. But I think I've seen this movie before. Shunned by human and vampire kind alike, our hero must fight a lonely war against the forces of darkness from the fringes of society. No, thank you! I want to be at the top *of society. Please, give me something better!*

His spirit body moved toward the orange glow.

[Ogre: You have shown a great love of battle, the bloodier and more violent the better. You're a consumer of human flesh and a consummate killer of your fellow man. Your next step will bring you to the pinnacle of brute physical force. The Ogre grinds humans up to make his bread and preys upon anything weaker than himself, which is most things. Accept a sharp penalty to Intelligence and minor penalty to Stealth in exchange for drastic increases to all physical Stats. Gain Iron Skin and Iron Muscles, as well as 6 points to each physical Stat with every new level in Race.]

No! Fail! Epic fail! Hell no! Do you think I'm a dumbass, System? He wanted to scream, but he didn't think he had a mouth here. After a few seconds, his wrath quelled enough for him to think more analytically. *I wonder if I got the Ogre and Dhampir because I consumed human flesh. Maybe Reptilian too. Fucking System tricked me! I hope there's at least some semi-humanoid Race. I would take "human but with fluffy ears and a tail," at this point.* He turned somber for a moment. *Will I really have to trade in my humanity to become one of these appalling* things?

He moved on to the yellow light, which he noted looked a bit like gaslight from a period movie. Just from looking at it, he expected something mystical, and in that, he was not disappointed.

[Wraith: You have demonstrated a great capacity for the destructive side of the mystic arts. You have also shown an affinity for the use of Stealth and a willingness to prey upon your fellow humans. Your next step removes you from humanity completely, casting aside your physical body with its weaknesses for the form of the Wraith. As a Wraith, you lose most of your physical power in exchange for becoming completely immune to physical attacks, but experience a sharp increase in Intelligence, Will, and

Stealth. You will need to feed upon souls to sustain your existence in this new form—but, happily, souls remain a plentiful commodity in the post-System world. Accept a slight weakness to light and certain magics and the loss of certain human abilities. In exchange, open the Soul Power Stat, and gain Shadow Affinity, Basic Shadow Magic, Basic Soul Magic, and 6 points to each non-physical Stat you have unlocked with every new level in Race.]

System, are you serious? Dhampir is starting to look really good right now. Do better at knowing your audience! Wraith is an even worse fit for me than Reptilian and Ogre, and I didn't think that was possible!

James moved and focused himself on the blue glow next, which he saw from closer up took the shape of a blue-colored lantern. The description appeared, and he was instantly relieved by the title.

[Evolved Human: You have struggled, and you have overcome. You have built your Stats one body at a time, until you reached this position. You have achieved the peak of what is possible for a System-Boosted Human, and you have become a peak life-form of that type. Now the time has come to accept your peak progress and convert your remaining potential into hard power, with all that exchange implies. Your final form is that of the Evolved Human, a life-form that dominates all System-Boosted Humans and sits atop the Orientation food chain, capable of besting even the hardiest foes from the Orientation setting in single combat. Gain 10 Free Points for every level in your Race that you have attained to this point. Enjoy your position at the pinnacle for as long as you can maintain it!]

Not remotely ideal, but at least I have an option where I remain human in name, James thought. *That choice is disappointing, only because it sounds too much like an endpoint for my growth. I'll be the strongest in Orientation, maybe. But surely I have to think about life beyond Orientation. Those ten Free Points per level are probably meant to sound generous, but they feel more like a bribe. It sounds like a one-time gain. I'd get super-strong for now, and then I'd have to worry about everyone who didn't take the Evolved Human route creeping up in my rearview mirror.* He considered the Dhampir option again. In the long run, that would certainly make him stronger.

He thought of Mina again. *Vampires are sexy, right?* But maybe not to her. She wasn't as into horror movies as he was, and he realized he didn't know if she'd ever read any vampire fiction. *With Evolved Human, at least I'd still be human, of a sort. Didn't think I'd be so attached to my species, honestly, but compared with the alternatives, I guess I really like what's familiar. And, let's be real, I don't want to be some kind of hideous monster. I hope the other option isn't so closed off.*

Next, James focused on the red glow, which he observed seemed to be moving. The other lights had appeared static, but this one moved like a flame. As he stared at it in the moment before the description appeared, the flame flickered slightly. It looked unstable.

[Evolver Human: You have struggled, and you will go on struggling. You have fought and overcome, and you must go on fighting and winning. You have yet to reach the pinnacle, but every day is a battle with your past self and with those who threaten to overtake you. Your new form is that of an Evolver Human, an unstable state of being that must either continue on to a new stage or collapse. Gain 2 points to each Stat you have unlocked up to this point with every new level in Race. If you fail to gain additional levels in your Race for an extended period, you will regress to the form of a System-Boosted Human and lose the Stat points you have gained since becoming an Evolver Human. Struggle on, struggler. Struggle, fail, and struggle again. If you ever cease advancing, death will not be far behind.]

The difference between the two human options was stark now that James had read both. The blue glow clearly offered security, at least for the short term, while the red glow was about the possibility for endless, perpetual growth. One would reinforce—for now—the status of strongest that he had just been thinking about. The other would require him to continually run a race to maintain and exceed his own efforts thus far. To keep gaining levels required greater accomplishments, which meant he would always have to surpass himself.

If I choose the red glow, it's unstable. If I had to guess my future trajectory, I either blow up to become one of the most successful humans in the new world, or I collapse into weakness and obscurity.

Given this train of thought, the choice was obvious. The option to challenge himself was what would take him the furthest in the long run. The System was testing his will and belief in himself. James had never encountered a test he couldn't pass in his life. There was no way he would allow himself to fail this time and, equally, no way he would pass up this opportunity.

James reached out to the red glow with his mind, and he felt the glowing red light pull itself into him.

[Evolver Human Evolution option selected! Initiating Evolution!]

James thought he saw another notification pop up, but he wasn't sure.

[You have chosen well . . .]

If it had existed, then it had flickered up and then disappeared.

And James couldn't be sure if he'd seen it, because as soon as he'd made his choice, James's world exploded with pain. The sensation could best be described as billions of paper cuts across his entire body, inside and out, as his cells seemingly spontaneously tore themselves apart.

But it was worse than spontaneous bodily self-destruction. He'd chosen this.

And Pain Resistance was apparently doing nothing.

Before, he had questioned whether his body was physically present within the void. He couldn't see anything or feel anything, including his own limbs. Now, he knew his body must be there because he was racked with agony. He screamed inside of his own mind. It felt as if he was coming undone.

His consciousness faded in and out, as unendurable pain forced his brain alternately to shut down and restart.

As he rebooted, James's memories intercut with the blackness in his vision. The images seemed to change color, melt, and stretch like taffy. He saw his father, alive and well again, and then he saw that his father was holding the cake that James vaguely remembered eating for one of his single-digit birthdays.

Then his father and the cake were stretching, bending and contorting at impossible angles, turning funny colors, going pink, then red, then auburn. Then James's vision went black again.

It didn't stay black for long. James flashed forward. There was his mother, standing over his father's grave. The mourners were gathered around them. None of them would help over the years to come, no matter what they said here. James's hallucination ignored them and focused on his mother.

Her skin, the same shade that James saw when he looked in the mirror, was young and flawless. *Beautiful.* Far too young to be a widow, alone in the world except for her children. This time, the vision had sound.

"You're the man of the house now, my son," she said. And he knew that it was true. Now it was his responsibility to take care of her and his baby sister.

Through the pain, through the awareness that this was a memory, a vision, a hallucination, James retained enough of himself to think, *No, it's not on you! Don't try to fill his shoes! You're only a kid. You can't do it . . .*

Then his vision was drawn to the grave. How had he not noticed that the grave was still open? Why was it open? Wasn't it closed by the time she said that in real life? As he looked into the deep hole, James felt himself pulled forward, as if the black void had a gravitational pull coming from somewhere deep down that he couldn't see.

Then he fell into blackness.

As he fell, he wondered if it was possible that he was being punished for his sins.

CHAPTER FORTY-FOUR

Remembrance of Things Past

James was pulled through the darkness of the grave until he found himself in a dimly lit room.

From the dingy yellow light, he recognized the setting even before he saw the furnishings or her face. It wasn't a place or a moment he ever wanted to revisit, but he didn't try to close himself off from it.

Focusing on the vision beat out focusing on the pain by a small margin, but only because the pain he endured was bone-boiling agony.

The scene was exactly the one that he had anticipated on seeing the scenery. Sure enough, there sat his dear sweet mother, teary, with dark circles under her eyes.

James had walked in on a scene he wasn't meant to, and his mother wiped moisture away from the corners of her eyes and tried to reassure him that things were fine. They were fine.

But even at thirteen, James was perceptive, precocious. In an instant, his eyes took in the overdue bills. His mind went to the ballet lessons his sister had been abruptly withdrawn from. And the surroundings provided context. The ugly little room with garish blue-green wallpaper. It was the only room in their new apartment where she had a little privacy. But not much privacy at all. Their circumstances had forced them to downgrade from their two-bedroom house.

Everyone experiences the discomfort of being poor in their own way. For James, it was the smaller amount and lower quality of food that initially stuck out. For Alice, it was less bathroom time, since they now all shared one toilet and one shower. For their mother, it was the loss of privacy.

The shame of it was that the door to her private space didn't close all the way.

It would jam every time she tried to close it, and opening it again made a terrible noise. So the door was rarely closed, and James never knew when she actually wanted to be alone there.

When he heard his mother weeping, he made up an excuse to enter.

The memory lacked sound, but James remembered the gist of their exchange that evening. Everything was all right. Work would come soon enough. Nursing jobs were a bit thin on the ground just then, but she would find something. No money for Alice's ballet slippers, but they would find a way. The family would find a way somehow.

But the family was only James, Alice, and their mother now. She was out of work.

So, who would find the way?

I paid for those goddamned ballet slippers, James thought. It was a bitter-sweet triumph because the slippers were only the start of something, but James clutched tightly to it.

The scene receded into darkness, like a curtain being drawn, and the pain engulfed him again until his conscious mind melted away.

The blessed oblivion of unconsciousness lasted for an indeterminate time until James became fully aware of himself again. He could feel that his body had finished dissolving.

Something new was happening. Something far less painful, thankfully. *Growth?*

He tried to assess it, but then another scene swam into view before James's eyes, or whatever visual organ was perceiving things. James wasn't sure if he had eyes at all anymore. He could swear that every cell in his body had self-destructed while he proceeded through his Evolution in the void.

The new vision became clear. James recognized what he was seeing immediately. Years had passed, and this memory was a bit fresher. Crisp. The image was a computer screen. The whole of the email exchange was displayed, but his eyes focused on the only words that mattered:

Sure thing. My account number is 2 6 8 - 5 9 4 7 - 8 6 5 9. PIN is 4989. Thank you so much for the opportunity!

With this disposable email account and a secondhand laptop, James was about to steal money through the Internet for the first time.

He had taken things before through petty shoplifting or picking pockets. But this was a new door opening. A different level of opportunity, coupled with a higher risk if caught. The easy money was intoxicating. The power of lies could get him anything he wanted. Today, he would clear out a juicy chunk of the money in this bank account. *Like taking candy from a baby, really*, he recalled.

And before the mark realized she wasn't getting the money back, let alone the return James had promised her, he'd already have tuition money for his sister's fancy private school, plus some groceries. His mother had already learned not to question how he was getting his contributions to the refrigerator or birth-day gifts.

Don't do it, present-day James thought. *Don't start on this track. It can get so much worse than a little petty theft . . .* But his past self's actions were already determined.

"Too easy," he heard young James crow. And that was at least part of the problem, present-day James knew.

Why are people so dumb? present-day James thought. *If not for gullible people like this—*

He stopped himself before he completed the thought, aware he was about to blame his victims for his own crimes. Victims to whom he had never made restitution. Perhaps he wasn't so different even now.

The picture below faded into darkness, and a new image emerged.

Even with his body now in the midst of a reconstruction that was almost painless, with most of James's nerve endings apparently already killed off, he was riveted by the scene.

"Excuse me, sir," a young woman said. "I am new here. Could you point me to Student Union?"

She was stunning. Perfectly kissable lips, nut-brown eyes, long dark hair. *So thin*, he thought, looking down at the scene. Mina had come from a poor family back home. She was one of seven siblings, so there was never quite enough food to go around. And the oldest was also generally uninterested in grabbing food before her younger sisters and brother could. If someone was going to go hungry, she wanted it to be her. Or so James had gathered over the years.

Until I started feeding her, James thought, *she could barely fill out those second-hand jeans. Beautiful, though. She was always beautiful.*

As the vision unfolded, James saw his younger self guide the foreign student to the Student Union. Then they exchanged numbers. He told her that he could guide her anywhere she wanted to go, on campus or off, and that she should call or text him with any questions.

His behavior in his first interaction with Mina had not been based on the purest of intentions. James found her attractive and thought she might be an easy lay. But the impression he came away with on the day they met was one of innocence. The more they spoke, the more that first impression solidified. Mina Danailova was a sweet, purehearted girl obsessively concerned with caring for her family. She wanted to make something of herself professionally so that she could buy her mother a house.

James was so lost in a string of memories about Mina that it took him some time to realize the vision below him had dissolved and changed at some point.

He reoriented himself in the timeline and realized that he was in his least favorite memory after the death of his father. Where the memory of his conversation with his mother had been tinged with a mixture of regret and stubborn pride, this memory was one of abject humiliation.

A police officer stood inside the apartment he shared with Mina, eight months into their relationship. The officer was speaking in a grave tone.

"We'll see if the victim wants to press charges. If not, you won't hear from us again. I'm not your father, so it's not really my place. But you're a university student. You're on a good trajectory. You have to know that your life could go very differently if you get a criminal conviction."

Below, younger James was just nodding along. Present-day James remembered how he'd felt. Numb. Disbelieving. He'd finally been caught stealing. Now his fate hinged on someone else's decision.

Finally, the police officer left.

Now it was just Mina and James. He couldn't look her in the eyes. She'd been there for the whole thing, and James hadn't even thought to ask the police officer to take the conversation elsewhere or spare her in any way. Mina already knew a little about what he did to earn pocket money, and she had rolled her eyes, made gentle but critical remarks, and left the room while he was in the middle of working on his illicit activities.

Now the reality and consequences of his bad behavior were made more real for both of them.

She made her case, sitting close to him, clutching his hand tightly in hers, staring up into his eyes.

"I love you, skapi. I don't care so much that you steal from other people, because you've never hurt me, and I know you never would. What I'm scared of is that the police take you away, and I never see you again."

Tears touched past-James's eyes.

Mina continued on, but present-day James didn't want to listen to it. He was so ashamed of the memory that he tried to drown the vision out. But it shone through. That awful memory was a turning point. It was the most important day of his life.

In the end, he had promised her that he would never break the law again. By the time the conversation ended, both Mina and James were in tears. His criminal career was over. And soon after, the pathway to his legal career had begun. They had never spoken of that day since.

The world blurred and slowly faded into darkness in present-day James's view, as though he was falling asleep through a haze of tears.

And he realized that all his physical pain had gone. The darkness of the void had gone.

Drained me of everything, he thought bitterly, pulse pounding. He missed Mina intensely now. The smell of her. The feel of her body against his. The soft sound of her voice.

But he could feel his body again. He existed somewhere again. There was that. *The new body better be worth all of that.*

James's body appeared in the area from which it had vanished. For the first time in days, he wished he could be out of this place. He quickly shook the feeling off, though.

He was back in Orientation now, and unlike whatever memory-world he'd been in before, this was a place of constant danger.

He could tell that he had reappeared from a different space because his body no longer fit properly into the space it had previously inhabited. He was significantly larger than he had been. His head was thrust violently into the silk he had wound loosely around his body and connected to the tree.

The loose cocoon has become a death mask, James thought. *I'll probably have to use Shed Skin just to keep it from sticking to my face, I'm pressed against it so closely!*

But that minor nuisance seemed unimportant next to the alerts that now appeared in James's vision.

[Race Evolution completed! Evolver Human Race obtained.]

[New Skills obtained: Skill Fusion and Skill Transfer!]

Skill Fusion, huh? Well, I guess my list was getting a bit long and not feeling quite as useful as I'd have hoped from Pillage. Maybe fusion is just what the doctor ordered.

He reviewed the Skills' descriptions.

[Skill Fusion: Permanently or temporarily fuse two or more Skills of your choice. Selected Skills must be compatible for successful fusion. Fused Skills may be greater or lesser than the sum of their parts.]

I'll have to be careful where I use that permanently, he thought. *Better to just experiment with temporary fusions for now.*

[Skill Transfer: Transfer Skills to and from yourself, items in your possession, and entities under your control. You may also use Skill Transfer to convey Skills from one consenting adult entity to another.]

I love the contractual language there, James thought. *The System thinks that's such a broken Skill that I need strict limits on who I can use it on.* And it really was. Skill Transfer or Skill Fusion would have been invaluable by themselves, but together—and coupled with James's existing Skill stack—he could imagine them making Pillage, his bread and butter self-improvement Skill, exponentially more valuable.

Hell, they'll even make me more effective as a Politician, James thought. *I can now offer a service that perhaps no one else can!* Though it was possible others would obtain similar Skills if they chose the Evolver Human path for their Race Evolution, James suspected that any new abilities were individually designed to enhance the person undergoing Evolution.

And how many other people could have Pillage?

He would try multiple different Skill combinations on his way back to camp.

But first, let's tear our way out of this stuffy cocoon! Though he'd been very interested in the new Skills, it was starting to be a little annoying having a silken mask stuck fast to all the contours of his face.

James didn't want to burn his way out of the cocoon this time. He didn't even want to use Predator's Armaments to cut his way out. He wanted to test his improved body.

Could he rip through the spider silk?

He pulled and tore at it for several minutes trying to answer that question, but it was more difficult than he'd been expecting. *This silk is a stronger Skill than I'd even realized,* he thought.

But finally, he tore it from all around him, ripping a layer of skin from his face and sending himself plummeting down the side of the tree in one swift, fierce motion. He hit a half-dozen branches on the way down before the last stopped him.

I seem to be getting heavier now, he thought. *Yet no more pain from the fall than I'd get from a bee sting.* Part of that might be that he was still wearing the Royal Exoarmor he'd obtained from the Spider Queen. *But ripping off the top layer of skin with the webbing on it didn't hurt much either. It's like all my Skills are a little stronger now that my base is better.*

James looked down and assessed his situation. His Predator—*and Evolver?*—Senses showed him what had happened after he began his Evolution. There were scores, maybe hundreds, of paw prints on the ground below him, mostly faint, but very visible to him.

The whole pack arrived, they circled the tree—James winced at the next realization—*and they ate their dead. Not that I have room to judge.* He looked off to the left. *They took off that way.*

I would hunt them, but I need to get back before the people I left behind starve, he thought. But he noticed it would be remarkably easy now for him to identify which way the pack had run. With his sensory abilities, it was as if he had a tracking Skill now. *If I'd had these abilities when Kurt Royersford escaped me, one of his Skills would be on my sheet at this very moment.*

James smiled wolfishly. His current circumstances seemed to recontextualize the bad memories that he'd been forced to relive. Back then, he had gone down a "wrong path." The sheepdogs that kept society safe from people like James had rebuked him, and he had felt real shame at his actions.

But now was a time for wolves. Time to put the shame behind him. Time to embrace his inner predator.

James pulled himself up and stood properly on the branch that he'd landed on. He gazed out over the Orientation forest, turning his head and body to get a good view in all directions.

His sense of direction seemed to have been enhanced by the Evolution as well as his Skills, Strength, and Perception.

He knew immediately which way he'd been walking pre-Evolution, and he knew that it was more or less the correct direction to find the Rodriguez camp.

James began flitting through the trees toward camp, jumping from branch to branch with perfect grace, never settling on a tree limb long enough to break it. As he jumped from tree to tree, he split his focus with Parallel Minds and reviewed his Skills for possible combinations.

He felt great. More powerful and free than ever before. As if reborn.

He wondered what Mina would think when they saw each other again.

Hero Worship

The figure approached, and Sierra recognized him now.

It's James after all, just about a foot taller and more muscular. Never thought I'd be relieved to see him.

She started to walk slowly toward him, hoping to intercept him before other people noticed and raised an alarm to Chava. Then a realization hit her that almost made her stop in her tracks.

If I was correct in my theory, James is under Chava's influence too. How do I deal with him?

A cold sweat rose on the back of her neck, and her hands started fidgeting of their own accord. She was seriously considering changing directions and getting Alan, Mitzi, and Cliff. She wasn't sure what they could do anyway, but at least there would be some other people around as witnesses in case James started acting aggressively.

Then her mind calmed.

I'll manage. What do I need other people for? Am I really afraid here? I've been training all my life for this, haven't I?

"You survived," were the first words James heard upon returning to the Rodriguez camp.

"Glad you noticed. Good to see you too, Sierra," he replied.

"I knew you would come back even if it defied common sense," Sierra said. Her tone sounded like rolled eyes, though her expression remained neutral. "You don't seem like the type of person common sense is really made for."

James couldn't tell if she was implying that he was very special or that he wasn't intelligent enough to use common sense. *Probably both.*

"Anything important change while I was gone?" he asked.

"Are you kidding?" Sierra replied. "How could anything important ever happen when you're not there?"

"I guess it would be difficult, but I'm glad that nothing did. Most of the important things I can imagine happening would involve death and destruction descending on you all."

She actually rolled her eyes at that, but he thought she was trying not to smile.

"How's the food situation?" he asked.

"Not great, actually. Some pretty strict rationing since you've been gone."

Is that why you seem a little bit off? he thought. She wasn't quite her usual self, he'd noticed. The conversation was just weird. He couldn't put his finger on exactly what was off, but maybe it was something as simple as hunger.

"Well, I killed a whole pile of animals while I was cutting my way through the spiders. We should have a couple of days' worth of food at least."

"A very successful hunt, then," Sierra said with a tone of interest. James read it as feigned interest.

She's pretending to be interested in how the hunt went? James thought. *This is weird. Are her reactions to things I say always this calculated, and I only just now leveled up enough to see through it? Or is something special going on right now?* He wondered if she was trying in a subtle way to slow his reentry into camp. Quietly signaling danger of some sort awaiting him? *What's that? A boy's fallen in the well?*

But he wasn't very interested in playing charades and he was losing patience at this guesswork. He cut to the chase.

"Yep, all spiders dead," he confirmed, "along with numerous other innocent forest creatures. The Spider Queen was actually able to talk, mourn her dead children, and scream at me for killing them."

James tried to smile nonchalantly, but he was aware that it must look wooden. It was still strange to think about the fact that some monsters were clearly sentient, not just the humanoid-looking creatures like the Corpse Eater. It bothered him a little to think that half the time he was killing something that might have its own thoughts, feelings, and goals. Something almost human. But she was the last person he wanted to see him vulnerable. There was a brief, uncomfortable silence before she spoke again.

"That must have been terrible for you," she said. "Having to kill an intelligent being with loved ones."

She didn't even sound sarcastic, which impressed him. A big jump in the acting quality there, assuming she didn't mean it. And it was obvious that she didn't, considering her phrasing.

"I've had worse," he said abruptly. "And anyway, the spiders ambushed me.

Hundreds of them. I *defended myself*. That's all I ever do. I defend myself *thoroughly* until the enemy dies or surrenders." He was aware that heat had crept into his voice and his face, but she had to know she was striking a nerve. *Why? Why is she bringing this up now? Because she feels safe in the Rodriguez camp? She doesn't need my protection, so she's going to make sure I remember what I did to her brother?*

It was enough to make him question his own decisions. *Why did I think it was a good idea to bring her with us?*

A seething rage threatened to overtake him, and he forced himself to turn his back on her, and on those destructive emotions. *Deep breaths.*

Aloud, he said, "I think I'll share the good news with the camp. I'm sure Chava will be grateful that I destroyed the menace threatening his family."

He started to walk, but his instincts flared up and told him something was approaching from behind him at breakneck speed—for a normal human, not for him. His body began moving defensively of its own accord, drawing a dagger and activating one of the temporary fusion Skills he'd created on his way back to camp. *Lightning Strike!*

One of his parallel minds read the sensory data that had alerted him to her movements. He wanted to gauge her intentions more clearly before he killed her.

Sierra fought for breath as she spoke with James.

Every moment was a struggle. It was as if in addition to growing visibly taller and stronger, he also had some sort of new ability to put pressure on other people around him, and he was testing it out on her at full blast.

Knowing him, maybe that was the case.

She'd meant to put him at ease and lower his guard, but as the conversation progressed, it was a struggle just to remain civil and get the words out. She began needling him instead. It was part shift in strategy, part reflex.

At least this way, even if he won't let down his guard, he'll be unfocused. It was hard to call it a coherent plan, just making him angry, but really, she wasn't capable of planning well in her current mental state. This was her best shot.

As he turned his back on her and stepped away, the pressure diminished slightly, and she took her shot. *Purification!*

She lunged at James's back, sprinting across the short distance he'd walked, green energy wrapped around her right hand.

He seemed to move in a flash, too quickly for her to see. He had a dagger drawn in his left hand, she saw, and it was shrouded in near-blinding yellow Mana.

As she closed in, her hand almost within touching distance of James's head, the dagger came dangerously close to her throat. It seemed blindsiding him hadn't worked, but she was too close to stop now, even if she'd wanted to.

Is this where I die? She wanted to clench her eyes shut.

Instead, she made herself keep going. Out of the corner of her eye, she saw James drop his dagger, and, impossibly quickly, grab her by the wrist. She tried to pull her hand away, but his grip felt like iron.

"What are you trying to do?" His voice was deadly cold.

"I'm a Healer," she breathed. "What do you think I'm trying to do with my bare hands?"

"I'm uninjured." A note of doubt in his voice.

"But are you, hah, free from external influences?"

James relaxed his grip for a second, and Sierra pushed forward. He didn't try to stop her this time, to her surprise. She touched his neck and released Purification.

He still had the dagger; she realized only once she'd made contact. He'd caught it with the other hand. As she touched his neck, he held the weapon next to her heart.

James held off on decapitating Sierra because, sifting through his sensory inputs, he realized there was no malice in her apparent attack.

Even if there had been, what could she really do to him now?

He still didn't quite trust her, though. He canceled his attack, switched his dagger to the other hand, and held it pressed to her heart. Even if she could somehow fry his brain with some new Skill, he thought that he might have a moment to plunge the weapon into her. And with his enhanced healing Skills, he would have at least as much chance of survival as her.

As the green energy swept over him, a brief flurry of unfamiliar memories played out before his eyes. He remembered entering Chava's tent. A brief conversation about the challenges of spider hunting. Uncomfortably sustained eye contact with Chava, which James abruptly found he couldn't break.

A battle of wills ensued. James had fought the old man in the arena of their minds, but Chava was surprisingly formidable for someone at level seven. There was crushing pressure, pouring into his mind like fire until the resistance was broken. And then there had been commands whispered into his subconscious mind.

So I had a reason to stupidly go and hunt the spiders alone beyond pure hubris, he thought. *It just wasn't my reason.*

Aloud, he said, "I should've known you were hiding something. I did *sort of* know. And there were so many clues too. I could even have smelled your sweat, if I'd been paying attention to my senses and not letting what you were saying distract me. How did you figure out I was being *controlled?*"

That last word was almost a hiss. James's anger had transferred cleanly onto a new target, and he was already thinking of how he would punish Chava for this.

She let go of him and backed away, out of dagger range, before she spoke again. She looked relieved—and, unless James misread her, slightly hurt. He put away the dagger.

"At first, it was just a suspicion," Sierra said. "I had no real basis for it. I just picked up on your behavior. It seemed out of character. Since I've been back here with the Rodriguezes, I've been gathering information. The whole family is under some kind of influence. I'm not sure if it's as strong as what he used on you, but it definitely traces back to Chava. He's the only one who benefits. I'm not sure what his end goal is. If I could mind-control people, I wouldn't have them sitting in place going hungry."

While Sierra spoke, James was visualizing different ways of killing Chava. His imagination impressed him with a feast of detail. As Sierra stopped talking, he realized she was probably waiting for him to say something. Fortunately, with Parallel Minds he could pay attention to two things at once. He continued enjoying the image of Chava's eyes melting inside of his skull and simultaneously formulated his reply.

What is he thinking right now? Sierra wondered. She still felt the same pressure from him that she'd noticed earlier, only now his expression matched. *Feels like he's imagining something awful.*

"I don't really care what his motives are," James said. "I'm just thinking about what I'm going to do to him."

Ah! That fits.

"Well," Sierra said carefully, "however you handle him, you have to do it quietly."

"Really? I was planning on leaving him in bloody pieces all over the ground." His face contorted with an icy wrath that she'd never seen before. *Scary!* Especially since he was almost a foot taller than he had been and built like a linebacker. "No one controls my mind but me. I could spell that message out very well with his intestines. Why do I need to be subtle?"

"It's just that I think he has a second mental power, one that's aimed at his family. Something more subtle than whatever he did to you. If you attack him, there's a chance the whole family will turn against you. They might riot or something. That's assuming the effects of the Skill don't vanish instantly upon his death."

"Sounds like you put a lot of thought into this," he said slowly. "Any other factors to consider?"

"Well, if you do kill him, it's possible that Camila could take over his role leading the family. He's been keeping her isolated, and I think it's because she might have her own ability that would rival his."

He nodded thoughtfully.

"Also, there is one more thing I feel the need to mention," she added. "You're giving off this pressure. And I don't know whether you know that you're doing it or not, but it makes me want to crawl into a hole in the ground and hide. So could you please turn that off?"

He looked surprised, then slightly embarrassed. "Sorry. Just got this new Skill I've been playing with. I had activated it to scare off monsters on my way here, but I forgot I still had it on."

How could you forget that? The Skill is that effective and has no cost to use?

The atmosphere changed suddenly, and Sierra suddenly stood straighter. She hadn't realized she'd been making herself smaller, hunching as if she didn't want to be seen. She also wiped away sweat from her forehead.

I'm drenched in sweat, she thought. *I probably stink. Need a bath as soon as we find a body of water.*

But mostly, she was exhausted.

"I'm going to go take a nap," she said. "Do what you want."

"Um, thanks for the magic, by the way. Guess I'll trust you next time." He sounded extremely uncomfortable saying that, but she was too tired to enjoy it.

"Yeah, thanks for not killing me."

She walked off.

James watched her retreating form.

She seemed to be in a strange mood, he thought. *Did Crushing Intimidation do all that?*

He had deactivated the Skill immediately upon Sierra's request. But he noticed there were another ten minutes left until it diffused into Intimidation and Basic Elemental Magic: Gravity. He didn't seem to have any way to diffuse the Skills early. *Honestly forgot I had it on, but it was nice seeing the forest creatures run away whenever I landed on a tree near them.*

Left to his own devices, he decided to be a bit sneakier about tackling Chava than he had been planning.

He entered the camp, and instead of heading straight to Chava's tent, he found a large, open area, and he began dumping the Exoshields from the hunt onto the ground. He kept going until there were none left in his satchel. It took a while.

As the Exoshields clattered and fell to the dirt, a crowd slowly gathered. James looked up from the pile of hundreds of shields, and he saw that the whole family was there to see him.

With the fall of the last shield, the Rodriguezes crowded around him and began talking over each other in an excited flurry.

"Did you really kill all of them?"

"How is it possible?"

"You've saved us!"

"Do you have any food?"

There were repetitions and variations of these questions, along with tight embraces from several members of the family. A few asked if they could have one of the Exoshields since they were still stuck on starter equipment. He was more than happy to oblige those requests. Indeed, James was quite enjoying the attention. Then *he* emerged.

"Hail the conquering hero!" Chava's voice cut through the hubbub. "How have you accomplished this, ah, miracle, James?"

James gave him a cheesy smile.

"Oh, I'm just the Little Engine That Could, Chava. Nothing but hard work and a positive attitude!" He strode through the crowd toward the old man, people parting for him like he was a celebrity back in the old world. James saw a flicker of fear in Chava's eyes, which was almost as gratifying as the other form of attention he'd been enjoying. He stepped in close to Chava, bent his back to get closer to Chava's height, and leaned to put his mouth next to Chava's ear.

"We'll talk about next steps later," James said quietly, giving him a reassuring nod. And he turned away again.

Facing the crowd once more, he opened the magic satchel and drew out all of the *non-human* meat he still had. As he handed out bundles of meat to the people around him, he spoke.

"The meat from all the monsters I killed while I was cutting my path to the Spider Queen," James said. "Please distribute this among your family. It will need to feed them today and while we're traveling unless we happen to catch something else."

At this, a real, spontaneous cheer erupted through the crowd. It grew louder as more people took it up.

"James! James! James!" They shouted his name over and over again as he passed out the food. As the shouting went on, the sound of the voices mingled with the sound of people banging on various Exoshields, which most of them had picked up. James turned his head to see more of their faces as they called out to him. He only noticed out of the corner of his eye that Chava was sneaking off toward his tent, making himself scarce.

He didn't care much for whether Chava felt comfortable or not just now. James would handle him later. But he put away his rage. He let himself soak in this moment.

There was an empty place in his heart, and the cheers helped fill it. *I wish my family could be here for this*, he thought. *I wish they could see me now.*

CHAPTER FORTY-SIX

Scream

James spent the next hour celebrating with the Rodriguezes and reconnecting with one of his original party.

"Good move solving the food shortage," Alan said. "You've won over everyone here, probably permanently. I hope you don't intend to go on many more solo missions, though. You have a fair number of people here who would happily fight and die beside you."

James read the words "including me" between the lines of that last sentence.

"I get it, Alan. Thank you. Really. I don't want to do this to you again. Next time I go somewhere dangerous, you'll be right there beside me." Then he changed the subject. "It's crazy that there was a food shortage. Hasn't anyone been hunting since I left?"

"People have tried," Alan shrugged. "Chava sent hunting parties out. He himself did not go on any of these expeditions, I noticed. The victims of his plan came back with nothing but spider bites to show for it. Which Sierra and I healed, naturally." He sounded as if he thought he'd shown saintly patience. James was noticing an edge to Alan these last few days that the old man had never shown before, and James was still deciding if he liked it.

"Of course. He *would* send them out and get people bitten before I exterminated the whole colony."

"It's still astounding that you did that." Alan at least sounded suitably impressed. His reaction was more gratifying than Sierra's. She'd seemed almost annoyed that he survived.

"Yep." James smiled grimly. "I got a special Title for driving a species to extinction too."

"Jesus. The shit this System rewards!" Alan went paler than usual.

I won't mention to him that I met a god, James thought. *Probably best to leave out the new immortality quest I unlocked too.* One shocking revelation at a time.

"Yes. It is quite brutal. Have you noticed anything else about the politics here?" James said. "And how have they been handling the low food supply?"

"They're being less active," Alan said. "They burn less energy that way. The men go out hunting. When they come back injured and empty-handed, they get healed. Chava has nixed any talk about leaving this spot since you left, so there's no real solution. And no one within the family seems particularly upset about it."

"And Camila? What's she saying about it?" James asked.

"Not much. Chava mostly keeps her in her tent. He says it's so she can recover faster."

"But you don't quite believe it?"

"I think what you, Sierra, and I did saved that woman's life. If she's still unwell, this is an awfully slow recovery compared to most of what we've seen since the System appeared."

"Sounds like Chava wants to keep things in stasis."

"That's about the size of it," Alan agreed.

"Thank you, Alan. Very helpful."

So, everything Sierra told me was true. He looked up at the sky, gauging the time. The sun was getting a bit low. *Almost time to uproot the family tree!* But he had another hour or two to socialize before then. He left Alan and went to look for Cliff.

James was still getting used to how it felt to move among people in his new body. As he walked past grateful Rodriguezes, nodding and smiling at their kind words, he towered over all of them. He felt graceful and strong. His new body was clearly better fitted to his current capabilities than his old body could ever have been.

Which was good since he suspected that if he was clumsy in this new body, he might accidentally kill people by bumping into them too hard.

He wondered if his face was any different. Or, more accurately, he assumed that his face was different, and he hoped the changes were improvements. He hadn't had the chance to look in a mirror yet.

As he walked past Chava's tent, there was a rustling within. Chava himself quickly emerged from the tent flaps, carefully making sure they were closed behind him. He looked nervous at the sight of James, but the older man quickly tried to hide it.

"James," he said quietly, "you survived. I'm so glad to see you came back all right!"

"Hey, Chava! People keep seeming surprised about that," James said affably, smiling broadly and throwing up his hands. "Almost as surprised as they are about me having wiped out all the spiders. It's like they didn't know how powerful I am. Well, I guess your family and I were strangers before, but everyone knows my name now, that's for sure! I'm glad to see you guys were able to hold down the fort here. I hear the hunting is quite dangerous in this neck of the woods."

"Oh, yes," Chava said mutedly. He looked queasy. "Dangerous."

"It's a good thing you didn't go yourself. The family needs to keep you and Camila very safe."

"Uh, yeah, right," Chava said. "That's what I've been doing. Keeping Camila safe, ah, very important. Listen, I wanted to talk to you about something, ah, alone. Wouldn't want to distract you from anything you're doing here, of course."

James nodded politely, trying to keep his expression blank. Inside, he was gleeful. *Permission to hasten my revenge, granted!*

"I'm happy to walk off with you somewhere private," James said. He gestured at the trees in the distance. "Do you need to give anyone any instructions or anything?" *Any last words?* He tried not to smile like a demon.

"Uh, no, everything is running itself for the moment. We can go right now."

What, worried I'll change my mind? James almost laughed, but he turned it into coughing.

"All right, how about we go that way?" James gestured at a dark patch of woods in the distance behind Chava's tent, where it would be difficult for anyone to see them.

"That seems fine," Chava said. A note of suspicion in his voice.

"I know we still have some *unfinished business* to take care of," James said confidentially, "about the camp's next steps." He gave his most charming fake smile.

"Oh, yes, of course. Exactly!"

Good, he sounds reassured. Chava took the lead, walking ahead of James. *I hope you enjoyed being a free man, Chava!*

James cracked his knuckles and followed; his smile evaporated as soon as he was out of view of the other family members.

They came to a dark place under the trees where the shade was thick enough that it would be difficult for people in the camp to see them.

James looked back, and he gauged that no one could see what was about to happen to Chava.

The old man looked James in the eye, and James suspected that he might be about to use the Skill he'd placed James under before. So he hauled off and slapped him in the face.

Chava went down like a sack of bricks, instantly unconscious from the open-handed slap. *Yep. The Strength differential is as big as I thought.*

And James dragged him farther into the woods, where they would definitely not be seen.

* * *

Drip. Drip, drop, drip.

Chava awakened to the sensation of water dripping on his head. He was sitting somewhere. Apparently somewhere with falling water? He felt woozy. Like he wanted to go back to sleep.

Then he was hit with a wave of pain. Shattering pain that largely washed out coherent thought. He hadn't felt pain that bad in—well, ever, probably. The closest he could grasp to it was a concussion he got playing baseball as a kid.

"Ohhh, my head," he moaned. "What's happened?"

He opened his eyes but realized that he was blindfolded. He tried to raise a hand to remove the blindfold, only to feel something binding his arms to his sides.

"Oh, shit. W-where am I?" he whimpered.

Only silence answered him.

He sucked in breath in preparation to scream, but that was when he felt a stabbing pain in his guts.

"*Aaahhhh!*" he squealed.

"How does your ability work?" a voice asked calmly. It took a moment for Chava to place it as James. "I thought I'd ask you that first."

"W-what are you doing? I swear, if you don't let me go, I'll—*aaargh!*" The pain in his intestines had just ratcheted up several notches.

"What was that, my friend?" James asked. "I couldn't quite hear you over the sound of my knife in your guts." He let out a low, sadistic chuckle. "Heh heh heh. Feel free to scream. In fact, go ahead and make all the noise you want. Where I've brought you, no one can hear you scream."

"Just kill me," Chava whimpered.

"Oh, no, you don't get off that easy," James said. "Not yet at least. We'll see where the evening takes us."

"You're enjoying this, aren't you, you sick bastard?" Chava felt the knife pull out of his body, and he sucked in air as he felt hot blood pour out.

"Why shouldn't I?" James whispered. Chava felt his hot breath close against his ear and shuddered involuntarily. "After what you've done."

"Don't kn-know what y-you're t-t-talking about," Chava managed. He felt like his body was shutting down, energy pouring out of him.

"You know, if you had invested some of your Stat points in Strength or Fortitude or Agility instead of putting them all in Will, you might have been able to resist a bit more effectively."

"How do you know what I did with my points?" Chava asked wildly, suddenly energetic, adrenaline pumping through his veins keeping him conscious at least for the moment.

"Well, it was obvious," James said.

Chava felt the blindfold lifted off his eyes, and he blinked in disbelief, not daring to hope. But there James stood in the dying light, not meeting Chava's eyes, holding the blindfold in his hands. They were still in the forest, clearly, but not in the clearing. There were trees all around, and Chava didn't recognize any landmarks besides his apparent kidnapper. The young man turned and faced away.

"Your mental manipulation power works with eye contact, does it not?" James asked. "And it requires you to out-power your opponent in Will?"

Chava nodded before he reminded himself that James had his back turned. He cleared his throat.

"Ah hem. Yes, that's how it works. You've got it right."

"Very good," James said. "Now you've answered those questions honestly, time to start the real interrogation. There's no point in refusing to answer or lying. All the truth is coming out tonight."

"I can just wait until I bleed out," Chava said.

"Let's forget about how slow and painful it is to die from a gut wound like that for a moment, because you have no way of knowing that," James said. "Old man, did I smack the sense out of you when I knocked you unconscious? Don't you remember how you and I introduced ourselves? The very first thing I did when I arrived at your camp, before you *sent me out to die alone?!*" Those last words were almost shouted. It was the first moment that James had broken his even tone.

"Before I—you—yes. Yes. I—I remember."

"Good. Then you remember what matters right now." James smiled so widely that Chava could see it even in the uneven dusky light, even with James's back turned, in the movement of his cheeks. "You remember that I can heal." A green glow surrounded him for a moment and abruptly died off.

"What do you want? Just tell me what you want! I'll give it to you."

"Answer my questions, like I said," James said. "Then I'll decide what to do with you."

"Whatever you say," Chava said, his voice betraying the trembling that had slowly overtaken him.

"Have you been controlling your family as well as me?" James asked.

"W-well, not control," Chava said. "Influence."

"Hmph. Fine. Good enough. What happens if you die?"

Chava saw a chance to lie, but he decided he'd be better off not taking it. "Nothing. Nothing happens. The influence just fades slowly over time."

"Good, good. That was what I thought. Why did you decide to send me off to die in the woods?"

Chava sucked in air sharply. "I just wanted to be rid of you. You were a threat to my headship. My leadership of the family. It's necessary for me to maintain that to keep my Job."

"Gods, so you were willing to risk your family's safety by throwing away their strongest protector, just so you could keep some of your power? Pathetic! You're even worse than I thought." He sounded almost impressed. "What was the Job, anyway?"

"Clan Leader."

"Uninspired name. All right. I also heard you sent some of your family members out hunting, but I know you never joined them. Why is that?"

"Like you said, my Stat points are all in Will. I'd be worse than useless!"

"Why all in Will, though?" James asked. "I don't really *need* to know, but I just don't understand. Will really is an almost useless Stat. It increases Mana, but so does Intelligence, and Intelligence is useful for more than just magic, obviously."

"You know why," Chava said lifelessly. The adrenaline was draining out of him, and he had given up. *Do what you want with me*, he thought. *Kill me or let me go. I don't care anymore.*

"No, I really don't," James said. "Tell me."

"It was so I could keep control of them. The situation. Everything. Anyone I came in contact with. I could bamboozle them, like I did you."

"Yeah, I thought as much," James said. "You wanted to control them more than you were ever worried about protecting them. That's just sick. A few last questions before I give you a chance to get out of this. What were you planning on doing, anyway? What was your end goal? Why were you keeping the camp in place? Were you ever going to go anywhere?"

"This is a fucking forest of death, you crazy motherfucker! Why would we ever move after we found a safe place? Me keeping us in this camp was me keeping my family safe!"

"That's either bullshit or bad reasoning, and I don't much care which anymore."

James turned back around to Chava without making eye contact.

"Well, I think we both know that the only way you're getting out of here with your nonexistent physical Stats is if I let you go," James said. "I'll give you a chance. Do you want to try your Skill out on me again? If you succeed, you could make me let you go. If you fail, assume the consequences are unspeakable. What do you think?"

James made direct eye contact with Chava then, and the old man grinned.

Instantly, James knew what he'd decided. The two were locked in a staring contest for almost ten seconds before they were pulled into the place of the mind where their Wills had struggled against each other before. A barren wasteland where two armies crashed against each other representing the respective sides. In one army, every soldier had Chava's face. In the other, each one was a clone of James.

Unlike the first battle, which had felt like it went on for hours in this place, this clash was quick.

Chava looked away, his expression pained.

Looks like I gave him a little bit of a migraine, James thought.

"I knew that wouldn't work," he said. "Just thought it would be interesting to let you believe you had a bit of a fighting chance. A real shot at getting out of what comes next."

And ensure that you feel your utter defeat, on your own chosen field, James thought.

"How did you know?" Chava asked.

"What, you don't remember how hard it was for you the first time? I remember. You barely won! Before we started this time, I used Identify to confirm you haven't increased your level one bit since our previous encounter. But while you've been sitting on your ass at camp, sending your own blood out to die, I've been improving! Multiple levels. Plenty of points in Will even though I didn't know I'd need them. That's what this place is really about. That is why you lose."

"Just kill me already, and quit your gloating, you son of a bitch!" Chava barked. "Spare me the sound of your fucking voice!"

"My pleasure," James said.

He used Predator's Armaments, and his fingernails became razor sharp. In one smooth, clean motion he cut Chava's throat. Thus began the night's real mission.

Pillage!

James first obtained a Skill called Familial Influence. It did just what the name suggested.

Disgusting, he thought. *Who would want to manipulate their own family that way?*

Laying on Hands restored Chava to full Health. James could have just brought him back from the brink of death, but he wanted to make sure, for purposes of using Pillage again, that Chava would be considered to have experienced a separate instance of dying each time.

James waited a few minutes for Chava's breathing to steady.

Then he stabbed him in the heart. *Pillage! Come on, luck be a lady tonight!*

But no. James acquired the Skill Familial Telepathy, which was interesting but not what he'd been looking for.

No big deal. Would be nice to actually have some music, though. He pulled the knife out and used Laying on Hands to mend Chava's broken heart.

He had enough Mana to continue this through the night if necessary.

CHAPTER FORTY-SEVEN

Compulsion

Sierra approached James as he stepped out of the forest. The sun was rising behind him. The new day found her tired and bleary-eyed. After her nap, she had barely slept during the night. She'd tossed and turned, guilty about the danger she'd placed Chava in.

He was a terrible leader. A coward who sent his family into harm's way while staying behind himself. Almost certainly a misogynist—*machista*, as Karla put it. *But did he deserve to die? I wonder what James did to him. "I was planning on leaving him in bloody pieces all over the ground,"* she recalled and shuddered.

Though she'd stood beside Kurt and his party when they'd led people to their deaths, she'd been able to tell herself she wasn't a real participant. She hadn't yelled to lure people toward the pit trap. She didn't do any fighting at all. She just healed people. Like a military nurse.

This time, she was the instigator.

You didn't have to tell him, Sierra, David's voice said, *but you'd all be in danger if you didn't.*

I know. Bad options. She was growing more accustomed to answering back when her brother spoke up, though she'd noticed that was less frequent, as if he was settling into a dormancy inside her mind. Or as if the voice was just a hallucination brought on by stress.

As she went to meet James, she tried to decipher his expression. But the sun behind him made his face almost unreadable.

Once she was closer, she saw a calm, slender smile. *Sort of his baseline face. A good sign?* She thought she heard him whistling for a moment. *Is that Frank Sinatra?* But he stopped before she could identify it.

"I assume your dark deed is done?" Sierra tried to say it lightly with an air of nonchalance. She had already concluded that he'd almost certainly murdered Chava. If that was true, then her role in this situation was either that of James's willing accomplice or the sole witness who would need to be silenced. Which one would depend on the next few minutes.

"I finished what I needed to do with Chava, if that's what you mean." His smile grew and spread to his eyes. Sierra swallowed involuntarily.

"That's great," she said, trying to cover her initial reaction. *I'm not ready to be an accomplice to murder!*

"Don't worry," James said, placing a firm hand on her shoulder. She flinched slightly at the touch, and he clearly noticed.

"I don't have to solve every problem with violence, you know." He sounded a little defensive. "I mean, I *did* solve this problem with a certain amount of violence, but I don't have to do that *every* time. I also didn't kill Chava."

Her eyes were drawn to the tree line behind James. The figure of Chava stumbled out of the forest almost on cue. There didn't look to be a scratch on him, though he walked with his head down.

Like a beaten dog, she noticed. It was scarier to her than if she'd seen his mangled body. She was getting used to death. *What could James have done to him?*

Images of gruesome torture played out in her mind's eye.

James leaned in a little closer and lowered his voice. "Thank you again for your loyalty to me and to the group, by the way. Don't think it goes unnoticed. This dude"—he gestured at Chava—"could have caused a lot of trouble if left unchecked. Now he'll never be a problem again."

He gave her what must have seemed to him a winning smile, and she forced herself to smile back and nod as if she understood. As if James hadn't inflicted some unspeakable horror that she did not yet comprehend on the man who stood behind him, expression blank.

"Mm-hmm, of course. Well done," Sierra said, barely aware of what she was saying.

There was an awkward silence in the air between them then, but she didn't think James was going to kill her at least. He hadn't even killed Chava.

After what seemed to her a decent amount of time, she turned and silently walked away.

James stood for a moment wondering if Sierra would be all right. She hadn't concealed her fear well, but he didn't think there was anything he could say that would reasonably reassure her.

He wouldn't deny what she must be imagining he'd done. He *had* tortured Chava. And he'd even turned the old man's own Skill on him at the end. It was the only way that James could justify leaving the man alive, so he considered it a lesser evil. But he was cognizant that others might not share his view.

He examined his newest Skill.

[Compulsion: Bend the mind of another into obedience to your whim. Initiation requires direct eye contact. Must possess a stronger Will than the other. Only one target at a time. Effectiveness reduced when a command goes against the other's core nature.]

It bothered him even to look at the description. In some ways, it was more repulsive than the Familial Influence Skill, which was less coercive but allowed the user to target all his blood relatives within range at once. James had used Skill Transfer to return Familial Influence to Chava since he wanted nothing to do with that.

But Compulsion, he told himself, was in good hands with him. He only intended to dominate Chava's mind. A taste of his own medicine, an effective prison sentence in a setting without iron bars and stone walls. All without alienating the Rodriguez family.

You're basically a slave owner now, a dark voice inside commented.

He tried to ignore it.

The next hour was spent with Chava, talking with Camila and other Rodriguezes.

"James!" Camila exclaimed as soon as she saw him. She pulled him into a warm hug that dissolved some of his uneasy feelings. *Her grip is surprisingly strong!*

Then she started chattering, asking how he was, how her family was doing, when they were leaving, and saying she hadn't been out of her tent for ages. Everything she said was still in Spanish, but the System was still translating, so James could just let the words effortlessly wash over him.

James had felt a little exhausted by the events with the Rodriguezes. Not that he wanted to leave them behind, but he had questioned whether the power of numbers and the value of allies were worth all the headaches that Chava had caused.

Now, in the midst of Camila's warmth, he felt affirmed in his decision to stick with them.

He also felt a bit better about what he'd done to Chava. The old man had confessed to using Compulsion to control Camila, though apparently the reasons were purely petty. Many family members liked her better, and they would have gladly listened to her over him if given the choice. At the very least, her presence among them would have weakened the effectiveness of his Familial Influence.

As she spoke, Camila reminded James a bit of his own grandmother before she passed. On her visits, she always made her grandchildren feel like they were the only people in the world; she listened to all their trivial concerns like they were adults and chattered away with them endlessly.

I'm glad the Rodriguezes are out from under Chava's yoke, he thought. *What a warm family they are, once they can really be themselves. Like what I want to make with Mina.* He smiled genuinely, barely aware of himself as he imagined his own family.

"You should really be lying down, sis," Chava commented uncomfortably. James had used Compulsion to command him to act as normal, and apparently, this was how he interpreted it—continuing to insist that his sister-in-law sleep and recover from an ailment that she was clearly over. But the effect of Compulsion over her was fading with the Skill now in James's possession.

"You and your rest," Camila said, her tone turning a little crabby. "I've had more than enough rest! Don't know why I've been laying up here like an invalid."

"Yes," Chava said tersely, clamming up a bit at James's mental command.

Interesting that she doesn't seem to remember that Chava used Compulsion on her, James thought. *Sierra's ability might be a requirement to break that aspect of the Skill.*

"I want to talk about moving camp," James said.

"The family has already lost—and come close to losing—members," Chava objected. "I cannot agree to—"

"The decision is not just up to *you,*" Camila interrupted. "Didn't I hear the young man say he killed off the monsters that attacked us before?"

"Yes, but—"

"It's true that I killed all the spiders," James interrupted. "They're not the only danger out there."

"Exactly!" Chava said.

"That's why we need to move the camp," James said.

"Come again?" Chava said.

"Yes, let's move the camp!" Camila said, immediately agreeing with James. She didn't even need to hear his reasoning, apparently. He smiled.

These two were the elders—the leaders in effect—of the Rodriguez family. It was amusing to watch their decision-making process when Chava was to act "as normal," and Camila was coming out from under Chava's influence. The two of them couldn't be more reflexively opposed than they had been in this short exchange where they were both finally behaving like their full selves.

But if they acted this way when discussing binary questions, he could only imagine the logjams that more complicated decisions would create. He thought he might actually be doing them a favor by taking the leadership role for himself.

Still, he took the time to explain actual reasons why they should agree to move camp, in case Chava ever drifted free from his control and wondered why he had gone along with James's plan. There would be the memory of this conversation, or so James hoped.

"This Orientation is a deathtrap. Half the people here are going to die by the end. We have to make sure we're not among them. This area your family cleared is not a safe place. There *is* no safe place."

"I understand my babies have gotten hurt hunting in this patch of forest anyway," Camila said. "And no food to show for it!"

James nodded. "That's right. It's been rough around here, I understand. The spiders that dominated this area weren't edible to begin with. And other monsters will arrive eventually, just like at the clearing in the beginning. There's no rule that they stick to the tree-lined areas. By then, everyone will be weakened from hunger. All staying would mean is guaranteeing a slow death for the sake of avoiding a quick one. And I can protect your family, just as I wiped out the spiders."

Camila expressed her agreement once again, and in a shocking twist, Chava followed suit.

"Thank you both," James said.

"Of course," Camila said. "I know you'll keep us safe."

"Let me know if there's anything else I can do," Chava said weakly.

"Oh, of course," James replied.

He allowed Camila and Chava to announce the move.

Walking away, James couldn't help but feel conflicted. He had seized control of the family's destiny by manipulating their elders. But he also felt righteous because he was all but certain he was leading the group in the right direction strategically, and he genuinely believed Chava was where he belonged: under James's tight control.

And they would surely all die if they stayed in place as Chava had wanted. Perhaps the ends justified the means.

His next order of business was ensuring he would never fight a battle alone again. For that purpose, he still intended to cultivate Cliff as a front-line fighter.

As he went off to find the older man, James happened to see the smoke column he intended to march them toward, visible in the distance. It hadn't changed its appearance much, just occasionally growing a little thinner or wider. Same location. He wondered what sort of group could have erected a signal fire so quickly.

But it was only a passing thought. *They must be doing very well.*

Then he was with his party again. They were all together when he spotted them outside of the tent that Chava had gifted them. Somehow it felt like a long time since he'd seen them all. *It's only been a couple of days, right? And, of course, I was just talking to Sierra this morning and Alan yesterday.*

"You grew!" Cliff commented upon seeing him. He seemed energetic and excited to see James back, which wasn't something James had ever expected.

"Apparently," James said. "Do I look different otherwise?"

"Better," Mitzi said, nodding. "Just generally better."

What, was I a big ugly bag of garbage before?

"Stronger jawline," Sierra said indifferently. Everyone but her looked to be in an elevated mood.

"You're ripped, man!" Cliff said.

"Almost like you're a different person," Alan assessed, smiling warmly. "You had gained a little muscle tone since Orientation started, but now you're suddenly multiple inches taller, and I'd say you put on twenty pounds of muscle. How do you feel?"

"Like I'm ready to take my shot at the heavyweight title," James admitted.

"How was the, uh, Evolution?" Mitzi asked.

"Uh, might be different for everybody . . ." James said. "It turns out that the Race Evolution process involves going to another dimension or something."

Better not mention that the System offered to turn me into a half-vampire. I already seem evil enough with the powers I actually have.

"But what was it actually like?" Cliff asked.

"Dark," James said. "Horribly painful." He looked off into the distance.

After that, no one asked him any more questions about Evolution.

When the group split up again to perform various tasks leading up to the move, James took the opportunity to speak with Cliff alone.

"Getting along well with the family?" James asked.

"The ones who will talk with me, absolutely," Cliff said. But he didn't sound terribly interested, which seemed slightly out of character. "I hear the killing spree went well?"

James opened his bag and spilled out twenty Exoshields of varying sizes onto the ground.

"Very successful, then!"

"This is just a sample," James said. "The spiders are extinct now."

"Whoa! You sure?"

"This species, definitely. I got a new Title out of it. Xenocide."

"You must have gotten quite a few levels out of that." Cliff sounded slightly down about it, and James wondered if he was jealous. It would be very understandable; the System had given James gifts that were probably rare, and Cliff was only falling further behind his former subordinate.

"I did," James acknowledged. "I wanted to see you about that, actually."

"Oh, yeah?" Cliff asked, raising his eyebrows. He seemed to be wondering if James wanted to rub it in, how their positions had reversed from prior to the System.

"Yeah. Two things. First, the group here is going to pick up and move campsites soon."

"I don't know about that," Cliff interrupted. "Old man Chava seems pretty bound and determined that this is where the family is going to stay, live or die."

"I know. I spoke with him. We're moving." James flashed a predatory smile. "I made him an offer he couldn't refuse."

"Badass." Cliff looked suitably impressed. "So, what's the other thing?"

"I was hoping that you could take the vanguard—the lead—when we march out of here. You would be the point of first contact with any enemies we encounter from the front. For that purpose, I have something for you." James opened his bag and drew the Ego Spidersword. He took a moment to examine the blade, which was the color of blackest condensed, hardened spider chitin. At the juncture between sword and hilt, there was a shiny orb that looked suspiciously like one of the Spider Queen's eyes. Perhaps it was precisely that.

"I'm lending you to my friend Cliff, here," James said aloud. "Help him keep us safe." The weapon didn't speak or anything, but he thought he felt a cold aura radiate from the eye orb.

James understood he looked like a madman, talking to the sword, so he added to Cliff, "It's an ego weapon, meaning it retains some of the Spider Queen's personality and power."

"I see," Cliff said, looking skeptical. "And you're just giving this to me?"

"*Lending* for an indefinite period of time," James gently corrected. "It's going to be good for you to have a better weapon to use. We'll see how it goes." He lowered his voice. "I want it to be in the hands of someone I trust. I think the Rodriguez family are good people, but I don't know them like I know you."

James did not, in fact, trust Cliff any further than he could throw him. With his Strength, James could now throw Cliff much farther than he had ever trusted him. James didn't even always like Cliff. But he *knew* Cliff, and that was, in many cases, better than trusting or liking. It would at least have to substitute for real trust until James was around people to whom that word applied. What he knew was that Cliff was vain, status-hungry, extroverted, and as far as James had ever seen, loyal to his leader.

That leader had been Brendan Barry. Now it was James, for as long as he could maintain the appearance of dominance. The reality of being strongest was preferable, but James couldn't count on that always holding. He thought he would at least have some warning if Cliff was ever going to try to make a play for leadership. The middle-aged attorney wasn't the type to act alone.

James Identified the weapon briefly before handing it over.

[Ego Spidersword: A sword crafted from the remains of the Wood Spider Queen, who James cruelly incinerated as she tried to avenge her fallen young. Contains the residual bitterness and vengeful instinct of the Wood Spider Queen, now twisted in service of the one who slaughtered her whole species. The weapon is intelligent and will protect its owner, moving independently when danger looms nearby. Boosts Strength, Fortitude, and Dexterity by 15 each when wielded. Grants access to the Skills Necrotic Strike and Shallow Wound Recovery.]

James only shook his head at the description. The System's labeling of these things couldn't surprise him anymore.

"I accept your generous loaner-weapon offer, sir," Cliff said eagerly, smiling.

"Excellent. You'll be a great vanguard, I'm sure!" James smiled back.

CHAPTER FORTY-EIGHT

Protection

The rest of the evening was spent in celebration.

The family gathered as a group to eat together, tell stories, sing, and dance. A couple of them even had instruments, a guitar and a harmonica. There was a festive atmosphere at dinner.

While Cliff and James sat and ate, Alan and Mitzi danced with a surprising spryness and energy. James found himself thinking that perhaps the System would bring a second springtime for many old-timers. It brought a smile to his face. He'd often thought about growing old with Mina, but perhaps they would remain forever young together instead, like elves in some fantasy world.

Even the more subdued Sierra looked to be cheered up by the music and the mood in the air, though she refused requests to dance from a couple of young men.

Ramon pulled James into a conversation with some of the other Rodriguezes gathered around the big central campfire, and they prevailed upon him to tell the story of the spiders' extermination. James tried to tell it almost exactly as it had happened without going into too much detail about his specific abilities. There were cheers at dramatic moments, and the men tried to press beer into James's hands, but he preferred to keep his pre-System habit of sobriety, so he politely declined.

Whenever James felt people out as to their mood about the travel plans that Chava and Camila had announced, they were almost uniformly positive. Only a few cast sidelong glances at the campfires, where words again appeared that night, imploring the reader to follow the smoke to safety.

James felt his first twinge of real apprehension about the planned course of action as he saw those words again. Someone was using powerful magic to communicate that message. *Is it really benevolent? Safety in numbers would be a good enough reason for me to do it if I had that magic, but can we really trust that safety is all that's on this person's mind?*

But he put away those doubts for now. He had already decided what they were doing, and there would be time to consider precautions when they actually made the journey. He wouldn't lead his group into danger the way Chava had.

After a festive evening of reunion spent celebrating the group's continued survival and James's successful return, the camp slept soundly.

The migration began promptly at the break of dawn the following morning. Happily, the universal possession of Small Bags of Deceptive Dimensions made the move significantly easier than any trip James had ever taken in the pre-System world. People just took down their tents and packed away all of their worldly goods in a matter of minutes.

James worked with Cliff to organize the formation the group moved in. Cliff took the vanguard position as planned, while Ramon and Jaime Rodriguez trailed at the back to protect the slowest moving among their family. As elders, Chava, Camila, Alan, and Mitzi were positioned more toward the center to ensure their safety from ambush. Sierra took a position close to the vanguard alongside Felicia, the archer, so they could act in a backup role. And James positioned himself somewhat removed from the front, but close enough that he could jump in if there was any real trouble.

Only if there's trouble the actual vanguard can't handle, though. Can't make them completely dependent on me.

This was a test for Cliff; it wasn't James's intention to steal his thunder. He needed to make sure he established that his whole party was competent in the eyes of the Rodriguez family, or the power dynamics of the situation could become tumultuous at any moment if James was taken out of commission.

And hopefully, Cliff would get some experience for a change. James was happy with whatever reflected glory he got from the migration's overall success. He had ensured that everyone was armed with spider weapons before the camp picked up roots, so even the teenagers had Small Exoshields and Spiderknives at the ready in case of trouble. James had saved the Medium Exoshields, Looted from the Command Wood Spiders, for the people at the rear or the front, all of whom had been selected as being stronger or more competent fighters than the average for the group.

James himself wore the Royal Exoarmor, which had better Stats than any other piece of equipment he possessed besides the Ego Antler Spear.

[Royal Exoarmor: Rigid armor that once protected the matriarch of an arthropod species before James killed her with fire. Now twisted to fit the human form, a species the matriarch despised. Contains a powerful

vitality-enhancing energy. **Boosts Agility and Fortitude by 20 each when worn. Grants access to the Skills Deep Forest Movement and Mild Passive Regeneration.]**

James was also armed with the Ego Antler Spear and a Wolfbone Dagger at each hip. He had finally stowed his Common Wolfskin Pelt because when worn with the Royal Exoarmor, it made him too hot for comfort. He felt ready for just about anything while equipped like this. At first, he was almost eager for a fight.

Yet the journey was fairly quiet for the first few hours or so.

James was able to spend time developing ideas for future experimentation with his Skills.

He was particularly interested in Monster Generation, Monster Control, and Venom Fangs, which seemed to have a lot of potential to make fighting easier. With Monster Generation and Monster Control, he might be able to create minions to do much of his fighting for him. With Venom Fangs, he could put his enemies on a timer so death would grow closer every passing moment without further effort, allowing James to just focus on dodging attacks.

James confirmed that he could use Monster Generation with even small pieces of his own biomass. He bit his thumb and spilled a single drop of blood, then used Monster Generation to transform it into a spider form. Unfortunately, when he crushed it just to see what would happen, he noted that it did not give experience, and it died much more easily than the spiders he'd met in the forest.

After spending a significant block of time going through his Status sheet and conducting similar experiments with his blood, James was a little surprised that he hadn't been interrupted.

He estimated that a few hours had passed with no random encounters. When he'd been walking through the forest by himself before, he'd experienced a rate of fights much higher than this while making much less noise, and that was before he started actively hunting. Why wasn't the noise of the group summoning any beasts?

James initially wondered whether the size of the traveling group was keeping the monsters at bay. But when he asked Chava about it, the old man explained that they had been attacked much more frequently when moving as a group before.

"I wouldn't credit the number of people moving with having any deterrent effect. Maybe it's your presence that's scaring the creatures away," Chava suggested with a smile, looking up at James. "You do seem to have a certain aura about you since wiping out the spiders. I think you might give off a red-flag signal to most creatures thinking about an attack. At least, I wouldn't want to fight you."

I'm not even using that combination Skill that had Sierra so freaked out the other day, James thought. But maybe the monsters could somehow sense his Xenocide Title. He wondered how intimidating he would have been if he'd chosen the other Evolution option. *I probably wouldn't be able to do any hunting for the rest of Orientation.*

Finally, though, when the sun was at its zenith, some creatures emerged from the forest and attacked the group from the front. Perhaps it would be more accurate to say that the group entered a species' territory, and that species defended its territory aggressively. A half-dozen beetles the size of Rottweilers flew down from the trees, and Cliff, alongside the other two vanguard fighters, met them head-on.

James thought about interfering briefly when one beetle flew at a Rodriguez family member's head behind the front lines, but one of the vanguard disengaged from the fight with the other five beetles, jumped back, and managed to draw its aggro to him.

James was most impressed by Cliff's performance. The first swing of his sword felled a beetle. The Ego Spidersword chopped right through the beetle's horn and into its head. The next swing penetrated deep into another beetle's center of mass, and James saw a black rot quickly take root there and spread to devour the rest of the beetle's flesh.

That must be the Necrotic Strike from the Ego Spidersword, James recognized. *Good thing I never let the queen bite me!* With those two beetles down, the fight became much more manageable for the vanguard fighters.

James didn't need to intervene after all. He was quite pleased with the vanguard's performance, and he wasn't the only one. The family had begun hooting and hollering encouragement at the start of the fight, and they let out a big collective cheer when it was over before the group returned to moving forward in relative quiet.

This was the beginning of a pattern. There were several more of these brief engagements over the next few hours. The vanguard was triumphant every time, and the cheers only grew more confident and enthusiastic. Aside from James mentioning to Cliff that he probably shouldn't use Necrotic Strike on any monster that was likely to drop edible meat—a tip that Cliff promised to take on board—James had no involvement.

It freed him up so he could spend his mental energy on viewing the forest as a tourist, without concern for potential threats. The woods were rather beautiful when one didn't have to think about being ambushed by monsters. The trees were a beautiful tapestry of earth tones, as one would expect from what James imagined was virgin forest, essentially untouched by human hand or axe.

He couldn't recognize any of the trees they passed in particular, and he couldn't help wondering if he had always been this bad at identifying flora or if he only would have known them if they were palm trees. *Or maybe there are new species here entirely.* It would make sense, given the many new and large species of animals that now made these trees part of their habitat.

Fortunately, whatever they were, the trees were well spaced out for unimpeded human and giant monster movement.

He found it charming. Maybe part of it was that he was accustomed to seeing forests intercut by roads. This one felt *unconstrained* and boundless, although surely there was an end to it somewhere.

Ultimately, Cliff did secure some meat for the group, as James had hoped. They were lucky enough near the end of the day to be attacked by three boars with what James judged to be very poor survival instincts. In a brief, well-coordinated defense, the vanguard engaged the three beasts, and the group as a whole quickly bled all three dry with attacks from multiple directions. Cliff didn't use Necrotic Strike even once, so they gathered enough meat to keep everyone well fed for another night.

Finally, with the sun drawing near the horizon, the group camped.

"Good work keeping us safe, man," James said to Cliff, clapping him jovially on the back. By the end of the day, Cliff had seemed quite dangerous with the Ego Spidersword. James thought it might be a worthwhile investment to leave the weapon in his hands permanently.

James was particularly pleased about the rate of their day's progress. He estimated that they would reach the source of the column of smoke by early afternoon the next day if the pace of their forward movement continued.

As he ate and then prepared to sleep, James thought the biggest hurdle he would face at this rate might be a boring forest. *Traveling with a group is just that much less dangerous.*

The next day started out as much of the same.

The forest was as beautiful as it had been when he had tried to look at it through tourist eyes the previous day. There were no monsters apparent in the immediate vicinity, and the column of smoke was tantalizingly close now. He sat, slowly taking in the nature all around him while others packed up their camping gear, appreciating his improved vision.

This apocalypse is really pretty all right so far, he thought carelessly for a moment. *The trees are gorgeous, the weather has been pretty consistently good, and the rate of wild monster attacks is super manageable.*

Then his thoughts darkened. *That's easy for me to say right now. I hope Mina and Yulia are in a position to appreciate the beauty of . . . wherever they are.* He frowned.

The caprice of the System to separate people by something as arbitrary as surnames did not bode well for the heavily pregnant woman and the petite teenager. He tried to remind himself that the only thing he could do for Mina or Yulia right now was to survive. But that continued to be a hard pill to swallow.

A tall shadow loomed over James and distracted him from his train of thought. He welcomed the distraction. He looked up and squinted through the bright sunlight for a fraction of a second until he recognized the man in front of him.

"What's new, Alan?"

"Just thought you and I should discuss objectives, James." He gestured at the column of smoke they'd been migrating toward. "We'll almost certainly reach those people today, I expect."

"I expect the same," James replied. He would let Alan spell out exactly what he was asking rather than volunteer a long explanation. Surely some people could hear them in this setting, and there was no need to give the Rodriguezes any reason to worry about how first contact would go with the new group.

"Well," Alan continued after a moment, "I'm wondering what the, uh, strategy is. You are a bit of a leader for the group right now—"

"And you are a trusted advisor, Alan," James interrupted. "If you're trying to gauge how I intend to interact with the new group, I will first reassure you that we're not going in willy-nilly without a plan. I will take a couple of our people, and we'll go and see the other camp up close. If we can establish that they're friendly, we'll go in with everyone else. If not, we're still not going to fight with them. We'll just leave."

"I see," Alan said, looking visibly relieved. "You have thought this through."

"I always have a plan." James smiled. "And I just told you yesterday that next time I went somewhere dangerous, you were going with me, didn't I?" James made firm eye contact with Alan and held it, despite the blinding sun in his eyes. After a weighty moment, Alan looked away.

The old man was smiling too, James saw. *I finally fixed that little bit of friction between us.*

Alan would, if James had his way, continue to be a key advisor and asset for long after the Orientation was done. Alan had been to war once, and he had much life experience James lacked. James imagined Alan being something like the Merlin to his King Arthur.

For that to happen, though, James would have to show that he was not only one of the most powerful people in this Orientation but also the most trustworthy and reliable. Alan seemed to James a very prudent man, not one to entrust his fate to just anyone.

"That you did," Alan said.

"Count on me, sir." James flashed his most confident smile.

The group arrived within what James gauged to be roughly two miles of the column of smoke. It had taken them a couple of hours since they set out.

James called for the group to halt.

He decided that the group should stay where they were for now, only sending out a hunting party, led by Cliff and Ramon, and a scouting party, which would hopefully make first contact with the originators of the smoke.

James had already decided who to take with him.

CHAPTER FORTY-NINE

To Bear Witness

Who's going with you while I lead this hunting party?" Cliff asked when James announced his plan. James wondered if he still felt excluded despite being given his own, similarly important task.

It was reasonable that Cliff might feel excluded this time; James *was* deliberately excluding him since Cliff's boisterous interpersonal style could complicate any negotiations with the other camp. And with James the current power in their own camp, proximity to him could be instinctively recognized as valuable and a good proxy for one's status in this group.

"Just two others," James said. "I wanted to bring the least threatening-looking people possible. I figured Alan and Mitzi. They're both older—*no offense*—and they look harmless, as compared to me. I'm a big bulletproof Black guy who's now over six feet tall. I need all the harmless I can get."

"No offense taken," Mitzi said, slightly coldly.

"I also like that, secretly, you can blow them all to kingdom come if necessary," James added to mollify her. "And I figured that the husband-and-wife combination would show that we value continuity with the traditions of the pre-System world." James was mostly just bullshitting now.

He did indeed want Mitzi for her firepower, but he wanted Alan to come along mainly because he knew Alan would be annoyed if he wasn't in a position to protect his wife, and because James had just promised him specifically that he would be included in James's next dangerous outing. Hopefully, this wouldn't be dangerous, and James would have fulfilled his promise.

The secondary benefit in James's mind was that Alan would be better able to advise him on future diplomacy with the other camp if Alan had met them himself, though James believed he could handle it even without advice.

"And if it turns out they're unfriendly?" Cliff asked.

"Then we run," Alan replied quickly. "Correct, James?"

"Yeah."

"The two old-timers are going to make a sprint getaway," Cliff said. There was no question in his voice, but James detected a hint of sarcasm.

Alan suddenly jumped back, then he turned and ran into the trees without looking back. He moved with the speed and suddenness of a much younger man.

Cliff and James watched in silence, while Mitzi stood by with a small smile on her face.

Alan walked back up from out of the woods, only a single bead of sweat visible on his forehead.

"I've been investing, ah, a lot of my Free Points into Agility," he said breathlessly.

"Same here," Mitzi added.

"Oh, yeah," Cliff said. He sounded distinctly unsurprised and unimpressed.

Should I be glad they're prepared for this eventuality or troubled that they're so concerned with being able to run away? James thought. He ultimately fell on the side of finding it funny.

"I guess that's how confident they are in my protection," he said finally, snorting with laughter. "Alan can hop away like a frog now if we're threatened."

"All right, fine. Whatever," Cliff said, relenting. "Just don't do anything I wouldn't do, guys."

Alan and Mitzi looked at each other, and James thought he and they were thinking the same thing: *If I find myself wondering what Cliff Rogers would do in my situation, I'll know I'm in real trouble!*

"Sure, man. Of course not!" James said.

"When do we leave?" Alan asked.

"We want to go soon," James replied. "Before the sun gets much lower. We don't want to travel in the dark, after all."

"We're really not taking anyone else?" Mitzi asked.

"The smaller the group, the easier it is for me to provide protection," James said. "We're well balanced with a Mage, a Healer, and a close-up fighter." He lowered his voice. "And no one else in the camp besides Cliff is strong enough yet to be a close-combat asset. I used Identify, and their levels have stagnated. Chava really did them a disservice by keeping them in place the last couple of days. From what I've seen, both the monsters and the other humans in the forest are only getting stronger." He turned to Cliff. "I'm relying on you to fix this. A couple of those people who were out fighting in the front with you have some potential. I'm hoping you can bring it out."

Cliff seemed more genuinely pleased with his role at that. "You can count on me!"

And, after a few more preparations and farewells to Chava, Camila, and Sierra, James led his mini party out of camp.

The walk from their camp to the other was uneventful. A couple of hours of hiking in silent anticipation.

James had chosen to dress down, wearing some of his backup basic Orientation gear rather than the improved items and weapons he had obtained from his spider slaughter. He didn't want to give the impression that he was Attila the Hun, come to wipe out the group they would likely be encountering. If he needed it, he had the rest of his arsenal in his magic satchel.

James, Alan, and Mitzi covered a lot of ground without seeming to suffer much from fatigue. It was amazing how the System had changed their collective physical fitness. Before, this would have been a challenging walk for James to take alone. Now, even the senior citizens were keeping up.

James himself was barely thinking about the walk, instead using his energy to contemplate Anansi's challenge.

I have to find him off the edge of the map, James recalled. *Does that refer to a place in this Orientation or out in the world? If it's back out in the world, where the hell is the edge of the map? The terrain is being altered somehow by the System, so old maps won't apply anymore, probably. But is the edge of the world changing specifically? Do I need to go to the Land of the Rising Sun or something?*

This would be much easier if the answer was somewhere in the Orientation, but so far, he had seen no hint of a place that could be called an edge of the map. The existence of the forest was a big problem in that regard. If there was some natural feature that could be considered the edge of the map, like the beginnings of an impassable swamp or desert or mountains, then he would at least have a clue. But the trees had made it impossible thus far for James to see much into the distance, and there didn't seem to be any mountains around at least.

As they approached, James noticed a smell rising in the air. *Barbecue?* It would make sense that they would use the fire for something if they always kept it going. As they walked closer, the smell grew clearer and more distinct. It almost made James hungry, but he didn't seem to need food as often since his Evolution. His mind returned to the Anansi question.

It was only when the three had clearly arrived at the source of the smoke that James pulled himself back to the present and shelved Anansi's challenge for later.

"Here we go," James said quietly.

The delegation of three stepped through a group of trees, and the outlines of another group of people came into view. At first, things appeared little different from the camp that James, Alan, and Mitzi had left behind.

A dozen or so men and women could be seen from their vantage point. They were relaxing or performing chores outside, cooking and laundry mainly. The sun was high, so James imagined it was around lunchtime for them.

These people didn't stand out generally from their appearance except that they were all dressed in white.

Most wore long, flowing garments, while others wore loose-fitting white shirts and pants. Something about this struck James as rather ominous. The color white was associated with purity in so many world religions, yet it was also a color of mourning in some cultures. And there was something austere about this group perhaps requiring its members to wear white. Did it mean they were hyper-religious?

"Let's stand back and watch for a little while," James said in a stage whisper. He sensed rather than saw Alan and Mitzi silently nod from his flanks.

A pair of the white-clad people were carrying bundles of wood, and as James followed them with his eyes, he finally saw the massive bonfire that had led him and his group all the way here. There was a depression in the ground, perhaps a pit, circular and wide enough for a large man to lie down in. The people in white fed the wood into the fire.

Above the pit loomed a tall statue, with the bonfire positioned in a gap between its legs. The statue had what appeared to be the head of a bull, the torso of a man, two angelic wings, and four humanoid arms. Two were outstretched to its sides as if ready for a fight; the other two were grasping in front of the figure as if expecting a gift.

The figure appeared to be stone, but James thought that shouldn't be possible in the brief time they had been in the Orientation. Unless the statue somehow predated the human presence there.

Made by another force entirely, suggested a voice in his mind.

Can gods act so blatantly in the Orientation? James questioned. *Putting up statues of themselves?* The god he presumed was Anansi had barely spoken to him, and yet that had seemed to cost some effort, to come with a strict time limitation, and to require that he take over the body of one of his subjects. Maybe Anansi could have achieved the same end result without going to all that trouble, but James doubted it.

Is this god more powerful, then? James felt like he should recognize the figure who stood above the fire, but he only vaguely felt that the horned figure standing above the pit of fire was probably ominous. *Really wishing right now that I paid more attention to world religions when I took AP World History.*

Another pair of figures in white approached the pit. They were notable at first because their white cloaks were smeared with red. Then his eyes were drawn to what the figures held between them: the bound, bloodied, nude figure of a young woman.

James couldn't see the victim's features well, only that she was a tall, slender brunette with pale skin. He thought he saw the slight swell of early pregnancy on her stomach.

As she was pushed forward, James saw long lines of red that someone had sliced into her back.

"Please! No! I repent!" she screamed.

"Guys, I think we need to get out of here," Mitzi whispered, alarmed.

James and Alan were both transfixed, mouths agape, by the sight in front of them, and Mitzi's whisper broke the spell.

"Yeah, let's get the heck out of Dodge," Alan agreed after a moment.

James managed to stop gaping at the atrocity unfolding before him for a moment and turn to look at Alan. But rather than replying, he found his head involuntarily swiveling back. The young woman had been tied to a stake, back turned to the hidden watchers.

The long gouges out of her flesh were on full display. They looked worse, deeper than they had when she'd been held between the two men.

Whoever cut those strips of flesh off her back could just as easily have killed her, James thought. *More easily, even. They're keeping her alive to torture her.* His face twisted into a snarl.

Alan was grabbing James's arm and gently shaking him.

"Is this really so much worse than everything else you've seen here?" Alan whispered urgently. "We really have to go."

One of the men in the clearing had taken a whip from a bag that hung from his waist, and James's eyes were stuck on that. He retained enough presence of mind to consider what Alan had said. *He's right, of course. I've seen much gorier scenes than this. I've* created *gorier scenes than this myself. But only when I had an enemy I needed to kill. This is* cold-blooded. *Fucked up.*

He had sometimes enjoyed fighting, killing, and even drawing out a fight, yes. But outright torture? He'd restrained himself even when dealing with someone like Chava.

Another reason this bothered him so much suddenly hit him. *She looks like Mina.* It was only a passing resemblance—tall, pale, long-haired brunette, slight hint at possible pregnancy—but he hadn't seen his wife in days.

He used Identify to get her name. *Just humanizing her more before you run away,* an inner voice chided.

[Isabelle Rose, Lv. 9]

"I want to save her," he found himself saying quietly.

"Jesus Christ, James!" Alan groaned quietly.

"I'll get you guys to safety first," James said.

"Goddamn right you will," Alan grumbled. "This is insane!"

"Let's retreat, then," Mitzi said. "I will gladly return with you in a supportive role if needed."

James could feel some tension in the air between husband and wife to either side of him, but he ignored it. There was something different all of a sudden about their surroundings. It was hard to exactly define the change, but his Predator's Senses and Situational Awareness were blaring a warning all the same.

"Quiet, guys," James hissed. "Something's wrong!"

Both of them froze, and then James pulled them roughly to the ground, twisting their bodies to fit under a bush. *Natural Camouflage!* He prayed the Skill would somehow protect the two older people from sight too, though he couldn't imagine how, since it involved his own vital signs diminishing drastically. At least there was a fair amount of shrubbery around to conceal them.

The feeling of wrongness shortly manifested in noticeable movement around the three. People were walking through the trees toward them.

"I don't see a goddamned thing around here," one voice grumbled.

"The Prophet said the ward in this area was set off. They've never once been wrong so far. Just stay focused on finding the intruders, Jeff." This second voice had a rather strong accent, but James couldn't place where it was from.

"Half the time his wards go off for beasts!" the first voice objected. "If this is another bloody Rodent of Unusual Size, I swear I'm going to—"

A third voice chimed in, cool and calm. "Gentlemen, I think we might be right on top of them."

A tense silence fell, and James's imagination filled it in with the worst-case scenarios. Three men staring directly down at him and the old couple, easily penetrating his camouflage and silently, perhaps telepathically, calling for backup. A dozen enemies or more gathered, all with weapons trained on James and his people, ready to let loose but waiting to shoot in sync to do as much damage as possible before they could move to evade. His heart was in his throat.

James focused and tried to become even more nearly invisible than he had been before. His heart slowed again. Even his consciousness seemed to change, as if he was slipping into meditation.

Then James felt a hand roughly grab and pull at Alan. The old man didn't clutch onto James at all, so his camouflage remained undisturbed. *Thank you, Alan*, James thought. *I'll get you out of this soon!*

"Well, looky what I found here," the voice they'd heard second said. "One humanoid intruder. Score one more for the Prophet. Eh, Jeff?"

Then James felt Mitzi pulling away from him too, but this time the movement was much smoother.

"You missed one," her voice pronounced firmly. "It's two intruders."

"Jesus H. Christ!" Jeff's voice groaned. "Lady, why didn't you stay hidden? Now we'll have to—have to—"

"Wherever my husband's going, I can go too," Mitzi replied. She couldn't keep her voice from shaking slightly.

"Jesus Christ," Jeff repeated. James thought the voice sounded a bit familiar now that he'd heard it a few times, but he still couldn't place it exactly.

"No more of you in there, are there?" the accented voice asked.

"Ain't nobody here but us chickens," Mitzi said, her voice self-consciously light but still shaking.

And thank you, Mitzi. James's mind immediately kicked into gear planning how he would rescue the two of them once the guards led them away. As long as these freaks didn't immediately sacrifice them to whatever god their prophet followed, he thought he could probably sneak into the camp once the sun got low.

He was already inside this prophet's wards, so hopefully they would only be set off once—by their arrival—rather than blaring out a constant signal with his continuous presence. If that was how it worked, the wards might be set off again on their way out, but the three would at least have a head start. Maybe he could wait until most of the camp was asleep too.

"All right. Well, we'll take you to the Prophet," the third man said.

"Why are you lot here anyway?" the accented voice asked. This one seemed dangerous to James. Altogether too interested in gathering information for his liking.

"Just looking for a safe place and people to gather with," Alan said. "We saw your smoke, and my wife and I thought that was here."

"No frickin' way!" the accented guy said. "You two old-timers made it across the forest by yourselves? The same woods we traveled through? The forest full of critters bigger than a man, with mandibles the size of my head, and claws the size of my arm? I don't believe it. You have to be jerking my chain! We literally wouldn't have made it ourselves if not for divine intervention."

One of the others, James couldn't tell which, made a shushing noise.

"What? It's not a secret, and they need to know why I'm calling bullshit on their story."

Smart, James thought, *but not smart enough to know that when you interrogate more than one person, you separate them so they can't cooperate on a story.*

Mitzi spoke. "We had other people with us. The spiders got them. Big, black things that came out of the trees. I think we're the last ones left."

Well done, James thought. *Next time we should have an agreed upon story in case this contingency happens again.*

"You satisfied now?" Jeff asked. "Can we get out of here? We're sitting ducks if anything that isn't human comes out of the woods. What if they led those spiders here?"

"You have no faith in the Prophet's protection, do you, Officer?" the third man asked. He sounded amused.

James realized suddenly where he recognized Jeff's voice from. *Officer Jeffrey Ross.* James had worked with him from time to time when he was a prosecutor. He was a good guy, or so James had always thought.

"I don't think it's infallible, if that's what you mean, Kassim. And I don't think it's heresy to say that either," Officer Ross replied, an undertone of contempt in his voice. "You let me know if the Prophet proclaims otherwise."

"Let's get out of here, as Jeff was saying," the accented man said. "I don't like lurking here in the woods either, Kassim."

"Fine, fine." Then this Kassim took a step, and James instantly had a problem. "What the hell is this I'm standing on?" A foot had landed right on top of James's right arm.

"What is it now, Kassim?" Officer Ross's voice was exasperated. "Forget how to walk?"

"No, it's not that. It's—"

"He's stepped on something," the accented voice pronounced, intrigued.

CHAPTER FIFTY

Chameleon

James could sense the speaker bending toward him, leaning in closer and closer to the ground. He had a split second to make a decision. It wasn't fight or flight; it was fight or give in.

"All right, you got me," he said, dispelling Natural Camouflage.

"Holy shit!" Officer Ross exclaimed. "There was a guy just blending into the ground!"

"The System works in fascinating ways," the accented man said. He laid a hand on James's shoulder. "Get up, then. Nice and slow, if you please, mister chameleon."

Was Natural Camouflage always that powerful? James wondered as he rose. The System still impressed him, even at moments when most of his mind was occupied with other things. Since he'd received Parallel Minds, multi-tasking was his normal.

As he wondered how his ability could function as well as it did, he took a good look at the people around him. The one called Kassim was closest. He looked vaguely Middle Eastern, a little older than James. James recognized Officer Ross. His hairline had receded slightly since they last saw each other. *Was that a flicker of recognition in his eyes?*

James's eyes moved on to the third figure, the man with the noticeable accent. He looked a bit like Sharlto Copley, and James guessed that the accent he'd heard was probably Afrikaans, from South Africa.

James's Predator Instincts gave him a guess at his odds of victory if his party engaged this group of people: roughly a 75 percent chance of victory, but only a 25 percent chance that they would all make it out alive.

It was his two companions who were in danger here. James felt an increasing sense since his Evolution that he could survive almost anything if he only worried about himself.

Mitzi and Alan were between Ross and the Copley lookalike. Perhaps not ideal positioning to be able to run away if James started something. The South African seemed to realize what James was thinking, and he drew visibly closer to Mitzi and put his hand to a dagger at his belt. Not one of the basic Orientation daggers like the one James was wearing. This one was either the South African's pre-Orientation possession or something he got from Looting a monster. Either way, the message in the body language was clear: *I know how to fight, and I'm ready to use this dagger, so don't test me.*

James relaxed and raised his hands above his head, finally standing straight to his full height. He stood taller than any of the men except Officer Ross, who was level with him.

He must have gone through Race Evolution too, James assessed. *He and I were about the same height before. I thought I was ahead of just about everyone else in the forest. How strong is this camp?*

"You're a big sucker," the South African observed.

"I eat my Wheaties," James replied. "So, what are we doing, guys?"

"You're going to go see our Prophet," Officer Ross said. He sounded uncertain. "Say, don't I recognize you from somewhere?"

"Yes. Yes, you do. We used to see each other in court quite a bit, Officer."

"Oh, yeah! You're a prosecutor, right?" Forgetting about the circumstances for a moment, he seemed happy to see James.

Good. I can maybe use that.

"That's right. Good to see you too. Wish we could've, uh, met up sooner."

Ross's face fell at that, as if he suddenly remembered they were not seeing each other under the best of conditions.

"Can I put my hands down?" James added.

"I don't know, can you?" the South African cut in, chortling to himself. James used Identify on him, Officer Ross, and the Middle Easterner in turn. He needed to at least know what he was dealing with here in terms of power.

[Jan Roest, Lv. 7]

[Jeffrey Ross, Lv. 10]

[Kassim Roukoz, Lv. 9]

Interesting. Very unfortunate that they all seem decently leveled, but at least Ross is the strongest. Maybe there's a chance at persuading him to turn on them?

But he didn't like the odds of that, much less so if the groups had to fight right here almost within spitting distance of the camp. And even if Jan and Kassim had been low level, a pre-Evolution Healer with an elderly body like Alan certainly wasn't going to do much good against them.

"Quit screwing around," Officer Ross said to Roest. "This guy was someone respectable back in the real world."

"This is the *real* world now, Officer," Kassim said. "I would think you'd have realized it by now, with how much blood you've gotten on your hands."

Crap, James thought. *He's a participant in this stuff? Is that where he got the levels from?*

"I just meant—" Ross seemed to deflate and didn't finish his sentence.

The sense of protection James had once felt in the Officer's presence evaporated instantly.

James slowly lowered his hands.

"We're not here to fight," he said. *And you don't want any of this, so just take me to your leader.* If they started any violence right here, he was ready to use Predator's Armaments and start cutting throats.

"Follow us, then," Kassim said, easing the tension a bit.

The three guards formed a circle around the prisoners and began escorting them through the brush toward their camp.

"All right. So, the three of you are taking us to see your leader," James said. "Anything you can tell us to help us hit it off with this prophet?"

"He's not that difficult to please," Kassim said. "You either strike his fancy, or you don't. If he or his god doesn't like you, then you wind up sacrificed."

"What a thoughtful process," Alan remarked.

"How did a man of the law like yourself wind up with a bunch of human sacrificers?" James asked, looking directly at the only person among their captors who he actually knew. There was genuine upset in his voice. *I can't believe what you've signed onto.*

"I wish I could say that it's complicated or a long story," Officer Ross replied, staring straight ahead, "but it isn't. It was just about survival. The Prophet was offering a guaranteed path, and the wife and I took it."

"When did this start?" James asked.

"How could you know he could guarantee you anything?" Alan questioned.

"Signs and wonders," Officer Ross said quietly.

"What was that?" Alan asked.

"On the first day, in the first fifteen minutes of this godforsaken place, the Prophet selected a group of people near him. It seemed like he picked almost at random, but he knew something that he could say to each of us to get us to go with him. No one refused him."

James resisted the urge to ask Ross what the prophet had said to him specifically. The conversation seemed uncomfortable enough for him already, and the details would undoubtedly be personal.

The important part was obvious already. *A god is putting its thumb on the scales for this prophet. I made the right call deciding not to fight for now. Even though he and his god are torturers, it would be better not to make them enemies if I don't have to.*

"From there, he led us down a primrose path," Officer Ross continued. "He knew a place where we could watch the slaughter in the starting area without being at risk. Then he brought us here. It was—"

"It was like Moses leading his people through the desert," Kassim finished for him. "He took us through perilous terrain without danger. We would see other people being torn limb from limb by strange, monstrous beasts, and we were left untouched." A tone of near worship infused his voice. "We traveled through the forest impossibly fast. He even led us to easy kills. We leveled up over and over, and no one did better from it than our friend Jeff here."

"He told us there would be terrible sacrifices," Ross said, "but he would lead us through. And he did. Impeccably. He was honest; he told us we would have to hurt people, but as long as we listened to him, we were absolutely certain to make it out of here. And eventually he led us here, and we started *making sacrifices.*" His voice broke there. "I'm in here with my wife. What would you have me do?" This last was spoken in a pleading tone and directed at James, with whom Ross could only barely bring himself to make eye contact.

"I'm not judging you," James lied. "We were just looking for a path to survival ourselves, and we figured safety in numbers was definitely the way. We have that in common. But it sounds like you found yourself something even better. I would hope that if he tells you to slit our throats, or do whatever he's doing to that young woman, you would at least hesitate. But I don't know what I would've done in your position."

As a brief silence settled over the group, James received two alerts.

[Sufficient experience accrued. Public Speaking leveled up!]
[Sufficient experience accrued. False Impression leveled up!]

They were arriving at the perimeter of the camp. As they approached the clearing, James and his companions could see it more clearly. The woman tied to the post was within spitting distance; James tore his eyes away with difficulty. That big signal fire—which James could now identify as a sacrificial fire, from the charred bones within its glow—was so close to him now that it warmed his skin.

There was a semicircle of animal-skin tents lining the perimeter of the camp. They formed a horseshoe shape at the opposite end of the clearing. *Set up*, James thought, *so every resident of the camp could see the sacrifices being made to this monstrous god without leaving the comfort of their bedrolls.*

"Time's up," Jan said, encroaching on James's thoughts. "Hope you enjoyed catching up! Better get ready to die!"

As he spoke, twenty or more white-clad people approached from all sides, men and women of all ages. James had never felt more self-conscious about being dressed all in black. He could see the woman from before—still bound to the stake, still bloodied and naked—but it seemed James, Alan, and Mitzi had at least interrupted her whipping with their arrival.

"Who are these people, Kassim?" asked a middle-aged woman with dark-bronze skin and high cheekbones who stood at the forefront of the gathered mass of people. From a flower wreath she wore around her head, James assumed that she was the leader.

Wait, didn't they use the masculine pronoun for their prophet? he questioned.

"Intruders," Kassim said briefly. "We must bring them before the Prophet for judgment."

Ah.

"The Prophet is resting," the woman said. "We'll need to throw them in the pit while he recovers his strength." She gestured somewhere behind her—away from the fire, to James's relief.

"The Prophet will want—"

"The Prophet has rested quite enough," a bemused voice cut off the disagreement. A tall man in a white, hooded robe approached, and the crowd parted for him. Clearly the leader. But James was less interested in this figurehead. He probably represented the genuine will of some savage, monstrous god. That was easy enough to understand. It was the interaction he'd just witnessed among the followers that he was turning over in his mind.

Fascinating internal politics, James thought. *Inside of a week, there are already rival factions within this cult, debating about what their leader wants despite the fact that he's still alive and available to be questioned. Absurd. Christianity, eat your heart out!* The whole secret to dissolving this band of zealots, it seemed to James, must lie in exploiting these preexisting divisions. Hopefully, he wouldn't have enough time around these people to test this theory.

Identify.

[Nikolai Rostov, Lv. 12]

Just like in my camp, the leader is the strongest one, at least on paper, James thought. His instincts gave him no indication of physical threat from this man, however.

"I see that my wards remain effective," Rostov said, his voice calming and steady. "At the risk of sounding cliche, dear guests, I've been expecting you." He said that, but James noted a certain degree of surprise in Rostov's face as he looked over James's group.

Whatever he was expecting, I don't think we were quite it.

James examined Rostov in turn. The man in the hood was roughly James's height, pale and lean with dark hair and a face that seemed neither young nor old, and wore a pointed salt-and-pepper beard. James thought he had a vaguely Eastern European look.

James used his Predator Instincts to try and gauge what his odds were of taking this man down successfully if he fought him one-on-one. The numbers that surfaced surprised him. His ability assessed only a 1 percent chance of victory but gave James a 99 percent chance of surviving such a fight.

He must have a strange set of abilities. Something entirely defensive? A Healer with support Skills and extremely high Health and regeneration? He must have had a lot of faith that his god wouldn't put him in a situation where he'd need to deal damage. With a build like that, he would need the group as much as the group needs him.

James himself wanted to play nice with the other people here so he could secure future alliances. But he could hack and slash his way through the remainder of the Orientation by himself if push came to shove.

James didn't know how he would use this information against Rostov, but he filed it away for later, nevertheless.

"Expecting them?" Jan asked. "As in, expecting these specific people?"

Interesting that a supposed prophet—presumably as in one who sees the future—is not someone they expect to know about specific people arriving in their camp. I would think that might be basic shit. His predictions must be quite vague usually.

"The Prophet is privy to many secrets," Kassim observed.

Their prophet ignored their back and forth and addressed himself to James directly.

"I'm sure you'll have many questions, James. Come and walk with me." Then he looked to Kassim, Officer Ross, and Jan. "We won't need an escort. You and our other two guests can wait here while I show our new friend around."

James was less impressed by Rostov knowing his name—since James had just gotten the very same sort of information by simply looking at Rostov himself—and more impressed by the instant obedience from the followers. *They'd let me walk off alone with their leader without question, even though he's been the only thing keeping them alive in here. Forget what I was thinking about factions. The leader here is an absolute dictator!*

"It would be my pleasure, Nikolai," James replied. Rostov showed no particular reaction to James casually using his given name. He just waited for the other to approach him. Finally, with one reassuring last smile at Alan and Mitzi, James did.

Rostov led James away from the group toward the line of tents.

Once they were a little distant, James asked, probing, "I take it I wasn't quite what you were expecting?"

"Oh, well, I was imagining you being a little older," Rostov hedged. "My god informed me that the Chosen of another deity would be coming my way sometime soon. From prior discussions, I've had the impression that I am on the younger end to hold such a position. A young buck achieving this amazing outcome improbably soon. But, to look at you, I'm less impressive. Not quite an old goat, but far from a prodigy!" He ended on a note of humor, and he spoke most of the words with a smile.

James thought this prophet was quite charming; charisma was a necessity for a radical religious leader—especially a cultist leader—if such a person was to be successful. But James had never witnessed it firsthand. More interesting was the designation of James as a Chosen, a Title James had stolen from a corpse.

Somehow, Rostov's god didn't seem to be aware, or hadn't bothered to inform the prophet, that James's Title of Chosen One of Apophis was a mere accident of fate. James needed to find a way to delicately explore that.

"Sadly, I am what I am," James said, trying to mirror Rostov's ironic tone. "You don't look that old to me, though, and I probably look younger than I am. Black don't crack, as they say. This is very interesting to me, though. Your god was interested enough in me to send you word that I was coming?"

"Honestly, it was more of a warning." Rostov's smile seemed to grow more forced before James's eyes. "Specifically, my god warned me that you might wish to kill my people and destroy my camp."

CHAPTER FIFTY-ONE

True Genius

Well, of course that's not my intention," James said. Perhaps not very convincingly, but that was all right. A plan was beginning to form in his mind.

There was an awkward silence for a few seconds after James's pronouncement, and then they passed through the area of camp with the line of tents. Rostov seemed to recall at this point that he was meant to be giving James a tour of the camp.

"You've already seen the statue, of course. And these tents house most of my residents here," he said. "What's most interesting is behind it, however."

He pointed out a long rectangular, grid-shaped wooden structure that was embedded in the ground. Grass and dirt poked out from beneath the lattice-like wooden structure.

"What in the world is that?" James asked, not bothering to hide his pure curiosity.

"Well, you came upon us in the middle of performing a sacrifice," Rostov said matter-of-factly. "Naturally, people who know they're about to be sacrificed can't simply be kept in the open air. They would run away. So we dug out an underground prison, and we keep them here."

"So this is the roof of an underground prison." James was surprised. And a little impressed, a little worried, and highly disgusted. Why had Rostov chosen to show him this?

"It is. It's difficult to lift the ceiling, even when we come and get the prisoners out ourselves, but it's worth it for the security. It makes escape very difficult.

Despite the low probability of anyone making it out, someone guards it at night. And we have a patrol around the outskirts of the camp. During the day, of course, we would be able to see any activity here." He gestured broadly at the open clearing. There was a good line of sight from the tents to the underground prison and beyond. "And of course, anyone coming to attack the camp from that side would be likely to stumble through this ceiling in the dark, even if they were somehow invisible to the guards. This is just a thin layer of wood, earth, and grass. It can't really support human weight." He pointed to the other side where the tents were, along with the statue of the god, the bonfire, and the female prisoner tied to the wooden post. "If someone snuck up from that side, they wouldn't really be sneaking, since we have a fire burning there constantly."

So, there it was.

"This is your way of discouraging me from making an attack on your camp," James said.

"It's a better way of discouraging you than trying to kill you, isn't it?" Rostov smiled wolfishly.

"Much better. I suppose you didn't choose that path, because you are still hoping for a productive relationship."

"At the least, I suspect my god is not well served by angering Apophis."

James swallowed. There it was. *He's basing his foreign policy here on our supposed religious affiliations. If he found out that I didn't have a legitimate tie to Apophis, would he order his men to try to kill me right now? Or worse, would he want to add me to his sacrificial fire?*

"I suspect you're right," James said, trying not to press the point too hard. "Before we go further on this subject, I must apologize for my ignorance. What god is that?" He gestured to the statue. "I never studied religions very much, and I did not expect I would be meeting the Chosen of another god today. I just thought I was finding a settlement of people."

"Oh, sure. My god is Moloch, lord of the cleansing fire. He can see everything done under the sun. That's literal since he's a sun god." Rostov smiled, and James was reminded of the history teacher he'd had in freshman year of high school. The other man seemed to really enjoy telling people about his god.

That's bad, James thought, *but how is it that Moloch gives his servant such incomplete information anyway? If he sees everything that's done—wait, that's not how Rostov phrased it. Moloch can* see *everything done under the sun. That doesn't necessarily mean he* does *see everything. Only that what he wants to see, he can see. Perhaps he was so focused these last few days on protecting and guiding Rostov and his flock, ensuring that his Chosen was perceived as infallible by these sheep, that he hasn't even bothered watching everything else that's been happening. That would explain why Rostov thought that I'd be older looking. He's only getting bits and pieces of information from Moloch, and I only popped up on Moloch's radar when he realized I was migrating in Rostov's general direction. He didn't bother giving a physical description. My bad luck is that I was traveling during the day and sleeping at night. I might have gotten the drop on these people instead of vice versa.*

James realized Rostov was looking at him expectantly, as if he thought James was going to share some details about Apophis with him in return for the religious-history lesson on Moloch. And James actually had just the right information to share in mind. A mix of truths and falsehoods that Rostov would hopefully never fully disentangle.

"Should I assume you have any knowledge about Apophis?" James asked.

"Only the very bare minimum. That he's a bit on the, uh, darker side, like Moloch, and that he represents a more chaotic element."

Perfect.

"That's putting it mildly, my friend." James put a hand on Rostov's shoulder. "He's an apocalyptic chaos god, and his entire thing within his own pantheon is trying to unmake creation."

Rostov's eyes widened. "I, ah, don't think Moloch would be accepting of that. He certainly likes the sacrifices, but I'm pretty sure he wants humanity to continue."

"Oh, of course! I completely understand. And you, as an instrument of your god's will, wish for the same thing. While I"—James winked and threw up his hands—"naturally wish for Apophis to destroy the world and bring on endless darkness. But that's not something I have much part in.

"Cutting to the chase, Apophis doesn't communicate with me quite as much as it sounds like Moloch does with you. I'm not really a player in his big designs yet, I don't think. If ever. Apophis gave me a mission, and it involves creating chaos, but I don't think that puts us at odds."

"Oh, no?" Rostov looked skeptical.

James smiled and shook his head. "No. First, I didn't come here to undermine the work that you and your god are doing to diminish the human population. If I had known who you were, I'd have headed in a different direction, frankly. The mission I have is to infiltrate groups within the Orientation, break them up from within, and cause them to self-destruct. Ultimately resulting in mass casualties and chaos." He tried to smile and look appropriately pleased with himself, as he imagined the enthusiastic supporter of an omnicidal god would.

"Then, those people you were traveling with?"

"They're the last survivors of the previous group. They don't know about my blessing, and I need to keep it that way, so I'd appreciate your discretion here. I infiltrated their group on day one. Day two, I was everybody's best friend. Day three, I had started to suss out some points of division within the group. These were people who knew each other, mostly, which meant there was a simmering cauldron of resentment already there to exploit just beneath the surface. The next day, I chose violence!" James chuckled. "Heh heh. I staged a crime scene so it looked like one faction within the group had killed a member of another. I added a little theft so the very distinctive stolen item could pop up in a suspect's sleeping bag when it was convenient for me.

"By a couple of days ago, the group was engaged in an open civil war. By the end, I had led the handful of survivors into the middle of some spider monsters' territory. There were so few of them that they all got picked off, except my buddies, um, Alan and, ah, Mitzi. I led them out of the spiders' territory since they both still trust me. I think having an elderly married couple with me will make me look a lot more approachable to the next group I infiltrate."

Rostov chuckled a bit. "So, the senior citizen couple aren't your hired help to assist in wiping out my little community? I had thought the idea of the three of you being here on a mission of destruction was pretty strange. Not quite what I expected from the Chosen of Apophis, at least. Now it makes sense. Pawns. Everyone needs them. Kind of you to spare the elderly."

"Eh, 'spare' is a strong word. They make a strong argument for my credibility right now, but once I'm in the next group, I'll have to get rid of them at some point. In fact, I was going to let you sacrifice them if I had to, in order to get in your good graces, but with your permission, I would like to take them alive and in one piece with me. Their presence makes such a strong argument that I'm a harmless, gentle soul, and since they're a married couple, they're much more valuable as a set than if one were to catch a bad case of being sacrificed. I can ensure they won't live long enough to tell anybody about your little community."

"Wow. That's—you're—" Rostov seemed taken aback for a moment, probably still absorbing everything James had said, not just the last snippet. He took a deep breath before saying with a chuckle, "Heh heh. You're a ruthless son of a bitch, aren't you?"

That's a bit rich coming from this human-sacrificing wannabe cult leader, James thought. But it was exactly the impression he was going for.

James threw up his hands and grinned. "Guilty as charged! Not that different from you, though, right? I mean, I can't imagine getting my two survivors to let me *sacrifice* people. You and your god put me to shame. And having that smoke constantly luring fresh victims—that's a stroke of genius! True genius."

Rostov chuckled a little at that. "Well, I swear I'm a nice guy just doing what I have to do. Humbly obeying my god's laws. Trying not to question too much. Speaking of which, why do *you* think my god believed you were coming to destroy me and my group, since it seems you intend to leave peacefully?"

"Well, I did intend to destroy you and your group when I set out here. At the time I made those plans, though, I just assumed the originator of the smoke was an ordinary group of Orientation survivors. Not followers of another destructive god. My plan now is to move on to another group and snuff them out. Our gods are both sort of dark, so I figure we're better off on the same page, at least for now. What I get out of it is knowing that you're whittling down the survivors in this place too. And you get the same from me. I'll be cutting down the number of cohesive groups that might threaten your dominance in here, and when I can, I'll direct survivors your way if it doesn't hurt my plans to do so. Who knows, maybe we can reconnect at the end of Orientation?"

"That *does* sound like it's to my benefit, ultimately. All right, then." Rostov looked pensive for a moment. He seemed to be chewing over this idea, looking for any flaws in it.

After a minute, he asked, "James, is there anything you and your party need while you're here, or would you like to be on your way sooner rather than later?"

James tried to be casual. "Nothing we need." He shrugged, as if he didn't want to grab Alan and Mitzi and literally run from this place. "Unless you happen to know of another population nearby that we can infiltrate?"

"Well, I'm afraid I don't. But if you're otherwise all right, then let's get you and yours on your way."

Confirmed that he's not aware of the Rodriguezes' presence, or he's unwilling to admit it, James thought. *And he'd have no reason to hide that information. His god is far from omniscient.*

"I did have one question about you and Moloch," James said.

"Go ahead and shoot! We've already shared so much."

"How do you pick who gets sacrificed? Is it random? Some specific set of criteria? Just any outsider, or what?"

Rostov seemed to light up at that. "That's an interesting question, actually! In the case of the woman there now, she was actually one of us originally. But she's gained an ability that's suited to consorting with demons, and weirdly, Moloch has no truck with that. Otherwise, we sacrifice outsiders, usually going from strongest to weakest to ensure minimal resistance as the process advances and it becomes clearer there will be no survivors."

So, demons exist too, James thought. *Not just gods. And also, Rostov is a monster. A real psychopath. If he takes this show on the road, he could grow up to be a religious version of Hitler. If I manage to escape here with Alan and Mitzi, I have to come back. Even if I can't save that woman, someone has to deal with Rostov. I don't want my family to exist in the same world as this bastard.*

"Very interesting," James said, smiling politely at Rostov's explanation. "Good future notes in the event I ever need to sacrifice people to please Apophis."

Rostov led James back to Alan and Mitzi, who stood holding each other close and smiling at the Moloch worshippers in a thin attempt to conceal their obvious discomfort. They were guarded by Officer Ross and two other tough-looking Moloch cultists.

As James approached, he Identified as many cultists as he could to gauge their real Strength. *Average level around seven, but three have been through Race Evolution. I can take them—hopefully?* All but one looked human. The non-human-looking cultist sported a pair of tiny horns and skin with a reddish hue.

James closed the distance with Alan and Mitzi and embraced them both. He felt relief surge through him, and he immediately passed it on.

"Don't worry. We're getting out of here shortly," he reassured them under his breath. "Just keep silent for now."

Rostov had a quiet word with the people who were guarding Alan and Mitzi, and the guards visibly relaxed.

"Safe travels, fellas," Officer Ross said, noticeably relieved that he did not have to sacrifice these people.

"I guess so," muttered one of the other guards, sounding disappointed they were letting them walk away.

Rostov waved. "We'll see you later, perhaps. If fate ordains!"

He and his people waited a moment, and then James began leading Alan and Mitzi away. As they made it to the tree line, the awkward silence was broken by the sound of the prisoner being whipped in the background.

James couldn't help but notice that she barely made a peep as the lash struck her, just sharp little intakes of breath. As if the fight had all been whipped out of her already. He resisted the impulse to shudder; someone might still be watching.

There, but for the literal grace of the gods, go I.

CHAPTER FIFTY-TWO

The Fox

So, are you going to explain what happened back there?" Alan asked once they were around a mile away from the camp.

"Yes, of course. The leader of the cult of Moloch—Rostov is his name—agreed to let us go, based on the understanding that the two of you are pawns in my evil schemes, and those evil schemes will not harm Moloch's interests directly in the short to medium term."

"Wait! Moloch, the evil god that people were sacrificing babies to in the Bible?" Alan exclaimed.

"That does seem consistent with what he told me, so I think that's probably correct," James said. "I never really studied the Bible."

"What evil schemes are we pawns in?" Mitzi asked.

"All sorts of diabolical stuff," James replied. "For one thing, we caused our last group to disintegrate into in-fighting and ultimately die out."

"Why on Earth would we do that?" Alan asked.

"Well, it's less of a 'we' thing and more of a 'me' thing. One of my Titles is that I'm the Chosen One of a certain evil god, so I used that as an explanation for why I'm going around infiltrating and destroying other groups."

"Which you're not actually doing, of course," Alan said. There was a question in his tone, but James ignored it.

The idea that it was possible he might actually be infiltrating groups and destroying them from within was a little insulting, and he would've thought Alan knew him better than that by now—or at least knew him well enough to know that he would never admit to such a thing if it was true. The question in Alan's tone was insulting either James's character or his intelligence, depending on how James chose to take it.

"Based on that premise, he agreed that it was in his best interests that I keep doing what I've supposedly been doing," James said.

"What an awful world they're creating," Mitzi said.

"You're not wrong," James said. "I don't want people being sacrificed either."

"Not just that. There are going to be people all around the world slaughtering each other in the names of who knows how many gods. It will be just like the ancient world, centuries past, except this time the gods are real, and obeying them will give you real advantages, so there's no reason to ever stop! Why would any divine being be cruel enough to think introducing this System and its gods into our world was a good idea?" Mitzi said, disgusted.

"It's possible that the System's representatives have lied to us about why it's come to our world," Alan said.

"Maybe there's some worse alternative that they're protecting us from," James suggested, suppressing the urge to shrug.

It was a thin thread, but if the System was telling the truth through its representatives, there had to be some worse alternative that they were avoiding by their integration into the System. It had presented itself as a blessing, and the System, whatever the faults of its divine beings, had never lied to James before as far as he knew. All the abilities he had been given worked exactly as the System described.

Recalling his initial interactions with the System Homunculus and Vinny as well as the descriptions that Identify gave him for abilities and items, James thought the System was, in fact, *brutally* honest—even unpleasantly so.

It had no reason to lie to them about the System's advent being a blessing; clearly it did not care about public relations. It was all powerful and authoritative, not reliant on public approval. There had to be a piece they were still missing.

"I don't know what could be much worse than this," Alan said quietly. "They'd better have a damn good reason for ripping us away from our lives."

"It has to be some end of the world shit," James murmured, as much to himself as to them. *But what kind of end of the world is the System averting? I wish it would just tell us. I would want to prevent the end of the world, regardless of what Apophis wants. The world is where my family lives!*

No one bothered to ask how James had come to be the Chosen One of an evil god. He hoped it was because that was obviously something he had stolen from someone else, but he also didn't feel in good enough spirits to proactively try and clarify the issue. *Let them draw their own conclusions.*

The three walked largely in a brooding silence for the rest of the journey back.

James informed Alan and Mitzi that he didn't want it to be obvious that they were going straight back to a camp they had just come from. If Moloch conveyed that they went directly to the Rodriguez camp, it would contradict some of what he'd told Rostov, which might provoke some future hostilities.

So James deliberately led them on a meandering route in case Moloch was watching from above. The column of smoke remained an excellent landmark for navigation purposes, and he thought he managed to convey the impression that they were lost, without ever actually feeling like that was the case.

They more or less wandered until near dark, resting liberally since there was no rush, and when the sun had almost set, James took them in a straight line for the last fifteen minutes until camp came into view.

James debriefed his inner circle in the largest tent, where Camila made her residence. James had quietly reassigned Chava's residence to the tent next door now that Camila was "recovered" and no longer "needed" his constant attention.

He expected that, in this place, Moloch's ability to see "everything done under the sun" would be blocked even though the sun was still setting. Therefore, any plans made would remain secret.

"So, you're telling me that the camp you had us walk all this way to reach turned out to be hostile," Chava summarized with a stone-cold gaze. "They're sacrificing random people to an evil pre-Christian god. And your diplomatic party was lucky to make it away with their lives."

"That's about the long and short of it," James said. "Fortunately for you, I didn't lead the whole camp into his hands, or we would probably all be dead or marked for death by now."

"James proved he's capable of playing the wolf as well as the fox here," Alan said in his defense. "If not for his quick thinking, I have no doubt we would all have been tortured and killed."

James appreciated the kind affirmation. He judged that Alan's faith in him was at a high point again, where it had been rocky a few days ago. He sent a mental command to Chava not to argue any further on this point. They had more productive things to discuss.

"I guess we'll have to be careful about dealing with other survivor groups," Chava said blandly.

For now, the group agreed that the Rodriguezes would camp where they stood.

The young had already done well clearing out the trees in a small area around them, making a quick and dirty replica of the campsite the family had prepared when James first encountered them. Chopping down trees to reduce the reach of the forest had been effective back in spider territory, and it seemed likely to be effective here too.

"The question is, what's next?" Cliff said.

"Definitely traveling in a different direction," Camila said.

"That's for sure," Alan affirmed.

"Yes, you should all prepare to move at first light. Not back toward the area we came from, but in a direction away from the smoke signal, for sure," James said.

"What do you mean, 'you all' should move?" Mitzi asked. "What will you be doing?"

James sighed. "That maniac back there has at least one prisoner he's torturing to death right now. Probably more. I have to do something about it, but I'll make sure that you and your family are not involved."

"Jesus Christ," Alan groaned. "James . . ."

"Why do you have to do this?" Camila asked. Her face looked tense.

"What if you don't get back to your family because you decided to do this alone?" Mitzi broke in. "How would you like us to explain to your wife that you decided to sacrifice yourself to save a bunch of strangers?"

"It wouldn't matter how you explain it. She wouldn't believe that," James said, trying not to laugh. *She knows me too well for that. I wouldn't go if I thought the situation was that dangerous.* "And you won't need to explain that because it isn't going to happen. Worst case scenario is either that I fail at killing their prophet, or I fail at saving the hostages. The idea of me dying isn't on the table." He imbued the words with slightly more confidence than he really felt.

Just sneaking into the Moloch camp would be a challenge, for the reasons Rostov had highlighted in James's tour of the place. Once he was there, he didn't think he would be spotted if he was alone. And he certainly didn't think they could kill him unless there were several people at higher levels than he was.

"How can you be so confident?" Cliff asked. "I know you wiped out the spiders, and that's *real cool*, but it's different to fight humans. People are intelligent. They'll come up with their own tactics to survive you."

I guess I never mentioned the sentient spiders to Cliff.

"For that matter, how can you guarantee that the prophet's wrath won't fall on this camp if you fail?" Alan asked.

"I've seen their defenses and their personnel. I've had the chance to gauge their strength. They're stronger than our camp, no question, but only because of a few exceptional individuals. I can at least take those people out, especially when I have the element of surprise. Even if I failed to get Rostov, he wouldn't be able to manage any reprisals with just the rabble he'll have left. His abilities aren't offensive in nature. He's a support Class. And in the event that I fail, they won't know where to strike for reprisals."

"How's that last part?" Cliff asked.

"Try to Identify me," James said. A demonstration would be quicker than an explanation, and anyway, he wasn't fond of explaining his Skills. Just doing things left a lot more mystery.

"Who the fuck is Octavius Root?" Cliff exclaimed after a moment.

"Probably not a real person," James said. "The important thing is that made up name doesn't lead back to us."

"I didn't know you could fool the Identify Skill, James," Alan said. He sounded faintly suspicious, as if he wondered what other deceptions James had been responsible for in the time they'd known each other.

But James didn't want to spend time reassuring him right now. *If you don't trust me now, you probably never will. You don't need to know what all my powers are to know I'm on your side.*

"If you're creative with your Skills, you'll surprise yourself with the things you can do, Alan." James held up a Small Exoshield. He'd used a dagger to drill a pair of crude eyeholes into it while he waited for everyone to gather in the tent. "I'll be wearing this to ensure it's impossible to visually identify me as well."

"You've clearly thought a great deal about this," Mitzi said, a little exasperated.

"Above all, I don't want to put the group at risk," James said firmly.

"I would still like to know"—Mitzi locked her gray eyes with James's brown ones; her look was stern—"what we should tell your family in the event that you don't come back from this suicide mission."

James didn't flinch.

"Tell my Mina that counter to all of our shared expectations, I died doing the right thing because I couldn't stand to do anything less."

That would be a good death, James thought. *It would be all too easy for me to live long enough to see myself become the villain. Better not to subject her and our children to that. In some ways, I might be better off dead.*

He took a breath and moved past that idea.

"Any other questions before I go and prepare for my suicide mission?" James asked, his tone ironic.

Heads shook. All but one.

"I want to know who's supposed to be in charge until you get back," Alan said. "Who will keep the group safe in the unthinkable event that you don't return?"

"Well, I think this group in general is the leadership group. That's why you're the ones I wanted to explain this decision to." James looked over the faces of the group members. They all looked unsatisfied with his non-answer. He sighed. "Cliff is probably the most dangerous besides me right now, so he can best keep you safe. If something happens to him, Mitzi is the next most lethal if not more dangerous, so I'd refer you to her. If that's all, let's adjourn this meeting."

Even in the System world, meetings were apparently inescapable. But finally, it broke off, and everyone went to their tents.

James was outside checking his gear and making sure he had everything he needed for both a stealth mission and a difficult fight when Mitzi found him.

"This is really stupid," the old woman said. "You going alone, I mean."

"Are you trying to volunteer to go with me?" James asked lightly.

"Better me than someone else," Mitzi replied. "Better that I die than a young man whose wife is about to have a baby. My life is mostly in the past already."

"If we were just going to rain death on the Moloch cultists, I would take you with me for sure," James said. "On a stealth mission, though, you'd mostly just increase my odds of being seen and captured."

"You could have me stand far back and just watch to see if you get captured!" Mitzi said. She was clearly very distressed by the prospect of being left behind again.

"All right," James conceded.

"I won't take no for an answer this time! I'm sick of you and my husband trying to keep me—wait, what was that?"

"I said all right. I'm okay with this idea. You can come with me on the suicide mission," James said. "You might die, but you know the risks as well as I do, and actually, if you're just standing way back looking to see if I'm spotted, you might be able to save me in the event that they get their hands on me. Raining death from the sky is probably the best way to deal with the Moloch camp. The only problem is that if *you* get captured, it's not just you that gets killed. They'll know for sure that at least Alan is in on this, and they'll go looking for him. They'll probably find the whole group. Whereas if it was just me, they'd probably be satisfied to just give me to Moloch as a sacrifice."

"So all you wanted to say is that you didn't really mean you're okay with me joining you. You just wanted to shut me up while you raised your objections," Mitzi grumbled. "You're a real piece of work, James." She exhaled a frustrated laugh.

"I was just thinking out loud," James said. "I'd be lying if I said I didn't want a fiery goddess of destruction with me on this mission. It just seems like a bad idea when I think about it a bit deeper."

"This whole *thing* is a bad idea!"

"Yeah, but your participation is the part that makes it a bad idea for the whole group, as opposed to it just being a bad idea for my personal survival. Which I'm confident in, by the way. You know what, forget that heroic death speech I wanted you to give to Mina on my behalf. If I don't come back from this, just tell her that I'll be a little late for dinner."

She threw her hands in the air and gave up.

"Fine, go on your suicide mission alone, then!"

CHAPTER FIFTY-THREE

God Complex

So, I hear you're going to go off and deprive us all of the pleasure of your company."

James turned and saw Sierra standing there in the twilight. Her expressions were usually harder for him to read than most people's, but he could barely see her face at all in this light.

"I'll be back."

"So you've been telling folks. I hear you're going to free a bunch of prisoners from an evil cult."

"That's about the size of it."

"Why?"

"Well, people being sacrificed to an evil god is bad."

"And?" She sounded suspicious. "No other reason?"

"Do I need another reason?" he asked, genuinely curious what she'd say.

"I would think you would," she said slowly. "But maybe I don't know you as well as I think I do."

"We've only known each other for a few days, and we've been apart for more than half of them," James pointed out.

"You know, you're an interesting guy." She settled herself on a log, one of many the family had left after clearing the forest for camp. "I thought that, over the last few days since we ran into this family, I'd started to figure you out. You're a guy who likes to dominate the people around him and kill things. Maybe you're a little more concerned about that than you are about getting back to that family you have somewhere. None of which is to say that you're a bad person. I kind of admire it. And you're definitely better than Chava. Better than Kurt. If I wasn't personally in danger, I'd definitely admire you. There's a logic to the way you work, and I can see you becoming someone important if you keep going the way you are."

"I feel as if you're coming to a point."

"Even when you killed my group members, when you killed *my brother*, you had a good reason for it. And I get it. I don't even blame you anymore. I logically can't. You *just* defended yourself. And now you're *just* trying to get the most out of this place that you possibly can. That includes pawns for after we get out of the Orientation. If I was a cynical woman, I would think that's what you want to do this for. And if you were a cynical man, I'd want to say something like, 'Don't do this thing. It's not worth the headache.' Because you might bring some heat back on us, and even if you don't, you might die a horrible death. Probably not worth it just to free a handful of people and build up your army here a little bit."

James took a deep breath. This was unexpected. "A little harsh, but understandable. I won't speak as directly as you, because I don't think we know each other that well yet, but I like that you feel you can be so open with me. And for what it's worth, I enjoy your company despite the fact that I feel certain you're holding a grudge. Even though you claim you're not. There is something about danger that I like, obviously. I don't think of Alan and Mitzi and Cliff as pawns. Or you for that matter. You all are more like valued allies to me. People I don't want to have to do without. If it feels like I'm managing the people around me, that's why. I want to maintain the current equilibrium and keep the group together. Maybe I'll feel similarly close to the Rodriguezes in a few more weeks."

I'm already unreasonably fond of Camila, James thought, *even if it's just because I keep picturing my grandmother when I'm with her.*

"And after the Orientation? What's your end goal? What are you going to do with all these people you're *collecting*?"

James snorted and shook his head. "You make it sound as if I'm some evil mastermind with everything planned out. Right now, I'm just trying to stay alive!"

Even in the bad lighting, he could tell she didn't really believe him. The moonlight was enough to convey that much. She shook her head, rose, and walked away. He smiled.

As far as he was concerned, Sierra was just making his life easier by being so much more open. One less variable he had to really focus on managing. He thought he understood her just a little bit better now. She clearly didn't want him dead. He imagined she wanted to remain under the umbrella of his protection, the same feeling he hoped to evoke in every member of his camp.

He finished choosing his gear for the trip, and he silently departed.

He left as soon after sunset as he could, to give himself maximum time to achieve his objectives out of the sight of Moloch. It was strange to think that he was hiding from an evil god by moving at night, but James didn't question that quirk of fate too much.

With the sun set and his makeshift mask secured to his face with his internally produced spider silk, his range of vision had drastically diminished. He focused most of his attention on simply looking where he was going. James moved alone, as silently and efficiently as he could only do alone.

Left to himself, he couldn't help but be distracted by his own doubts.

He knew that this was a bad idea. Maybe Mitzi would end up delivering that stupid message he'd given her for Mina and Yulia because James would be roasting in Moloch's stupid bonfire. Or maybe she'd say he died because of his ego. A hero complex. Or a god complex.

There was a lot running against him. Even the moon. James had never had much cause to notice the moon in the Orientation space before, but in apparent simulation of Earth's moon, it seemed to have phases. Tonight, it was full, bright, and milky white. It even seemed to loom larger than he remembered from the other times he'd vaguely noticed it.

If the Moloch cultists were just killing people, James would've left them well enough alone. He didn't like sticking his neck out. But he couldn't ignore the barbaric, torturous methods they employed. He wanted to roast them all alive. Let them see how it felt. And he wanted to save their prisoners.

It was the first time since getting to this place that he felt called to do something for nearly selfless reasons, though he was also conscious that the prisoners would likely turn into devoted followers afterward.

Still, Mitzi was right that this was as near a suicide mission as James could imagine. He could not pretend it was anything else. He had no idea what the Moloch cultists' real strengths were, let alone any of their weaknesses or points of vulnerability. He knew only what he'd seen and what Rostov had been cocky enough to show him.

James imagined that Rostov wasn't actually trying to dissuade any kind of future attack by him when he described the Moloch camp's defenses. James thought he understood Rostov a bit because he had the same weakness. *He was bragging. He badly needed someone else to know how clever and dangerous and secure he is in his fortified camp.* That level of arrogance was beyond what James would let himself indulge in. Hopefully, it would be a fatal weakness.

A similar level of knowledge had been enough to wipe out the spider nest, but the spiders weren't strategic thinkers. Besides the Queen, they didn't seem very intelligent except that by the end, they had managed to work together to capture James. Even then, a simple trick like playing dead was enough to penetrate their defenses.

Just have to hope that arrogant prick showed me the better part of his security system and didn't hide any surprise giant three-headed dogs. Given how Moloch had seemingly put a heavy finger on the scale in Rostov's favor thus far, James had no faith that the cultists' defenses would be as reasonable—or as penetrable—as they seemed.

If James was Moloch's prophet, there would be layers of defense that no one knew about, including other members of the cult. After all, Moloch's human sacrifices were bound to draw a lot of negative attention from people who found the practice as *distasteful* as James did.

For the fourth or fifth time, James wondered what the limitations of Rostov's wards were. No power that he'd seen thus far was limitless in duration and effectiveness. Elemental magic was limited by the amount of Mana poured in. Spider silk and similar abilities consumed calories or Stamina or both to use. His Predator in Human Skin abilities were all basically enhancements of his existing human capabilities—or rather, his Evolver Human capabilities.

As he trudged through the darkness, James developed his plan to get around each of the known layers of Rostov's defenses.

Finally, he arrived in the area he recognized as the near outskirts of the Moloch camp. The column of smoke remained a useful signal of the enemy's position.

Unwilling to get close enough to actually see the camp itself just yet, he paused.

He adjusted his Flame Resistant Wolfskin Pelt—a moderately strong piece of equipment, and one Rostov hadn't seen him use earlier—wrapping it more loosely around his body. He made sure the False Impression falsification of his identity was still in place. He'd decided to go with showing up as Jeffrey Ross, to ensure he would initially appear to be an ally if anyone besides Ross spotted him and used Identify. He began Silent Spellcasting.

Slowly, wind Mana gathered around him until, finally, he felt that he had enough. James unleashed the power, and the wind wrapped around him, blowing under the wolfskin pelt and propelling him into the air.

James shot up, then hovered far above the trees and gradually descended into the Moloch camp. He guided himself to a soft landing right in front of the Moloch statue so that he could use it for cover. The best guess he had for a weakness to Rostov's wards was that they either wouldn't work after sundown, in which case they were a non-factor, or they might not catch something above or below a certain altitude.

Since digging underground would be much more Mana-intensive and probably much noisier than simply lifting his body weight, he flew. He landed where he did because who would expect an intruder to appear right next to Moloch's statue?

As James landed, nothing appeared to be stirring. But Rostov had mentioned guards. James wanted to get a sense of their shift timing and where they patrolled.

He pulled himself very close to the left leg of Moloch, and he activated Natural Camouflage. His heart rate slowed, and his body relaxed. It was as though James had melted into the statue's leg. He felt a deep patience settle over him, and he simply observed.

The first thing he noticed was Isabelle Rose, still alive. He hadn't noticed her when he landed because he was only looking out for threats. By contrast, she was barely still clinging to life. Her chest rose and fell in weak, subtle movements. She lay on a stone table a few feet away from Moloch's bonfire. Someone apparently had had the decency to take her down from the whipping post. Perhaps they simply thought she might die in the night if she wasn't placed in a less unpleasant posture.

Then again, perhaps placing her on this table was just about presenting her in the way that Moloch preferred his victims, or about making it easier to torture her. Rose's skin was flayed to ribbons in long, dark-red strips across her chest, stomach, and thighs. James winced at the sight.

All I need to do is get close to her to save her, James thought. He felt confident that his healing would pull her back no matter how close she was to death. He just needed to make sure the coast was clear first.

It was painful to remain in place and do nothing after noticing her just a few paces away. But for an interminable period, that was what James did.

He crouched in Moloch's shadow for long minutes, waiting, until a flicker of the bonfire showed him two other people walking along the outskirts of the camp. The two figures wore the same white hooded cloaks James had seen some of the cultists wearing earlier. A few seconds later, he heard them.

"Waste of time," one yawned.

"Shut up, and let's get this over with," the other said. "Our shift is over as soon as we check on the prisoners and wake the next two."

"What's the point?" the first asked. "Where are the prisoners going to go? Deeper underground? I don't even understand why we left *her* alive tonight." He gestured at Isabelle Rose.

"Shut up about that!" the second said, apparently a bit louder than he intended. He looked around to see if he'd woken anyone before he continued. "You know Moloch prefers sacrifices at first light or at sunset, and thanks to those senior citizens lost in the woods from earlier, we didn't get the timing right for sunset."

"I don't know jack about Moloch," the first griped, "except that we sure are taking a lot of bullshit orders about his preferred sacrificial methods. If I wanted to take orders like this, I'd have become a short-order cook!"

"Revered Moloch guided us through the dangers of the forest," the second insisted, glancing around them again as he spoke.

"Yes, he did," the first agreed. "That was what we needed him for. Now, though—"

The two men began to move out of James's easy hearing range. *Who are those guys?* One of them at least seemed far from the loyal Moloch cultist he expected to find. James used Identify on the first and second man, respectively.

[Max Roper, Lv. 7]

[Philippe Rousseau, Lv. 6]

He filed the information away for later use, and then, slowly and cautiously, he moved. There must be a short lag between this patrol and the next, while the two guards checked on the other prisoners and then awakened the relief shift. In that time, he had to heal Isabelle Rose and maneuver into position to be able to free the other prisoners when the coast was clear.

Still crouching, he approached the half-dead woman. The first thing he noticed as he got closer was that she was tied to the table with thin cords, as if her injuries didn't secure her well enough on their own. James thought that he could hack through the cords fairly quickly, but it would add an extra minute to an already delicate rescue operation.

The second thing he noticed was that her wounds were even worse than he'd noticed on first inspection. There were injuries to her back that he couldn't completely see because she was lying face-up. Those injuries looked to be worse than the gouges cut out of her front side; the table beneath her was a mess of semi-congealed blood—too much for the more visible front wounds to account for. If he had to guess without flipping her over, James thought her whole back must have been flayed open.

Recalling how long Cliff had needed to recover from regrowing a severed hand when James and Alan healed him, James recognized that Isabelle Rose would probably be of no help at all in her own rescue. He would have to rely on the other prisoners.

Since he was already close, however, James used Laying on Hands and began healing the injuries that were within his reach. The long gouges out of her front began to heal, and the flesh slowly knitted itself back together.

As her body repaired itself, the woman stirred.

"Ugh—ahh! Hurts so much," she whimpered. Fresh tears ran along her face in tracks formed by now-dried ones.

"Shhhh," James whispered, pressing one hand to her mouth. "I'm here to help, Isabelle. Just need you to be quiet, and I'll heal you and get you out of here."

"Just—just kill me," she managed. "My brother. S-save my brother!"

Her body went limp, but James could hear her racing pulse and knew she'd only lost consciousness again. Healing her to the degree that he had had taken a surprising amount of Mana, and though the gouges to her front were reduced to angry red welts, he'd done almost nothing to the wounds on her back.

James recognized he couldn't finish the job now and still be ready for a possible fight to get the prisoners out of here. At least after the work he'd just done, she shouldn't die while he detoured to secure the other prisoners. And she still looked messed up enough that if the next shift of guards approached her, they might not notice from a cursory glance that he'd healed her.

Hopefully, her brother's a Healer, he thought.

Keeping low, he crept away from Isabelle Rose's body, moving away from the bonfire and the Moloch statue and toward the tree line without actually entering it. He guessed entering the tree line would probably set off Rostov's wards.

He moved in a wide arc around the cultists' tents toward the underground area Rostov had identified as the enclosure where the prisoners were kept.

The next set of guards, a male and a female, were already starting off on their patrol, fortunately moving in an arc going in the opposite direction from James's path. He should have a little time unless they discovered that some of the sacrifice's injuries had been healed.

Cold sweat trickled down James's neck as he passed by the biggest tent. It was closest to the tree line, on the side he was moving through. James could sense that beneath this thin frame of animal skin and fabric, Rostov was sleeping peacefully. He wasn't sure how he knew this was Rostov's tent, apart from the size of it, but then his nose twitched. He realized that he smelled a trace of something that he'd also caught earlier when he met Rostov.

Something spicy and slightly sweet. *Incense?*

A powerful temptation came over James. *He's asleep. I could kill him right now and never have to deal with this madness again.* And good sense asserted itself. *Never have to deal with it until Moloch creates another prophet anyway. A prophet who will probably be informed that I'm public enemy number one.* Still. It was tempting.

Who knew if the next Chosen One of Moloch would be as effective as Rostov had been at carrying out his grotesque will? And James could practically hear Rostov's pulse. It would be all too easy to end him. Then he could free the prisoners with one fewer threat. If anyone found out that Rostov was dead, it would destroy the camp's unity in an instant. They'd be in no shape to round up the prisoners without his guiding hand.

After a few long moments of inner turmoil, James walked away. He was here on a rescue mission. He wouldn't jeopardize it for a chance to kill the enemy's leader.

He approached the underground prison and began Silent Spellcasting.

CHAPTER FIFTY-FOUR

Run

Once the appropriate amount of earth Mana had settled around James's body, he directed it downward, shaping the earth according to the image he had in his mind.

The lattice-like ceiling of the underground prison slowly, subtly lifted off the ground until there was enough space for a crouching man of James's height to step under it. And the wall of the pit closest to James formed itself into stairs, the steps descending into the darkness. Earth Affinity, he had noticed, came with extremely fine control of earth Mana.

After casting one last look around to make sure he wasn't seen, James hunched down, ducked under the raised ceiling, and stepped down into the shadows. Two things hit him at once: a wave of fetid human stench and the sound of a human voice.

"It's not morning yet," a voice yawned, breaking the relative silence.

James froze on the stairs for a half-second. Then he realized stopping was pointless. These people had been in complete darkness until he opened the ceiling up; there was no way they'd fail to spot him while he was still on the staircase, especially when that was where the moonlight shone most brightly.

He descended more quickly.

"Shhhh!" he whispered. He repeated it, the first whisper having been muffled under his mask. His Evolution had substantially improved his night vision, so as he moved into the pit, he could scope out the general shape of it and count how many shapes were present before his eyes had fully adjusted to the darkness. The pit was larger than he had anticipated from the size of the ceiling, but the space was still tight. There were around two dozen people crammed into the cavernous space. Most of them rested, seated shoulder to shoulder, using the earthen walls and each other for their pillows. There wasn't enough room for them to all lie down.

Most of them remained asleep. The one who had noticed James stood out because he groggily shook his head as James got closer. Maybe he thought he was dreaming.

"*Urk!*"

James looked down and realized his foot was pressing into someone as he took his first step off of the stairs. It was incredibly tight down here, and as he breathed in, he again noticed the smell. He realized there was no separate space for the prisoners to relieve their biological needs. The pit was toilet as well as house for these people, and it smelled more strongly of shit and piss the more he inhaled. An atrocity worthy of the trans-Atlantic slave trade.

As if I didn't already think the Moloch cultists were savage enough. Rostov deserves to rot in a thousand hells for this. James didn't need any more reasons to dread the prospect of falling into their hands, nor to justify this prison break. But the reasons kept presenting themselves, nonetheless.

He pulled his foot back, then crouched low, facing the person he'd stepped on.

He whispered urgently, "Sorry I hurt you! I'm here to set you guys free! I need you to wake up your neighbor and pass the message on. We have to sneak out quietly as a group. If anyone makes noise, we're all screwed together!"

"Thank you, man! Thank you so much!" The woman's voice came out in a raspy whisper.

She seemed to understand the urgency of the situation, so James moved onto the one he'd awakened first. The yawner was staring at him curiously, looking half-asleep.

"This is not a drill." James tried to keep his voice low. "I'm here to save all of you. You need to get up and—"

"What's the point?" the man said, interrupting. His voice was much less sleepy now. He sounded upset. "You're just going to piss off that prophet and get us sacrificed faster. It's not like we can get away. We're starved, thirsty, weak—"

"Would you rather die now or live to run?" James asked. "Because I can mercy kill you if you don't believe you have a chance at getting away."

The man shrank away from James at that but said nothing.

"Wake up the next guy," James hissed. "Don't waste our precious window. We don't have unlimited time!"

The naysayer began gently shaking the man next to him.

James went around the pit, roughly shaking and waking various prisoners, explaining the situation, and telling them to rouse more of their neighbors. The whole process took a few minutes at most, and he thought they were off to a good start. Virtually everyone understood the magnitude of the situation almost instantly upon waking.

So far, no one had broken the stillness of the night.

James leaned down to wake one more prisoner. He shook the man vigorously before catching movement out of the corner of his eye. James turned and saw that the naysayer from earlier was shaking his head emphatically from side to side.

Do I have to come over there and knock you out? James questioned to himself. *I can't afford the distraction right now.* Then he realized the man was mouthing some words.

"Don't wake him up," the naysayer subvocalized. "He's a plant!"

"Prophet! Prisoners escaping!" James looked down. The man he'd just been shaking was yelling at the top of his lungs.

James groaned to himself and slapped a hand over the man's mouth. He continued trying to yell, but it was muffled by James's palm.

"Poff! Tum kick! Pissoners!" James could sort of make the muffled words out still, and it was a problem. He used his knee to drive the air out of the sitting man's lungs.

Then he turned to the naysayer and growled, "Lead your people out of here right now! Run for the forest, away from the fire!"

There was a stirring as the prisoners began moving up the stairs to obey. James felt a sharp pain in his side, and he looked down to see that the tattletale had drawn a knife and stuck James under the ribs.

Fortunately, he didn't get anything important, James thought optimistically. He could tell he wasn't critically injured. It hurt like hell getting stabbed, though.

He pressed his knee down harder into the man's chest, and there was a rewarding hiss of air out of the cultist's mouth. James pulled his palm away from the man's mouth, brought it to the knife stuck in his side, and pulled it out from his wound. He exhaled sharply. With both hands, he plunged the blade into the cultist's neck with his upper body's full weight behind the thrust.

There was a quiet sound of cracking bone, a gurgle, and the feeling of warm blood trickling down over his palms and then onto his pants. Then the notification came.

[You killed Sid Rohan, Lv. 8. You gained 140 exp!]

Well, that's one down. Hopefully, the next cultists I kill don't manage to ventilate me further before I can finish them. There was no time to Pillage.

James sensed someone approaching him from the side, and he swiveled his head sharply, wary now. He felt a bit of blood trickling from his torso wound as he moved, but keeping his bleeding to a minimum was not as important right now as avoiding further surprise attacks.

But it was only the naysayer.

"Hey, man, you need help?" he asked.

"Absolutely!" James snapped. "I need you to get your people out of here! Try to find the Rodriguez camp. It's about a mile or two away, in that direction." He pointed off in the direction he'd come from. "Tell them when you get there that they need to take you guys and get out of this area. The Moloch cultists will be after you guys, even if they never figure out that another camp existed very close to them, and they have eyes in the sky. It would be best for them to move at night to avoid being seen."

"You're not going to kill the cultists?" the other asked.

"Didn't you just go on about how starved and weak you all are?" James gestured at the man and the other prisoners, who were still cautiously making their way out up the stairs and through the gap between ceiling and earth that James had created.

"Well, but you're—"

"What about my sister?" another man interrupted. "Have you seen my sister?" James used Identify.

[Moishe Rose, Lv. 9]

Hopefully, strong enough to be useful, James thought.

"I have seen her," James said. "She's in very bad shape. She needs a Healer right away."

"Did you get her out?" Moishe asked. He spoke with a noticeable tremor of anguish.

"She was too weak to be moved, and she wanted me to get to you."

"Ugh!" Moishe covered his face with a hand. James thought he saw tears tracing a path through the dirt on his cheeks.

"I'll do my best," James said. "Just hurry up and get out of here with the others." Everyone else had made it to ground level in the time James had been dealing with Moishe and the naysayer. He used Identify so he'd know for later who the naysayer had been.

[Theodore Rowe, Lv. 6]

"I'm a Healer," Rowe said. "Do you need me for anything?"

"Just stick with your group," James said. "They'll need some healing, and—"

"Jeff! We need some help up here!" It took James a moment to recognize that the voice calling down into the pit was calling for him. False Impression was still active, causing anyone who used Identify on him to see him as Jeffrey Ross.

He scrambled up the stairs, and he saw the prisoners huddled together around the entrance. *Why aren't you idiots leaving?* he thought.

Then he saw why.

A half dozen of the Moloch camp's finest guards stood in a semicircle, loosely surrounding the prisoners.

"What's the meaning of this, Ross?" one of the guards called as James looked around and took in the sight.

"Just thought Moloch didn't seem like such a great boss after all!" he called back. To the people around him, the weakened, disheveled prisoners, he rasped, "I'll make you an opening between these guys. Then you have to run for the tree line. Move that way"—he gestured in the direction he'd come from—"and don't stop until you meet another group of people. Join up with them. Safety in numbers."

"What about you?" Moishe Rose's voice sounded from behind him.

"Are you in a position right now to worry about what I'll be doing?" James hissed. "Lead everyone out of here, keep them alive, and I can rest easy." He paused. "I'll see what I can do for your sister, but I'm not optimistic."

Then James focused on the guards around him. Four men, one woman. There had been another before, but that person seemed to have run away to alert yet more people. James had to make whatever moves he was going to make quickly.

He drew the Wolfbone Dagger from its sheath, and instantly, the two closest men stepped backward. This might be easier than he'd thought. *Maybe they haven't seen any real stand-up fights, just ambushes arranged by their prophet.*

He Identified those two.
[Leonard Robie, Lv. 7]
[Antony Roku, Lv. 6]
Then he heard one of the guards farther away whispering to another, "We should stay back until the Prophet gets here. He can heal us."

With that, James leaped into action. Time was really not on his side.

He closed with Roku first, using Quick Strike to jump within a foot of the other man. Before Roku could react to the sudden movement, James slashed his throat with such force that he could feel he'd almost decapitated the man.

Heal from that, he thought, wiping blood from his face with the back of his hand.

He turned to where the next closest man had stood, but before Roku had even crumpled to the ground, Robie had turned and run. James didn't have to look around much to see the other so-called guards were giving him distance now too. None of them wanted what Roku had gotten.

James had made the promised opening.

The prisoners needed no further prompting. They ran past James and Roku's corpse and into the tree line.

James only had a few seconds to enjoy the feeling of success before he was rushed. Two guards approached at once. *Must be feeling brave*, James thought.

Identify.
[Mustafa Roshan, Lv. 10]
[Fatemeh Roshan, Lv. 9]
Siblings, he guessed.

He dodged a sword swing from the man and slashed the woman's arm with his dagger, opening a long, red line in her white cloak.

These white cloaks are terrible for fighting at night, James thought as he moved around another very telegraphed sword swing, getting inside Mustafa's guard. *They almost glow in the moonlight.*

He leaned into Mustafa, so close that he could kiss the man, and in the same moment, James lifted the bottom of his mask up, just enough to expose his mouth. And then—*Venom Fang!*—James sank his teeth deep into the warrior's neck.

Mustafa dropped his sword and collapsed to the ground, clutching at his throat. But even as one opponent fell, James felt the sting of a blade sinking into his lower back.

Perhaps this was a suicide mission.

CHAPTER FIFTY-FIVE

Nameless, Faceless

The blade pulled out of James's back, and he thought, *Now! I need to get out of here now! I can still move well enough. I just need to heal and—*

Predator's Instincts screamed at him to move to the side, and he dodged just in time. A spear thrust pierced the space where James had just been standing. He felt an ominous heat coming off the red-hot spearhead, along with a sound as if it had singed the air around it.

In a single smooth motion, James pulled his mask back down over his face and turned his head to look at the spearman. Jan Roest stood next to a swordswoman dressed in white armor and holding a longsword that dripped with James's blood.

"Well, who do we have here!" Jan Roest exclaimed. He wore a broad grin as he pulled the spear back and readied for another attack. Then he frowned. "Wait, Jeff? The fuck are you doing here?"

"Betraying you," James growled, doing his best False Impression-fueled impersonation of Officer Ross's voice. In the moment that Roest hesitated, James closed the distance between them, grabbed him by the throat, and *squeezed* tight, using Predator's Armaments to strengthen his grip. He remembered that Roest was a lower level than him and hadn't been through Race Evolution, so it was unlikely he had the Strength to endure James's grip.

The swordswoman reacted too slowly to stop him.

Sure enough, in the seconds he squeezed, James heard a cracking sound from Roest's neck—but then James felt something *extremely hot* approaching from behind him. He was forced to pivot and use Roest to shield himself from the incoming fireball.

"*Aaaargh!*" Roest remained alive enough to scream, at least, and the flames didn't fully envelop him; they were licking up the left side of his body. As Roest dropped to the ground, James assessed that the wounds were probably survivable with immediate medical help, but he couldn't afford to focus too much on killing this one man.

He looked around himself. More people had gathered. He was almost surrounded, and the mass of men and women were closing in. With Predator's Instincts, he could somewhat feel where all the people behind him were, and James kept moving, trying to avoid giving anyone an easy shot at stabbing him again. The wound he already had didn't seem to be remotely debilitating, or perhaps his new body was just that much hardier than a normal human one.

None of the unevolved cultists were likely to match his speed, and Predator's Insight seemed to indicate that there were several weak points where he could carve his way through the enemies and escape.

James started to wonder if Rostov had instructed them to hold back on attacking him seriously until the prophet could get there himself. After all, the average of the group was quite weak compared to James.

But no. It made more sense that they had all only just awoken and gathered to see the enemy that threatened their camp.

Most of them had not had time to do more than position themselves. And maybe they were afraid of getting too close to the intruder who had already dispatched a couple of people in only a few seconds.

Then the situation got much worse.

"Take heart, my friends!" an all too familiar voice boomed. "He is just one man. Nothing before the might of Moloch!"

James saw the prophet's silhouette emerge in the center of the group of enemies closest to the tents. *The one we've all been waiting for*, he thought.

James had a very bad feeling about this. The group of people all around him suddenly felt more menacing, as if they'd grown taller from Rostov's pronouncement. Somehow, those words—which sounded very confident but quite empty to James—had injected steel into their spines. And some other effect that James couldn't quite explain.

And James realized that rather than projecting his chances of victory and survival, Predator's Insight was now just screaming at him to *run!* Surely, his odds couldn't have declined that much, just from the addition of one supporting player to the enemy group.

Don't be stupid, James, he told himself. *Of course they could. Rostov is a higher level than you. Even if he's only some kind of support Class, his support abilities must be incredible.*

"Lord Moloch, please protect your servants with your holy light!" Rostov chanted.

James had felt the presence of a god descending into a mortal body before, and without experiencing any of the same visual or sound effects he associated with that phenomenon, he now felt a small fraction of that same energy in the air around him.

Oh, crap.

James dove toward what Predator's Insight had identified as the weakest section of the line of cultists, thinking he would be able to penetrate through it. A pull at his ankle stopped him abruptly, almost sending him careening to the ground.

James looked down to find Roest. He'd locked onto James's ankle with the arm that wasn't horribly burned.

"Fuck me," James swore.

"I intend to," Roest growled, his half-burned face contorted in a horrific grimace.

James lunged downward, swiftly plunging his dagger toward Roest's unprotected neck. The blade struck something—and stopped.

This feels uncomfortably familiar. Can I please get a fucking break? He now saw that Roest emanated a golden glow. Through his peripheral vision, he could tell that the surrounding area had grown brighter in the last few seconds. Worst case scenario, everyone else would be glowing golden too. But he didn't look around right now to check.

Instead, James braced himself to exert his full Strength. He swung down with the dagger clasped in both hands, right at Roest's head. The man released James's leg and raised his arms to defend himself, but he was too slow.

The dagger came down at faster-than-human speed, struck the golden light in front of Roest's face—and snapped in two. The broken tip of the blade spun off into the night, whizzing harmlessly past James's face.

I really can't win this, he realized. *How do I escape?*

He swung his head in a wide arc and took in as much as he could of the situation around him.

The Moloch cultists approached on all sides, moving slowly but surely and glowing golden with apparent invincibility. A few were almost close enough to touch him.

They look like a goddamn zombie horde, James thought. *If zombies had a weird holy aura.* But fortunately, most of them were at least slow. The two closest cultists tried to grab him, and he dodged back and forth, keeping out of reach without moving very far from where he'd started. As he weaved around the closest ones and looked for a gap in the wall of people that he could pass through, he noticed something strange.

As his followers advanced all around James, Rostov stayed away. He hung in the background like a mascot at a sports match. There had to be a reason why.

James focused his eyes on Rostov for a moment. He could barely see him around the other people, but he thought he caught a good image of him between the moving bodies. Rostov was glowing golden, just like his cultists, but he was also sweating as if he was the one fighting.

Of course! He's the one who's fueling this. Maybe if I target him, the shielding will disappear. He tried to use Predator's Insight, but it continued to scream at him that he needed to escape as quickly as possible. So he deactivated the Skill. *I'll have to improvise.*

James bent to grab Roest, who yelped with surprise as James lifted him overhead. James couldn't stab the other man with his knife, but the glow did not prevent James from getting hold of him. Though James could sense he wouldn't be able to do any damage by grabbing Roest, holding onto him was good enough for his purposes.

James charged the weakest place he could find in the enemy encirclement, using Roest's body as a battering ram. It worked to push the closest people backward, though James could sense they hadn't taken any damage.

He dropped Roest on the ground as soon as he was through the human obstacles.

James bobbed and weaved through the few cultists in the weak area of the line he had broken through, and he made a beeline for where Isabelle Rose still lay on the stone table. He knew what he had to do. He was already drawing another Wolfbone Dagger from his bag.

I'm sorry I couldn't do better for you, he thought. Given the change in circumstances, his mission in regard to her was no longer rescue but merely to bring an end to suffering.

"Why leave so soon?" Rostov's voice came from James's elbow.

Really? James thought. *I thought you were a coward, or at least that you could only fight through others. If you're going to come to me, though . . .*

He turned and seized Rostov by the collar. The golden glow around the leader was stronger than that around any of the followers. It seemed obvious now that James wouldn't be able to pierce it unless Rostov ran out of Mana or whatever resource it consumed.

But every ability he'd seen in the System thus far did have some limit or other.

James slammed Rostov head first into the ground. Then he lifted Rostov's head off of the ground and smashed it down again. And again.

As the cultists rushed toward him, James slammed Rostov's head against the ground once more and scraped it forward, trying to create maximum friction. But as soon as James stopped to see if there was any damage or weakening of the shield, Rostov pushed against the ground, trying to raise himself from his prone position.

James got a good look at him. There wasn't a hair out of place. Aside from the sweat that continued to pour down the side of his face in greater and greater volumes, Rostov looked the same as before.

The only damage their clash had done was to the ground, which James had landscaped with a small crater connected to a trench, both dug in the shape of Rostov's head.

I give up, James thought. He took off running toward Isabelle again, only to feel a sudden twinge of tension. He half turned back, and an arrow tore through his left bicep.

If I hadn't moved, that would've gone right through my heart! He covered the wound with his right hand in an attempt to slow the bleeding, and he began Silent Spellcasting. He needed some magic that would definitively put an end to this fight. It was time to rely on good old Apophis again.

At the same time, he ducked low and continued the rush toward Isabelle, dodging slightly from side to side as he moved to make himself a harder target. Projectiles repeatedly zoomed by him as he ran, but none of them landed this time. Either their poor aim or his heightened instincts protected him. It didn't matter which. He made it to Isabelle.

As he reached her, he sensed Rostov's mob continuing to press closer around him. Tightening the noose. He had no time to say anything to her. To apologize or explain. To try to wake her or free her from her bonds. He only had time to do what he had resolved to do.

Just think of her like a piece of meat, he thought. *Nameless, faceless. No one's sister. No one's daughter.* His eyes fell upon the slight swell of her stomach. *No one's mother.*

He swallowed. Then he raised the dagger up as high as he could and plunged it straight down toward the hollow between her breasts. *Forgive me.*

As if possessed by some superhuman instinct, Isabelle stirred at the last moment. Her eyes flew open, and their gazes met for a moment.

He thought he saw a flash of *contentment* there, and then the knife was in her chest. He pulled it out and quickly, numbly slashed her throat as well. *Have to be sure.* He wouldn't put it past these people to heal her just so they could sacrifice her according to their perverse rituals.

Then he rose to his normal height.

"He has stolen the Sun God's sacrifice. We must capture him alive!" Rostov declared.

James felt a pit form in his stomach. He wanted time to process what he'd just done, but that would have to come later. He wanted far more desperately not to take Isabelle's place on the table.

He looked around and assessed his situation again. It wasn't so bad. He was almost surrounded, but he'd been more surrounded when he broke through to reach Isabelle. Everything he'd done in these moments of heated action since he'd freed the prisoners had taken less than a minute.

Only a few of the enemy had caught up to him as he paused to kill Isabelle. Those three figures stood just a body's length away, waiting for more of their group to catch up to them. Even with the golden light protecting them, none of them wanted to fight him one-on-one.

Most of the cultists couldn't compare to his speed, power, or sheer unrelenting energy. He just had to stay out of reach of those few who could actually keep up with him. Then he could escape, just like the prisoners. Or he could stay out of reach long enough to blow them all to kingdom come. His Mana was charging a bit more quickly than it had pre-Evolution, and in the state of mind he was in right now, he'd happily blow up most of the forest to take all of them down with him. He was focusing hard on that thought for Apophis's benefit.

Then there was a new light. A bright and sharp canary-yellow hue, approaching from the distance behind the line of cultists. Rectangular in shape. Roughly as wide across as a small house. Around the height of a one-story building. He could see through it, but it gave a sense of solidity. And it moved forward ominously slowly.

Whatever the light was, it was different from the golden light that surrounded Rostov, and it gave James a foreboding feeling.

After all, it certainly wasn't backup for James.

"Ah, excellent!" Rostov said.

James noted most of the cultists turn their heads, apparently as surprised as he was by the light.

A group of figures appeared, outlined against the light. *More cultists? They have more people than I realized.* Then he saw.

No! How?! The woman wearing the flower wreath was the first figure he could see, and the yellow light shone brightest around her. But also wreathed in the light were all of the prisoners James had just freed. The glowing yellow wall of light followed behind them. They hadn't made it very far after all.

CHAPTER FIFTY-SIX

A Thousand Suns

James and the cultists stood transfixed; the fighting was on pause for the moment as the prisoners slowly approached the battlefield.

James didn't mind the pause, since he was still charging Mana as they all stood there. But the moment of reflection was dispiriting. The escaped prisoners' postures said it all. They were slumped, defeated. Any resistance within them had broken.

They gave in so quickly, James thought. *I guess I shouldn't have expected more out of people who allowed themselves to be held captive pending human sacrifice. It's my own fault for thinking they'd liberate themselves if I just distracted most of the cultists. Shit! I didn't help anyone by coming here, except maybe Isabelle. I wasn't prepared for this at all. Got cocky.*

A few other figures, including Officer Ross, stood guard around the prisoners, but they didn't appear to have much agency in the situation anyway. As James watched, the slowest one of the prisoners, a man with a bad limp, almost fell behind. When he did, he struck the yellow wall, and the yellow light dragged him forward like it was a solid, moving structure.

It's like a Green Lantern construct or something, James assessed. *This group has way too much power for so early in Orientation! I guess I understand why the prisoners gave up.* He quietly gave up on freeing the prisoners. There was no way out for them. *At least I didn't try to bring Alan or Mitzi or any of the Rodriguezes. I would've led them straight into a massacre.*

He glanced down by his foot for a moment, just to make sure Isabelle was gone. And she was very clearly dead.

Now to figure out my escape. Or how to keep them from killing me while I finish charging my attack.

James only had a fraction of a second's warning from Predator's Instincts. And he couldn't move quite fast enough to dodge completely. A bullet careened through the corner of his mask as he threw himself to the side. It missed his head completely, but the fact that it penetrated through the spider exoskeleton boded poorly.

So, guns aren't useless yet after all.

He saw the smoking gun in the distance—a police service pistol. Officer Ross was the shooter. James grimaced behind the mask. *I guess False Impression isn't going to work to mimic* his *identity anymore. That was fun while it lasted.*

He didn't bother changing the name that displayed, though. Instead, while he was down he grabbed Isabelle's body and pulled it close to use as a human shield.

He felt a little bad desecrating the body, but not enough to stop him doing it. She was level nine, after all. There would surely be some defensive value.

Then he rose, effortlessly holding her up in front of his body with one hand. Sure enough, he heard another couple of shots, and the corpse shook slightly in his hand with each impact, but he didn't feel anything go through and strike him.

She was tougher than the average spider, James assessed. *She would've probably done well here if she wasn't in their hands.* But his attention was drawn to his sides. With the ring of the first gunshot, the other cultists around him had started moving again too. On his right, the first cultist to move was almost close enough to grab James.

The cultist was holding his knife hesitantly, pointed at a low angle toward the ground, as if he really didn't want to fight. James assessed the man wasn't a true threat. Just an obstacle, with that golden glow surrounding him and making him unkillable. James stuck his dagger in his belt and leaped the short distance toward the man. He grabbed the surprised cultist and dropped Isabelle as he landed.

Now I have a completely bulletproof human shield, he thought. He turned and held the man up. A couple of bullets immediately pinged off of the cultist's body. The golden glow around him didn't go away. James's shield was clearly unharmed. He didn't think there was any chance a weapon would pierce through his hostage's body and get to him.

James assessed again. He was almost surrounded now. *Almost enough Mana to blow them all away, though*, he thought optimistically. The plan wouldn't be escape now. He'd had a moment's doubt, but now he knew. He had to kill these people and stop what they were doing.

Another shot rang out, and James felt it hit his mask and penetrate right through, striking him in the center of the forehead. The mask began to fall away in pieces around the hole. The impact to his head hurt like hell, and he thought he might have a concussion in the morning.

But the bullet only barely broke the skin; a trickle of blood falling across his nose was the only clear indicator of damage.

If the mask hadn't hidden his face, the cultists might have paused at the sight of their enemy grinning like a madman. *Good shot! But I really am almost bulletproof now. Just a little more Fortitude, and shots from pistols will bounce right off like I'm Luke Cage or Superman!*

Then the pounding headache wiped his smile away, and he held his hostage up a little higher to try and prevent a recurrence. The man in his grip wiggled and writhed, trying to get loose, but James was using both hands to hold him, gripping him by the arms—in a Strength contest, no one here was likely to beat him.

"Grab him! Pull him back toward the table!" Rostov's voice echoed through the camp, and the cultists began to move a little more quickly.

Just need to stall a little longer, he thought. *Blow them all away.* His body glowed brightly now, rivaling the bonfire at the center of the camp. Brighter than any glow of Mana he'd ever prepared before. Once this was over, he'd have next to nothing left, but he wouldn't need anything more. He hoped. If he had the chance to charge enough Mana.

But the cultists were getting closer and closer now—perhaps emboldened by the fact that his hands were occupied—pressing at his sides and back, everywhere he wasn't blocking with the hostage.

It was like *Night of the Living Dead.*

Dead, hostile eyes surrounding him. He could feel at any moment, the crowd would swallow him whole.

And then they started grabbing onto him.

Hands clutched at his arms, his legs, and the sides of his clothes. Unarmed hands, so there were no weapons for him to fear. They were just trying to hold onto him, to secure him for their leader. For their god.

Over two dozen hands latched onto James. He was finally forced to release his hostage because the sheer number of people grabbing onto him made it difficult to move and exert himself, and he needed his hands free as he resisted the pull of their hands.

The man turned around as soon as James let go, and he grabbed for James's mask.

James had to duck and dodge despite the hands holding him. Above all else, he couldn't let Rostov figure out who he really was.

If he had to run away instead of wiping the cultists out, that was fine. Just so long as Rostov didn't know where to go for revenge.

As he danced in the grip of the cultists, trying not to be publicly unmasked, James caught sight of what was going on far behind the man grabbing at his head. Officer Ross and another servant of Moloch were leading the prisoners back to the underground prison.

That wasn't so bad. As long as they were underground, James imagined the explosion he planned to unleash probably wouldn't kill them. He was already prepared for collateral damage, and the cultists were unknowingly minimizing it for him.

But something else was happening that gave him pause. The woman with the flower wreath was moving her hands, and the glowing yellow wall she'd placed behind the prisoners was growing. No longer behind the prisoners, it now blocked the direction James had come from. Beaming, she walked away from the wall toward James and the cultists surrounding him.

And James saw two other figures attired similarly to that woman walking in opposite directions away from her—a man and a woman, also wearing flower wreaths. James could guess what they might be doing.

If they have the same ability as her, they could cut off my retreat entirely. No way out of their killing box except by killing all of them or running deeper into the forest, away from the direction I came from.

A disturbing thought occurred to James. *Do they know which direction I came from? Or are they just blocking the directions the prisoners were running toward?*

As he had this thought, the cultists who gripped his arms and legs lifted him bodily off the ground and began pulling him forward.

"Secure him to the tablet!" Rostov was shouting. "We will give him to Moloch at sunrise. He must not escape!"

Escape? James thought. He almost wanted to laugh. *He must be incredibly confident in this magic aura he's surrounded everyone with.* At this point, James glowed so brightly that he thought he rivaled the sun itself. And with Apophis's power multiplying the effectiveness of his Mana, he imagined that the camp would be completely destroyed when he unleashed his power.

They're the ones who should be worried about escape! He felt it then as the cultists dragged him back almost to within touch range of the table, the Moloch statue, and the bonfire.

I have enough.

And James released the fire Mana.

A massive explosion originating from his body burst through the air in all directions. In an instant, James felt no more hands gripping him, no more bodies beneath him. Only fire and flame as far as the eye could see.

He fell from where the human hands had held him, above their heads, but he smiled as his body came crashing down.

I did it, he thought. The light of his own flames was so blinding that he had to rub and blink his eyes for a minute before he could see properly again.

The visual that presented itself before his eyes was an astonishing one: a column of fire bursting forth in all directions. At its inception it had blinded him. The brightness reminded him for a moment of Oppenheimer, who had compared his atomic bomb's brightness to the radiance of a thousand suns.

James had expected the insane power of the explosion to ripple through the forest, destroying everything in its path for a mad radius all around.

And the flame was wreaking havoc. It had destroyed the table in an instant. It continued pressing forward, destroying trees in its path in all directions except where it was blocked by human figures or the statue of Moloch.

But most of the human figures, James saw, were still very much alive.

Many of them looked almost unharmed, in fact.

The golden glow around them had completely dissipated. A few of them who had been the first to be hit by the explosion were actually dead, horribly scorched, including one of the flower-wreathed people. But most of them had only minor burns. People who had been further away were completely unharmed.

James saw, after a moment's searching, that Rostov lay on the ground, either unconscious or dazed.

I can't believe Moloch's barrier was that powerful.

One of the cultists raced toward Rostov and began shaking him.

And the yellow barriers that he had anticipated the two other flower wreathed individuals would erect suddenly blazed into life.

There were now three walls all around him, and James knew he had to get out of there before he was cornered on the fourth side.

He was all out of Mana. Surrounded by dozens of people, several of whom were close to him in level, who wanted nothing more than to see him dead. And his best trick hadn't killed more than a few of them.

Rostov stirred. He blinked his eyes open. He turned his head. His and James's eyes met.

"Get that bastard!" Rostov yelled.

James turned and ran.

CHAPTER FIFTY-SEVEN

No Way Out

James raced through the dark into the tree line, away from the yellow walls of light, and toward the one side of the camp that wasn't blocked off by those structures. The only way out.

Need to get far away, out of hearing, out of sight. Then hide. Stay hidden during the day. Probably need to be underground, so Rostov's stupid god won't spot me for him. The next night, I can double back, maybe fly the distance back to the Rodriguez camp. That should make it difficult for anyone to follow. None of them will have the kind of Mana reserves I have, even assuming one of them has wind magic to fly with.

And if one or two people in the Rostov camp had the requisite abilities and could follow him, James would enjoy taking his frustrations out on that person anyway. It wasn't as if anyone in the Rostov camp could match him. It was their sheer numbers that was the problem.

An arrow whipped by the side of his head, tearing through the silk on one side. But the mask held tight to his face for now.

Thank goodness for that silk, he thought. *If I can't get somewhere underground by daybreak, I could at least stick myself to a tree with it and use Natural Camouflage until night comes again.*

The air around him fairly burst with intense, fiery heat as James rushed through the trees. The forest was burning again, thanks to James once again. *But I didn't even get the kills this time.*

He grew somber. Everything about tonight was a terrible, ugly failure.

But at least he would escape to lick his wounds. *He who fights and runs away can live to fight another day.*

A shot rang out and tore through the silk on the other side of James's mask, and he felt the mask almost ready to fly off of his face. He grabbed it to keep it where it belonged, then darted through a small gap between two trees.

I don't seem to be losing them as quickly as I'd expect with my Agility.

But he was being chased by a lot of people, coming from several directions. The forest was alive with the sound of snapping twigs and branches, and he could hear even the ones that were far away. He had to be gaining some distance.

More shots rang out, but they went wide.

James picked up his pace, dashing farther and faster through the forest.

He kept going at a full sprint for another several minutes, silently thanking the System for his insane Stamina. The air became quieter and quieter as he outpaced both his pursuers and the forest fire.

He kept running, mostly in a straight line, as the silence predominated. He started to feel like he might be able to stop soon. He should be far enough ahead now. *Just get as much distance as possible before you stop*, he told himself. His Stamina wasn't at the bottom yet, although it had been dropping much faster for the minutes he spent sprinting.

James was so preoccupied with getting away that he almost missed it. He came very suddenly to the end of the forest.

Rather than a new biome in front of him, he saw nothing.

A vast gulf. A chasm filled with nothing but black emptiness.

James was running at such high speed that he had to dig in his heels to stop, and he barely managed in time. His momentum carried him to the edge of the cliff.

As he stood there, he looked straight down. Besides the sheer cliff itself, he couldn't make out a single detail as far as his eyes could see.

Only darkness.

He tried to peer across the chasm to spot what was on the other side. Maybe he could throw a weapon with some spider silk, establish an anchor on the opposite end of the chasm, and pull himself across.

But he saw only darkness in the distance. There was no apparent end to it, though with his vision, he would expect to see some hint of the other side even if it was far away. *And the moon is bright tonight.*

He shuddered slightly. *It reminds me of what the ancients supposedly believed. That the world was flat.* In reality, pre-Columbus Europeans already knew that the world was curved. It was nineteenth century thinkers who reinvented the Middle Ages as a period when people were so backward that they believed the Earth was flat.

But this was like the edge of the world that those pre-Columbians supposedly believed they would sail off of.

Nothingness. *The edge of the map.*

Slowly, carefully, James backed away from the edge. He didn't want to look at it. The void was too disturbing. With his enhanced sight, he should be able to see deep down into it. But it was as if there was nothing at the bottom.

It seemed impossible. Nothing like this should exist on the Earth he knew.

One more confirmation, if I needed it, that Orientation is in another universe or a separate dimension or something.

James heard noises of movement from back the way he'd come: snapping twigs and voices that were trying to be quiet but didn't seem to account for his superhuman hearing.

How? I haven't stopped here that long, have I? How could they have found me so quickly?

He looked around. There was nowhere to run except back the way he'd come or along the cliffside. That seemed dangerous. Considering their numbers, he'd just run into more cult members if they were so determined to follow him.

He looked at the tracks he'd left in the ground. *They'll definitely know I was here.* Maybe he could use that to his advantage. The ground near the cliffside was dirt, but he'd just been running through an area of forest full of clover.

I have a minute or two before they get close, he estimated. *Just enough time?*

James walked forward several feet along the cliff side, deliberately making heavier footfalls than usual. He kept going until he'd walked from the dirt that lined the cliffside to the clover that marked the reentry into the forest.

He looked back. *Perfect. An easy-to-follow trail.*

He stepped backward through his footsteps until he was close to the cliffside again. Then he stood in the treads he'd made when he'd stopped himself from running off the edge of the cliff. And he jumped up the side of the closest tree.

As soon as he was secure in a branch, he affixed his mask more firmly on his head with a hastily applied new layer of spider-silk. With that done, he activated Natural Camouflage. His pulse slowed, his breathing grew shallow, his body relaxed, and he felt as if he was melding into the tree. And he waited.

A few seconds passed, and he heard voices.

"Definitely came this way," a voice he didn't know said.

"The Skill says he's still somewhere over here," Officer Ross said. "It's a little general. Kind of like reading radar, I think."

"You haven't had to use this Skill very often before, have you, Officer?" Rostov testily replied. "Perhaps there's been a bit of a learning curve?"

Seven figures materialized from the darkness into James's field of view. He was slightly gratified to see that they each looked more exhausted than he felt. Their white clothes were dirty. Several of them looked annoyed. One of them was the wreath-wearing man. Another was the man with the reddish skin and the tiny horns. And Jan Roest, looking hideously burned but considerably healed up compared with how James had left him.

Shit, they brought the A-team. And me, almost in the red on Mana. It had been recharging as he ran away, and much faster than pre-Race Evolution, but it was nowhere near enough for James to get into a fight. Certainly not the kind of flashy fighting he'd done back at the cultists' camp earlier.

"No, I haven't had to use the Skill very often," Ross shot back. "Normally *Moloch* gives us the location data. What's up? His GPS not working?"

"How dare you blaspheme against my god to my face? My god who has saved your life time and time again! You presume too much, Officer!" Rostov fumed. "If you are not capable of tracking down our enemy, then perhaps I no longer need you, eh? Remember who is keeping who alive here! I doubt Catherine would appreciate your blasphemy either."

"Leave my wife out of this, Rostov!" The policeman grabbed Rostov by the collar and looked like he wanted to strike him.

There was a moment of tense silence as the two held eye contact, clear hatred in Ross's expression. Rostov's face, however, revealed nothing. James wondered if Rostov was using a Skill on Ross right now, to place him back under control. It would be strange if a cult leader didn't have some powers in the same vein as what he'd experienced from Chava.

Finally, Rostov broke the silence.

"He is a *sun god*, anyway, so how is he supposed to help us at night?" A note of humor. That same sly, charismatic way of putting people at ease that James had noted before.

Even Officer Ross, who clearly hated Rostov's guts, seemed affected. He snorted derisively but released Rostov's collar.

"We'll look until we find him, in any case," the wreath-wearer said, stepping forward to place himself between the two.

"Yes," Rostov agreed. He sounded much calmer now. "There is no need for alarm. The other searchers will signal if they find him. We have him so thoroughly boxed in, there can be no way out."

The seven figures moved on, and James let out a breath he hadn't realized he was holding.

Just have to wait a little while now to make sure they won't come back and that the next patrol isn't following immediately after. Then I'll sneak down from this tree and dig a hole for myself on the side of the cliff. I can keep the entrance to the hole open, so I'll be able to breathe. No one will be able to see me unless they somehow cross to the other side of the cliff. And as far as I know, there's nothing on the other side of the cliff. Just void. It's the edge of the map.

Something about the plan sounded odd as he thought it out, but he couldn't see anything wrong with it. Just something that felt strange, and he had no time now to try and drill down to figure out whether it meant anything.

He started counting in his head. *One-Mississippi, two-Mississippi, three-Mississippi, four-Mississippi, five-Mississippi. I'll go until I get to ten, and then I'll hop down from this place and start climbing down the cliff side. Shouldn't take much Mana just to dig out a human-sized hole.*

As he had these thoughts, he heard the sound of approaching humans again. It felt slightly muffled this time, as if they were trying to be quiet, but there was no mistaking it.

Damn it, I missed my window! What little there was of one. I'll just have to wait a bit longer . . .

Then he heard more footfalls. These were coming from the opposite direction.

Two groups were converging on this one spot.

This can't be a coincidence. He recalled the exchange earlier about Officer Ross's tracking ability. It must have something to do with that. They knew he was here.

Can't risk my life testing what's on the other side of that cliff. Can't stay here and hope they go away. Not when they're gathering in numbers.

He moved from a prone position, to a crouch, to standing.

Then he took a running leap, jumping from the branch he stood on—and this time he felt the bullet almost at the same time that he heard the shot ring out.

James collapsed to the ground, clutching his side.

Not completely bulletproof, then. He'd suspected as much. It was only a shallow wound, and hopefully, the shooter would be running out of bullets about now. But he didn't want to bet on it.

As another shot rang through the air, James quickly sprang back toward the tree and took cover behind it.

"There's no point in hiding anymore, heathen!" Rostov's voice taunted loudly. "Did you think we didn't know you were there?"

"You had me fooled!" James called back. *Just need them to give me a little time. I'll come up with something.*

"Do you prefer to surrender or fight?" Rostov asked, maintaining the same elevated volume. "We've made sure we have plenty of people in case you prefer the fight."

"For me personally, I prefer the fight!" Jan Roest pronounced in his distinctive accent. "Come on out and let us fuck you up!"

James could hear the pain in his voice even through the sneering. *Sounds like you're the one who's fucked up.* Normally, he would want to taunt an opponent in a situation like this.

But here, there was just no point. They had the numbers to beat him; he was almost certain. There was no point in winding them up. He thought furiously, trying to come up with some way to escape. Some way he could win or flee back through the forest behind him.

Before he could come up with a plan, he saw them drawing closer all around him. He could only guess there were some on the other side of his tree, but the ones he could see were enough of a problem. A baker's dozen of Rostov's people, with his strongest—except for the other two wreath-wearers—all represented.

Then things got worse. Someone kindled a yellow glow, emanating from behind him.

A wall to cut off any possible retreat.

"Brought you that fight you were looking for, intruder." Rostov's voice came from behind James, presumably behind the yellow barrier wall.

Of course he waits to gloat properly until he's protected again, James thought. *I must have scared the crap out of him with that explosion. Bloody coward!*

"Coward!" James spat. "Get out from behind that energy field and fight me yourself. Like a real man!"

"I'm more of a support role, but thank you for thinking of me," Rostov replied. He sounded completely unperturbed.

James had known the cheap shot wouldn't work. *Still worth a try.*

As he spoke, the thirteen on the same side of the barrier as him positioned themselves, evenly spaced, to better cut off any escape. With the wall behind him and the tough fighters all around him, James was surrounded.

Ross was one of those who had him encircled. He had put his pistol back in its holster, James saw, and drawn a small club. Since Ross had been through Evolution, James anticipated this was going to hurt.

Roest was another of those poised to attack. James got his first good look at the man's weapon: a gleaming red spear that glowed slightly in the darkness.

The man with the little horns was there too, holding a big club that James could vaguely see was covered in intricate carvings.

A woman with a longsword and pristine white armor.

A stocky man with two long knives.

"Get him!" Roest snarled.

The other faces all blended together as the thirteen charged in unison. The fight wasn't polite, like what he'd seen in movies when the hero was attacked by a gang. There was no choreography, no taking turns. Everyone wanted a piece of James at once.

Clubs struck his head and shoulders, spear thrusts pierced through where he'd just been standing, and a sword swing almost took his head off. He dodged what he could, weaved around deadly attacks, and simply took the blows from the clubs.

The bad thing was simply that he was too overwhelmed to go on the offensive.

James had been in several one-sided fights over the last week. It was just unfortunate that this time he was on the wrong side.

Slowly but surely, the repeated blows whittled down his Health. Stab wounds that were barely dodged pulled back and turned into slashes that grazed him. Bludgeoning weapons gradually achieved their purpose and broke several of

James's weaker bones after repeated blows. A rib, several fingers on his left hand, the left wrist.

And then he found an opening. James dove through a gap that briefly appeared between the attackers.

As he dove, his Predator's Instincts went wild. But it was impossible for him to dodge in midair without magic charged to protect him.

Roest's spear pierced through James's back, and he felt the searing heat explode through his lung. He was on fire from the inside.

He wanted to scream, but the air had all gone out of him.

He managed to crawl forward, spear still stuck through him, but it was agony.

The weapon finally pulled out of his chest cavity, and James felt Roest's breath as the man leaned in close.

"I told you, didn't I? Heh heh."

In a flash, James sprang up, grabbed Roest by the throat, and turned him around to use him as a human shield. Even with his left hand almost fully disabled, the Strength difference was insurmountable. With his left arm wrapped around Roest's throat and his right hand crushing the wrist of the hand that held the spear, Roest dropped the weapon.

"How does this feel?" James asked. "Bring back any memories?"

"Motherfucker," Roest sputtered, uncomfortable in the role of repeat hostage. "I'll kill you, you piece of *aaaaahhhh*—"

He let out a pained yelp as James tightened his grip and broke Roest's wrist.

"Don't just stand there, you sons of bitches. Do something!" Roest croaked at the others. They shuffled indecisively, slowly moving to form a new circle around James. But Roest had been at the farthest reach of their semicircle before, close to the edge of the chasm.

Now James had the advantages of a hostage in hand and his back to the cliff. He couldn't be surrounded, and he could only be attacked with great peril to Roest.

Still, James knew his situation was shit, and it was only going to deteriorate from here. The cultists would undoubtedly sacrifice a pawn like Roest to kill an obviously high-value target like himself. He would've made the same call if he had to.

He weighed his options, and he decided there weren't any good ones. And only one that was somewhat acceptable.

He yanked backward on Roest, and the two of them tumbled together over the edge of the cliff and into the murky blackness below.

As they fell into darkness, James threw his head back and began to laugh.

Epilogue

Kurt Royersford crawled on all fours, desperately trying to get away from the blazing inferno, tears boiling up at the corners of his eyes.

Oh, my God! That friggin' psycho blew them all up! I have to get away before he tries to kill me. Screw these guys! I have to escape!

He screamed, both aloud and inside his own brain.

Once, Kurt's Skill had linked his mind to the Corpse Eater's. But the bond had been severed in one fiery instant.

Now, the psychic scream seemed to tear the sky and ripple far and wide through the invisible world.

Kurt barely managed to drag his body away from the burning clearing before he collapsed to the ground, landing on his badly burned lower half. A few flickers of fire still licked at his back, but he was too far gone to do anything more to save himself.

He whimpered quietly, tears streaming from his eyes. And the world went dark.

The next moment that Kurt was aware of himself, he found that he was mobile. His body was being jostled back and forth. It was the still-fresh burn on his back that woke him. The one carrying him had scraped his back carelessly against a low-hanging tree branch.

"Aaahhh! Fu—jeez! Careful there, buddy," Kurt whined.

He slowly blinked his eyes open and realized that he was several feet off the ground, hanging upside down. He lifted his head and looked backward, where he saw that the smoke and flames were retreating into a safe distance.

He breathed a sigh of relief before he realized that he had no idea who was carrying him. Who did he know that was this tall and strong?

"Uh, hey, David? Could you put me down, man? And does that sister of yours have any Mana left? Could really use a quick heal. That fire did a number on me. I can't feel all the places he burned, but I know it's going to hurt like hell tomorrow."

There was no pause in the forward march.

"Hey, David—"

Kurt reached to grab his rescuer's shoulder and pulled himself up enough to turn and face him. What he saw shocked him.

Greasy gray skin stretched over a skull that seemed two sizes two large. Strands of coarse black hair sprouted from its scalp in scrubby chunks. Cloudy blue-yellow eyes. A jaw that seemed stuck in a mindless, endlessly gaping grin.

He screamed.

A moment passed, and he reminded himself that there were probably many intelligent creatures in this forest that he might not enjoy looking at.

"I mean, um, uh." He swallowed. "W-who, or what, are you?"

"*Urk!*" the creature croaked.

This one can't speak? Kurt realized. *Shit. Did it take me to eat me? But then why is it bothering to carry me away?*

He thought of reaching out with Contract Formation, but an alien thought interrupted.

Relax, human, an unfamiliar voice intruded into his head. The voice was confident, warm, and smooth as caramel. *Murk is there to help you. If I wanted him to smash your skull in, he would've done that already. But I feel it's fate that brings us together. We're both quite fortunate.*

"You can speak into my mind," Kurt said aloud, stunned.

How powerful is this thing? he wondered.

Yes, I can speak into your mind, it said. Kurt detected a condescending tone now. *And so many other things. Have no fear. We'll take good care of you.*

"That's wonderful, mighty one," Kurt said, unconsciously rubbing his hands together. The pain he was in couldn't distract him from self-preservation. "How do you think I might be of service?"

Already, he imagined how he might work with the originator of the voice to get his revenge on the guy who'd left him in this condition. *How many minions must this guy have? I wonder what the terms of the contract would be . . .*

Don't trouble yourself about how you will serve right now, the voice said. *Time enough for that once we meet. For now, rest.*

Kurt felt the fatigue wash over him then. It was only pain from his wounds and anxiety about what was happening that kept him awake. *It's fine, right?* he told himself. *And there's nothing I can do even if he wanted to kill me. I'm in bad shape. Soon I'll be right as rain.*

The darkness overtook him again.

When Kurt awakened, he was lying on his back. His eyes stared up into mist and darkness. His vision was slightly blurry. Everything around was shrouded in shadow and speckled with flickering green and yellow light. There was a horrible smell that he couldn't identify in the air. It pulled him back to a specific afternoon, when he was a boy.

His family had brought him to the memorial for his great-grandmother. Kurt had barely known the old woman. He took the first opportunity he could to sneak back into the funeral home's off-limits area. He entered a cold white metal room, and he smelled—

Where am I?

He tried to move, but his body did not respond.

There's no need for that, Kurt, the voice sang into his mind. It sounded joyous. Relieved? Something was very wrong. *You're under my sedation anyway. Don't worry about moving around.*

A shadow fell over Kurt's face, and he could finally see a few details of the other life-form near him. Creepy gray skin, like Murk. *And like the Corpse Eater.* Except this thing's skin was a lighter shade of gray. Closer to a human color. And the skin fit better than Murk's had. Like this thing was the original owner.

Its eyes looked human, except that the irises shone with an eerie golden yellow. A long, unkempt mane of gray hair. Pointed ears. A mouth that had been sewn shut.

"What are you?" Kurt said. Or tried to say. His body remained almost fully nonresponsive, though he heard himself emit the dull grunts of the words without any enunciation. His face had moved slightly at his attempt to speak, he noted. Just a twitch, but it showed that he wasn't entirely immovable flesh.

Me? the voice transmitted into his head. It remained as soothing as Kurt remembered, and he instinctively calmed a bit at the sound of it. *I am called Roscuro. As for what and who I am, that question is more complicated. My memories are mere fragments. I have no idea how I found myself here. I know that a witch cursed me and made me the way I am. I know that I have been reborn with a particular set of Skills. And I know that I must use them. I need to, so that I may survive. But I find that I am talking too much.*

He sounds human, Kurt thought, *regardless of how he looks.*

Roscuro moved out of Kurt's sight, and Kurt heard a rustling sound coming from around his lower body.

"Are 'ou 'ealing me?" he tried to pronounce. The little moans came out slightly more clearly this time.

Oh, don't worry, my friend! the voice replied. *We're almost done working on you. Just need to replace some fluids. I'm no Healer, but I'm quite proud of the work that I've done on you!*

Kurt felt a chill run down his spine. It was a strangely dull sensation, but he had the unmistakable sense that something was going terribly wrong.

"Pease, I don' zink I wan' dis," he attempted.

Soon you'll be better than new, the voice promised, either ignoring or not understanding the muffled sounds Kurt had produced.

More sounds of movement.

Out of his peripheral vision, Kurt perceived Roscuro suspending clear tubes from supports that he couldn't see. The tubes could've been anything—plastic, rubber, animal intestines. He only knew that they dangled somewhere at the edges of his vision.

More fiddling around in the general vicinity of his lower body. Kurt could see and feel nothing outside of an outline of Roscuro moving around in his peripheral vision.

Then Kurt saw, rather than felt, one of the tubes begin filling up with a red fluid. After a moment, he recognized it as his own blood.

He unleashed muffled wails as the blood continued draining, flowing somewhere beyond his view. Roscuro seemed to ignore him. A moment later, green and yellow fluids began flowing in the opposite direction through another set of tubes.

Kurt felt *that.* He thought his body had gone almost completely numb. But then a cold sensation filled his veins. If he could have writhed in discomfort, he would have.

Don't try to resist, came Roscuro's voice. Kurt detected a malevolent edge to it. *The fluids are saving your life! Where were you ever going to find a proper Healer in time, anyway?*

Kurt wanted to disobey, but he could hardly move so much as an eyebrow. The sensation continued, and the fight slowly drained out of him. Long minutes passed, and the cold spread throughout his body.

Roscuro wandered away somewhere out of view while the liquids took effect. And then . . .

[Necromantic energies detected within your body. Accept Undead Transformation? Y/N]

Kurt tried to select "N," but his interface didn't do anything. The question remained in his field of view, as if he hadn't answered it.

Kurt heard movement outside of his range of vision, and then he saw Roscuro's frame lumber into view.

Why are you resisting? Roscuro thought at him. *You can become stronger, better, fully recovered. Have your revenge on whoever did this to you. All you have to do is accept the change.*

Kurt used Identify. It was strange he hadn't thought to do it earlier, with his body all but paralyzed.

[Soul Eater Roscuro, Lv. 19]

Soul Eater? Jesus, I'm so screwed!

Well, I don't want to eat your soul, Roscuro sent. *Some other humans, perhaps. But in your case, you have quite a useful Skill that I want you to make use of, for our mutual benefit. But first you must accept the transformation!*

The situation seemed inescapable to Kurt. And he decided to give in.

He selected "Y."

You won't regret this, Roscuro sent. *You will be one of my most distinguished servants.* The tone was consoling, but Kurt found it extremely cold comfort.

And darkness overtook his vision once more.

When he awakened, the green and yellow light that had played across his vision during the necromantic procedure was gone. The air felt calm. Still.

He quickly discovered that he could move again. He tried lifting his head up and found that he could move it around with an even fuller range of motion than he had enjoyed before Roscuro's procedure. As if the connection between skull and spine was almost unimportant.

The pain was all gone from his body now, he belatedly noticed. Kurt felt gratitude for that, but the feeling was dull, distant.

In moving from his supine position, Kurt observed that the space he was in wasn't empty at all. Strewn around nearby him were the remains of a partially disemboweled body with graying skin. He saw that a large amount of that skin had been flayed off. Imagery that would have turned his stomach not long ago, and yet he didn't sense any disgust rising within him.

As he looked down at his lower body, he saw that Roscuro had grafted a new layer of skin onto the burned places. He could see the border between the two regions outlined in stitches, one side gray and the other his normal pale flesh. There was a dull surprise at that observation, but it was even more distant than the gratitude had been. Like he was looking at feelings on the floor of the ocean through a glass-bottom boat.

Of course it was necessary to graft on new skin, and it wasn't as if they were in a hospital.

There were notifications, and Kurt saw that he had completed his transition to a new Race: Ghoul. That didn't sound so desirable. Yet Kurt realized he didn't care nearly as much as he should.

That's strange, he thought clinically. Now that he thought about it, he didn't seem to feel very strong emotionally about anything.

He tried to revisit some strong emotions from his memories. A girl rejecting him. Losing his virginity. His dog getting hit by a car. Getting accepted to veterinary school. Every one of those memories was clear. If anything, they were clearer than they had been, as if somehow, they were better preserved now than before.

But Kurt felt very little about any of them now. Veterinary school had been a great point of pride for him for years.

All of his feelings were watered down.

All but the physical ones, he realized. He pinched himself and experienced roughly the normal amount of pain.

And then his stomach growled. Kurt realized he felt hungry. Ravenously hungry.

About the Author

D. J. Rintoul was born and raised in Orlando, Florida. He obtained his law degree from the University of Florida and subsequently returned to Pennsylvania, where he had met his wife and obtained his undergraduate degree. Rintoul now lives with his family in eastern Pennsylvania. He enjoys history, books, board games, Christmas lights, and, occasionally, sunlight.

Podium
DISCOVER
STORIES UNBOUND
PodiumAudio.com